WRASSLE CASTLE

PUT A LYD ON IT

WONDERBOUND®

WONDERBOUND

Missoula, Montana
www.readwonderbound.com
@readwonderbound

PUBLISHER, **DAMIAN A. WASSEL**
EDITOR-IN-CHIEF, **ADRIAN F. WASSEL**
SENIOR ARTIST, **NATHAN C. GOODEN**
MANAGING EDITOR, **REBECCA TAYLOR**
DIRECTOR OF SALES & MARKETING, DIRECT MARKET, **DAVID DISSANAYAKE**
DIRECTOR OF SALES & MARKETING, BOOK MARKET, **SYNDEE BARWICK**
PRODUCTION MANAGER, **IAN BALDESSARI**
ART DIRECTOR, WONDERBOUND **SONJA SYNAK**
ART DIRECTOR, VAULT **TIM DANIEL**
PRINCIPAL, **DAMIAN A. WASSEL SR.**

LIBRARY OF CONGRESS CONTROL NUMBER: 2022900210

PRINT ISBN: 978-1-63849-099-9

FIRST EDITION AUGUST 2022
10 9 8 7 6 5 4 3 2 1

PRINTED IN THE USA BY VERSA

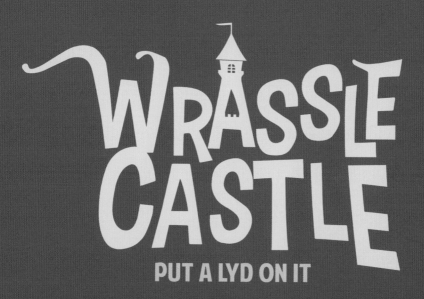

WRASSLE CASTLE

PUT A LYD ON IT

WRITTEN BY
COLLEEN COOVER & PAUL TOBIN

ILLUSTRATED BY
GALAAD

COLORED BY
REBECCA HORNER

LETTERED BY
ANDWORLD DESIGN

DESIGNED BY
BONES LEOPARD & SONJA SYNAK

EDITED BY
REBECCA TAYLOR

WONDERBOUND

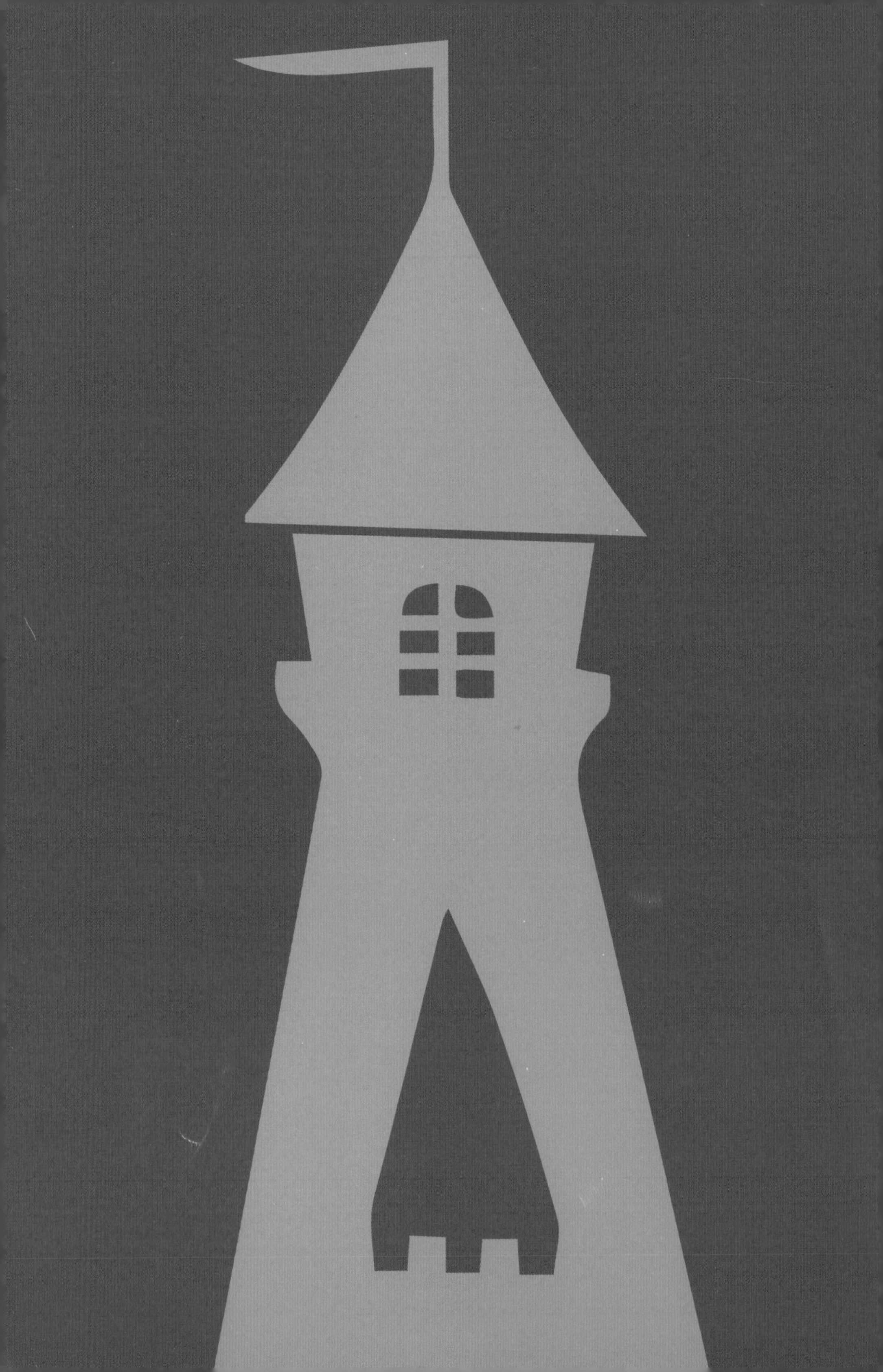

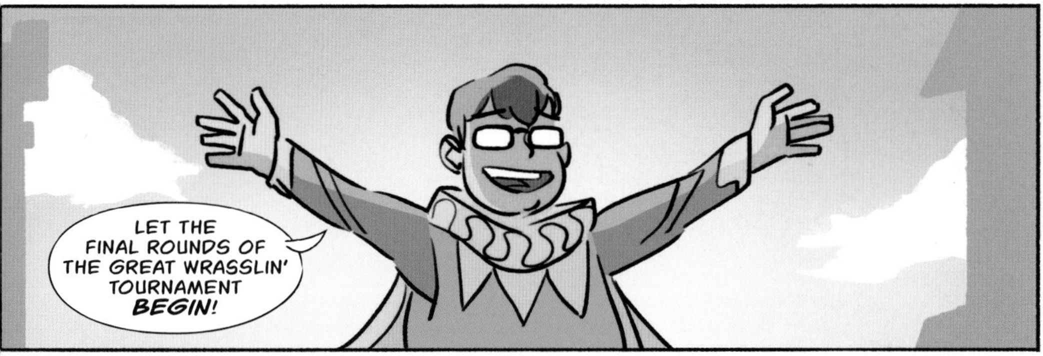
LET THE FINAL ROUNDS OF THE GREAT WRASSLIN' TOURNAMENT **BEGIN**!

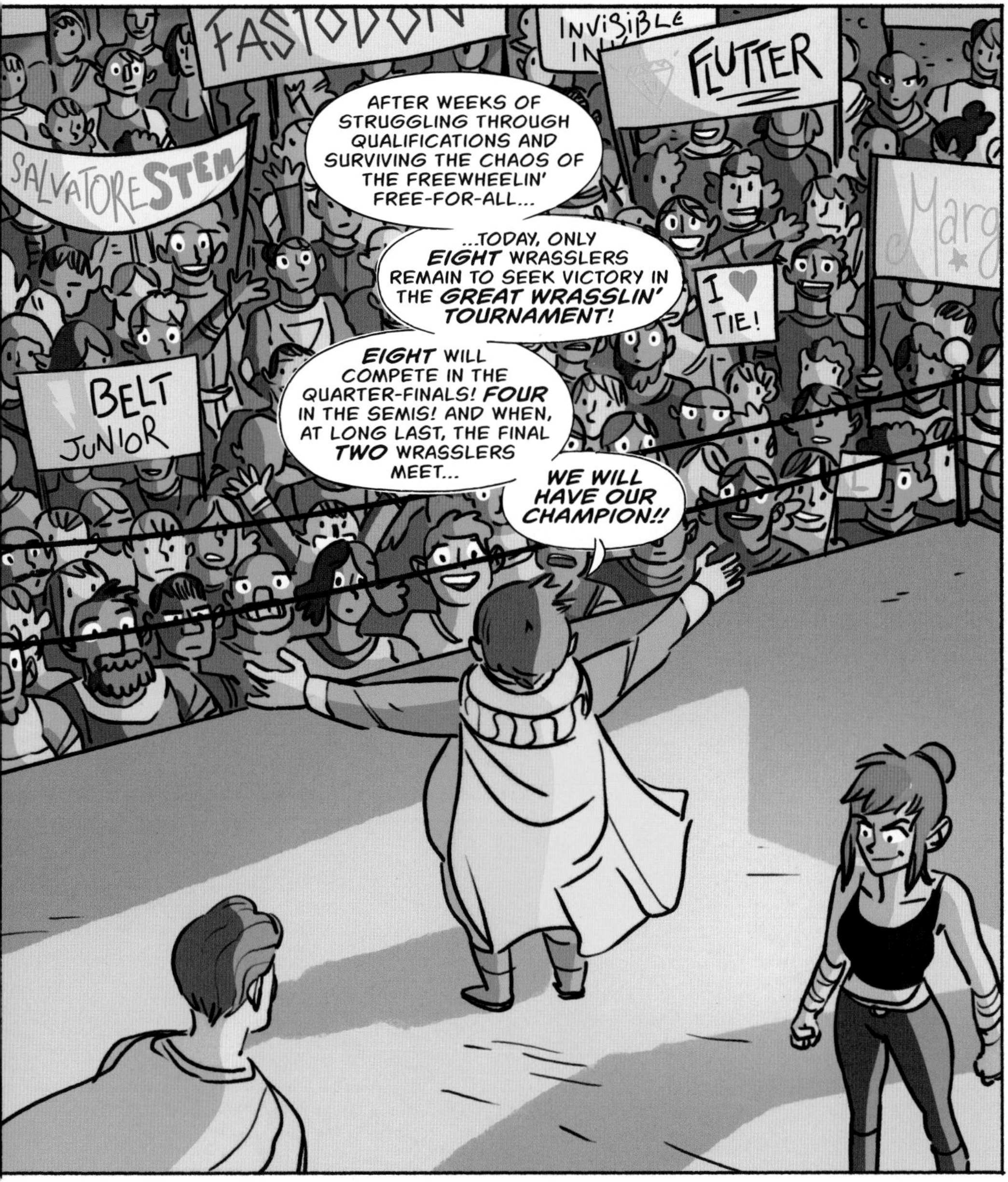
FASTODON
INVISIBLE INK
FLUTTER
SALVATORE STEM
Marg
BELT JUNIOR
I ♥ TIE!
AFTER WEEKS OF STRUGGLING THROUGH QUALIFICATIONS AND SURVIVING THE CHAOS OF THE FREEWHEELIN' FREE-FOR-ALL...
...TODAY, ONLY **EIGHT** WRASSLERS REMAIN TO SEEK VICTORY IN THE **GREAT WRASSLIN' TOURNAMENT**!
EIGHT WILL COMPETE IN THE QUARTER-FINALS! **FOUR** IN THE SEMIS! AND WHEN, AT LONG LAST, THE FINAL **TWO** WRASSLERS MEET...
WE WILL HAVE OUR CHAMPION!!

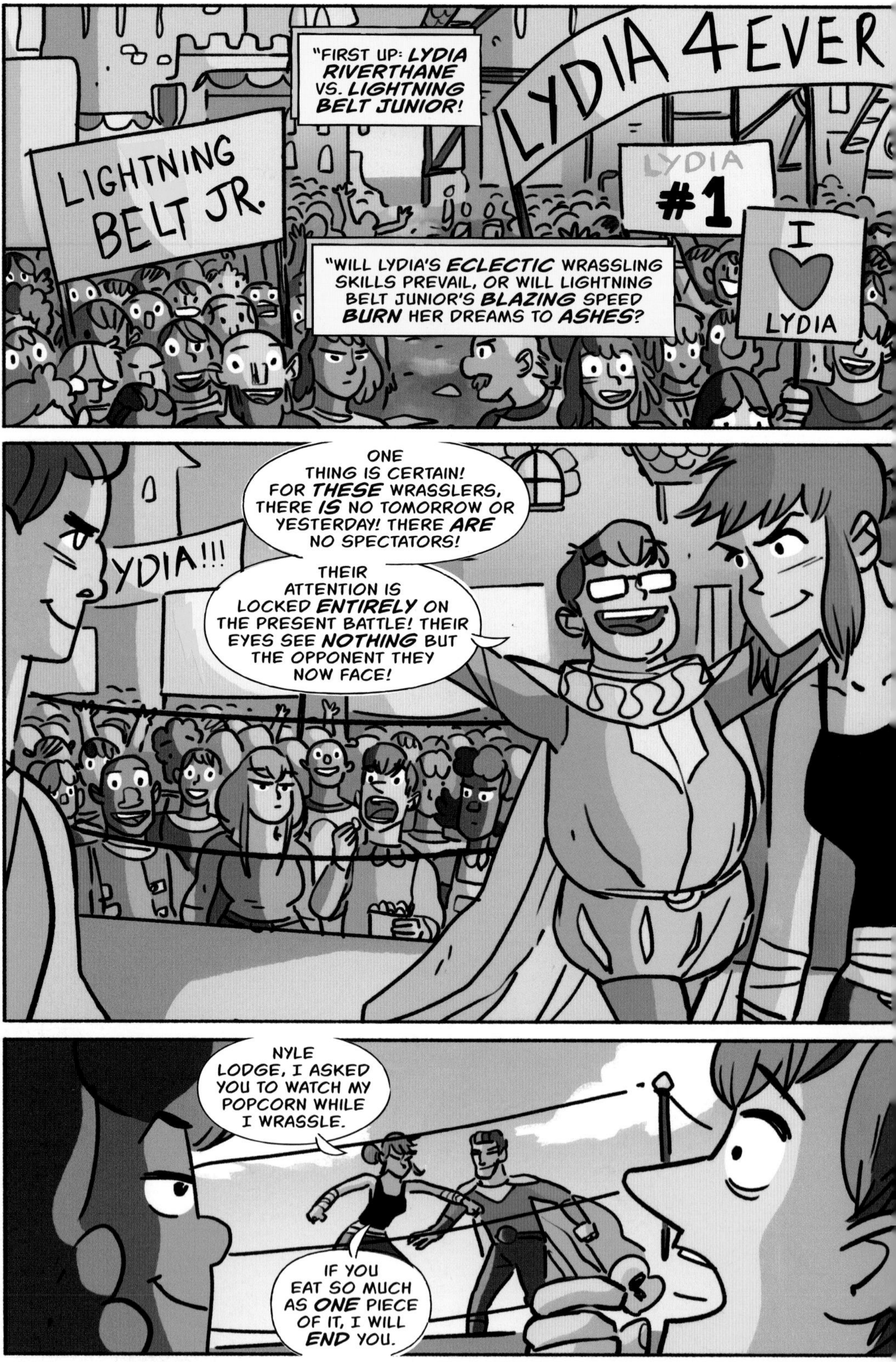
LIGHTNING BELT JR.
"FIRST UP: LYDIA RIVERTHANE VS. LIGHTNING BELT JUNIOR!
LYDIA 4 EVER
LYDIA #1
I ♥ LYDIA
"WILL LYDIA'S ECLECTIC WRASSLING SKILLS PREVAIL, OR WILL LIGHTNING BELT JUNIOR'S BLAZING SPEED BURN HER DREAMS TO ASHES?
YDIA!!!
ONE THING IS CERTAIN! FOR THESE WRASSLERS, THERE IS NO TOMORROW OR YESTERDAY! THERE ARE NO SPECTATORS!
THEIR ATTENTION IS LOCKED ENTIRELY ON THE PRESENT BATTLE! THEIR EYES SEE NOTHING BUT THE OPPONENT THEY NOW FACE!
NYLE LODGE, I ASKED YOU TO WATCH MY POPCORN WHILE I WRASSLE.
IF YOU EAT SO MUCH AS ONE PIECE OF IT, I WILL END YOU.

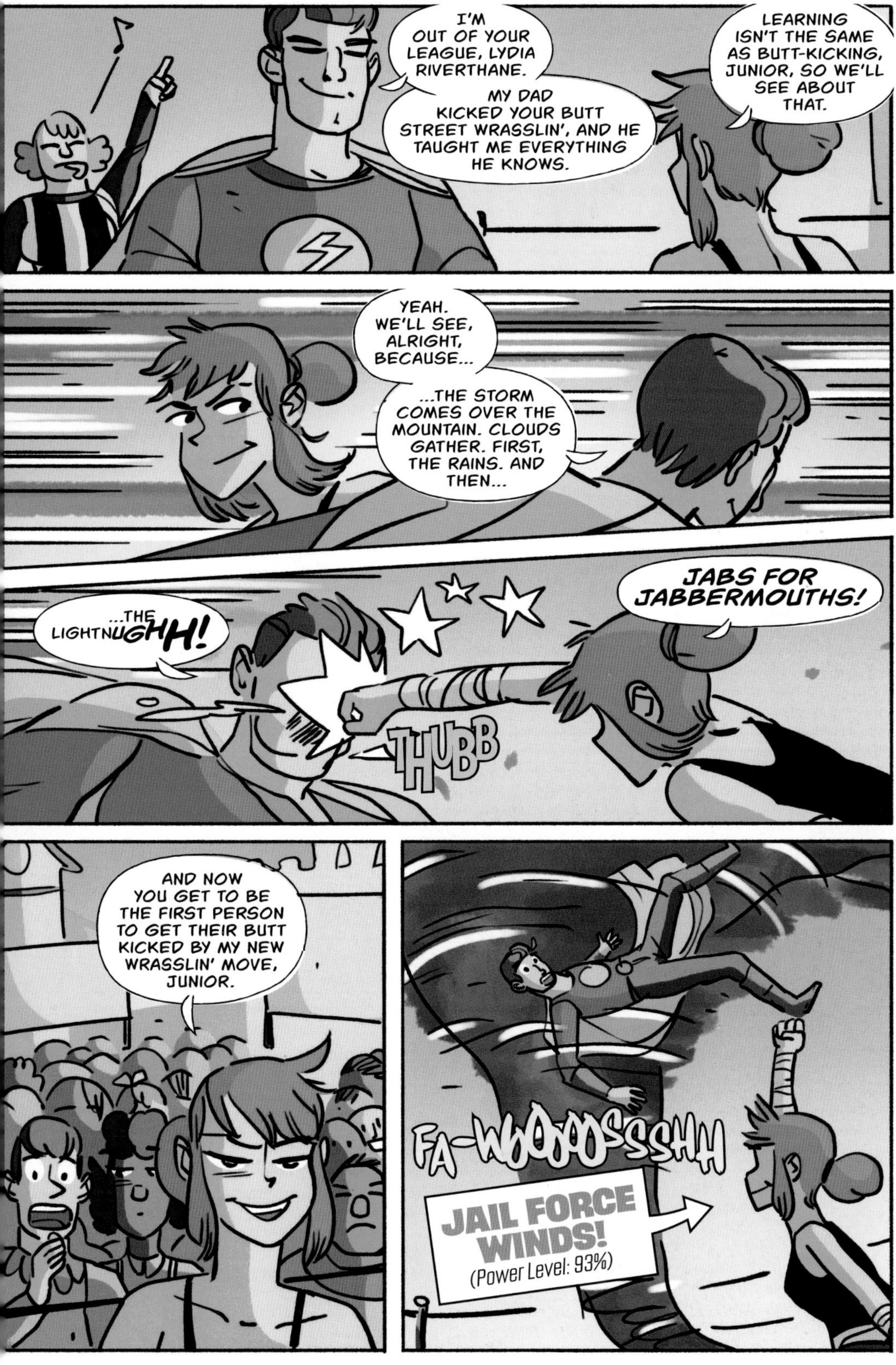
I'M OUT OF YOUR LEAGUE, LYDIA RIVERTHANE.
MY DAD KICKED YOUR BUTT STREET WRASSLIN', AND HE TAUGHT ME EVERYTHING HE KNOWS.
LEARNING ISN'T THE SAME AS BUTT-KICKING, JUNIOR, SO WE'LL SEE ABOUT THAT.
YEAH. WE'LL SEE, ALRIGHT, BECAUSE...
...THE STORM COMES OVER THE MOUNTAIN. CLOUDS GATHER. FIRST, THE RAINS. AND THEN...
...THE LIGHTNUGHH!
JABS FOR JABBERMOUTHS!
THUBB
AND NOW YOU GET TO BE THE FIRST PERSON TO GET THEIR BUTT KICKED BY MY NEW WRASSLIN' MOVE, JUNIOR.
FA-WOOOOOSSSHH
JAIL FORCE WINDS!
(Power Level: 93%)

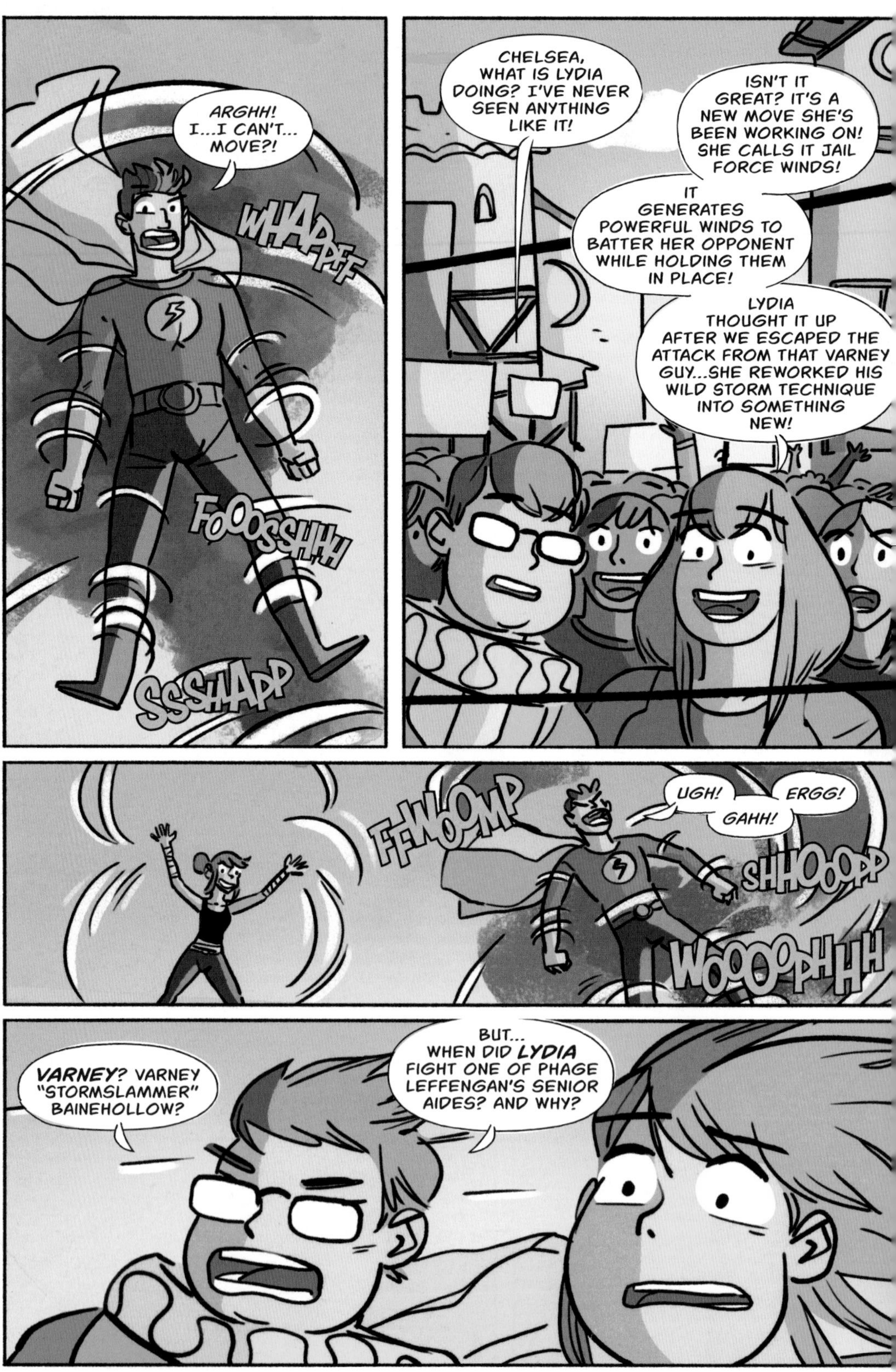
ARGHH! I...I CAN'T... MOVE?!
WHAPFF
FOOOSSHHH
SSSHAPP
CHELSEA, WHAT IS LYDIA DOING? I'VE NEVER SEEN ANYTHING LIKE IT!
ISN'T IT GREAT? IT'S A NEW MOVE SHE'S BEEN WORKING ON! SHE CALLS IT JAIL FORCE WINDS!
IT GENERATES POWERFUL WINDS TO BATTER HER OPPONENT WHILE HOLDING THEM IN PLACE!
LYDIA THOUGHT IT UP AFTER WE ESCAPED THE ATTACK FROM THAT VARNEY GUY...SHE REWORKED HIS WILD STORM TECHNIQUE INTO SOMETHING NEW!
FFWOOMP
UGH!
GAHH!
ERGG!
SHHOOPP
WOOOPHHH
VARNEY? VARNEY "STORMSLAMMER" BAINEHOLLOW?
BUT... WHEN DID LYDIA FIGHT ONE OF PHAGE LEFFENGAN'S SENIOR AIDES? AND WHY?

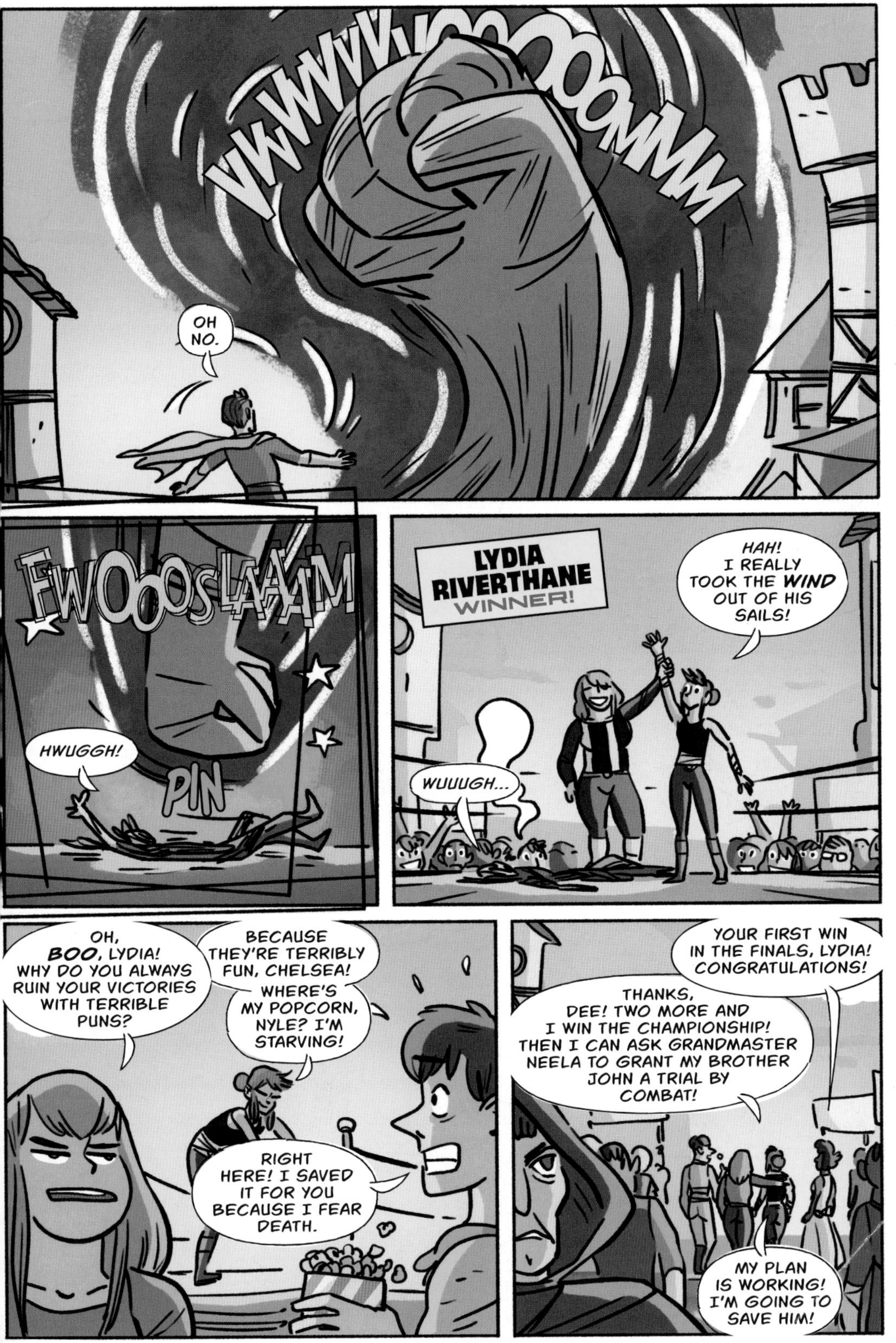
VWWVVVOOOOOOMMMM
OH NO.
FWOOOSLAAAM
HWUGGH!
PIN
LYDIA RIVERTHANE WINNER!
HAH! I REALLY TOOK THE WIND OUT OF HIS SAILS!
WUUUGH...
OH, BOO, LYDIA! WHY DO YOU ALWAYS RUIN YOUR VICTORIES WITH TERRIBLE PUNS?
BECAUSE THEY'RE TERRIBLY FUN, CHELSEA!
WHERE'S MY POPCORN, NYLE? I'M STARVING!
RIGHT HERE! I SAVED IT FOR YOU BECAUSE I FEAR DEATH.
YOUR FIRST WIN IN THE FINALS, LYDIA! CONGRATULATIONS!
THANKS, DEE! TWO MORE AND I WIN THE CHAMPIONSHIP! THEN I CAN ASK GRANDMASTER NEELA TO GRANT MY BROTHER JOHN A TRIAL BY COMBAT!
MY PLAN IS WORKING! I'M GOING TO SAVE HIM!

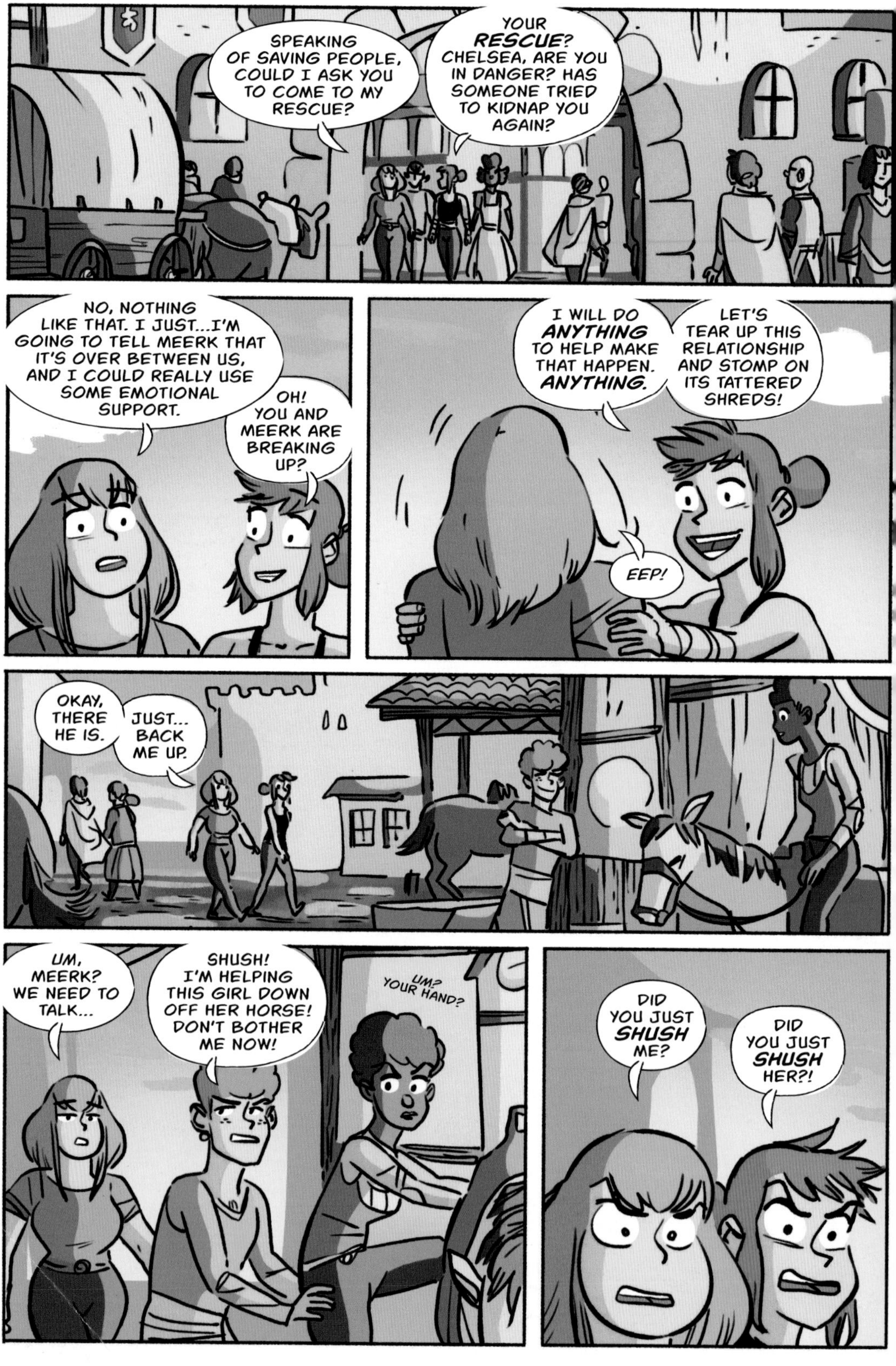
SPEAKING OF SAVING PEOPLE, COULD I ASK YOU TO COME TO MY RESCUE?
YOUR RESCUE? CHELSEA, ARE YOU IN DANGER? HAS SOMEONE TRIED TO KIDNAP YOU AGAIN?
NO, NOTHING LIKE THAT. I JUST...I'M GOING TO TELL MEERK THAT IT'S OVER BETWEEN US, AND I COULD REALLY USE SOME EMOTIONAL SUPPORT.
OH! YOU AND MEERK ARE BREAKING UP?
LET'S TEAR UP THIS RELATIONSHIP AND STOMP ON ITS TATTERED SHREDS!
I WILL DO ANYTHING TO HELP MAKE THAT HAPPEN. ANYTHING.
EEP!
OKAY, THERE HE IS.
JUST... BACK ME UP.
UM, MEERK? WE NEED TO TALK...
SHUSH! I'M HELPING THIS GIRL DOWN OFF HER HORSE! DON'T BOTHER ME NOW!
UM? YOUR HAND?
DID YOU JUST SHUSH ME?
DID YOU JUST SHUSH HER?!

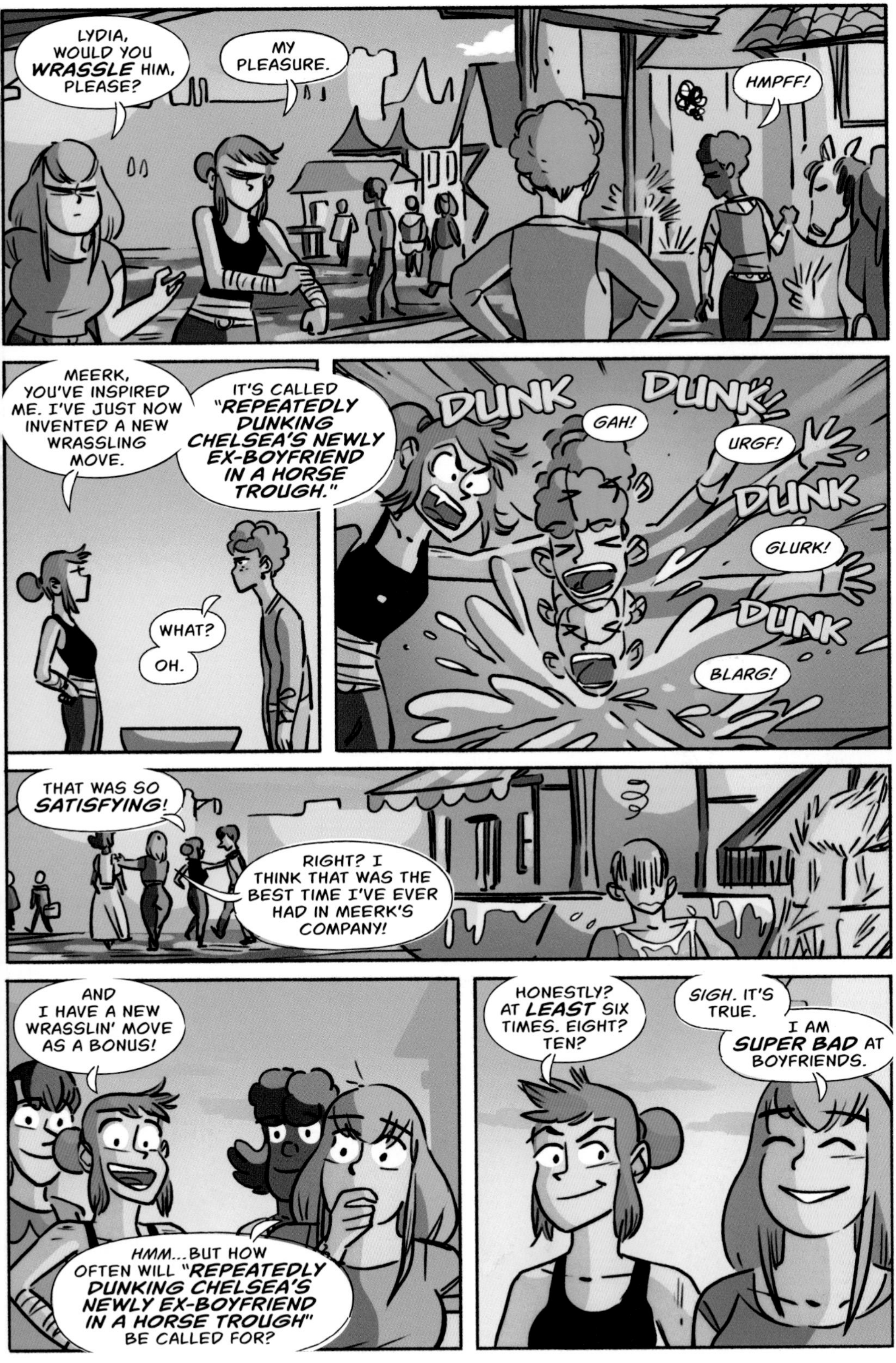
LYDIA, WOULD YOU WRASSLE HIM, PLEASE?
MY PLEASURE.
HMPFF!
MEERK, YOU'VE INSPIRED ME. I'VE JUST NOW INVENTED A NEW WRASSLING MOVE.
IT'S CALLED "REPEATEDLY DUNKING CHELSEA'S NEWLY EX-BOYFRIEND IN A HORSE TROUGH."
WHAT?
OH.
DUNK
DUNK
GAH!
URGF!
DUNK
GLURK!
DUNK
BLARG!
THAT WAS SO SATISFYING!
RIGHT? I THINK THAT WAS THE BEST TIME I'VE EVER HAD IN MEERK'S COMPANY!
AND I HAVE A NEW WRASSLIN' MOVE AS A BONUS!
HMM... BUT HOW OFTEN WILL "REPEATEDLY DUNKING CHELSEA'S NEWLY EX-BOYFRIEND IN A HORSE TROUGH" BE CALLED FOR?
HONESTLY? AT LEAST SIX TIMES. EIGHT? TEN?
SIGH. IT'S TRUE.
I AM SUPER BAD AT BOYFRIENDS.

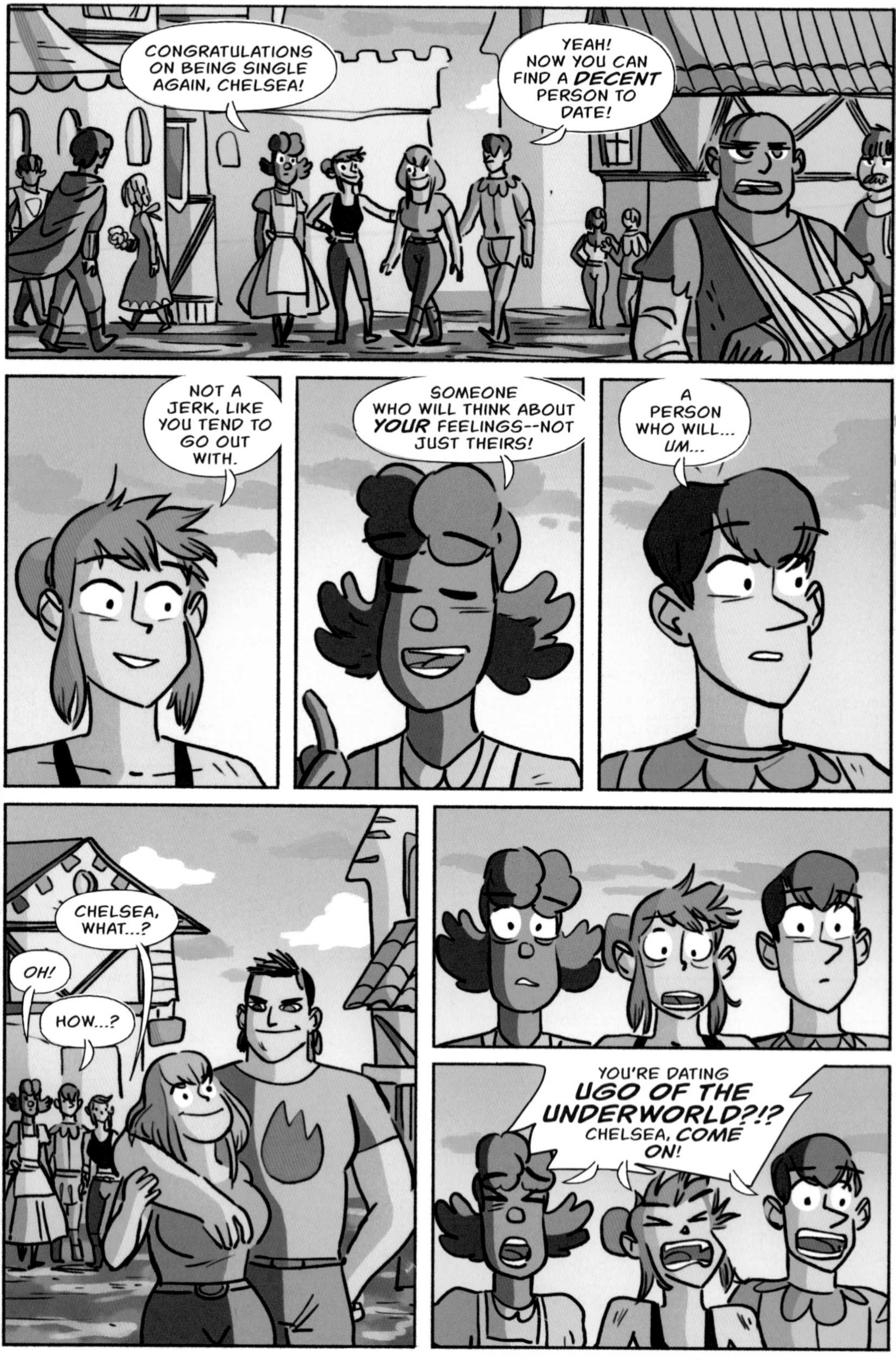
CONGRATULATIONS ON BEING SINGLE AGAIN, CHELSEA!
YEAH! NOW YOU CAN FIND A DECENT PERSON TO DATE!
NOT A JERK, LIKE YOU TEND TO GO OUT WITH.
SOMEONE WHO WILL THINK ABOUT YOUR FEELINGS--NOT JUST THEIRS!
A PERSON WHO WILL... UM...
CHELSEA, WHAT...?
OH!
HOW...?
YOU'RE DATING UGO OF THE UNDERWORLD?!? CHELSEA, COME ON!

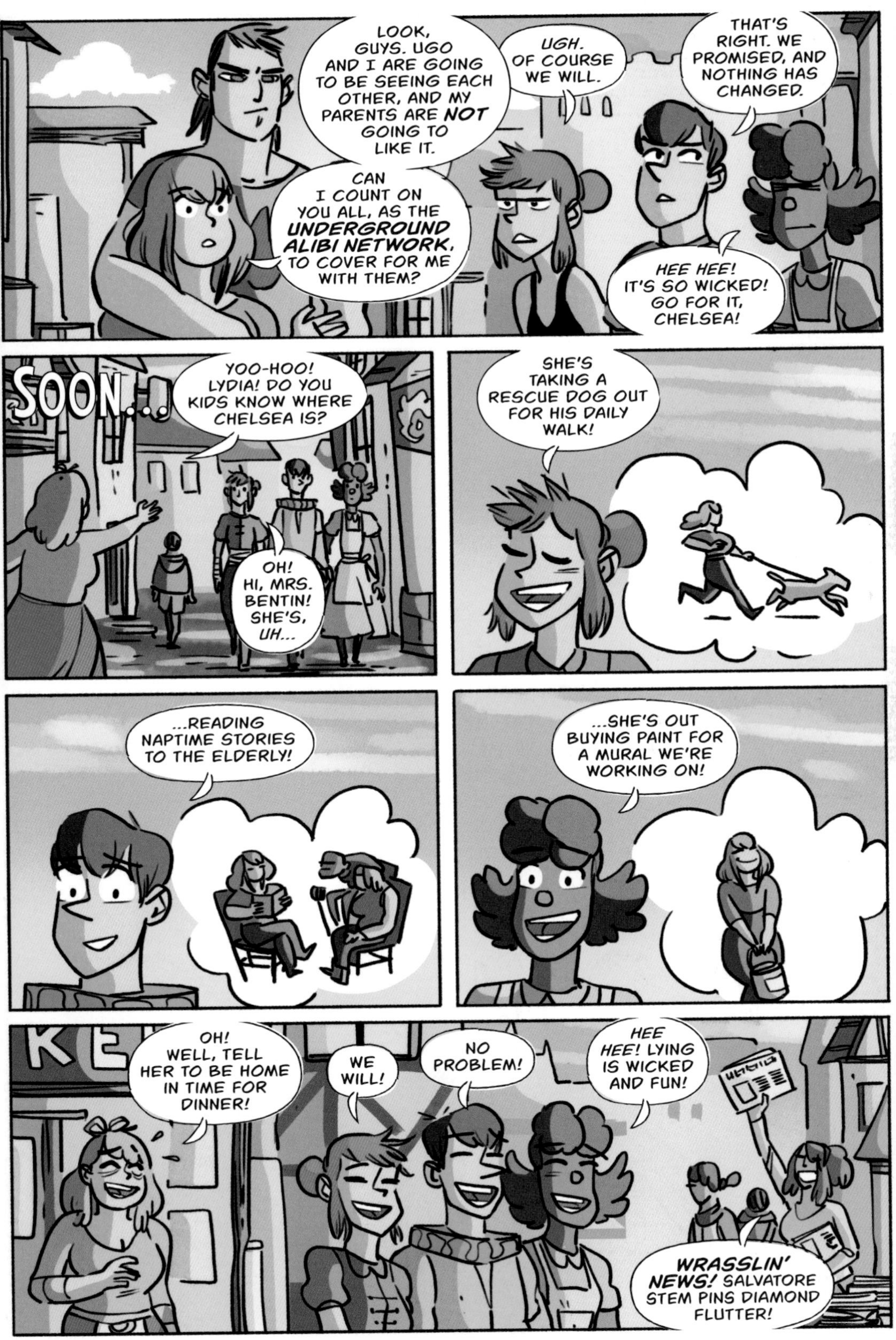
LOOK, GUYS. UGO AND I ARE GOING TO BE SEEING EACH OTHER, AND MY PARENTS ARE **NOT** GOING TO LIKE IT.
CAN I COUNT ON YOU ALL, AS THE **UNDERGROUND ALIBI NETWORK**, TO COVER FOR ME WITH THEM?
UGH. OF COURSE WE WILL.
THAT'S RIGHT. WE PROMISED, AND NOTHING HAS CHANGED.
HEE HEE! IT'S SO WICKED! GO FOR IT, CHELSEA!
SOON...
YOO-HOO! LYDIA! DO YOU KIDS KNOW WHERE CHELSEA IS?
OH! HI, MRS. BENTIN! SHE'S, UH...
SHE'S TAKING A RESCUE DOG OUT FOR HIS DAILY WALK!
...READING NAPTIME STORIES TO THE ELDERLY!
...SHE'S OUT BUYING PAINT FOR A MURAL WE'RE WORKING ON!
OH! WELL, TELL HER TO BE HOME IN TIME FOR DINNER!
WE WILL!
NO PROBLEM!
HEE HEE! LYING IS WICKED AND FUN!
WRASSLIN' NEWS! SALVATORE STEM PINS DIAMOND FLUTTER!

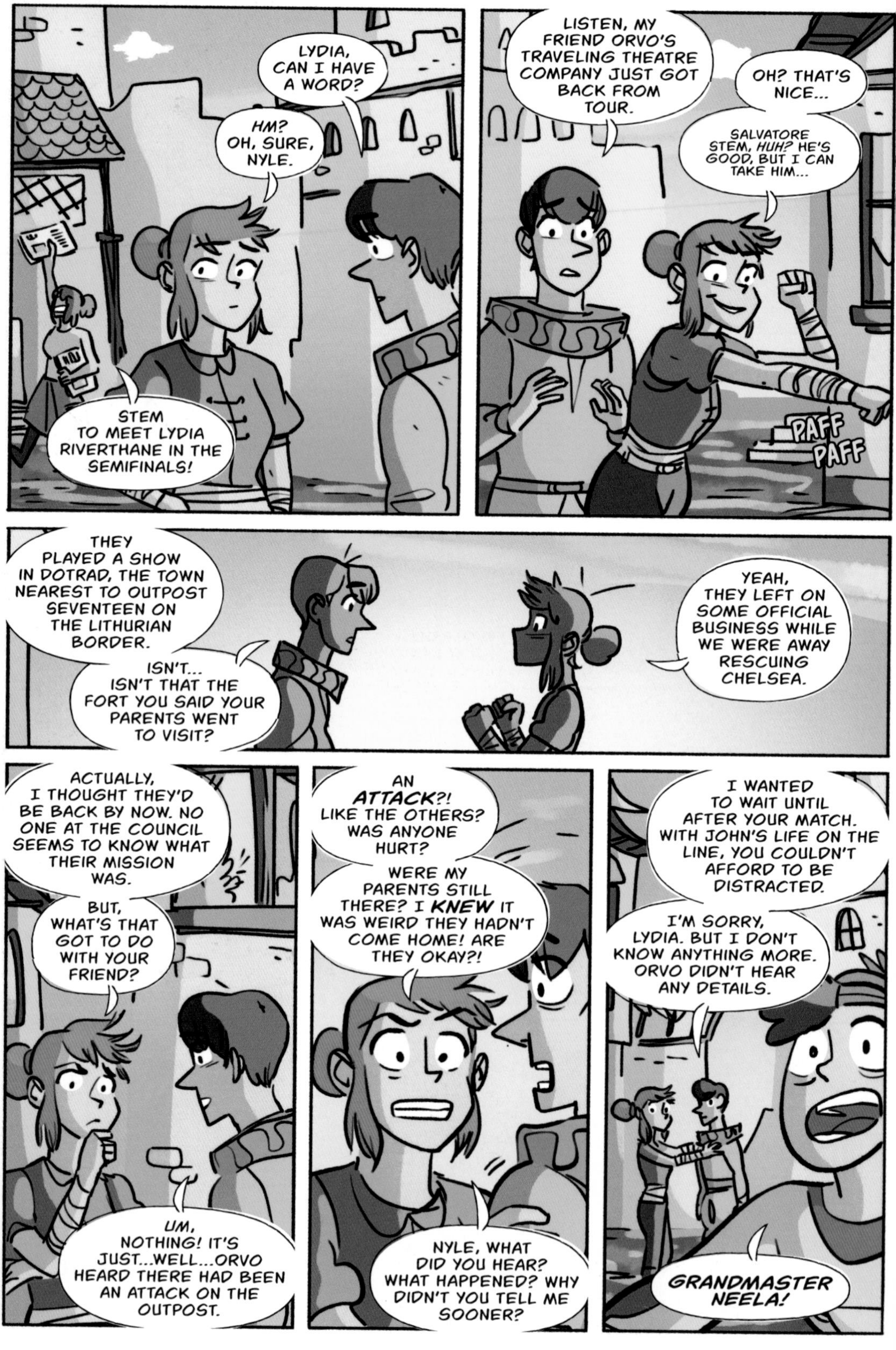
LYDIA, CAN I HAVE A WORD?
HM? OH, SURE, NYLE.
STEM TO MEET LYDIA RIVERTHANE IN THE SEMIFINALS!
LISTEN, MY FRIEND ORVO'S TRAVELING THEATRE COMPANY JUST GOT BACK FROM TOUR.
OH? THAT'S NICE...
SALVATORE STEM, HUH? HE'S GOOD, BUT I CAN TAKE HIM...
PAFF PAFF
THEY PLAYED A SHOW IN DOTRAD, THE TOWN NEAREST TO OUTPOST SEVENTEEN ON THE LITHURIAN BORDER.
ISN'T... ISN'T THAT THE FORT YOU SAID YOUR PARENTS WENT TO VISIT?
YEAH, THEY LEFT ON SOME OFFICIAL BUSINESS WHILE WE WERE AWAY RESCUING CHELSEA.
ACTUALLY, I THOUGHT THEY'D BE BACK BY NOW. NO ONE AT THE COUNCIL SEEMS TO KNOW WHAT THEIR MISSION WAS.
BUT, WHAT'S THAT GOT TO DO WITH YOUR FRIEND?
UM, NOTHING! IT'S JUST...WELL...ORVO HEARD THERE HAD BEEN AN ATTACK ON THE OUTPOST.
AN ATTACK?! LIKE THE OTHERS? WAS ANYONE HURT?
WERE MY PARENTS STILL THERE? I KNEW IT WAS WEIRD THEY HADN'T COME HOME! ARE THEY OKAY?!
NYLE, WHAT DID YOU HEAR? WHAT HAPPENED? WHY DIDN'T YOU TELL ME SOONER?
I WANTED TO WAIT UNTIL AFTER YOUR MATCH. WITH JOHN'S LIFE ON THE LINE, YOU COULDN'T AFFORD TO BE DISTRACTED.
I'M SORRY, LYDIA. BUT I DON'T KNOW ANYTHING MORE. ORVO DIDN'T HEAR ANY DETAILS.
GRANDMASTER NEELA!

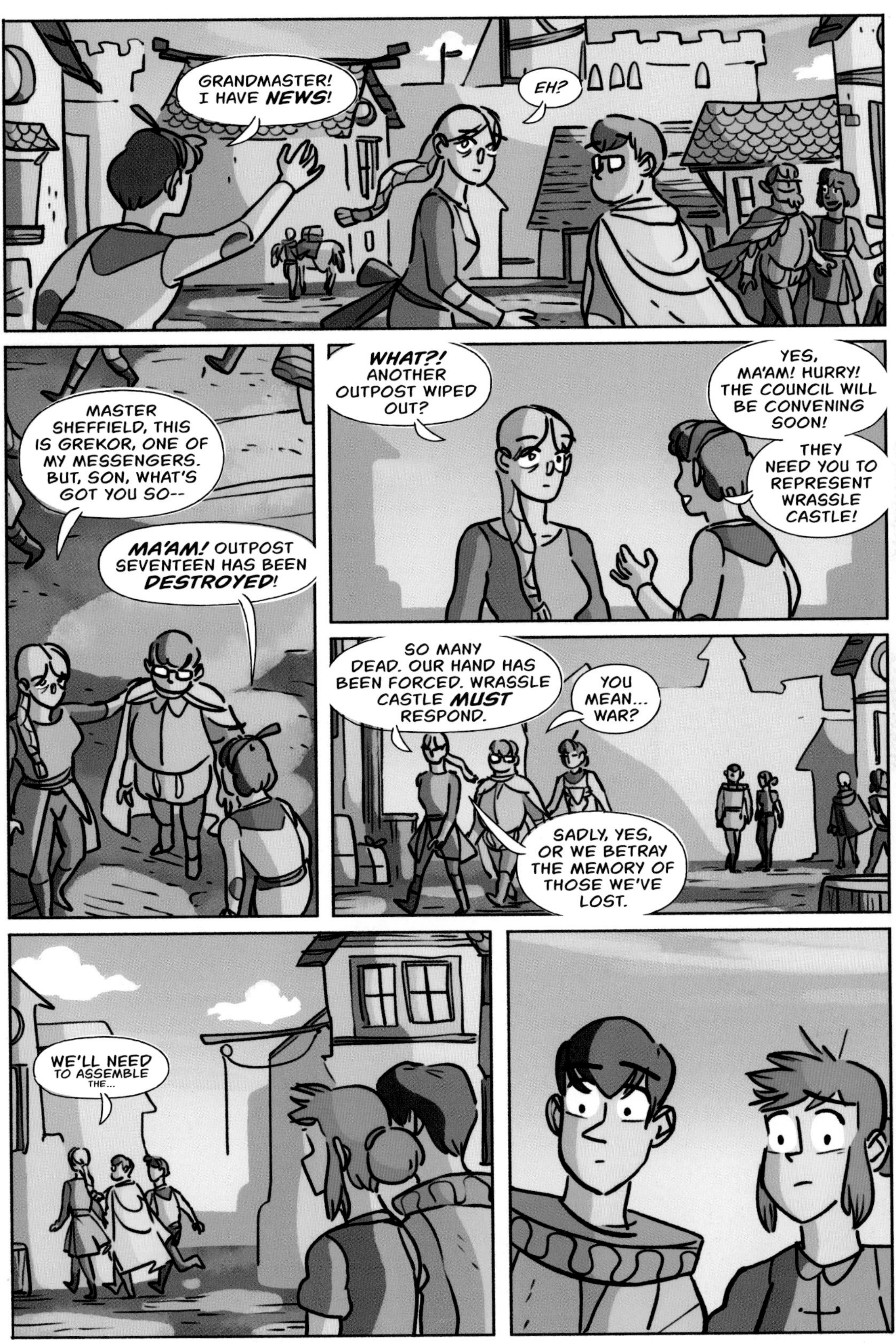

GRANDMASTER! I HAVE NEWS!
EH?
MASTER SHEFFIELD, THIS IS GREKOR, ONE OF MY MESSENGERS. BUT, SON, WHAT'S GOT YOU SO--
MA'AM! OUTPOST SEVENTEEN HAS BEEN DESTROYED!
WHAT?! ANOTHER OUTPOST WIPED OUT?
YES, MA'AM! HURRY! THE COUNCIL WILL BE CONVENING SOON!
THEY NEED YOU TO REPRESENT WRASSLE CASTLE!
SO MANY DEAD. OUR HAND HAS BEEN FORCED. WRASSLE CASTLE MUST RESPOND.
YOU MEAN... WAR?
SADLY, YES, OR WE BETRAY THE MEMORY OF THOSE WE'VE LOST.
WE'LL NEED TO ASSEMBLE THE...

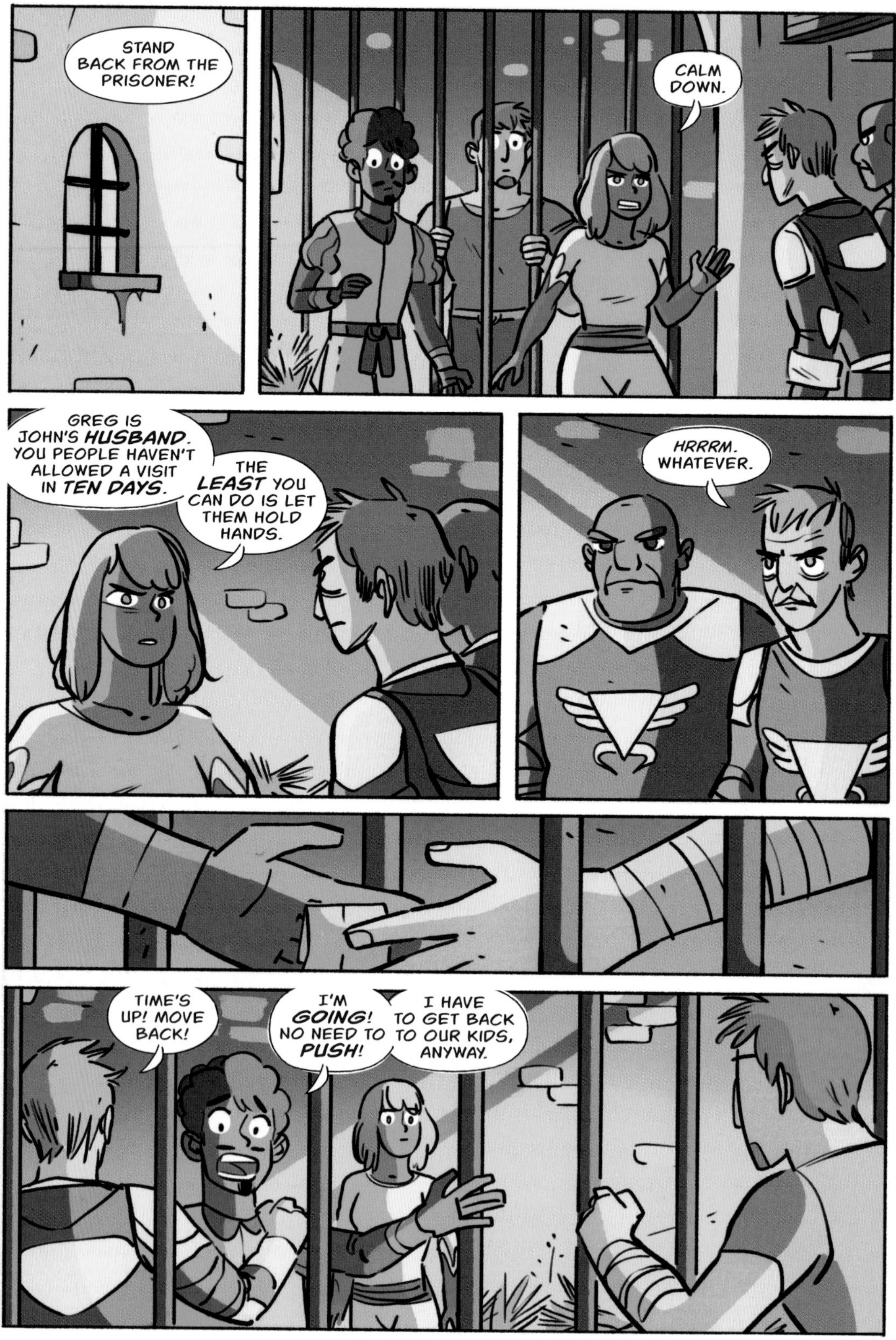
STAND BACK FROM THE PRISONER!
CALM DOWN.
GREG IS JOHN'S ***HUSBAND***. YOU PEOPLE HAVEN'T ALLOWED A VISIT IN ***TEN DAYS***.
THE ***LEAST*** YOU CAN DO IS LET THEM HOLD HANDS.
HRRRM. WHATEVER.
TIME'S UP! MOVE BACK!
I'M ***GOING***! NO NEED TO ***PUSH***!
I HAVE TO GET BACK TO OUR KIDS, ANYWAY.

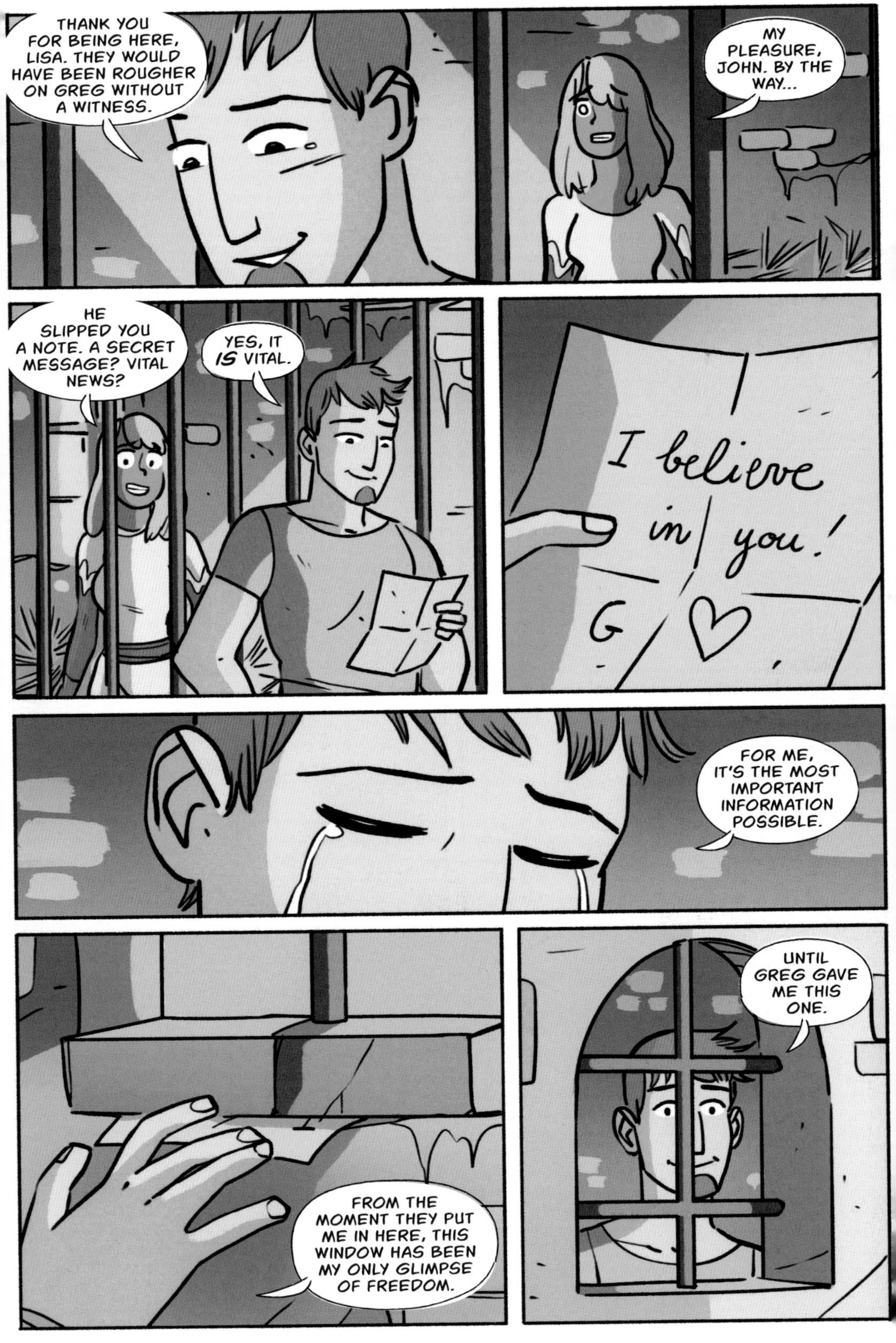
THANK YOU FOR BEING HERE, LISA. THEY WOULD HAVE BEEN ROUGHER ON GREG WITHOUT A WITNESS.
MY PLEASURE, JOHN. BY THE WAY...
HE SLIPPED YOU A NOTE. A SECRET MESSAGE? VITAL NEWS?
YES, IT *IS* VITAL.
I believe in you!
G ♡
FOR ME, IT'S THE MOST IMPORTANT INFORMATION POSSIBLE.
FROM THE MOMENT THEY PUT ME IN HERE, THIS WINDOW HAS BEEN MY ONLY GLIMPSE OF FREEDOM.
UNTIL GREG GAVE ME THIS ONE.

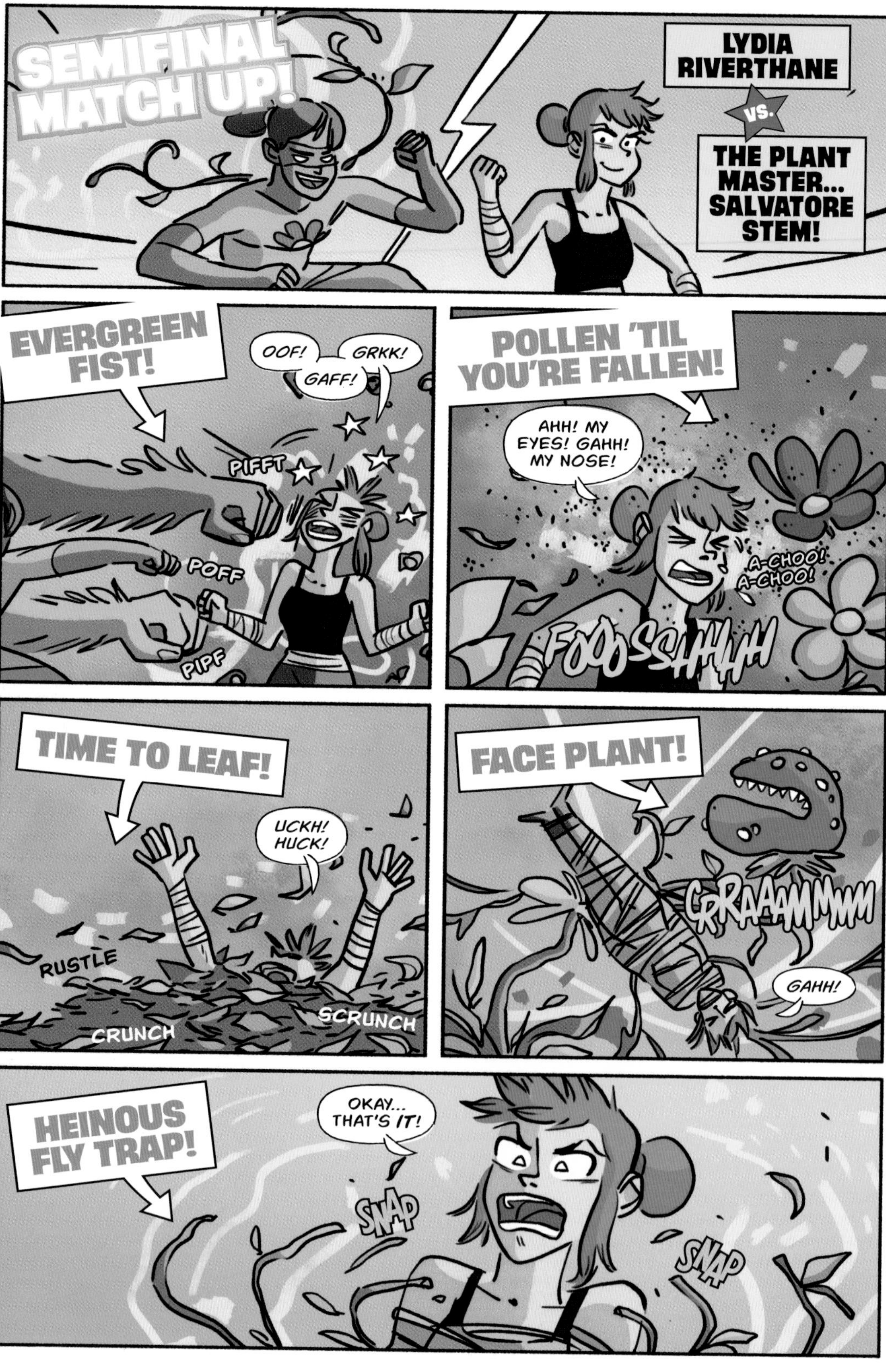
SEMIFINAL MATCH UP!
LYDIA RIVERTHANE
VS.
THE PLANT MASTER... SALVATORE STEM!
EVERGREEN FIST!
OOF!
GAFF!
GRKK!
PIFFT
POFF
PIPF
POLLEN 'TIL YOU'RE FALLEN!
AHH! MY EYES! GAHH! MY NOSE!
A-CHOO! A-CHOO!
FOOOSSHHHH
TIME TO LEAF!
UCKH! HUCK!
RUSTLE
CRUNCH
SCRUNCH
FACE PLANT!
CRRAAAMMMM
GAHH!
HEINOUS FLY TRAP!
OKAY... THAT'S IT!
SNAP
SNAP

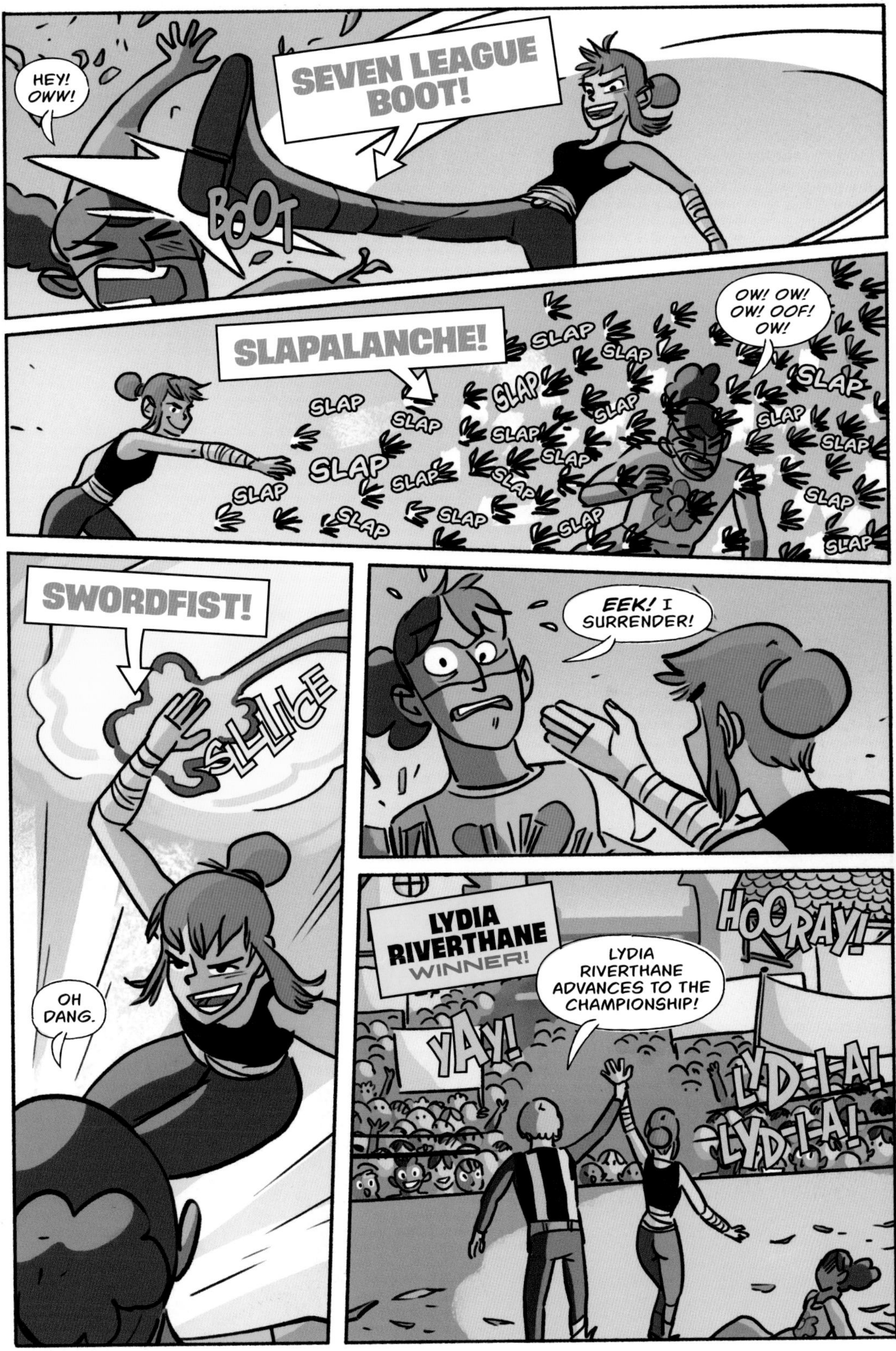
HEY! OWW!
SEVEN LEAGUE BOOT!
BOOT
SLAPALANCHE!
OW! OW! OW! OOF! OW!
SLAP SLAP SLAP SLAP SLAP SLAP SLAP SLAP SLAP SLAP SLAP SLAP SLAP SLAP SLAP SLAP SLAP SLAP SLAP SLAP
SWORDFIST!
SSLLLICE
OH DANG.
EEK! I SURRENDER!
LYDIA RIVERTHANE WINNER!
HOORAY!
LYDIA RIVERTHANE ADVANCES TO THE CHAMPIONSHIP!
YAY!
LYD-I-A! LYD-I-A!

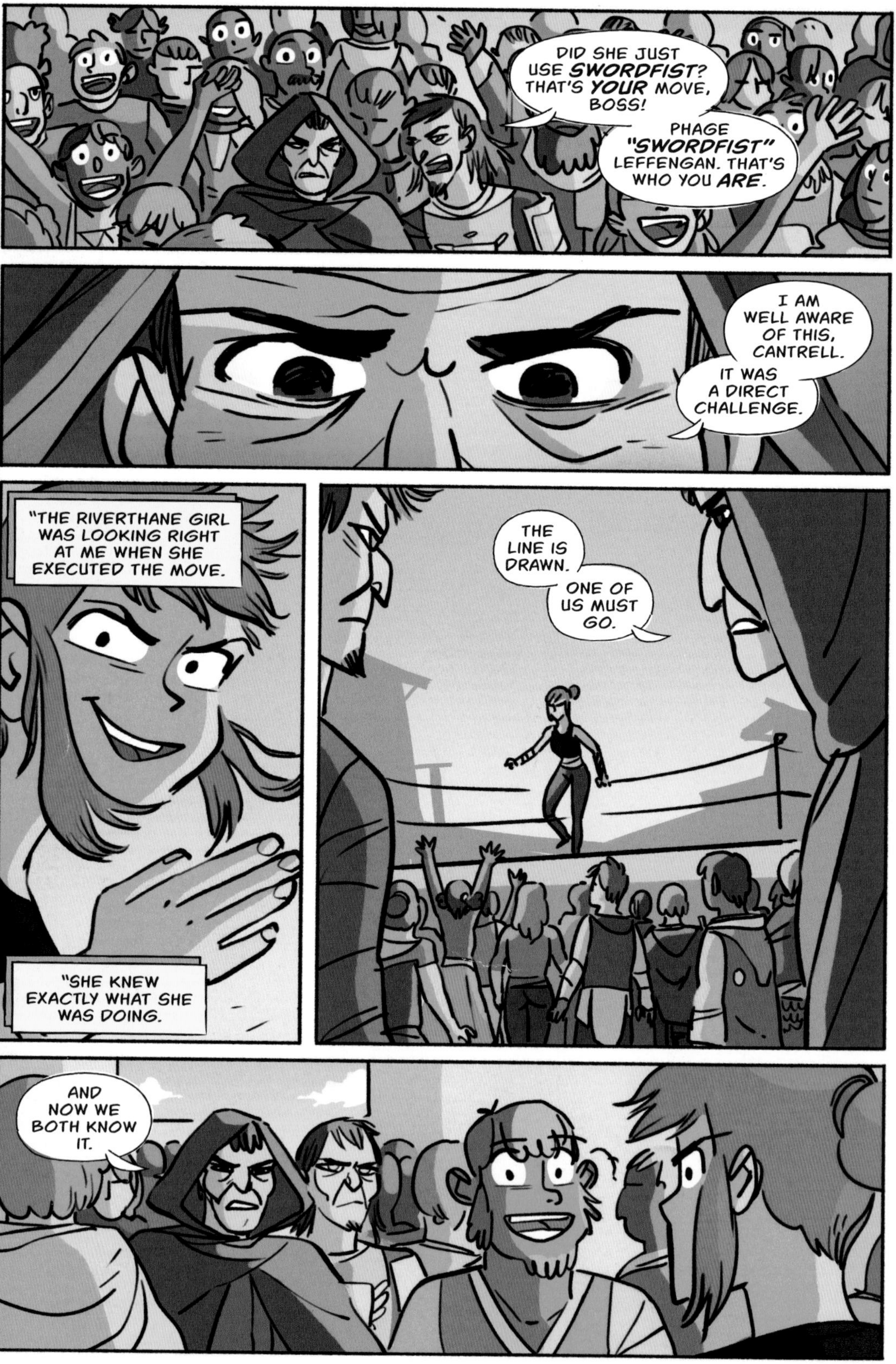
DID SHE JUST USE SWORDFIST? THAT'S YOUR MOVE, BOSS!
PHAGE "SWORDFIST" LEFFENGAN. THAT'S WHO YOU ARE.
I AM WELL AWARE OF THIS, CANTRELL.
IT WAS A DIRECT CHALLENGE.
"THE RIVERTHANE GIRL WAS LOOKING RIGHT AT ME WHEN SHE EXECUTED THE MOVE.
"SHE KNEW EXACTLY WHAT SHE WAS DOING.
THE LINE IS DRAWN.
ONE OF US MUST GO.
AND NOW WE BOTH KNOW IT.

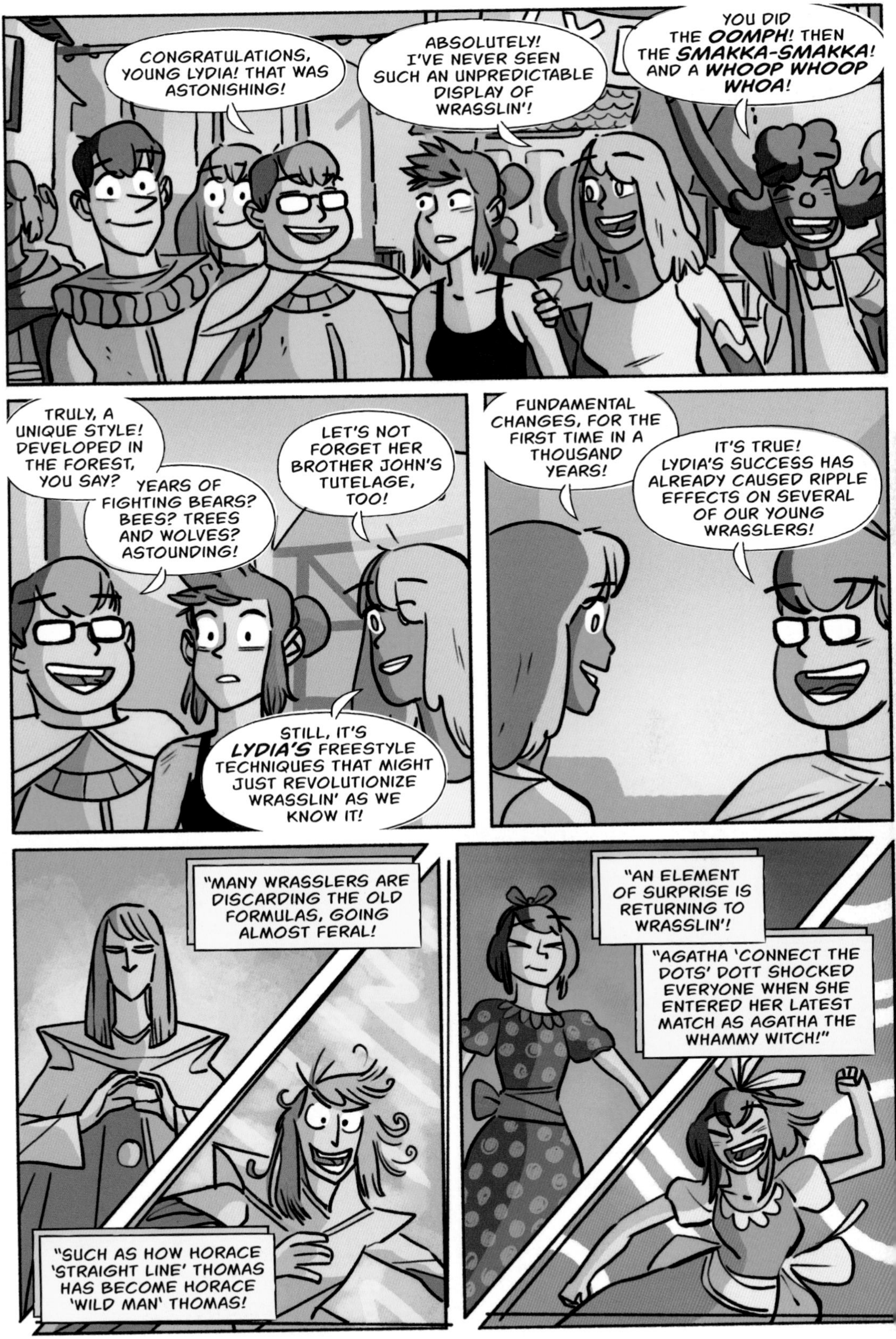
CONGRATULATIONS, YOUNG LYDIA! THAT WAS ASTONISHING!
ABSOLUTELY! I'VE NEVER SEEN SUCH AN UNPREDICTABLE DISPLAY OF WRASSLIN'!
YOU DID THE *OOMPH*! THEN THE *SMAKKA-SMAKKA*! AND A *WHOOP WHOOP WHOA*!
TRULY, A UNIQUE STYLE! DEVELOPED IN THE FOREST, YOU SAY?
YEARS OF FIGHTING BEARS? BEES? TREES AND WOLVES? ASTOUNDING!
LET'S NOT FORGET HER BROTHER JOHN'S TUTELAGE, TOO!
STILL, IT'S *LYDIA'S* FREESTYLE TECHNIQUES THAT MIGHT JUST REVOLUTIONIZE WRASSLIN' AS WE KNOW IT!
FUNDAMENTAL CHANGES, FOR THE FIRST TIME IN A THOUSAND YEARS!
IT'S TRUE! LYDIA'S SUCCESS HAS ALREADY CAUSED RIPPLE EFFECTS ON SEVERAL OF OUR YOUNG WRASSLERS!
"MANY WRASSLERS ARE DISCARDING THE OLD FORMULAS, GOING ALMOST FERAL!
"SUCH AS HOW HORACE 'STRAIGHT LINE' THOMAS HAS BECOME HORACE 'WILD MAN' THOMAS!
"AN ELEMENT OF SURPRISE IS RETURNING TO WRASSLIN'!
"AGATHA 'CONNECT THE DOTS' DOTT SHOCKED EVERYONE WHEN SHE ENTERED HER LATEST MATCH AS AGATHA THE WHAMMY WITCH!"

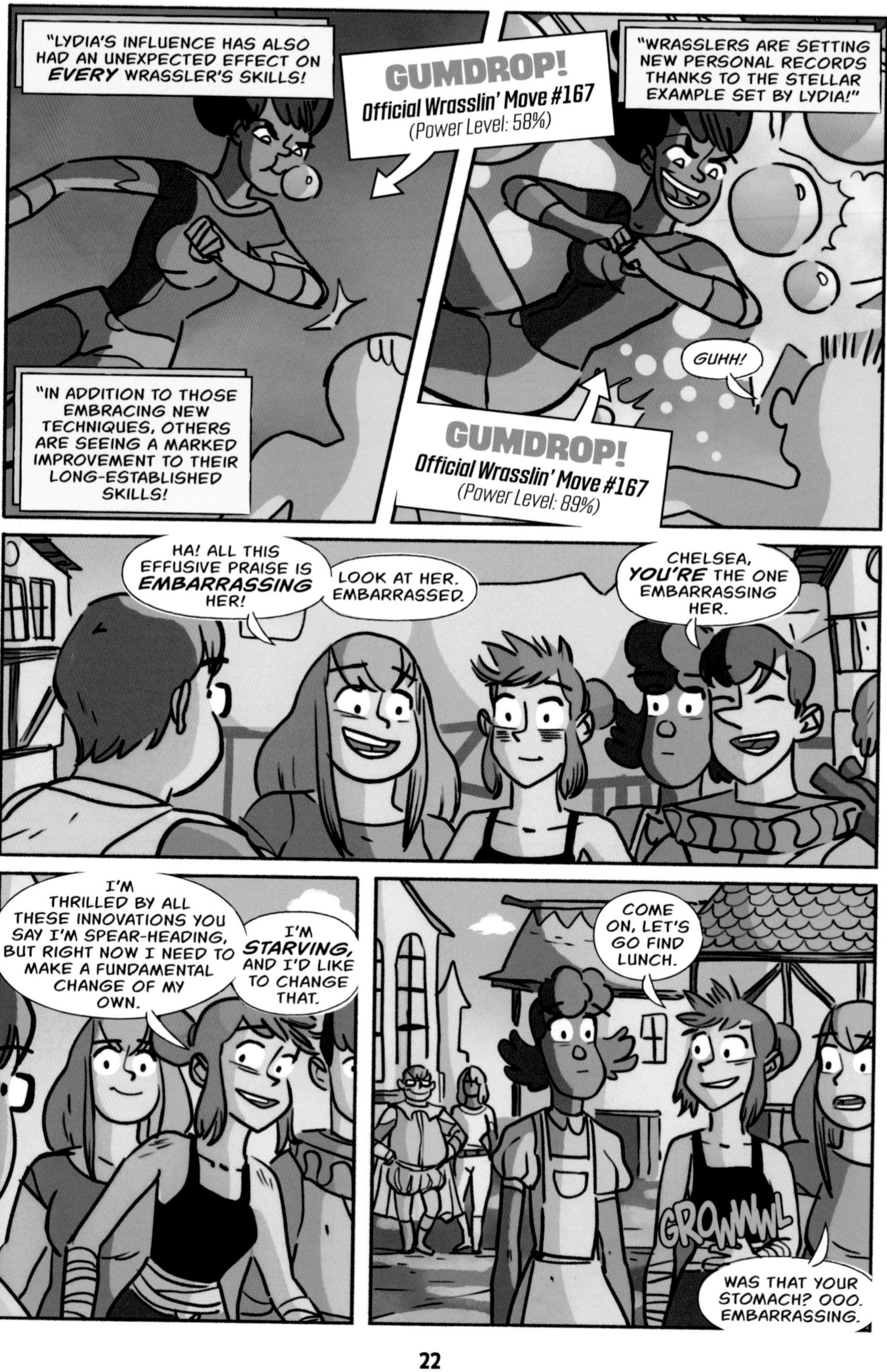
"LYDIA'S INFLUENCE HAS ALSO HAD AN UNEXPECTED EFFECT ON EVERY WRASSLER'S SKILLS!
GUMDROP! Official Wrasslin' Move #167 (Power Level: 58%)
"IN ADDITION TO THOSE EMBRACING NEW TECHNIQUES, OTHERS ARE SEEING A MARKED IMPROVEMENT TO THEIR LONG-ESTABLISHED SKILLS!
"WRASSLERS ARE SETTING NEW PERSONAL RECORDS THANKS TO THE STELLAR EXAMPLE SET BY LYDIA!"
GUHH!
GUMDROP! Official Wrasslin' Move #167 (Power Level: 89%)
HA! ALL THIS EFFUSIVE PRAISE IS EMBARRASSING HER!
LOOK AT HER. EMBARRASSED.
CHELSEA, YOU'RE THE ONE EMBARRASSING HER.
I'M THRILLED BY ALL THESE INNOVATIONS YOU SAY I'M SPEAR-HEADING, BUT RIGHT NOW I NEED TO MAKE A FUNDAMENTAL CHANGE OF MY OWN.
I'M STARVING, AND I'D LIKE TO CHANGE THAT.
COME ON, LET'S GO FIND LUNCH.
GROWWWL
WAS THAT YOUR STOMACH? OOO. EMBARRASSING.

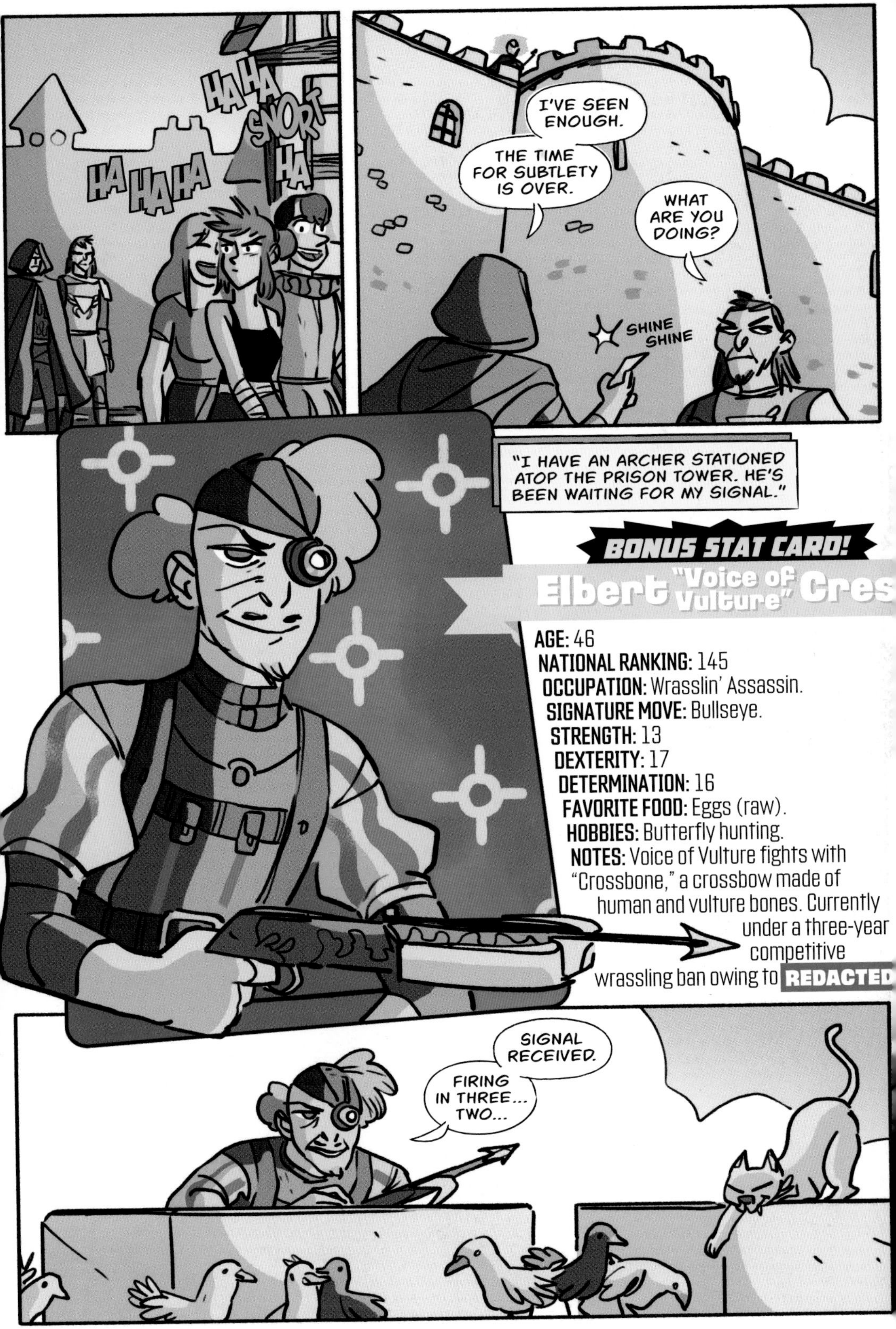
HA HA SNORT HA
HA HA HA
I'VE SEEN ENOUGH.
THE TIME FOR SUBTLETY IS OVER.
WHAT ARE YOU DOING?
SHINE SHINE
"I HAVE AN ARCHER STATIONED ATOP THE PRISON TOWER. HE'S BEEN WAITING FOR MY SIGNAL."
BONUS STAT CARD!
Elbert "Voice of Vulture" Cres
AGE: 46
NATIONAL RANKING: 145
OCCUPATION: Wrasslin' Assassin.
SIGNATURE MOVE: Bullseye.
STRENGTH: 13
DEXTERITY: 17
DETERMINATION: 16
FAVORITE FOOD: Eggs (raw).
HOBBIES: Butterfly hunting.
NOTES: Voice of Vulture fights with "Crossbone," a crossbow made of human and vulture bones. Currently under a three-year competitive wrassling ban owing to REDACTED
SIGNAL RECEIVED.
FIRING IN THREE... TWO...

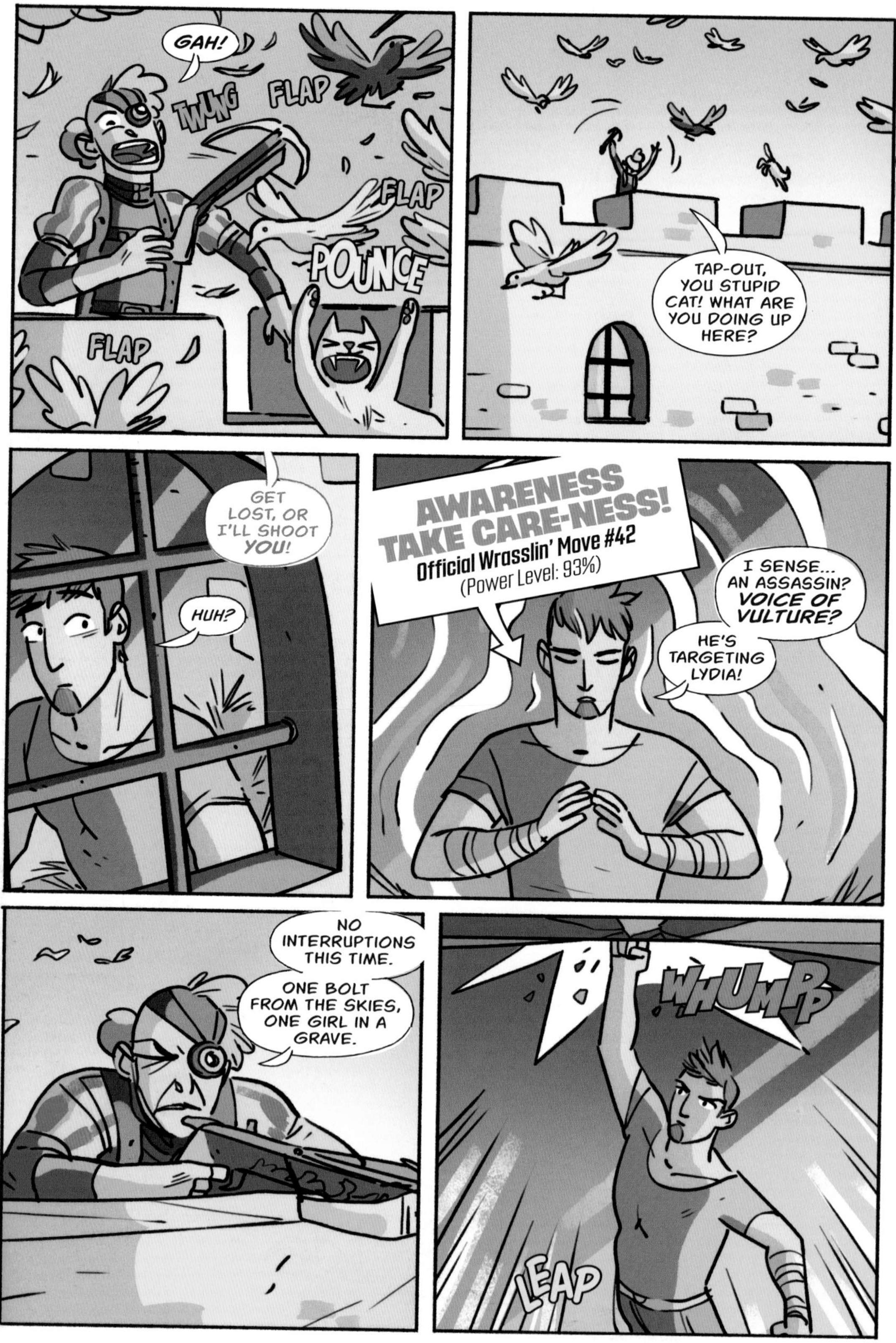
GAH!
TWUNG
FLAP
FLAP
POUNCE
FLAP
TAP-OUT, YOU STUPID CAT! WHAT ARE YOU DOING UP HERE?
GET LOST, OR I'LL SHOOT YOU!
HUH?
AWARENESS TAKE CARE-NESS!
Official Wrasslin' Move #42
(Power Level: 93%)
I SENSE... AN ASSASSIN? VOICE OF VULTURE?
HE'S TARGETING LYDIA!
NO INTERRUPTIONS THIS TIME.
ONE BOLT FROM THE SKIES, ONE GIRL IN A GRAVE.
WHUMPP
LEAP

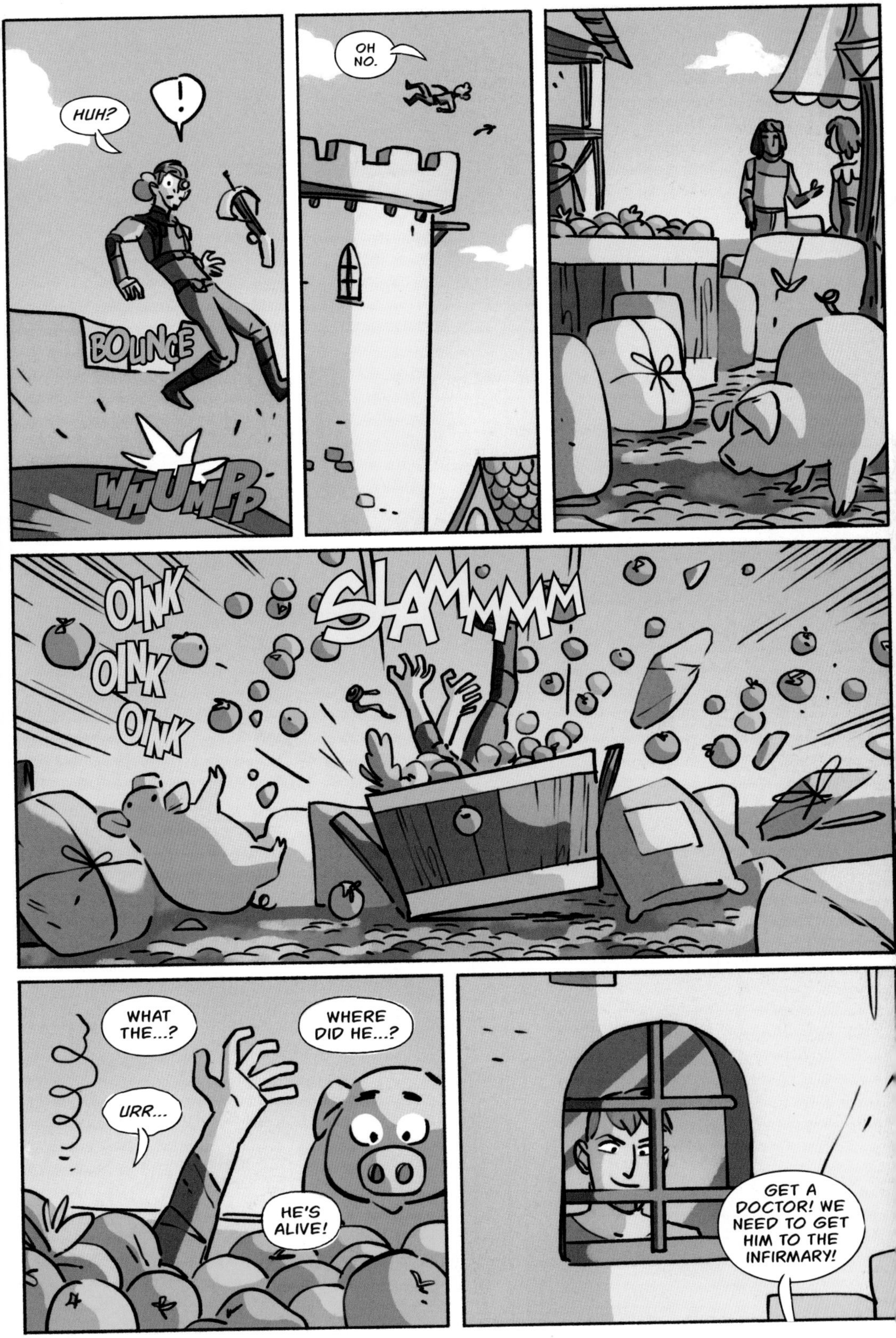
HUH?
!
BOUNCE
WHUMPP
OH NO.
OINK
OINK
OINK
SLAMMMM
WHAT THE...?
WHERE DID HE...?
URR...
HE'S ALIVE!
GET A DOCTOR! WE NEED TO GET HIM TO THE INFIRMARY!

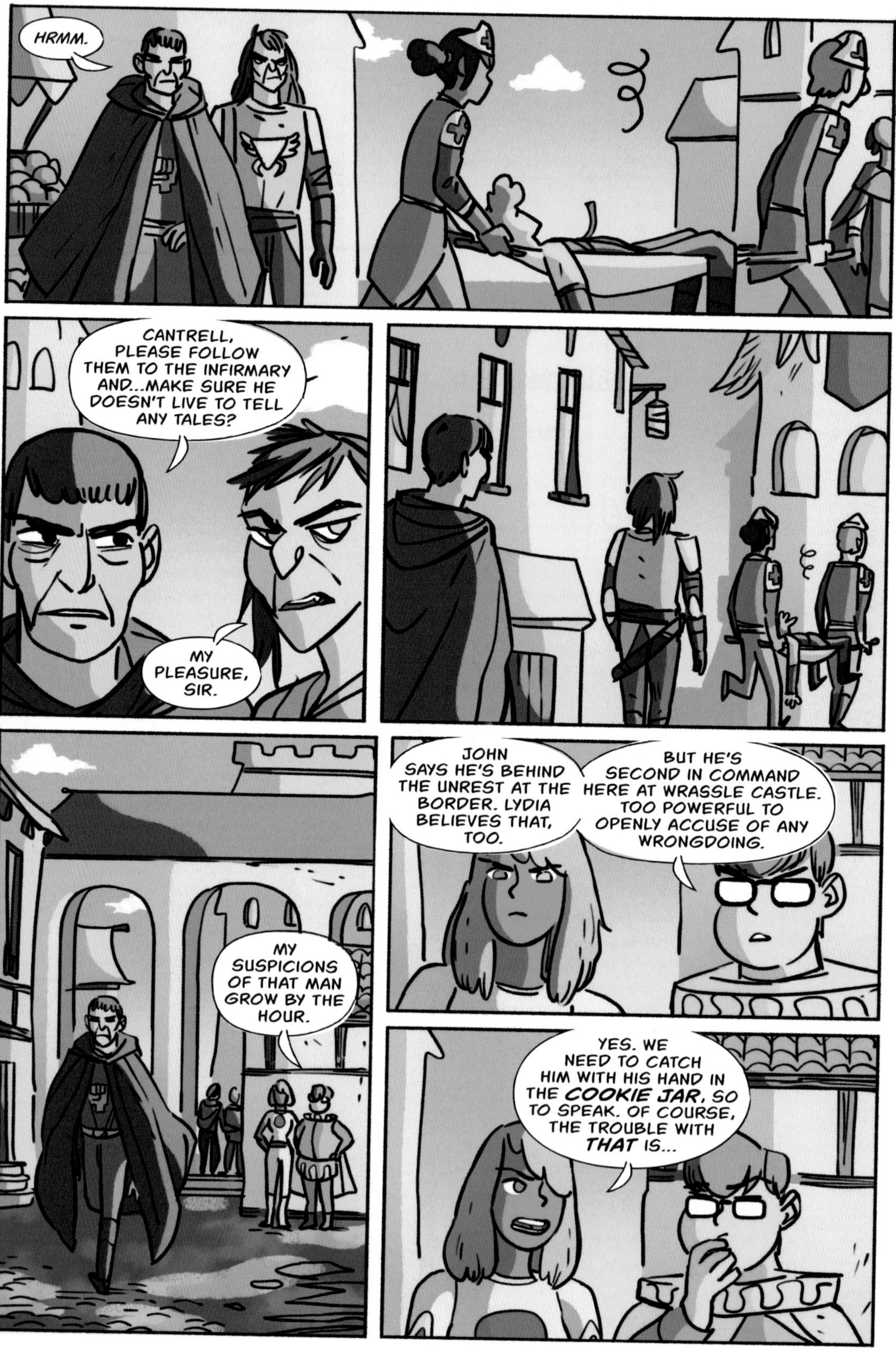
HRMM.
CANTRELL, PLEASE FOLLOW THEM TO THE INFIRMARY AND...MAKE SURE HE DOESN'T LIVE TO TELL ANY TALES?
MY PLEASURE, SIR.
MY SUSPICIONS OF THAT MAN GROW BY THE HOUR.
JOHN SAYS HE'S BEHIND THE UNREST AT THE BORDER. LYDIA BELIEVES THAT, TOO.
BUT HE'S SECOND IN COMMAND HERE AT WRASSLE CASTLE. TOO POWERFUL TO OPENLY ACCUSE OF ANY WRONGDOING.
YES. WE NEED TO CATCH HIM WITH HIS HAND IN THE ***COOKIE JAR***, SO TO SPEAK. OF COURSE, THE TROUBLE WITH ***THAT*** IS...

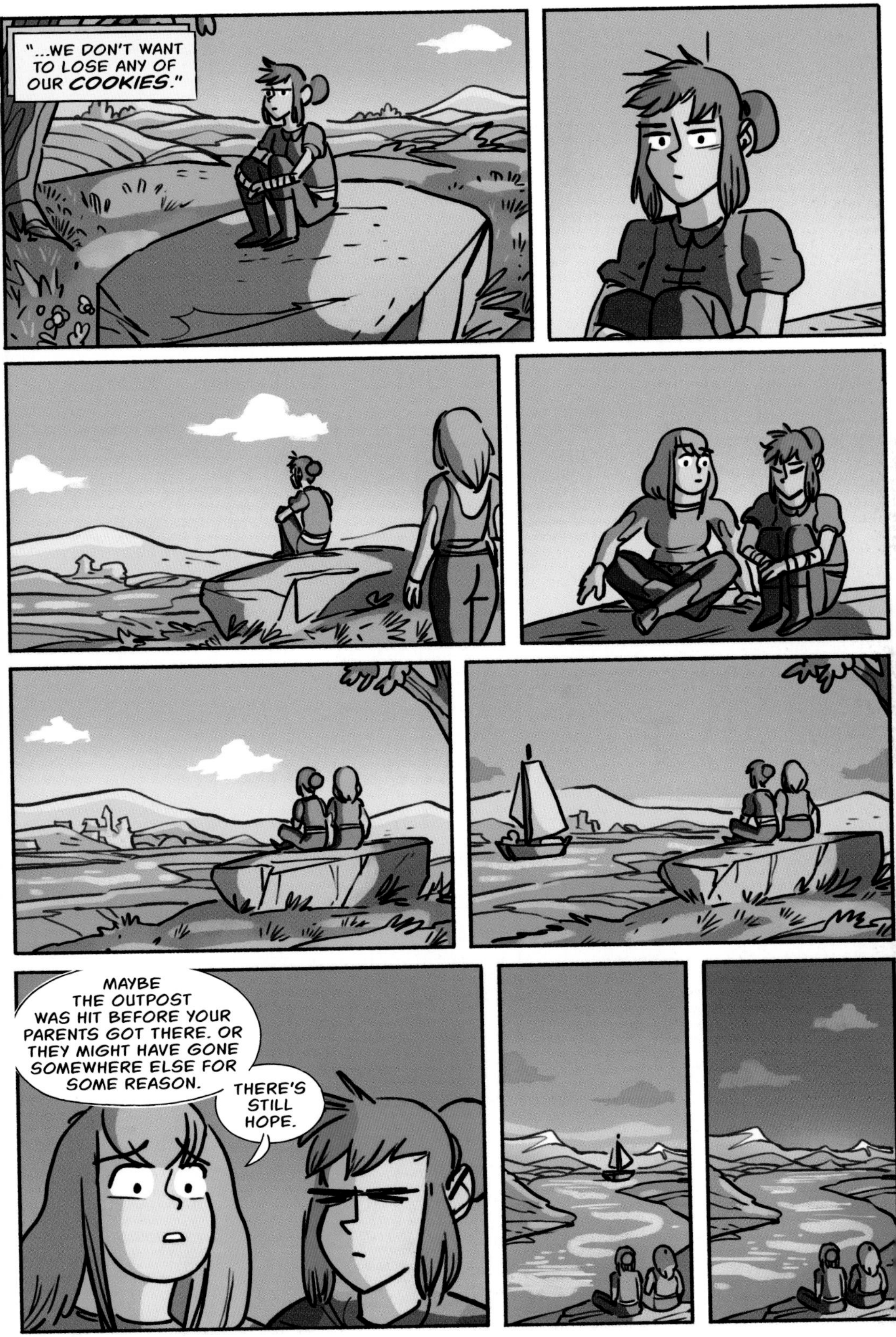
"...WE DON'T WANT TO LOSE ANY OF OUR COOKIES."
MAYBE THE OUTPOST WAS HIT BEFORE YOUR PARENTS GOT THERE. OR THEY MIGHT HAVE GONE SOMEWHERE ELSE FOR SOME REASON.
THERE'S STILL HOPE.

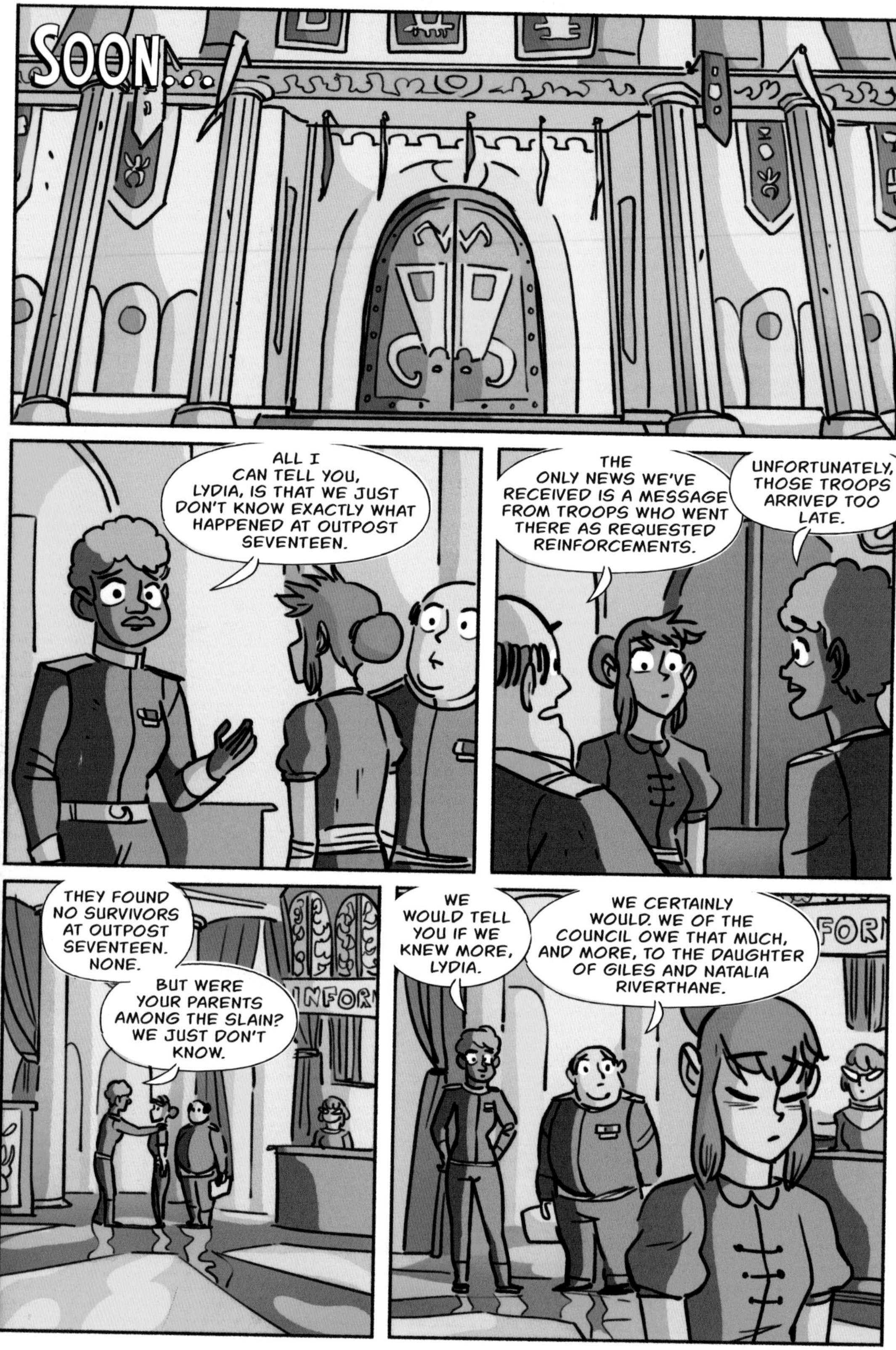
SOON...
ALL I CAN TELL YOU, LYDIA, IS THAT WE JUST DON'T KNOW EXACTLY WHAT HAPPENED AT OUTPOST SEVENTEEN.
THE ONLY NEWS WE'VE RECEIVED IS A MESSAGE FROM TROOPS WHO WENT THERE AS REQUESTED REINFORCEMENTS.
UNFORTUNATELY, THOSE TROOPS ARRIVED TOO LATE.
THEY FOUND NO SURVIVORS AT OUTPOST SEVENTEEN. NONE.
BUT WERE YOUR PARENTS AMONG THE SLAIN? WE JUST DON'T KNOW.
INFOR
WE WOULD TELL YOU IF WE KNEW MORE, LYDIA.
WE CERTAINLY WOULD. WE OF THE COUNCIL OWE THAT MUCH, AND MORE, TO THE DAUGHTER OF GILES AND NATALIA RIVERTHANE.
FOR

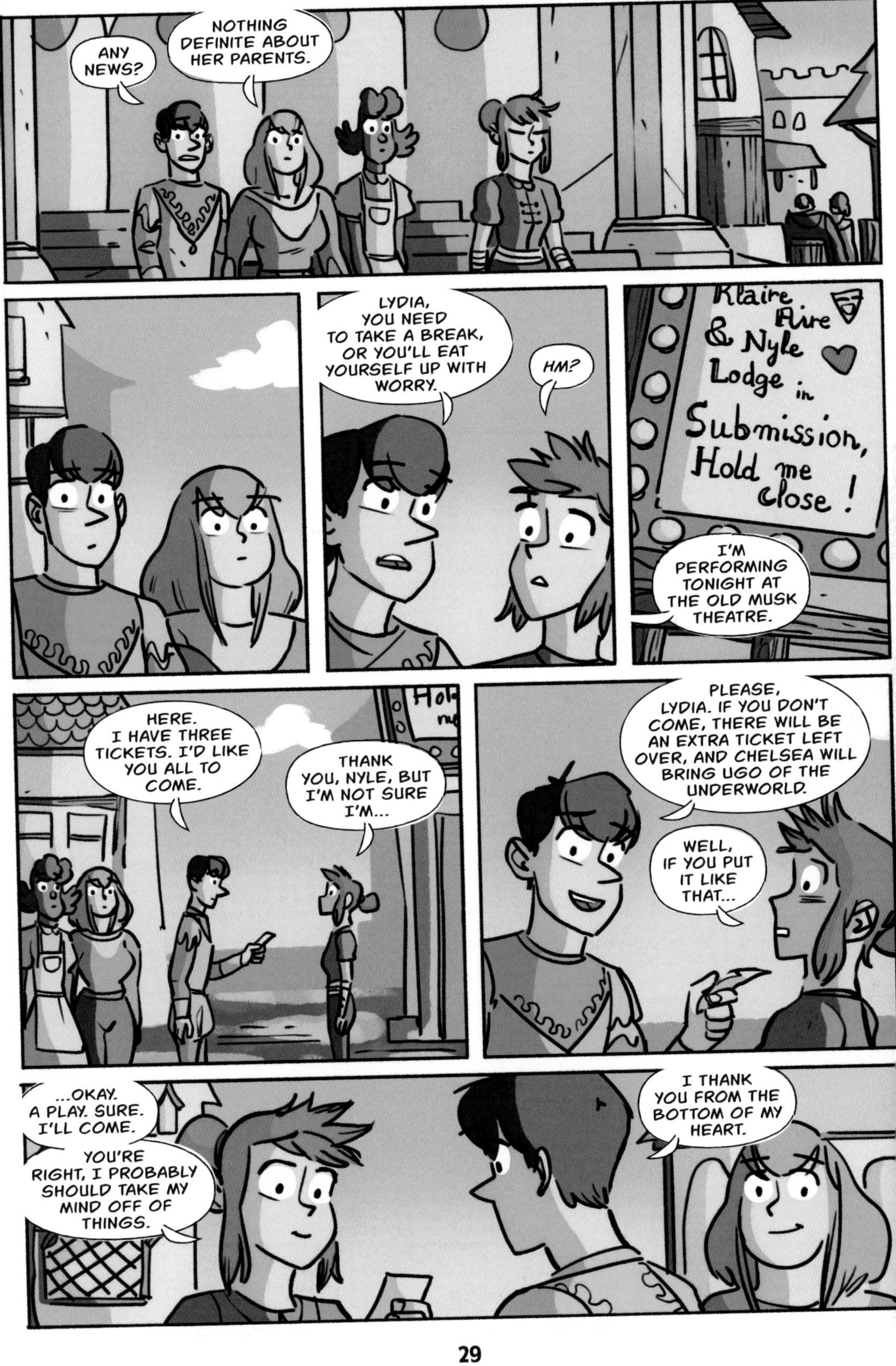

ANY NEWS?
NOTHING DEFINITE ABOUT HER PARENTS.
LYDIA, YOU NEED TO TAKE A BREAK, OR YOU'LL EAT YOURSELF UP WITH WORRY.
HM?
Klaire Aire & Nyle Lodge in Submission, Hold me close!
I'M PERFORMING TONIGHT AT THE OLD MUSK THEATRE.
HERE. I HAVE THREE TICKETS. I'D LIKE YOU ALL TO COME.
THANK YOU, NYLE, BUT I'M NOT SURE I'M...
PLEASE, LYDIA. IF YOU DON'T COME, THERE WILL BE AN EXTRA TICKET LEFT OVER, AND CHELSEA WILL BRING UGO OF THE UNDERWORLD.
WELL, IF YOU PUT IT LIKE THAT...
...OKAY. A PLAY. SURE. I'LL COME.
YOU'RE RIGHT, I PROBABLY SHOULD TAKE MY MIND OFF OF THINGS.
I THANK YOU FROM THE BOTTOM OF MY HEART.

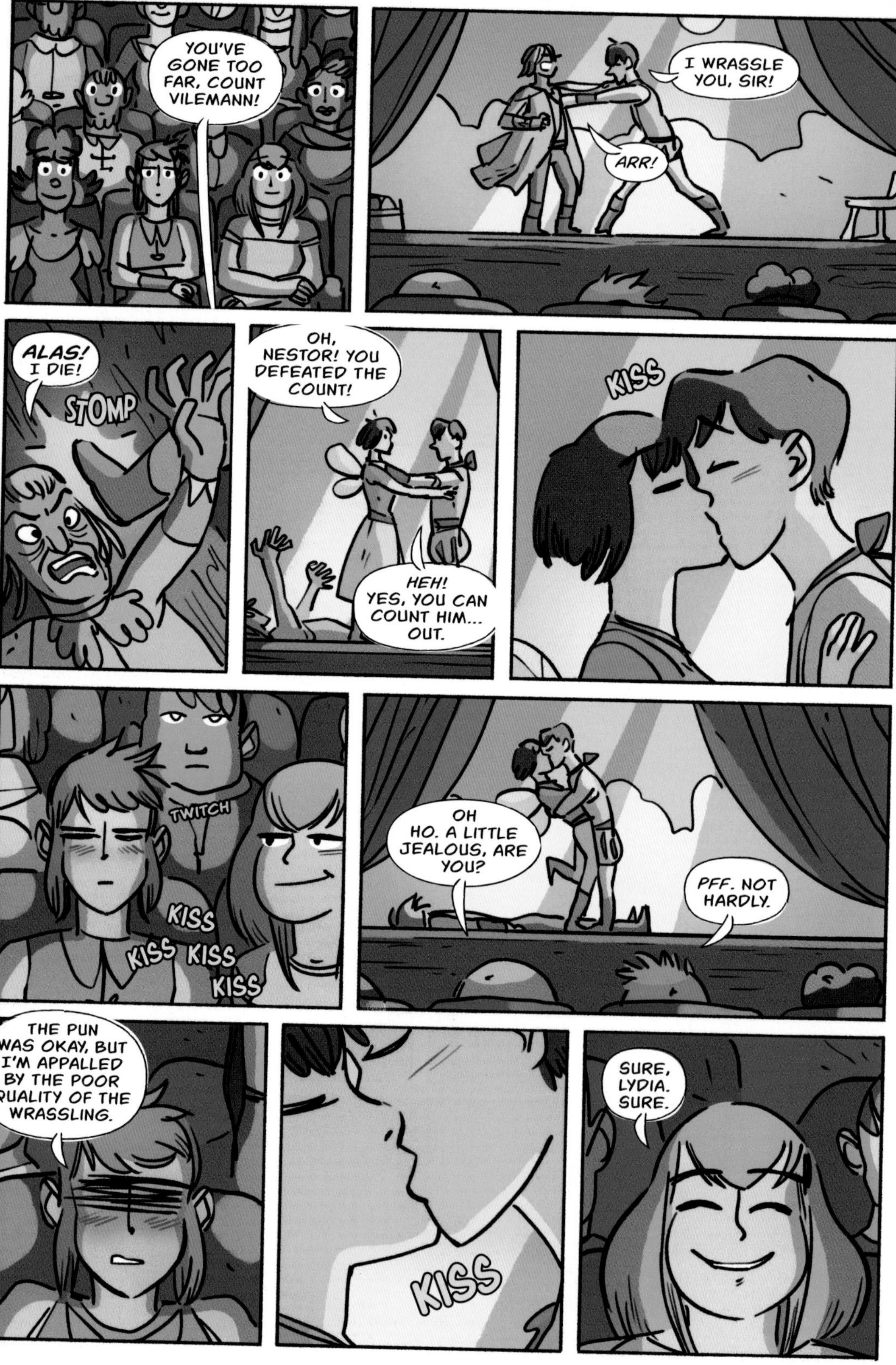
YOU'VE GONE TOO FAR, COUNT VILEMANN!
I WRASSLE YOU, SIR!
ARR!
ALAS! I DIE!
STOMP
OH, NESTOR! YOU DEFEATED THE COUNT!
HEH! YES, YOU CAN COUNT HIM... OUT.
KISS
TWITCH
KISS
KISS KISS
KISS
OH HO. A LITTLE JEALOUS, ARE YOU?
PFF. NOT HARDLY.
THE PUN WAS OKAY, BUT I'M APPALLED BY THE POOR QUALITY OF THE WRASSLING.
KISS
SURE, LYDIA. SURE.

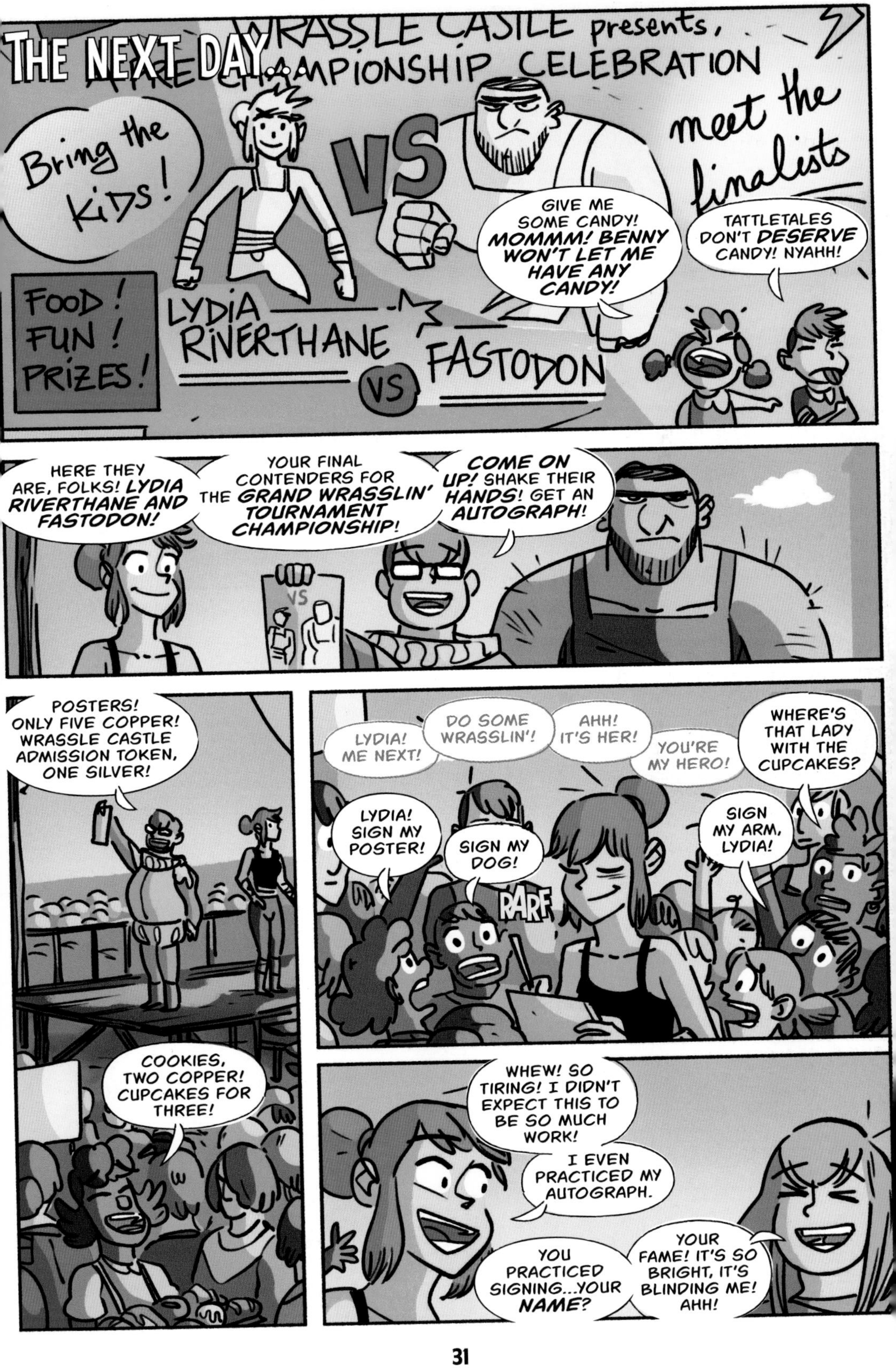
THE NEXT DAY...
WRASSLE CASTLE presents,
CHAMPIONSHIP CELEBRATION
Bring the KIDS!
VS
meet the finalists
GIVE ME SOME CANDY! MOMMM! BENNY WON'T LET ME HAVE ANY CANDY!
TATTLETALES DON'T DESERVE CANDY! NYAHH!
FOOD! FUN! PRIZES!
LYDIA RIVERTHANE
VS
FASTODON
HERE THEY ARE, FOLKS! LYDIA RIVERTHANE AND FASTODON!
YOUR FINAL CONTENDERS FOR THE GRAND WRASSLIN' TOURNAMENT CHAMPIONSHIP!
COME ON UP! SHAKE THEIR HANDS! GET AN AUTOGRAPH!
VS
POSTERS! ONLY FIVE COPPER! WRASSLE CASTLE ADMISSION TOKEN, ONE SILVER!
LYDIA! ME NEXT!
DO SOME WRASSLIN'!
AHH! IT'S HER!
YOU'RE MY HERO!
WHERE'S THAT LADY WITH THE CUPCAKES?
LYDIA! SIGN MY POSTER!
SIGN MY DOG!
RARF
SIGN MY ARM, LYDIA!
COOKIES, TWO COPPER! CUPCAKES FOR THREE!
WHEW! SO TIRING! I DIDN'T EXPECT THIS TO BE SO MUCH WORK!
I EVEN PRACTICED MY AUTOGRAPH.
YOU PRACTICED SIGNING...YOUR NAME?
YOUR FAME! IT'S SO BRIGHT, IT'S BLINDING ME! AHH!

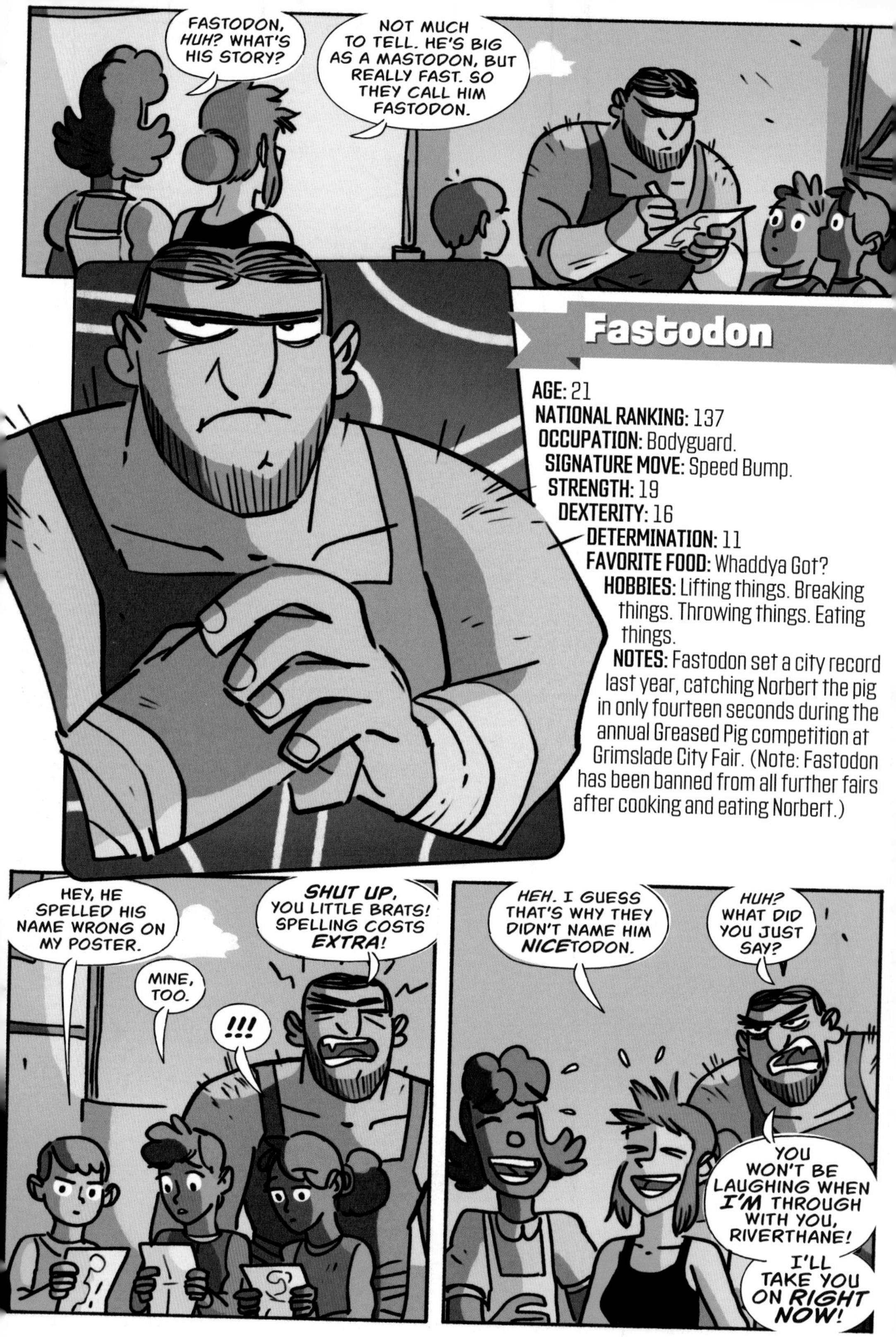
FASTODON, HUH? WHAT'S HIS STORY?
NOT MUCH TO TELL. HE'S BIG AS A MASTODON, BUT REALLY FAST. SO THEY CALL HIM FASTODON.
Fastodon
AGE: 21
NATIONAL RANKING: 137
OCCUPATION: Bodyguard.
SIGNATURE MOVE: Speed Bump.
STRENGTH: 19
DEXTERITY: 16
DETERMINATION: 11
FAVORITE FOOD: Whaddya Got?
HOBBIES: Lifting things. Breaking things. Throwing things. Eating things.
NOTES: Fastodon set a city record last year, catching Norbert the pig in only fourteen seconds during the annual Greased Pig competition at Grimslade City Fair. (Note: Fastodon has been banned from all further fairs after cooking and eating Norbert.)
HEY, HE SPELLED HIS NAME WRONG ON MY POSTER.
MINE, TOO.
!!!
SHUT UP, YOU LITTLE BRATS! SPELLING COSTS EXTRA!
HEH. I GUESS THAT'S WHY THEY DIDN'T NAME HIM NICETODON.
HUH? WHAT DID YOU JUST SAY?
YOU WON'T BE LAUGHING WHEN I'M THROUGH WITH YOU, RIVERTHANE!
I'LL TAKE YOU ON RIGHT NOW!

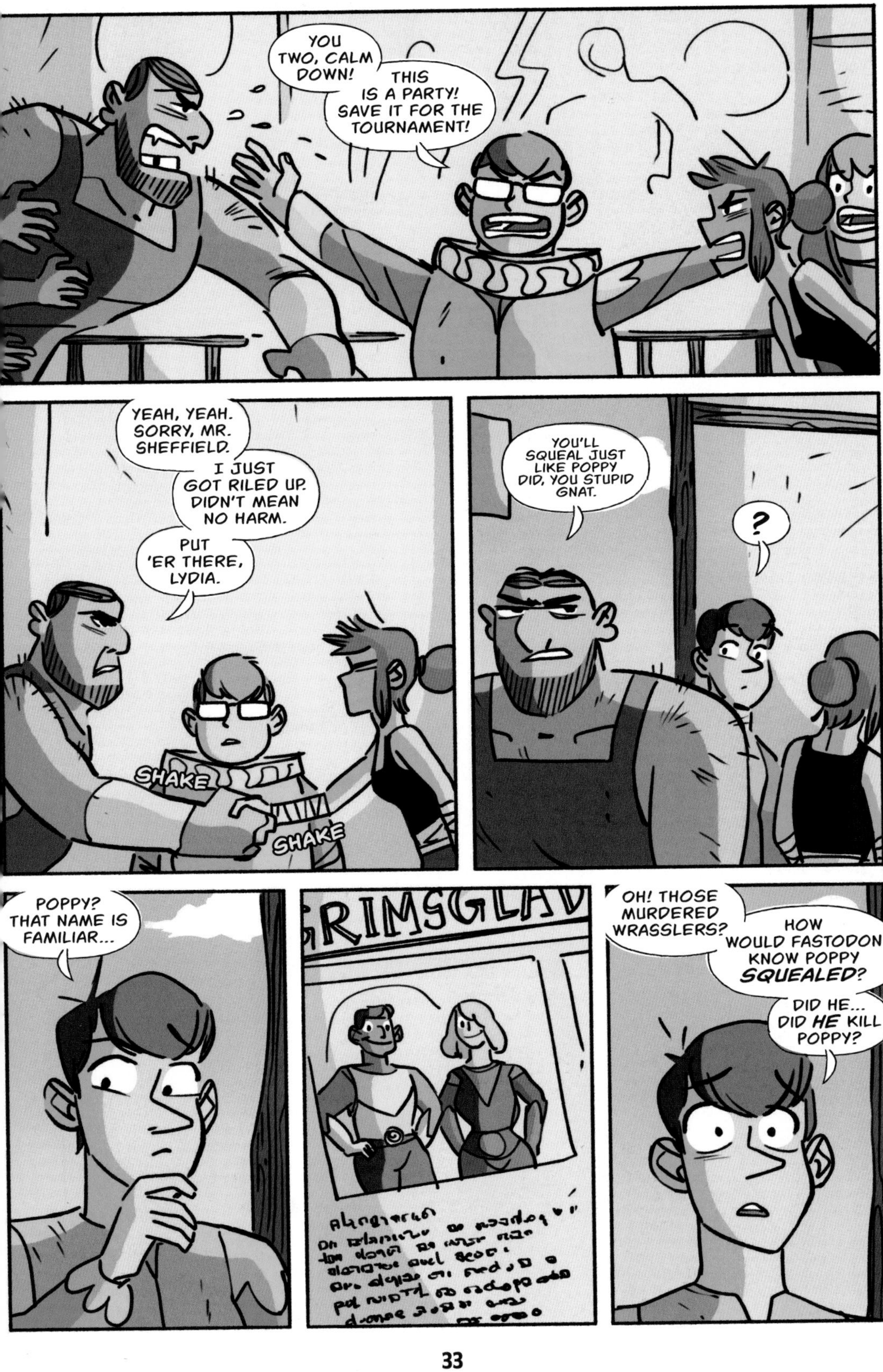

YOU TWO, CALM DOWN!
THIS IS A PARTY! SAVE IT FOR THE TOURNAMENT!
YEAH, YEAH. SORRY, MR. SHEFFIELD.
I JUST GOT RILED UP. DIDN'T MEAN NO HARM.
PUT 'ER THERE, LYDIA.
SHAKE
SHAKE
YOU'LL SQUEAL JUST LIKE POPPY DID, YOU STUPID GNAT.
?
POPPY? THAT NAME IS FAMILIAR...
GRIMSGLAD
OH! THOSE MURDERED WRASSLERS?
HOW WOULD FASTODON KNOW POPPY *SQUEALED*?
DID HE... DID *HE* KILL POPPY?

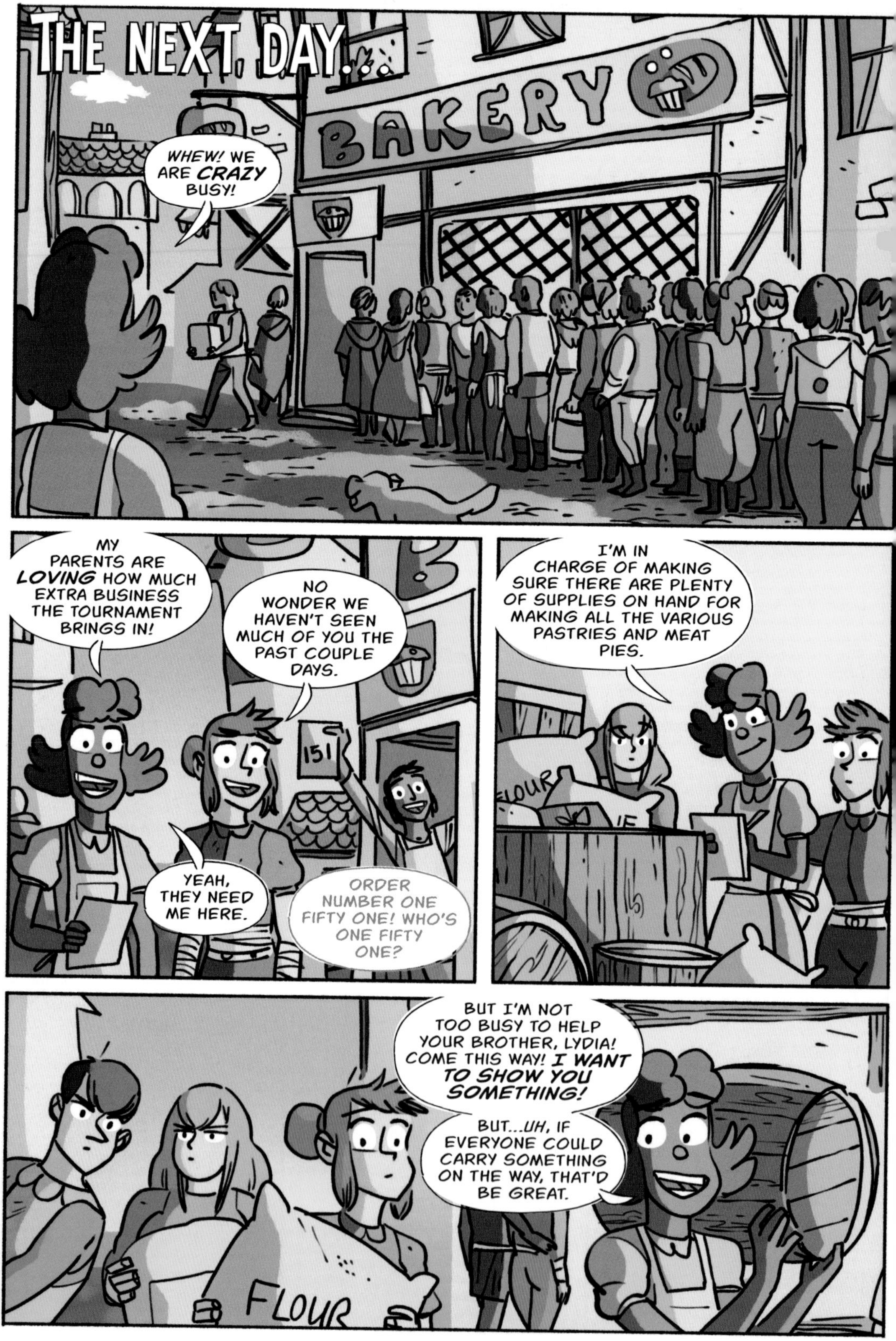
THE NEXT DAY...
BAKERY
WHEW! WE ARE CRAZY BUSY!
MY PARENTS ARE LOVING HOW MUCH EXTRA BUSINESS THE TOURNAMENT BRINGS IN!
NO WONDER WE HAVEN'T SEEN MUCH OF YOU THE PAST COUPLE DAYS.
151
YEAH, THEY NEED ME HERE.
ORDER NUMBER ONE FIFTY ONE! WHO'S ONE FIFTY ONE?
I'M IN CHARGE OF MAKING SURE THERE ARE PLENTY OF SUPPLIES ON HAND FOR MAKING ALL THE VARIOUS PASTRIES AND MEAT PIES.
BUT I'M NOT TOO BUSY TO HELP YOUR BROTHER, LYDIA! COME THIS WAY! I WANT TO SHOW YOU SOMETHING!
BUT...UH, IF EVERYONE COULD CARRY SOMETHING ON THE WAY, THAT'D BE GREAT.
FLOUR

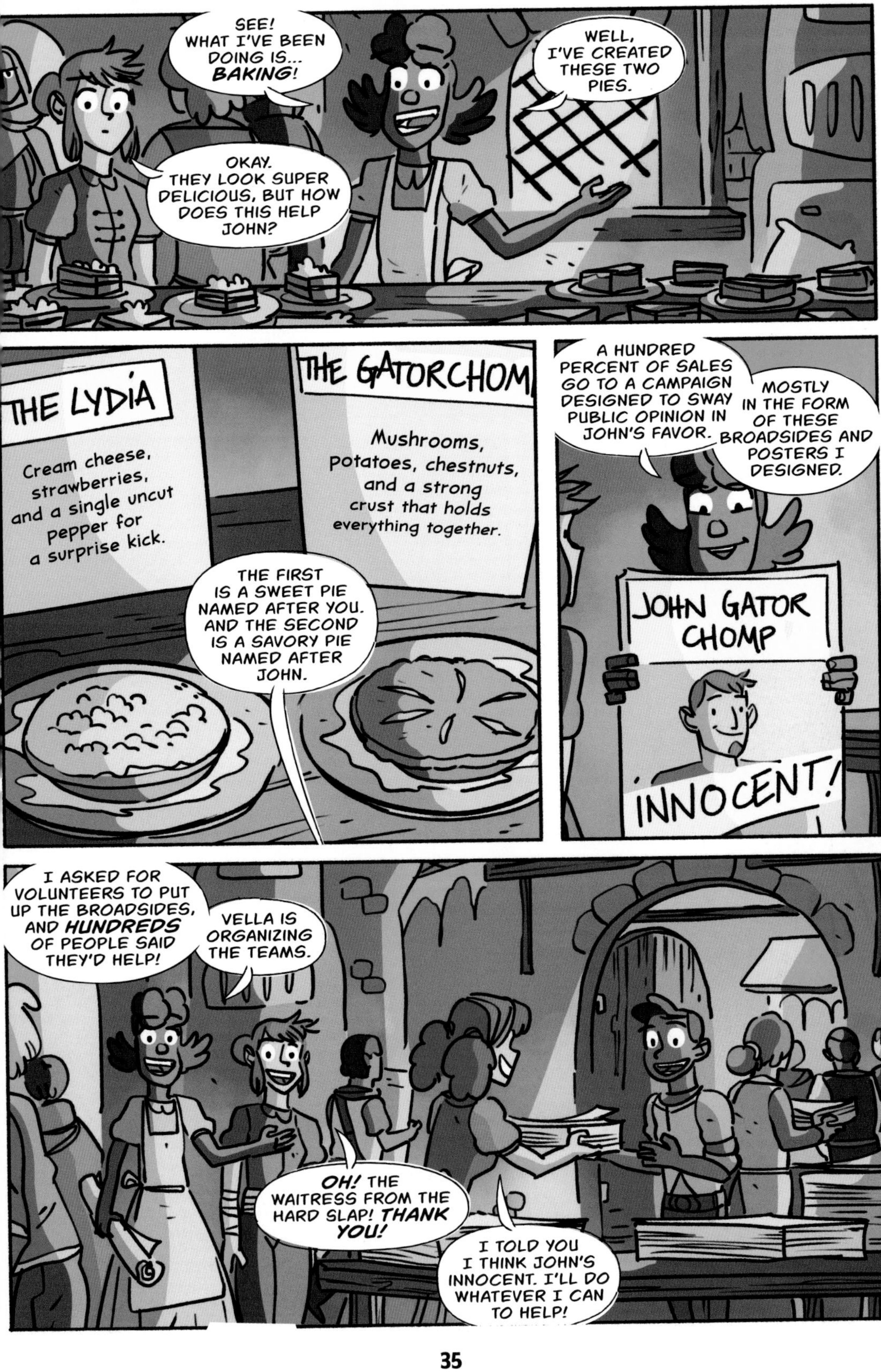
SEE! WHAT I'VE BEEN DOING IS... BAKING!
WELL, I'VE CREATED THESE TWO PIES.
OKAY. THEY LOOK SUPER DELICIOUS, BUT HOW DOES THIS HELP JOHN?
THE LYDIA
Cream cheese, strawberries, and a single uncut pepper for a surprise kick.
THE GATORCHOMP
Mushrooms, potatoes, chestnuts, and a strong crust that holds everything together.
THE FIRST IS A SWEET PIE NAMED AFTER YOU. AND THE SECOND IS A SAVORY PIE NAMED AFTER JOHN.
A HUNDRED PERCENT OF SALES GO TO A CAMPAIGN DESIGNED TO SWAY PUBLIC OPINION IN JOHN'S FAVOR.
MOSTLY IN THE FORM OF THESE BROADSIDES AND POSTERS I DESIGNED.
JOHN GATOR CHOMP
INNOCENT!
I ASKED FOR VOLUNTEERS TO PUT UP THE BROADSIDES, AND HUNDREDS OF PEOPLE SAID THEY'D HELP!
VELLA IS ORGANIZING THE TEAMS.
OH! THE WAITRESS FROM THE HARD SLAP! THANK YOU!
I TOLD YOU I THINK JOHN'S INNOCENT. I'LL DO WHATEVER I CAN TO HELP!

HEY, LYDIA!

GREG! YOU'RE HELPING WITH THE POSTERS, TOO?

SURE AM. AND SO ARE PHINA AND LUCIA!

I'VE PUT UP *TWENTY.* LUCIA ONLY PUT UP *FIVE!* I'M HELPING DAD THE MOST!

I STUCK ONE TO MY FACE!

WIFFLE

WIFFLE

JOHN CHOW INNOCENT

INNOCENT

I'VE SOLD ONE HUNDRED AND FIVE "LYDIA" PIES, AND TWO HUNDRED AND SEVEN "GATOR-CHOMPERS."

UGH! JOHN BEATS ME *AGAIN!*

BUT THIS IS GREAT. I'D THOUGHT PEOPLE HAD DESERTED JOHN.

IT'S GOOD TO SEE HE'S NOT ALONE.

THUMP

JINGLE

I'D LIKE TO PLACE AN ORDER FOR ONE HUNDRED OF EACH OF THE SPECIALTY PIES, PLEASE.

SHEFFIELD? LISA?

WHOA! YOU TWO, *THANKS!*

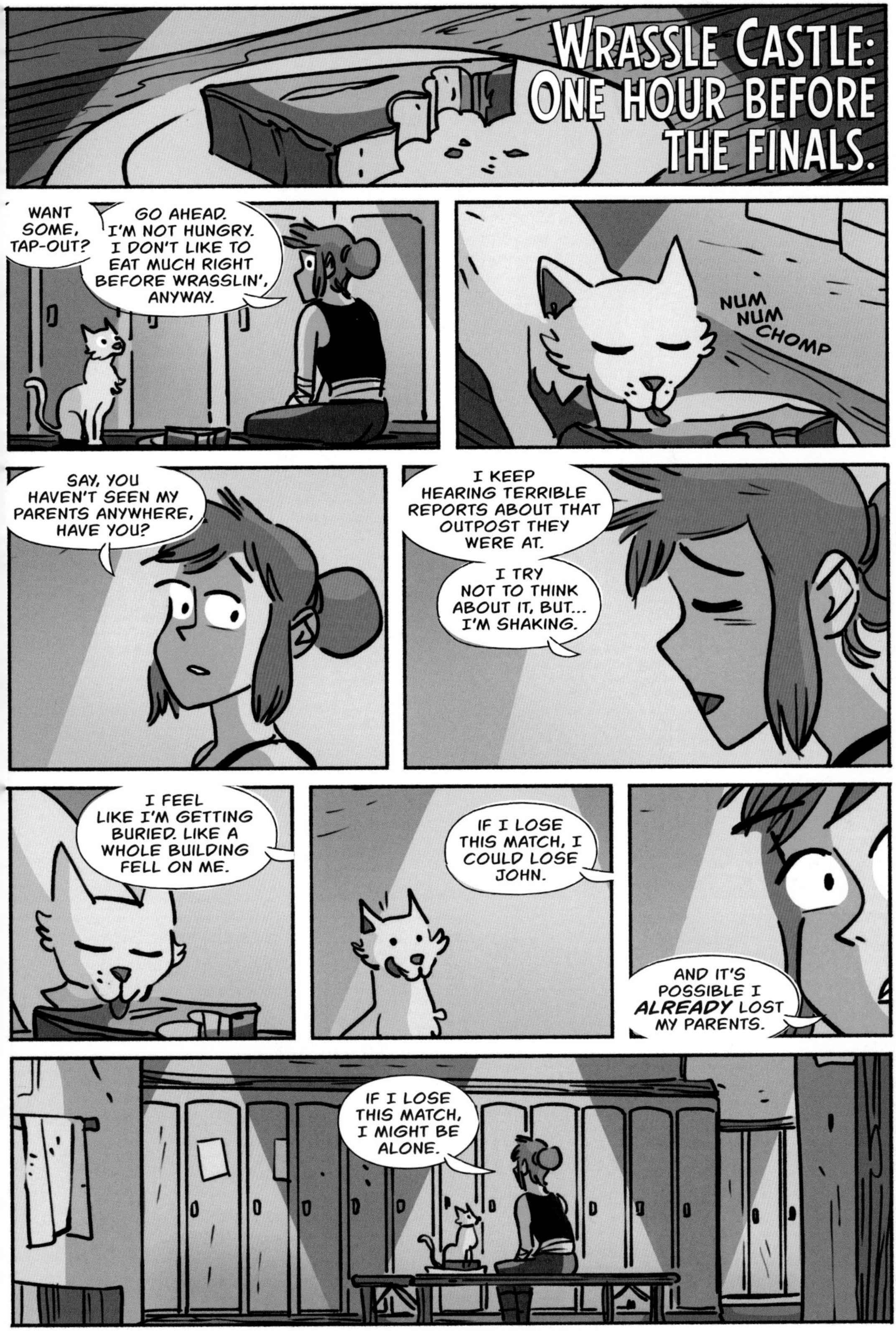
WRASSLE CASTLE: ONE HOUR BEFORE THE FINALS.
WANT SOME, TAP-OUT?
GO AHEAD. I'M NOT HUNGRY. I DON'T LIKE TO EAT MUCH RIGHT BEFORE WRASSLIN', ANYWAY.
NUM NUM CHOMP
SAY, YOU HAVEN'T SEEN MY PARENTS ANYWHERE, HAVE YOU?
I KEEP HEARING TERRIBLE REPORTS ABOUT THAT OUTPOST THEY WERE AT.
I TRY NOT TO THINK ABOUT IT, BUT... I'M SHAKING.
I FEEL LIKE I'M GETTING BURIED. LIKE A WHOLE BUILDING FELL ON ME.
IF I LOSE THIS MATCH, I COULD LOSE JOHN.
AND IT'S POSSIBLE I ALREADY LOST MY PARENTS.
IF I LOSE THIS MATCH, I MIGHT BE ALONE.

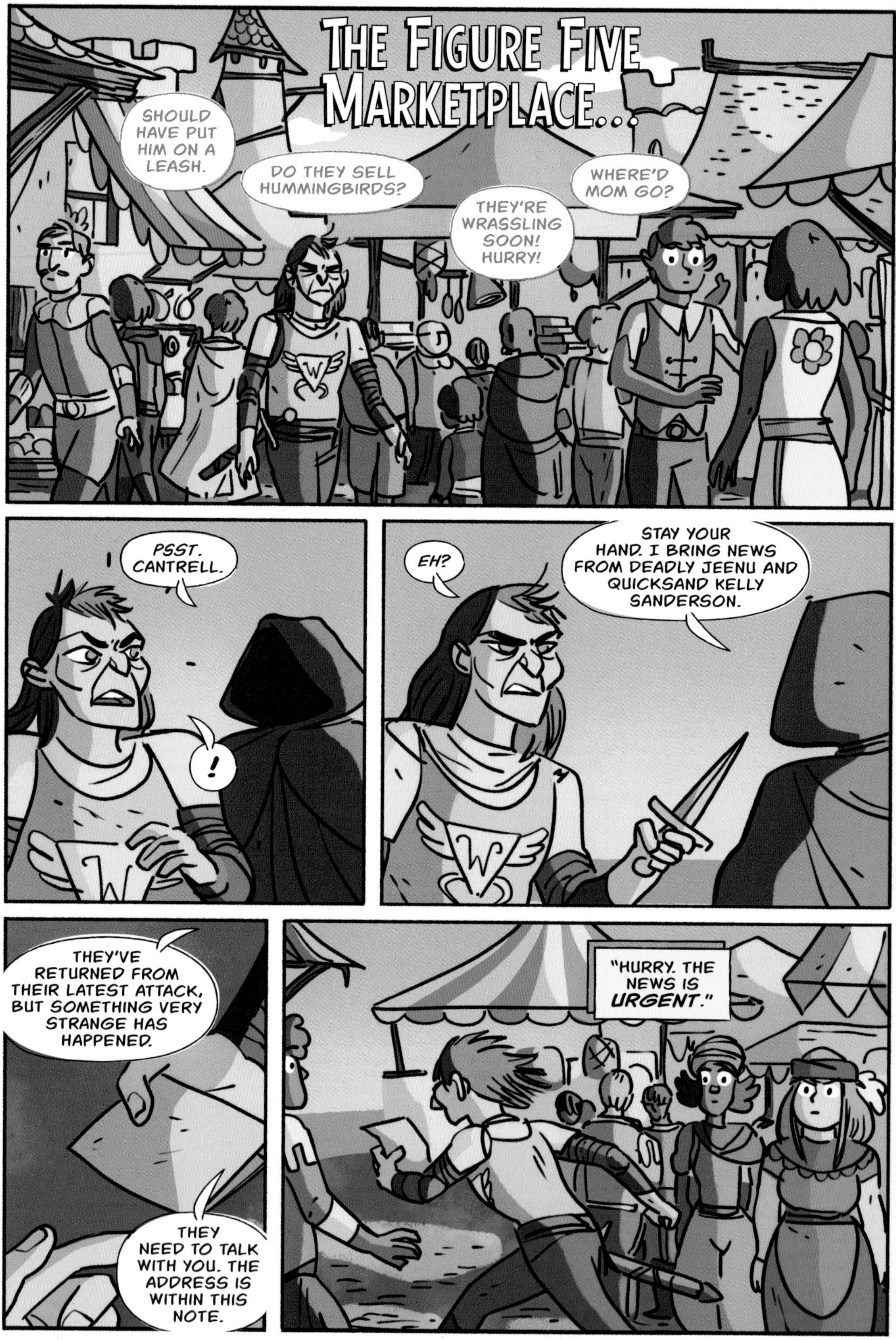

THE FIGURE FIVE MARKETPLACE...
SHOULD HAVE PUT HIM ON A LEASH.
DO THEY SELL HUMMINGBIRDS?
THEY'RE WRASSLING SOON! HURRY!
WHERE'D MOM GO?
PSST. CANTRELL.
!
EH?
STAY YOUR HAND. I BRING NEWS FROM DEADLY JEENU AND QUICKSAND KELLY SANDERSON.
THEY'VE RETURNED FROM THEIR LATEST ATTACK, BUT SOMETHING VERY STRANGE HAS HAPPENED.
THEY NEED TO TALK WITH YOU. THE ADDRESS IS WITHIN THIS NOTE.
"HURRY. THE NEWS IS URGENT."

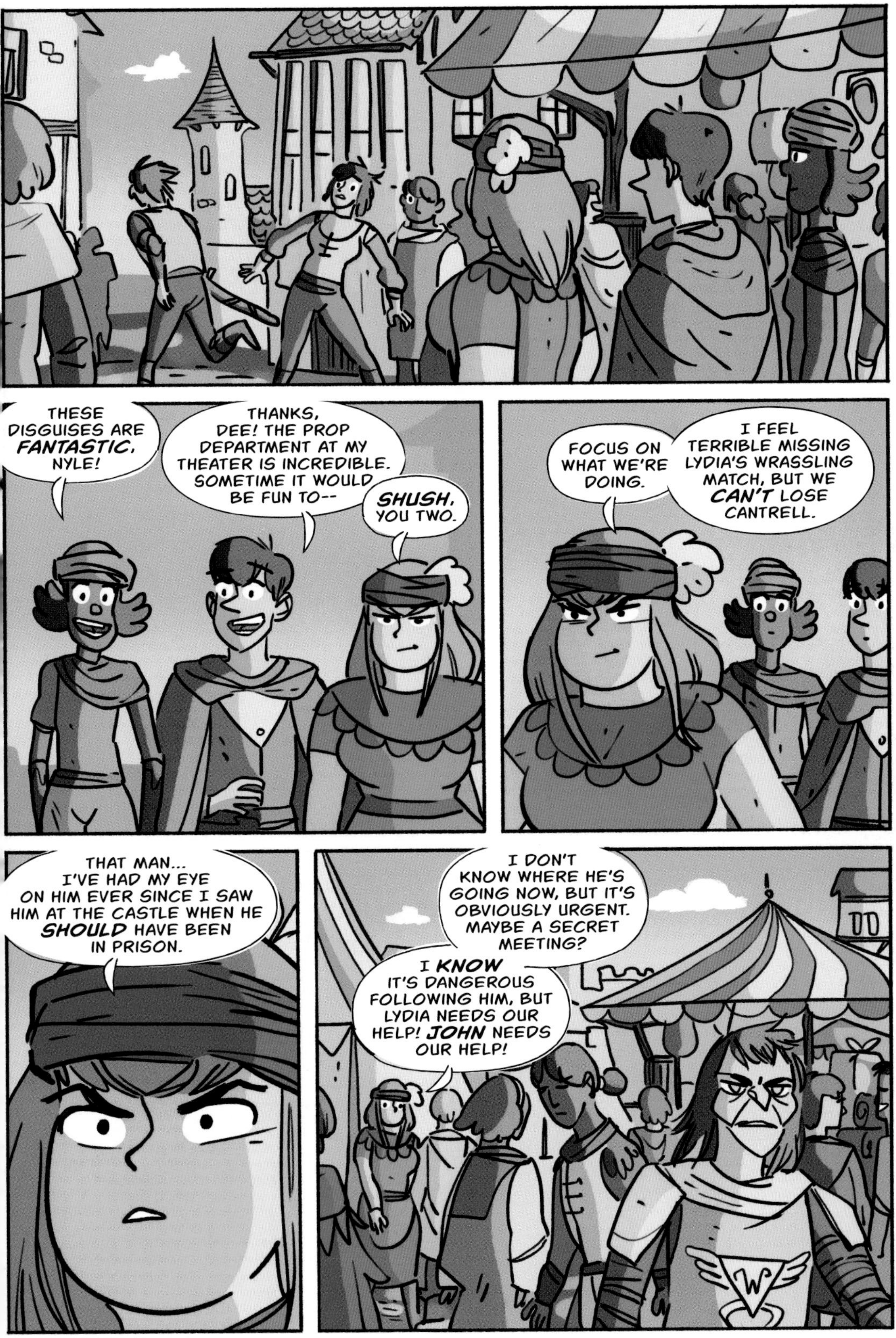
THESE DISGUISES ARE FANTASTIC, NYLE!
THANKS, DEE! THE PROP DEPARTMENT AT MY THEATER IS INCREDIBLE. SOMETIME IT WOULD BE FUN TO--
SHUSH, YOU TWO.
I FEEL TERRIBLE MISSING LYDIA'S WRASSLING MATCH, BUT WE CAN'T LOSE CANTRELL.
FOCUS ON WHAT WE'RE DOING.
THAT MAN... I'VE HAD MY EYE ON HIM EVER SINCE I SAW HIM AT THE CASTLE WHEN HE SHOULD HAVE BEEN IN PRISON.
I DON'T KNOW WHERE HE'S GOING NOW, BUT IT'S OBVIOUSLY URGENT. MAYBE A SECRET MEETING?
I KNOW IT'S DANGEROUS FOLLOWING HIM, BUT LYDIA NEEDS OUR HELP! JOHN NEEDS OUR HELP!

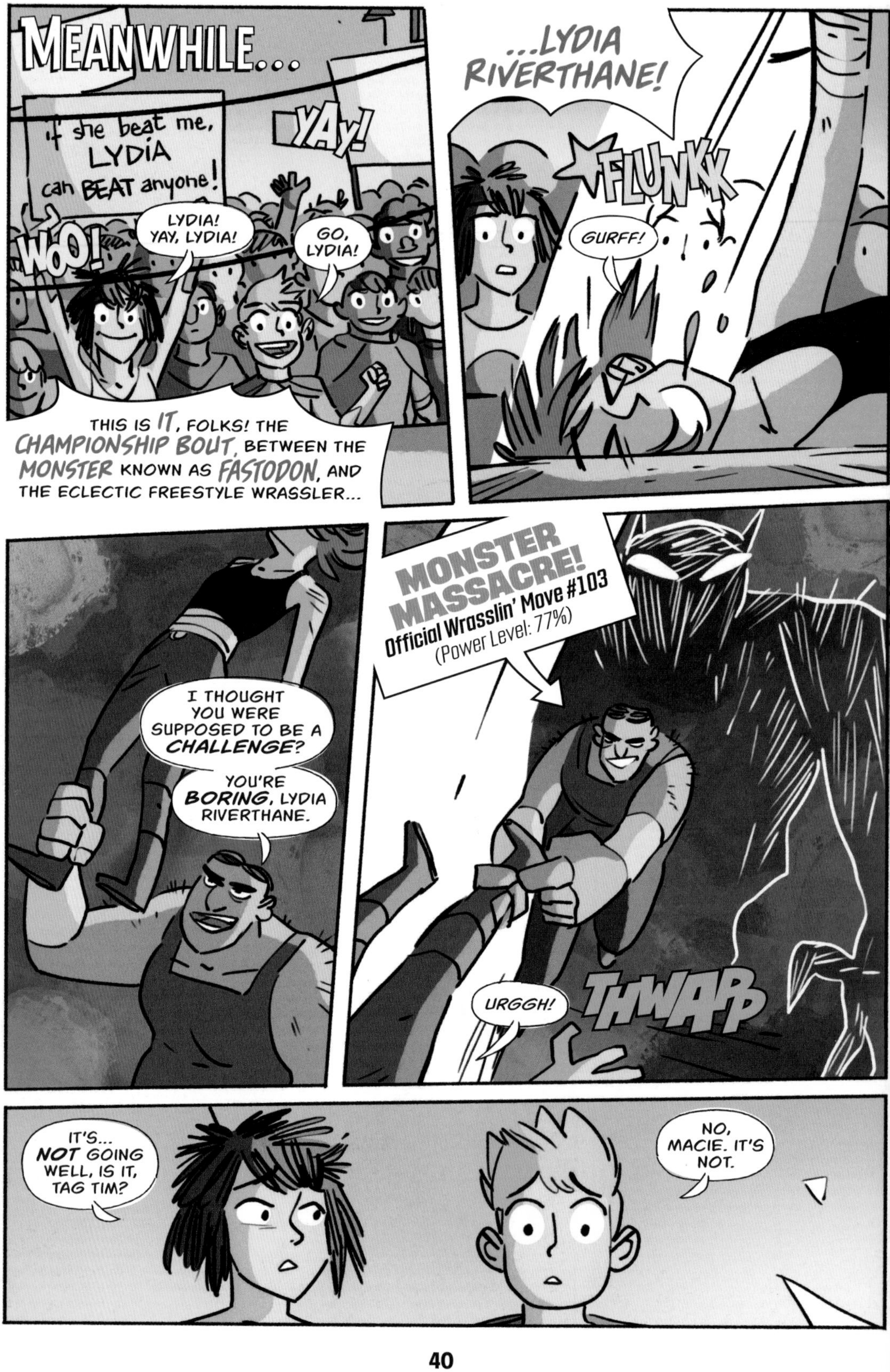
MEANWHILE...
if she beat me, LYDIA can BEAT anyone!
YAY!
WOO!
LYDIA! YAY, LYDIA!
GO, LYDIA!
THIS IS IT, FOLKS! THE CHAMPIONSHIP BOUT, BETWEEN THE MONSTER KNOWN AS FASTODON, AND THE ECLECTIC FREESTYLE WRASSLER...
...LYDIA RIVERTHANE!
FLUNKK
GURFF!
I THOUGHT YOU WERE SUPPOSED TO BE A CHALLENGE?
YOU'RE BORING, LYDIA RIVERTHANE.
MONSTER MASSACRE!
Official Wrasslin' Move #103
(Power Level: 77%)
URGGH!
THWAPP
IT'S... NOT GOING WELL, IS IT, TAG TIM?
NO, MACIE. IT'S NOT.

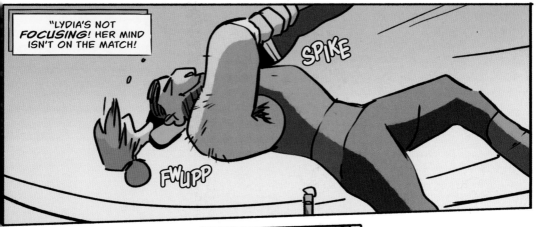

"LYDIA'S NOT *FOCUSING!* HER MIND ISN'T ON THE MATCH!"

SPIKE

FWUPP

"I TALKED TO HER BEFORE IT STARTED, AND ALL SHE DID WAS WORRY ABOUT HER MISSING PARENTS!"

SHAKE

SHAKE

WOBBLE

SHAKE

SHAKE

AND *NOW,* WHERE ARE HER *FRIENDS?* CHELSEA? NYLE? DEE?

THEY WERE *SUPPOSED* TO BE RINGSIDE DURING THE MATCH! CHEERING HER ON!

WE'LL HAVE TO DO IT, NOW.

if she beat or *LYDIA* can BEAT anyon

WAVE

WAVE

"WE'RE ALL SHE'S GOT."

FWOOSH

SLAP

PUNCH

FWOOSH

ELBOW

URF! AH! GUHH!

41

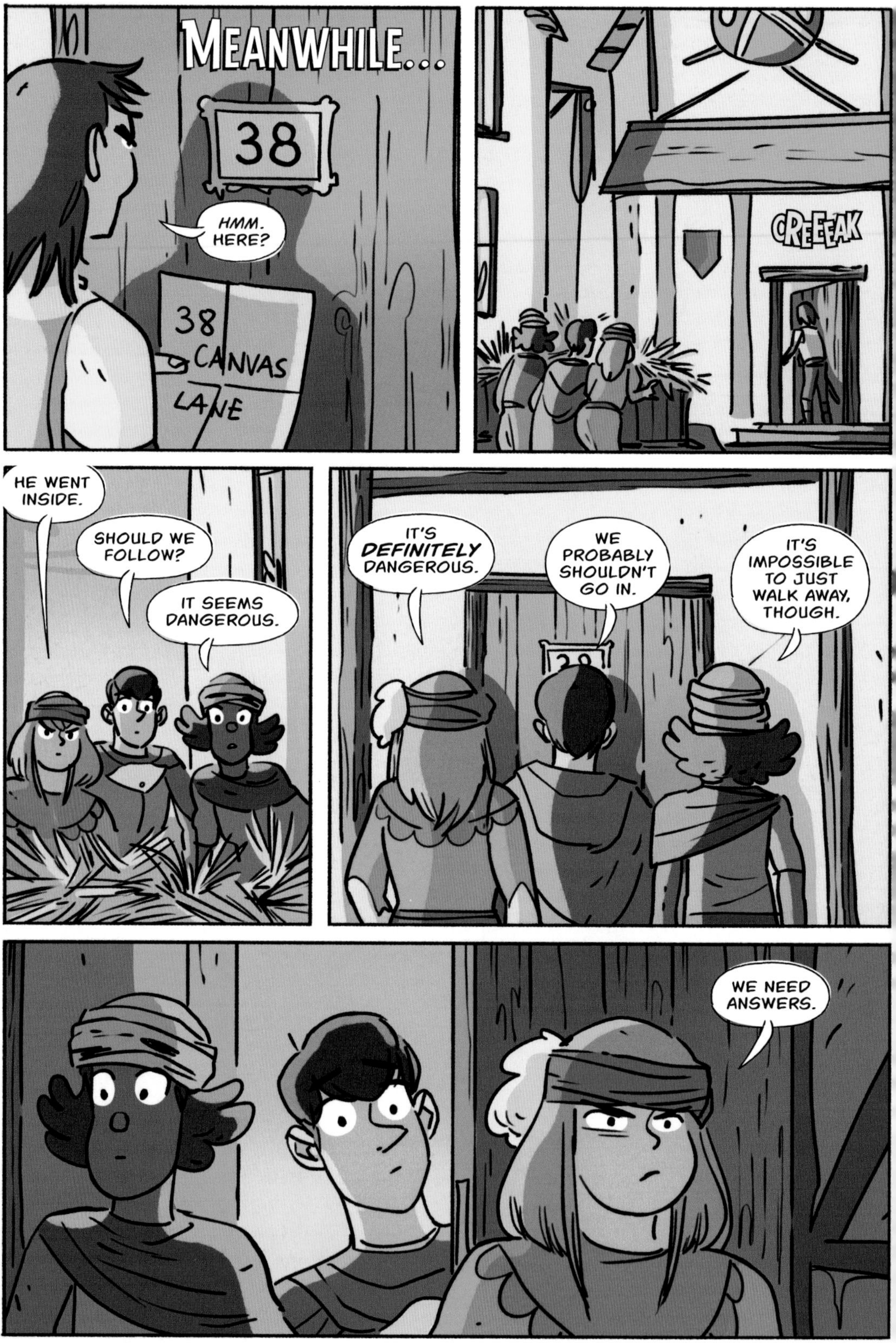
MEANWHILE...
38
HMM. HERE?
38 CANVAS LANE
CREEEAK
HE WENT INSIDE.
SHOULD WE FOLLOW?
IT SEEMS DANGEROUS.
IT'S *DEFINITELY* DANGEROUS.
WE PROBABLY SHOULDN'T GO IN.
IT'S IMPOSSIBLE TO JUST WALK AWAY, THOUGH.
WE NEED ANSWERS.

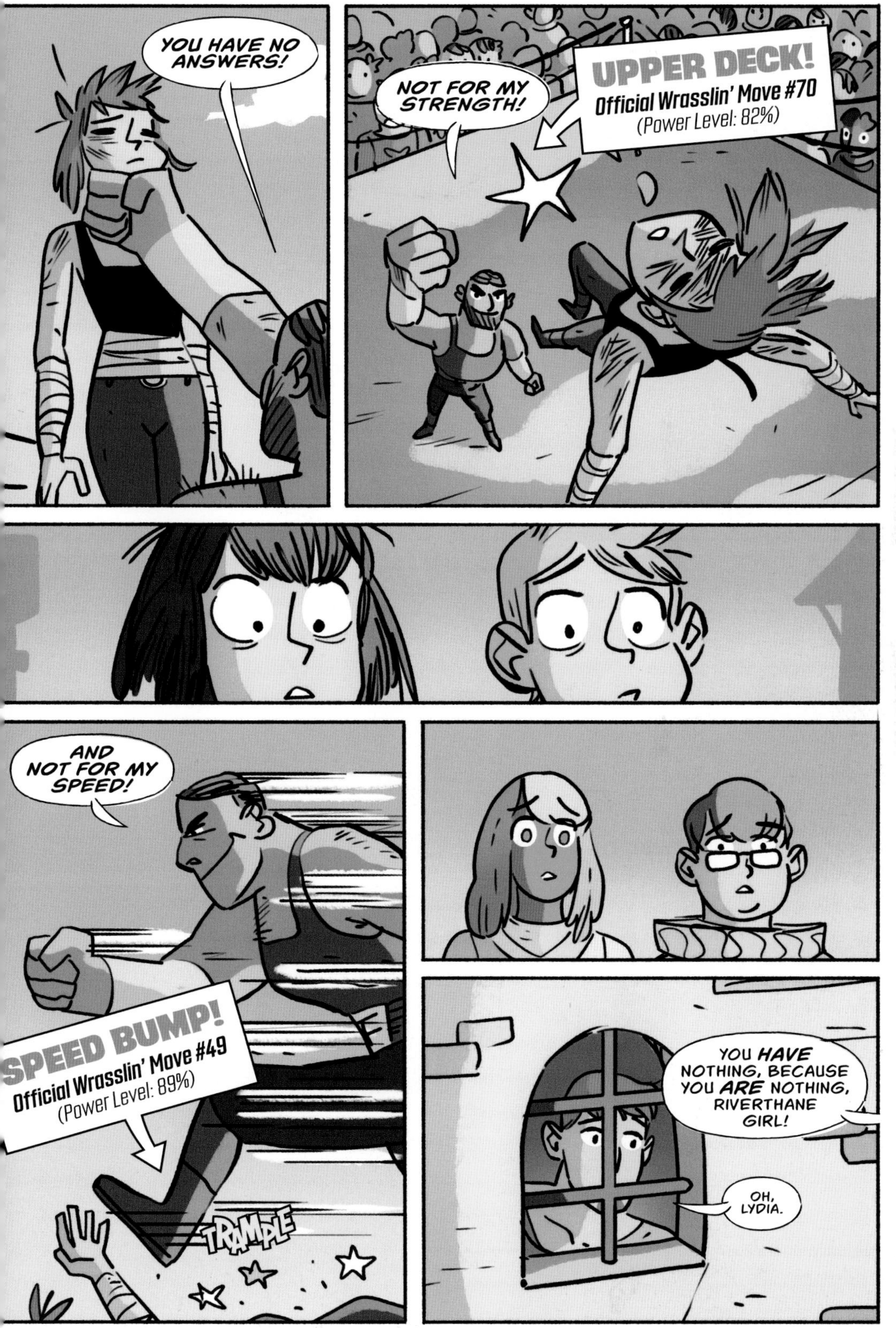
YOU HAVE NO ANSWERS!
NOT FOR MY STRENGTH!
UPPER DECK!
Official Wrasslin' Move #70
(Power Level: 82%)
AND NOT FOR MY SPEED!
SPEED BUMP!
Official Wrasslin' Move #49
(Power Level: 89%)
TRAMPLE
YOU HAVE NOTHING, BECAUSE YOU ARE NOTHING, RIVERTHANE GIRL!
OH, LYDIA.

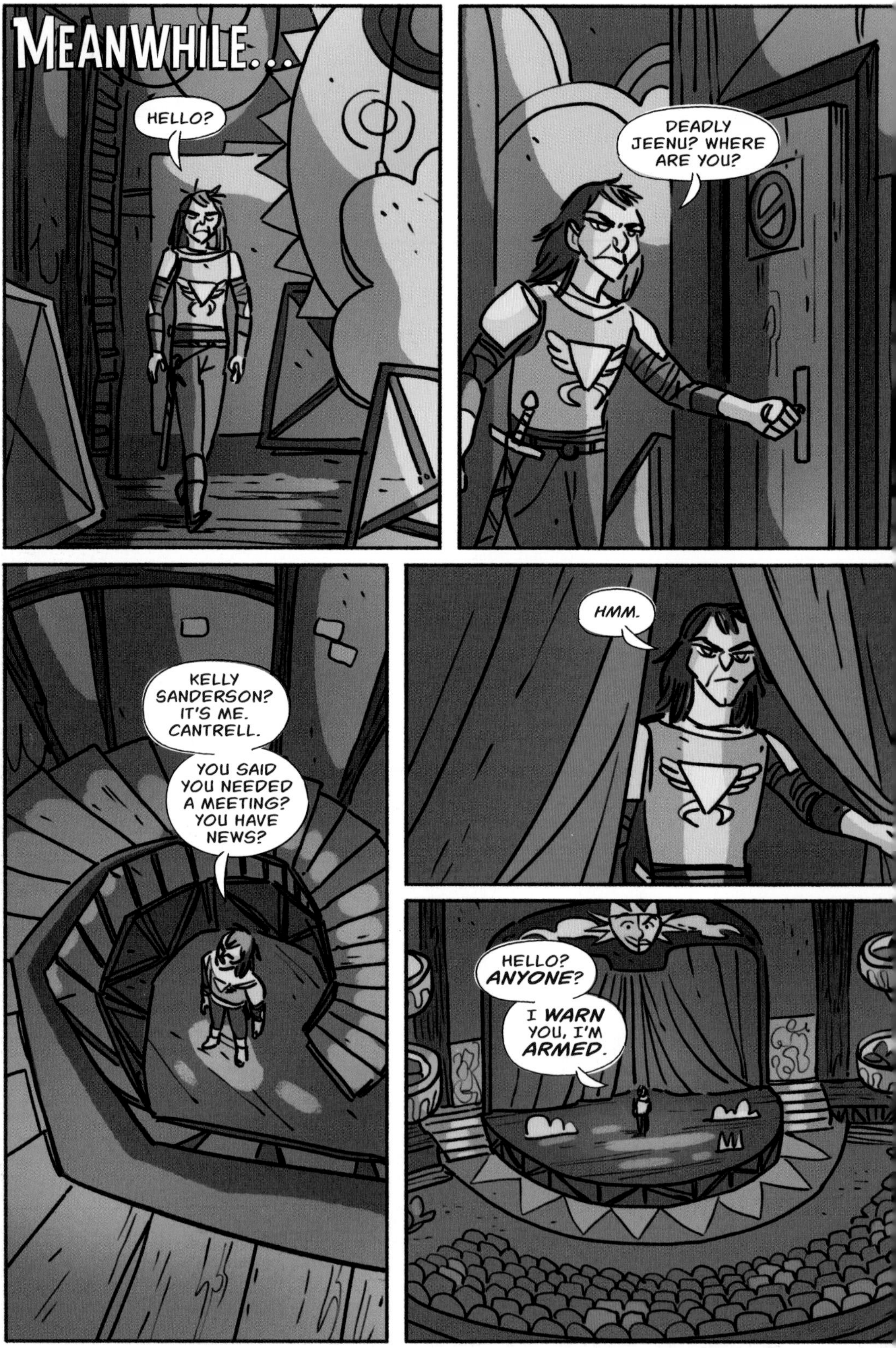
MEANWHILE...
HELLO?
DEADLY JEENU? WHERE ARE YOU?
KELLY SANDERSON? IT'S ME. CANTRELL.
YOU SAID YOU NEEDED A MEETING? YOU HAVE NEWS?
HMM.
HELLO? ANYONE?
I WARN YOU, I'M ARMED.

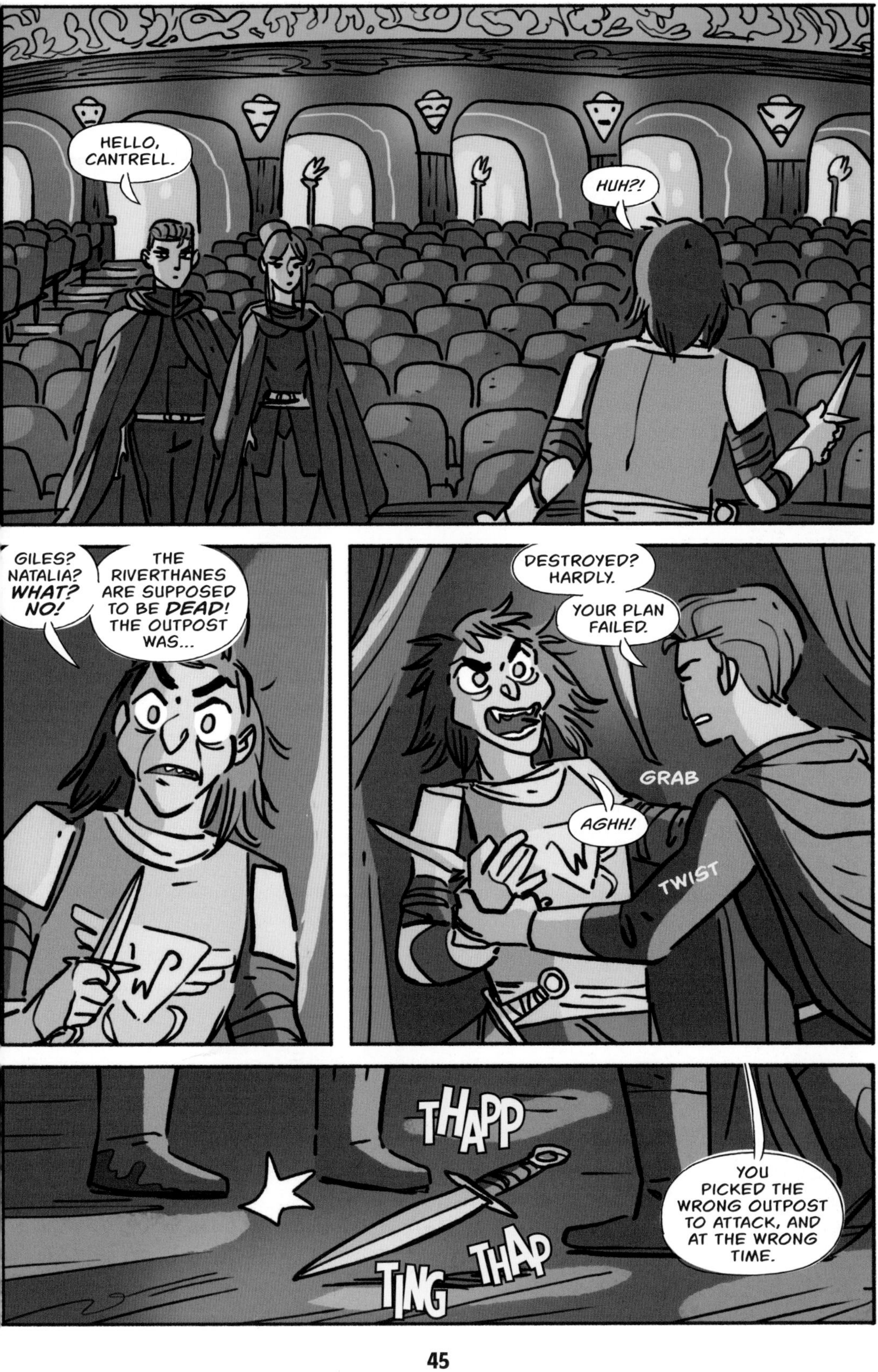
HELLO, CANTRELL.
HUH?!
GILES? NATALIA? WHAT? NO!
THE RIVERTHANES ARE SUPPOSED TO BE DEAD! THE OUTPOST WAS...
DESTROYED? HARDLY.
YOUR PLAN FAILED.
GRAB
AGHH!
TWIST
THAPP
TING
THAP
YOU PICKED THE WRONG OUTPOST TO ATTACK, AND AT THE WRONG TIME.

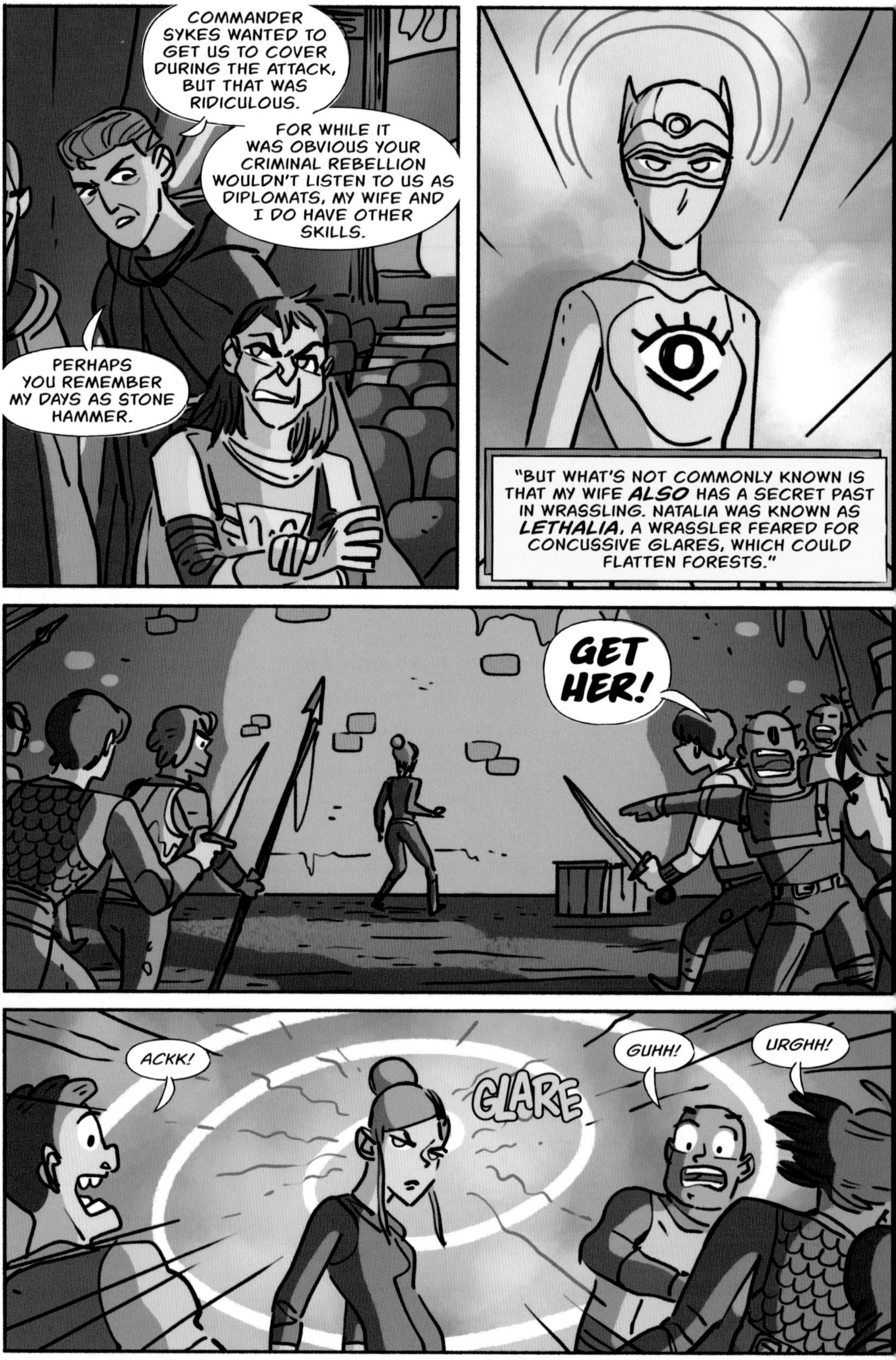
COMMANDER SYKES WANTED TO GET US TO COVER DURING THE ATTACK, BUT THAT WAS RIDICULOUS.
FOR WHILE IT WAS OBVIOUS YOUR CRIMINAL REBELLION WOULDN'T LISTEN TO US AS DIPLOMATS, MY WIFE AND I DO HAVE OTHER SKILLS.
PERHAPS YOU REMEMBER MY DAYS AS STONE HAMMER.
"BUT WHAT'S NOT COMMONLY KNOWN IS THAT MY WIFE ALSO HAS A SECRET PAST IN WRASSLING. NATALIA WAS KNOWN AS LETHALIA, A WRASSLER FEARED FOR CONCUSSIVE GLARES, WHICH COULD FLATTEN FORESTS."
GET HER!
ACKK!
GLARE
GUHH!
URGHH!

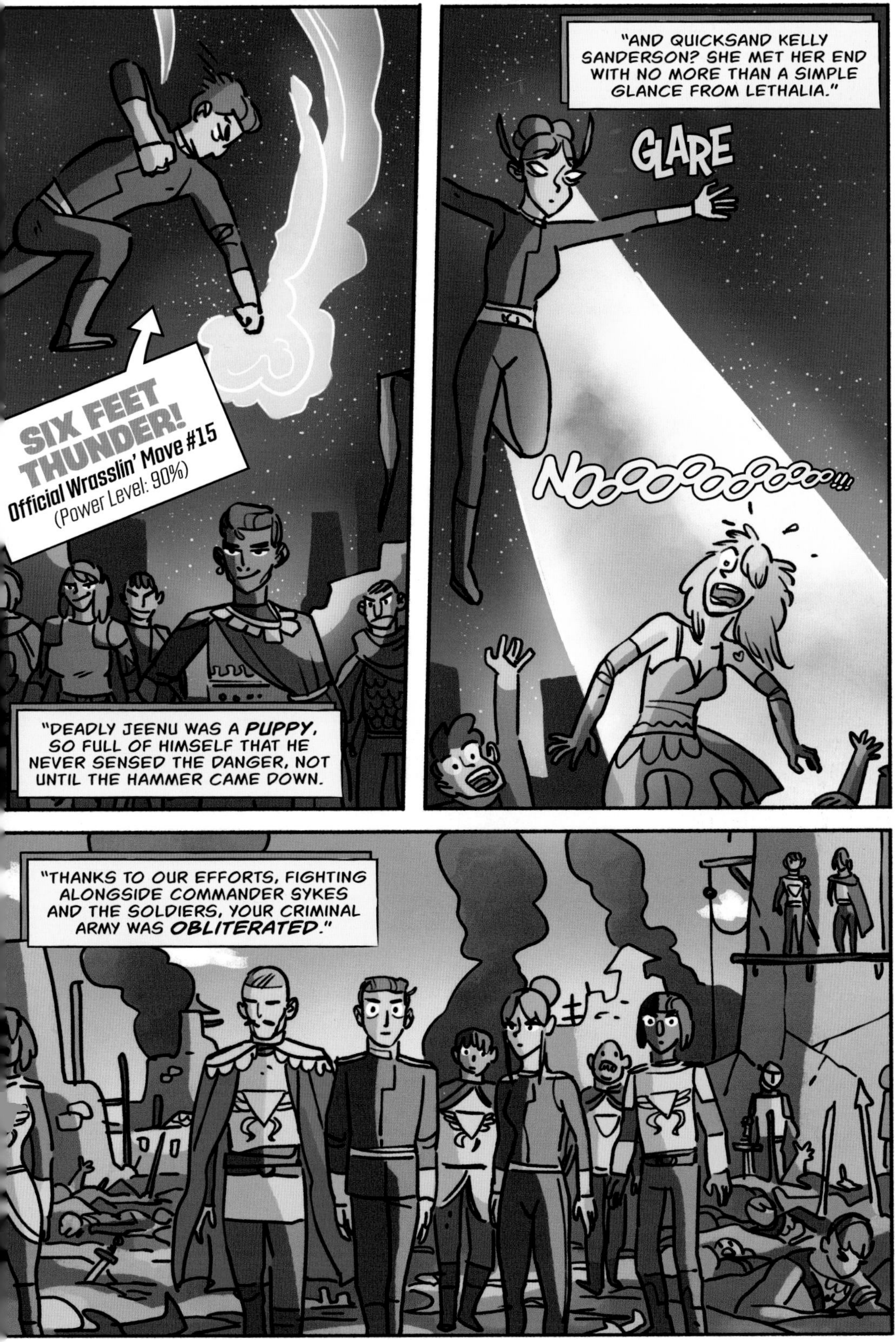
SIX FEET THUNDER!
Official Wrasslin' Move #15
(Power Level: 90%)
"DEADLY JEENU WAS A PUPPY, SO FULL OF HIMSELF THAT HE NEVER SENSED THE DANGER, NOT UNTIL THE HAMMER CAME DOWN.
"AND QUICKSAND KELLY SANDERSON? SHE MET HER END WITH NO MORE THAN A SIMPLE GLANCE FROM LETHALIA."
GLARE
Noooooooooooo!!!
"THANKS TO OUR EFFORTS, FIGHTING ALONGSIDE COMMANDER SYKES AND THE SOLDIERS, YOUR CRIMINAL ARMY WAS OBLITERATED."

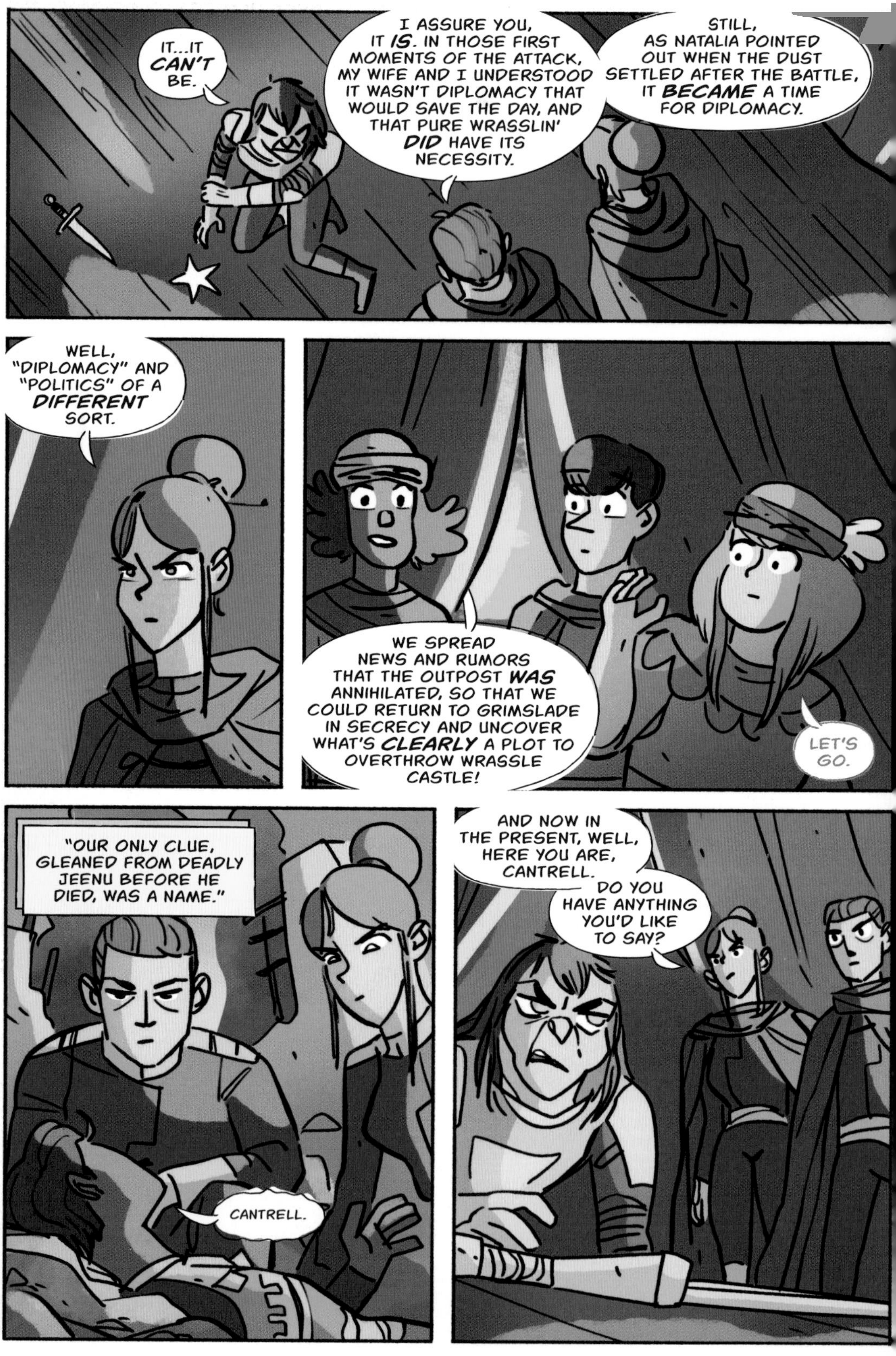
IT...IT CAN'T BE.
I ASSURE YOU, IT IS. IN THOSE FIRST MOMENTS OF THE ATTACK, MY WIFE AND I UNDERSTOOD IT WASN'T DIPLOMACY THAT WOULD SAVE THE DAY, AND THAT PURE WRASSLIN' DID HAVE ITS NECESSITY.
STILL, AS NATALIA POINTED OUT WHEN THE DUST SETTLED AFTER THE BATTLE, IT BECAME A TIME FOR DIPLOMACY.
WELL, "DIPLOMACY" AND "POLITICS" OF A DIFFERENT SORT.
WE SPREAD NEWS AND RUMORS THAT THE OUTPOST WAS ANNIHILATED, SO THAT WE COULD RETURN TO GRIMSLADE IN SECRECY AND UNCOVER WHAT'S CLEARLY A PLOT TO OVERTHROW WRASSLE CASTLE!
LET'S GO.
"OUR ONLY CLUE, GLEANED FROM DEADLY JEENU BEFORE HE DIED, WAS A NAME."
CANTRELL.
AND NOW IN THE PRESENT, WELL, HERE YOU ARE, CANTRELL.
DO YOU HAVE ANYTHING YOU'D LIKE TO SAY?

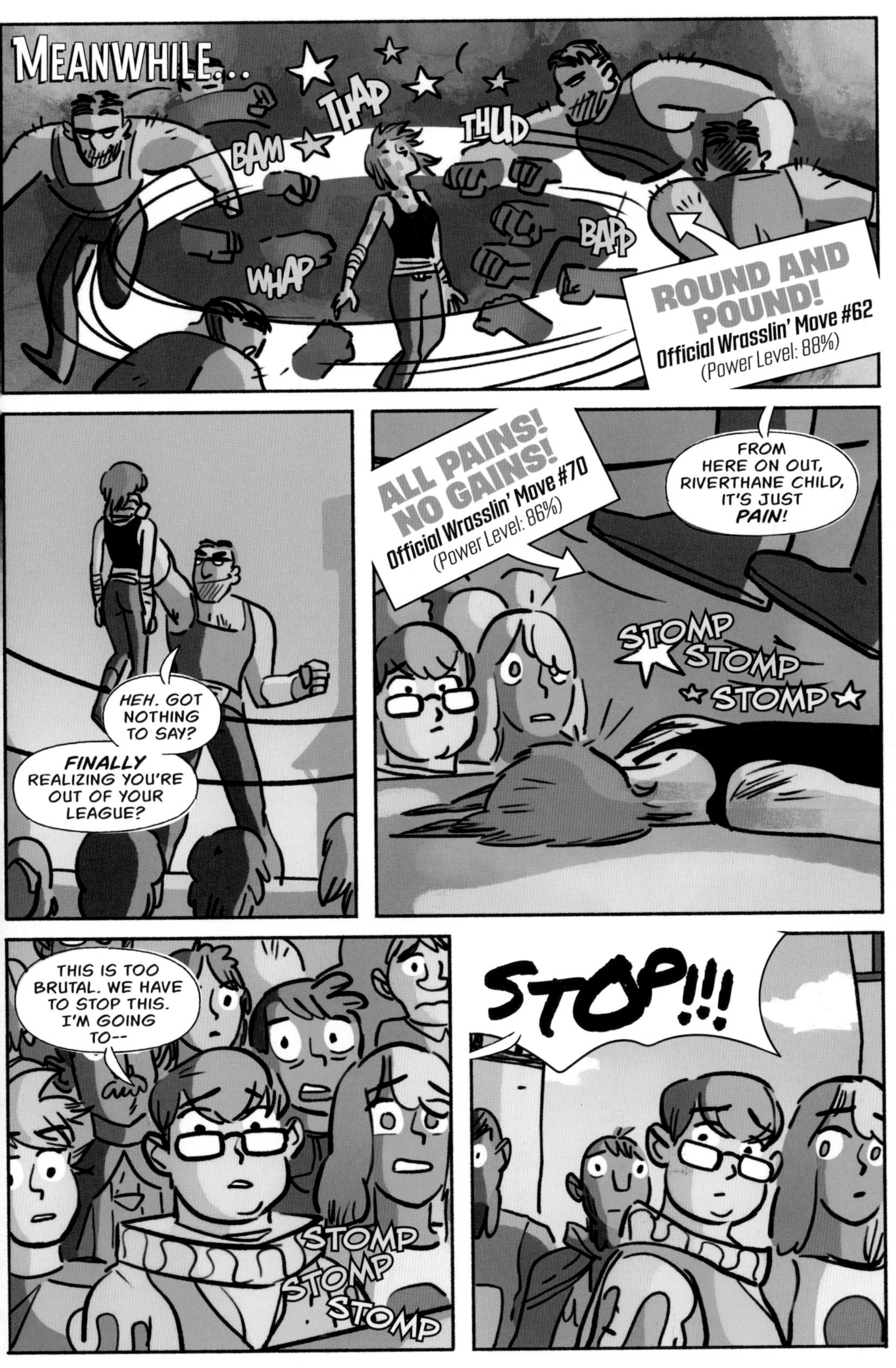
MEANWHILE...
BAM
THAP
THUD
BAPP
WHAP
ROUND AND POUND!
Official Wrasslin' Move #62
(Power Level: 88%)
HEH. GOT NOTHING TO SAY?
FINALLY REALIZING YOU'RE OUT OF YOUR LEAGUE?
ALL PAINS! NO GAINS!
Official Wrasslin' Move #70
(Power Level: 86%)
FROM HERE ON OUT, RIVERTHANE CHILD, IT'S JUST PAIN!
STOMP
STOMP
STOMP
THIS IS TOO BRUTAL. WE HAVE TO STOP THIS. I'M GOING TO--
STOMP
STOMP
STOMP
STOP!!!

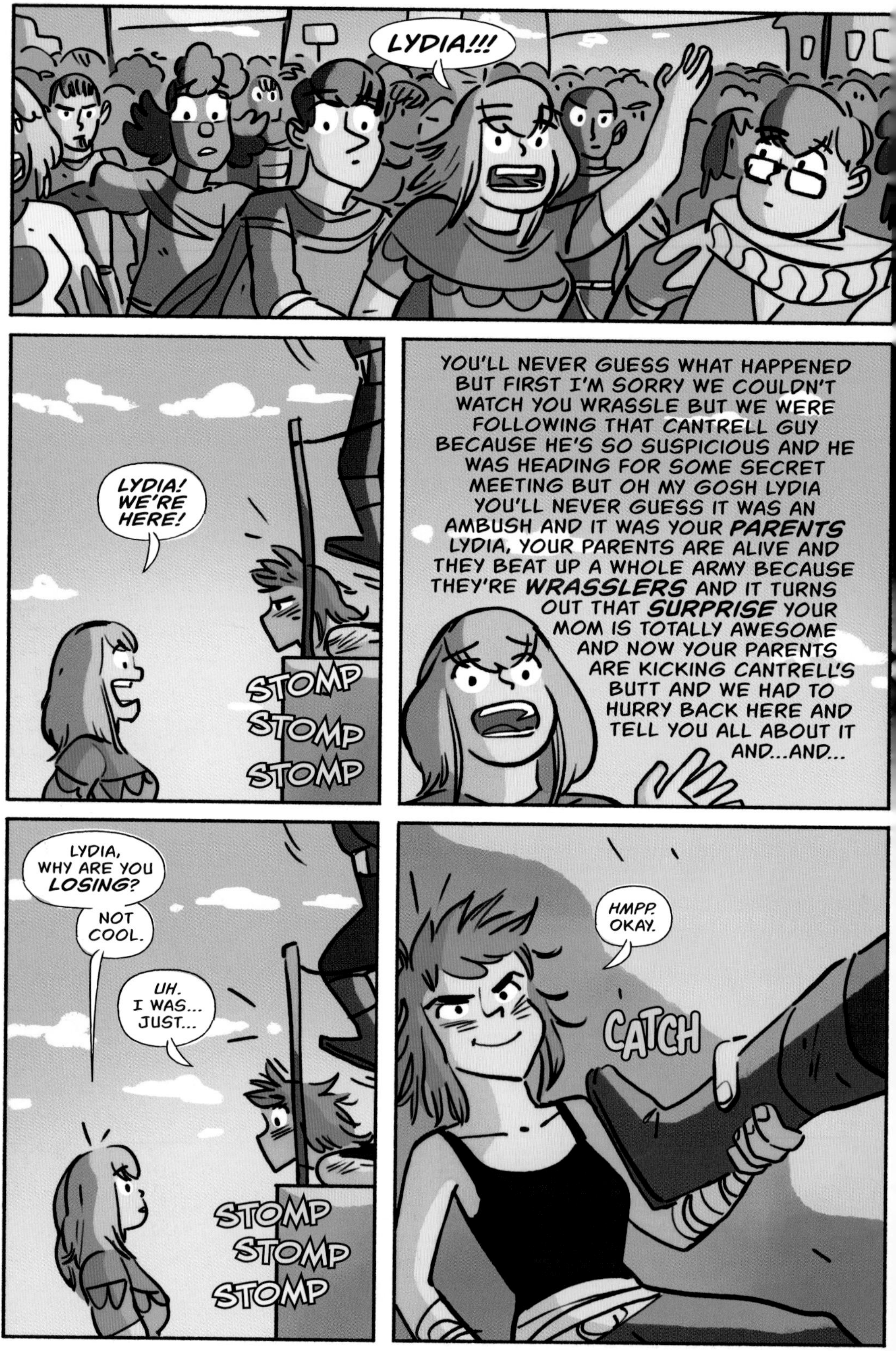
LYDIA!!!
LYDIA! WE'RE HERE!
STOMP
STOMP
STOMP
YOU'LL NEVER GUESS WHAT HAPPENED BUT FIRST I'M SORRY WE COULDN'T WATCH YOU WRASSLE BUT WE WERE FOLLOWING THAT CANTRELL GUY BECAUSE HE'S SO SUSPICIOUS AND HE WAS HEADING FOR SOME SECRET MEETING BUT OH MY GOSH LYDIA YOU'LL NEVER GUESS IT WAS AN AMBUSH AND IT WAS YOUR PARENTS LYDIA, YOUR PARENTS ARE ALIVE AND THEY BEAT UP A WHOLE ARMY BECAUSE THEY'RE WRASSLERS AND IT TURNS OUT THAT SURPRISE YOUR MOM IS TOTALLY AWESOME AND NOW YOUR PARENTS ARE KICKING CANTRELL'S BUTT AND WE HAD TO HURRY BACK HERE AND TELL YOU ALL ABOUT IT AND...AND...
LYDIA, WHY ARE YOU LOSING?
NOT COOL.
UH. I WAS... JUST...
STOMP
STOMP
STOMP
HMPP. OKAY.
CATCH

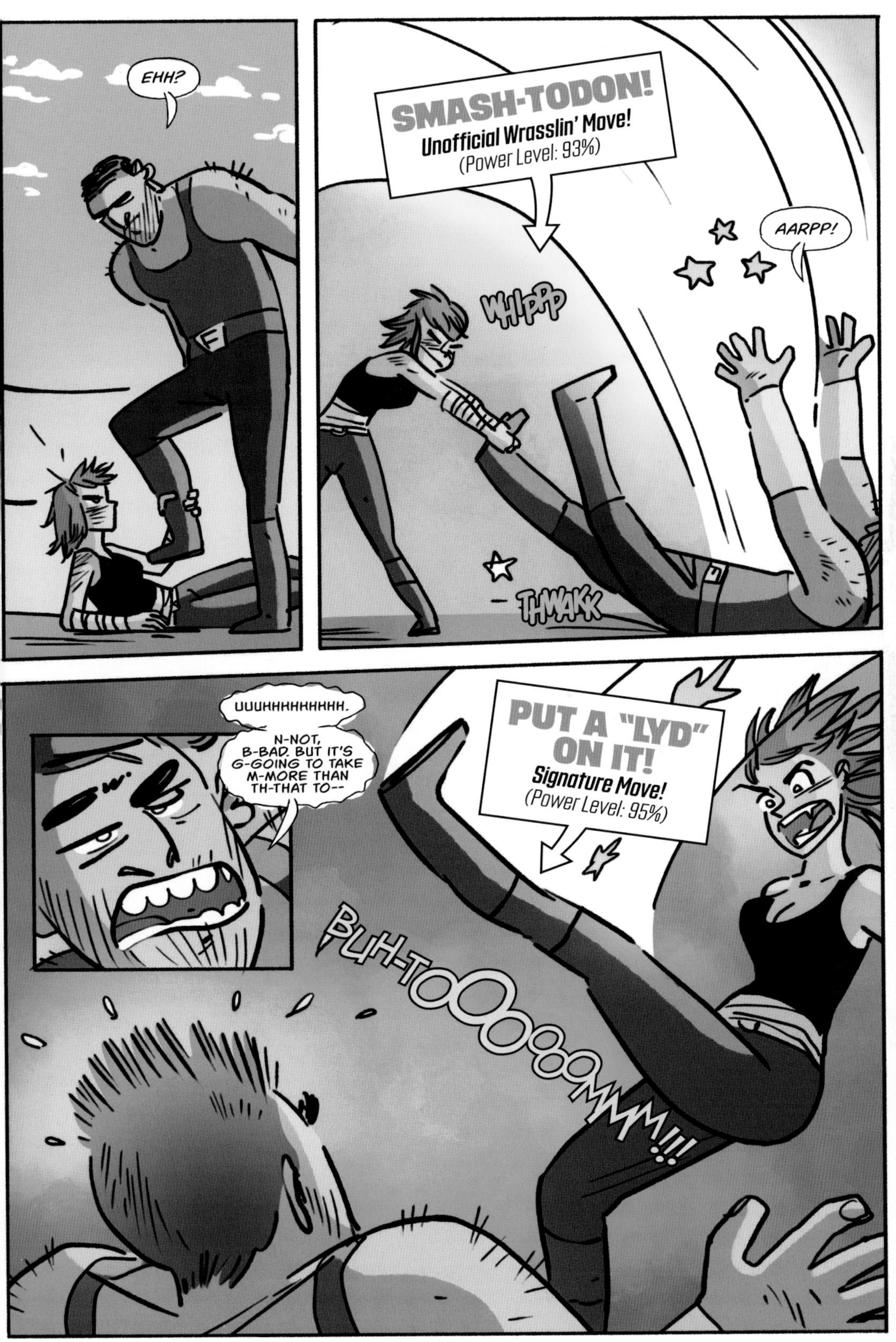

EHH?
SMASH-TODON!
Unofficial Wrasslin' Move!
(Power Level: 93%)
AARPP!
WHIPPP
THWAKK
UUUHHHHHHHHHH.
N-NOT, B-BAD. BUT IT'S G-GOING TO TAKE M-MORE THAN TH-THAT TO--
PUT A "LYD" ON IT!
Signature Move!
(Power Level: 95%)
BUH-TOOOOOOMMM!!!

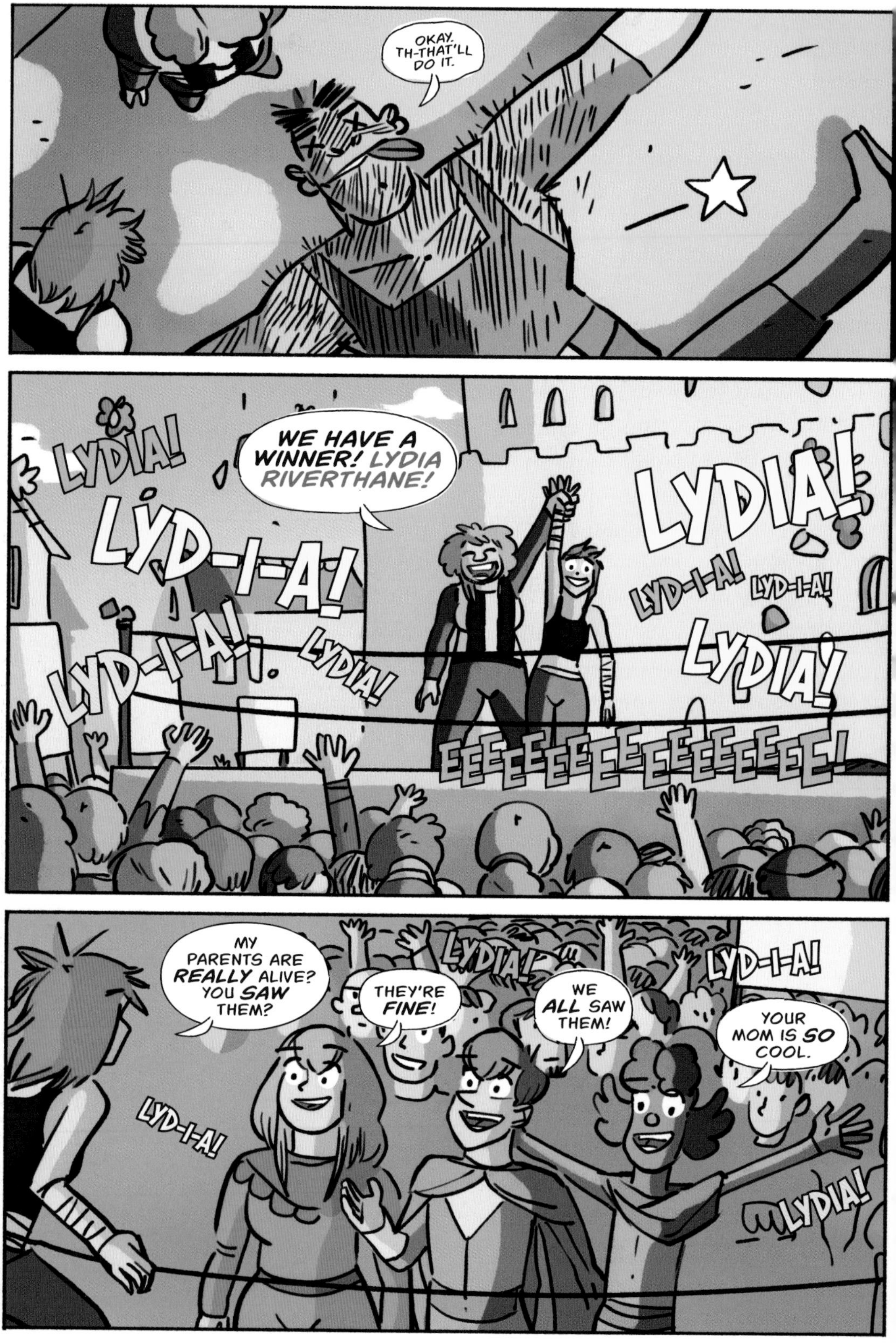

OKAY. TH-THAT'LL DO IT.
LYDIA!
WE HAVE A WINNER! LYDIA RIVERTHANE!
LYD-I-A!
LYDIA!
LYD-I-A!
LYDIA!
LYD-I-A!
LYD-I-A!
LYDIA!
EEEEEEEEEEEEEEEEE!
MY PARENTS ARE REALLY ALIVE? YOU SAW THEM?
LYDIA!
THEY'RE FINE!
WE ALL SAW THEM!
LYD-I-A!
YOUR MOM IS SO COOL.
LYD-I-A!
LYDIA!

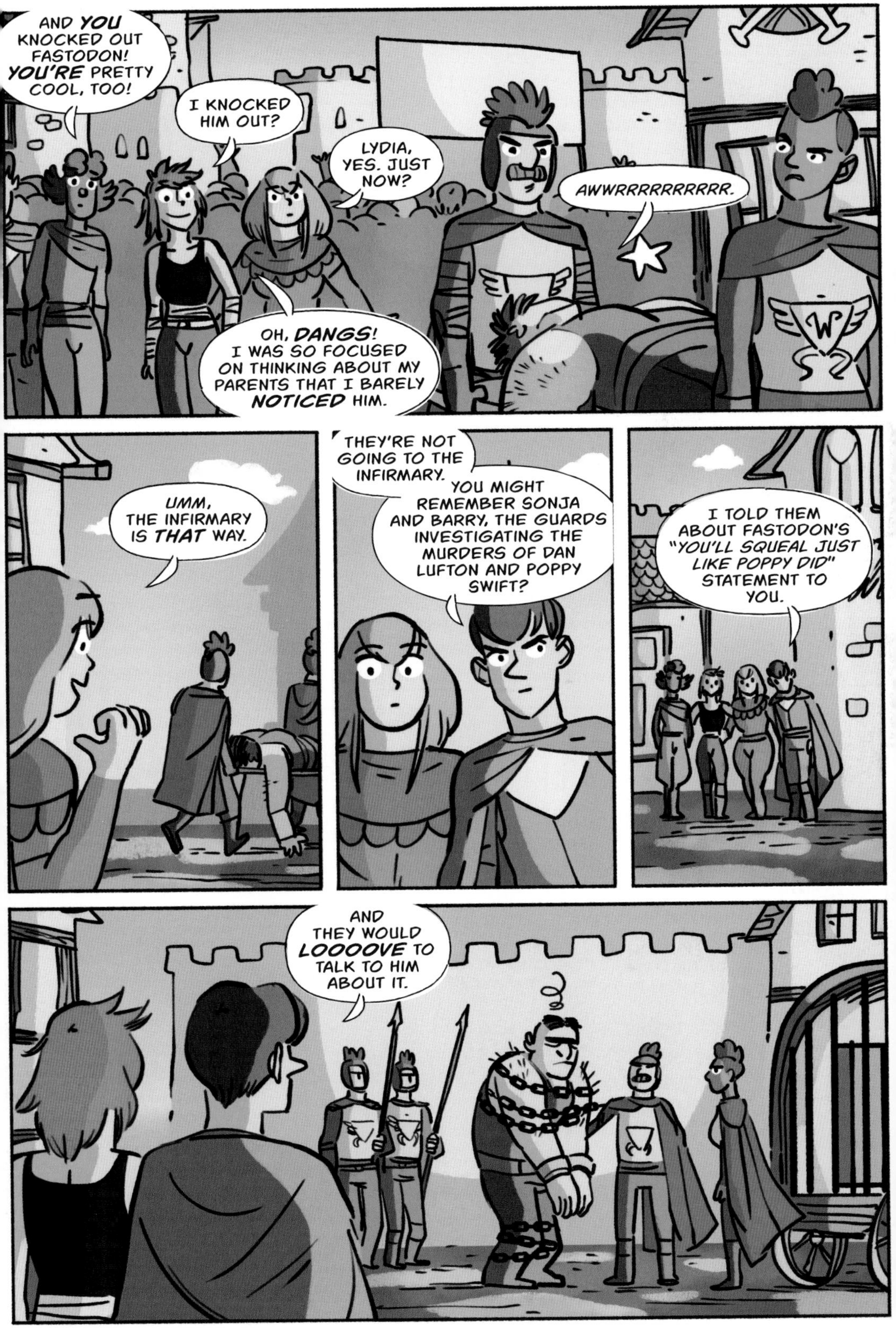
AND YOU KNOCKED OUT FASTODON! YOU'RE PRETTY COOL, TOO!
I KNOCKED HIM OUT?
LYDIA, YES. JUST NOW?
AWWRRRRRRRRRR.
OH, DANGS! I WAS SO FOCUSED ON THINKING ABOUT MY PARENTS THAT I BARELY NOTICED HIM.
UMM, THE INFIRMARY IS THAT WAY.
THEY'RE NOT GOING TO THE INFIRMARY.
YOU MIGHT REMEMBER SONJA AND BARRY, THE GUARDS INVESTIGATING THE MURDERS OF DAN LUFTON AND POPPY SWIFT?
I TOLD THEM ABOUT FASTODON'S "YOU'LL SQUEAL JUST LIKE POPPY DID" STATEMENT TO YOU.
AND THEY WOULD LOOOOVE TO TALK TO HIM ABOUT IT.

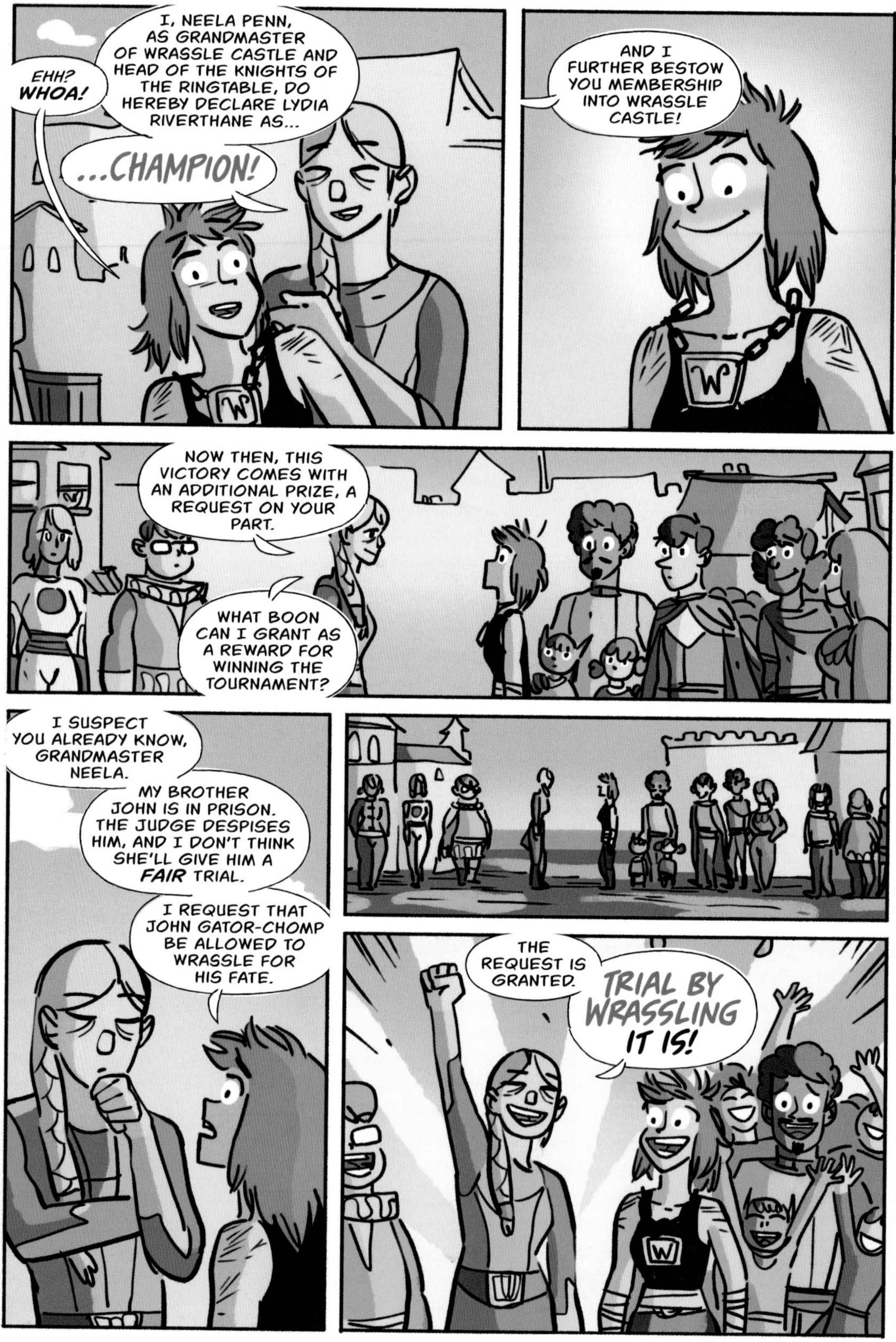
EHH? WHOA!
I, NEELA PENN, AS GRANDMASTER OF WRASSLE CASTLE AND HEAD OF THE KNIGHTS OF THE RINGTABLE, DO HEREBY DECLARE LYDIA RIVERTHANE AS...
...CHAMPION!
AND I FURTHER BESTOW YOU MEMBERSHIP INTO WRASSLE CASTLE!
NOW THEN, THIS VICTORY COMES WITH AN ADDITIONAL PRIZE, A REQUEST ON YOUR PART.
WHAT BOON CAN I GRANT AS A REWARD FOR WINNING THE TOURNAMENT?
I SUSPECT YOU ALREADY KNOW, GRANDMASTER NEELA.
MY BROTHER JOHN IS IN PRISON. THE JUDGE DESPISES HIM, AND I DON'T THINK SHE'LL GIVE HIM A FAIR TRIAL.
I REQUEST THAT JOHN GATOR-CHOMP BE ALLOWED TO WRASSLE FOR HIS FATE.
THE REQUEST IS GRANTED.
TRIAL BY WRASSLING IT IS!

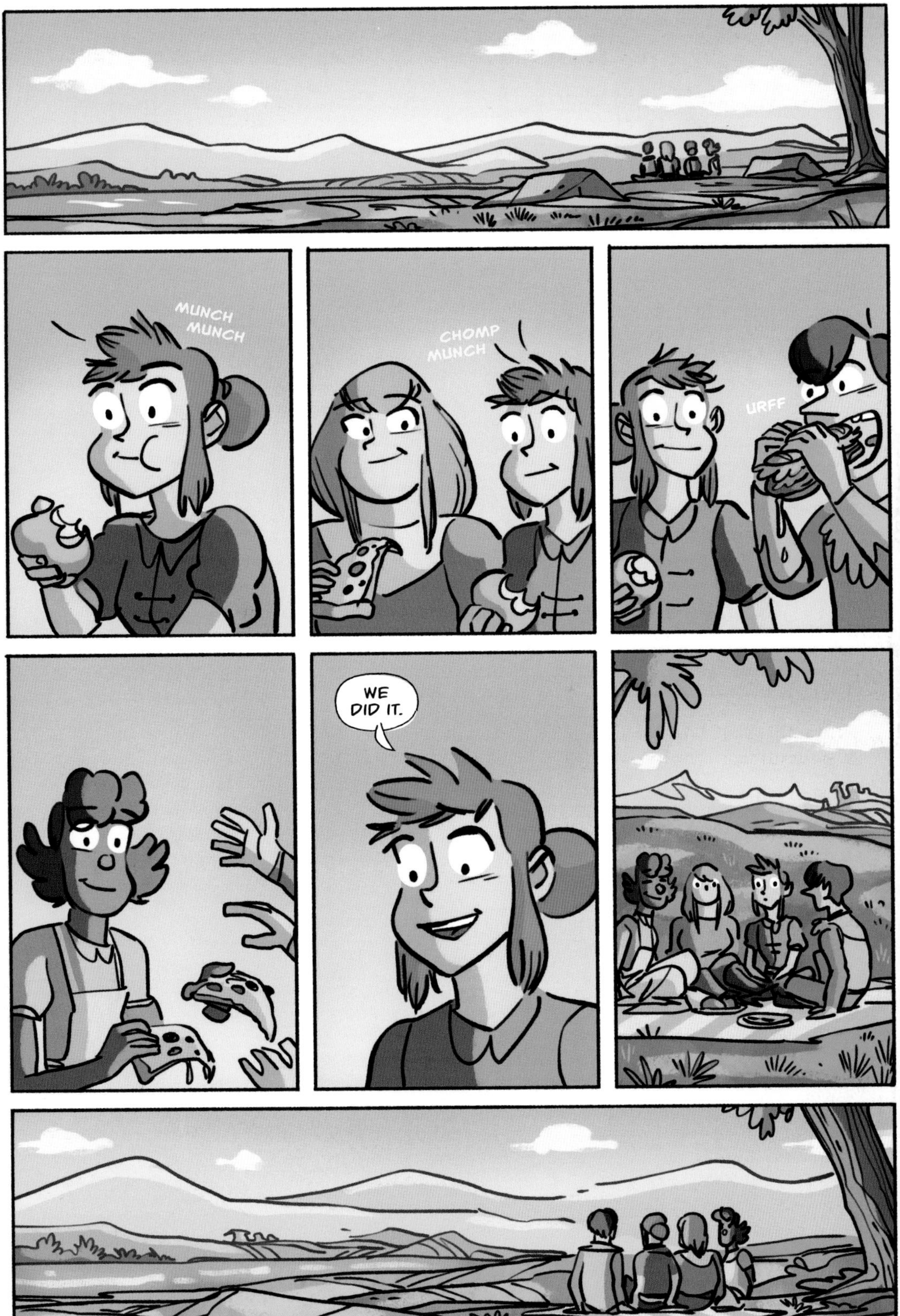
MUNCH MUNCH
CHOMP MUNCH
URFF
WE DID IT.

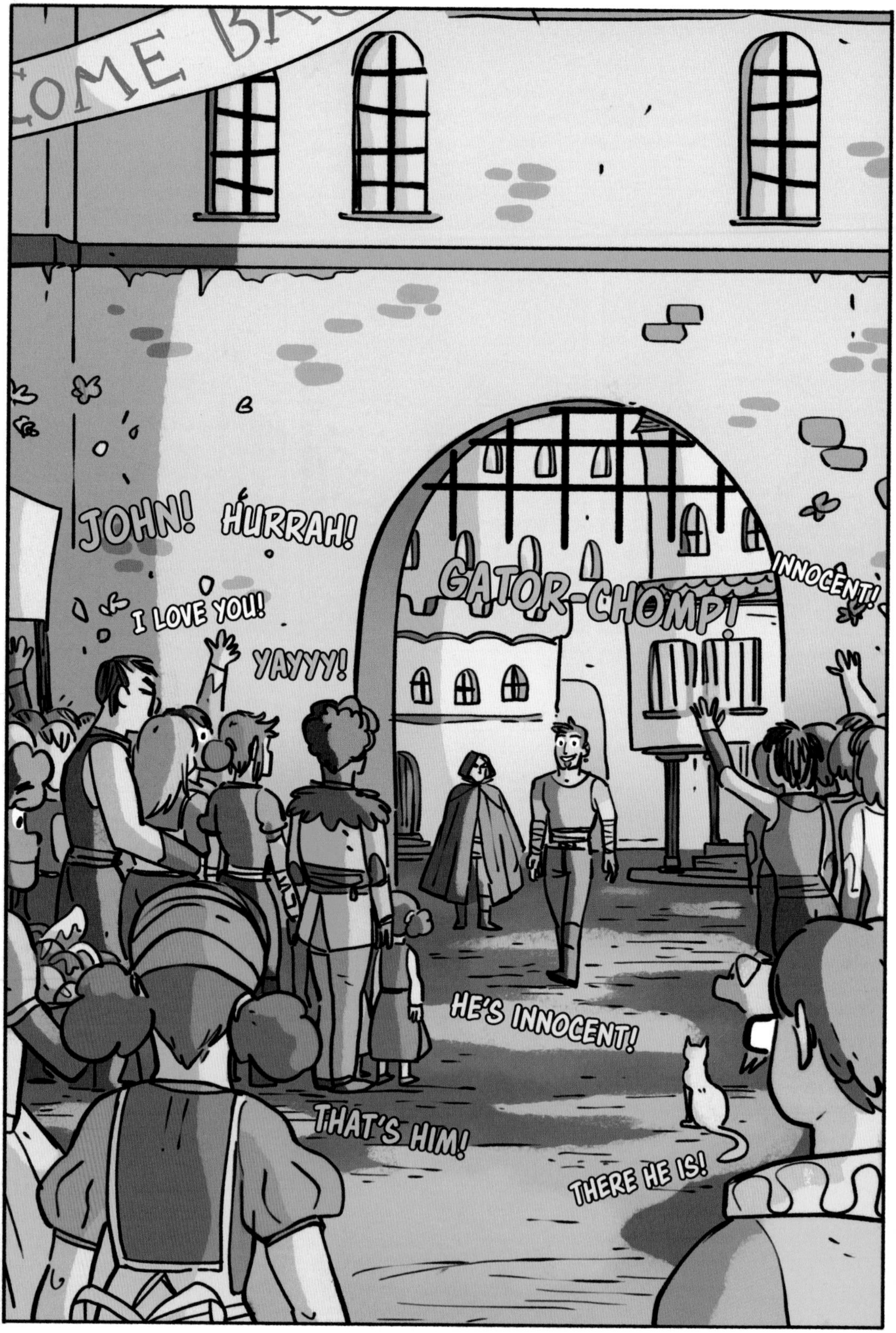
COME BA
JOHN!
HURRAH!
I LOVE YOU!
YAYYY!
GATOR-CHOMP!
INNOCENT!
HE'S INNOCENT!
THAT'S HIM!
THERE HE IS!

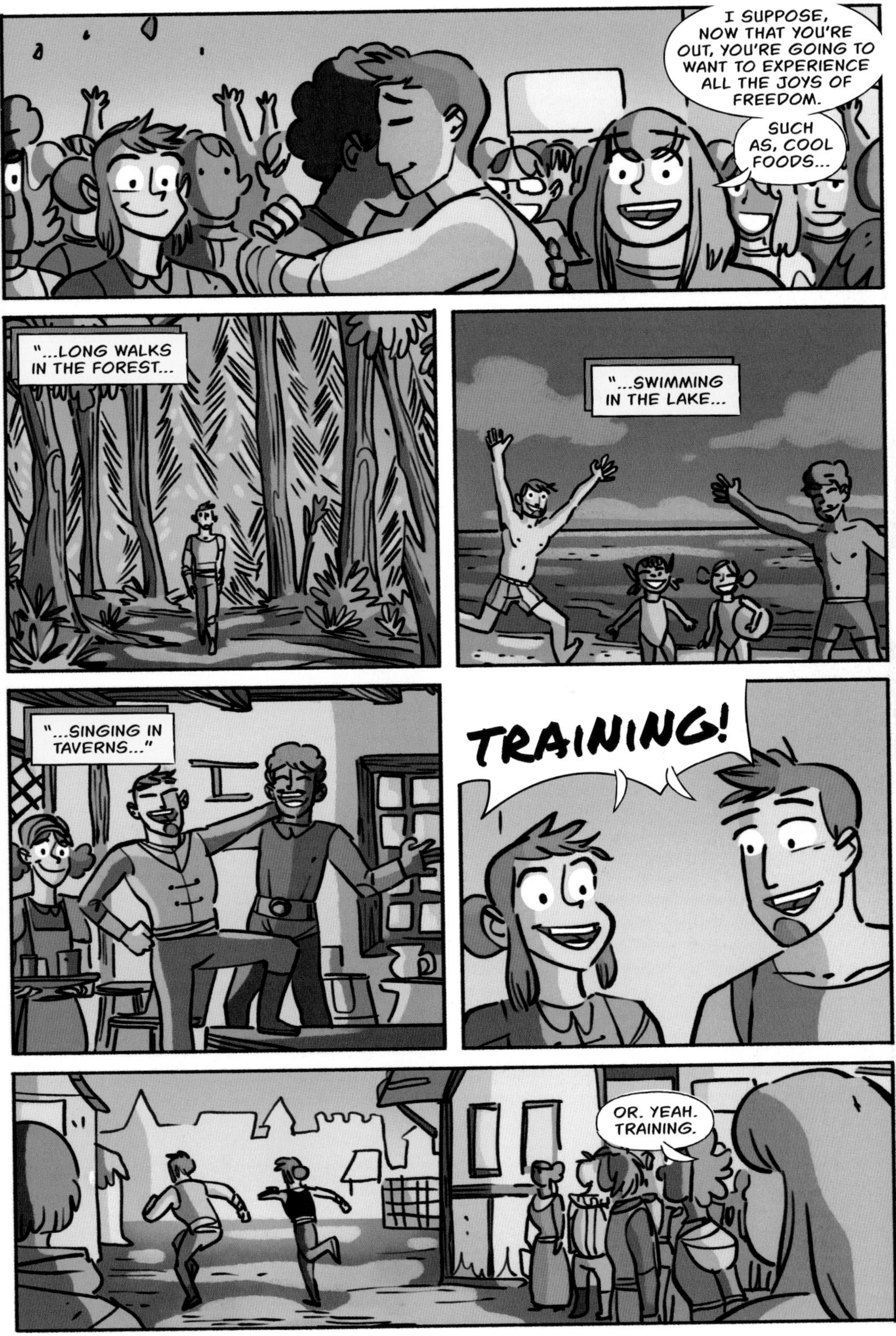
I SUPPOSE, NOW THAT YOU'RE OUT, YOU'RE GOING TO WANT TO EXPERIENCE ALL THE JOYS OF FREEDOM.
SUCH AS, COOL FOODS...
"...LONG WALKS IN THE FOREST...
"...SWIMMING IN THE LAKE...
"...SINGING IN TAVERNS..."
TRAINING!
OR. YEAH. TRAINING.

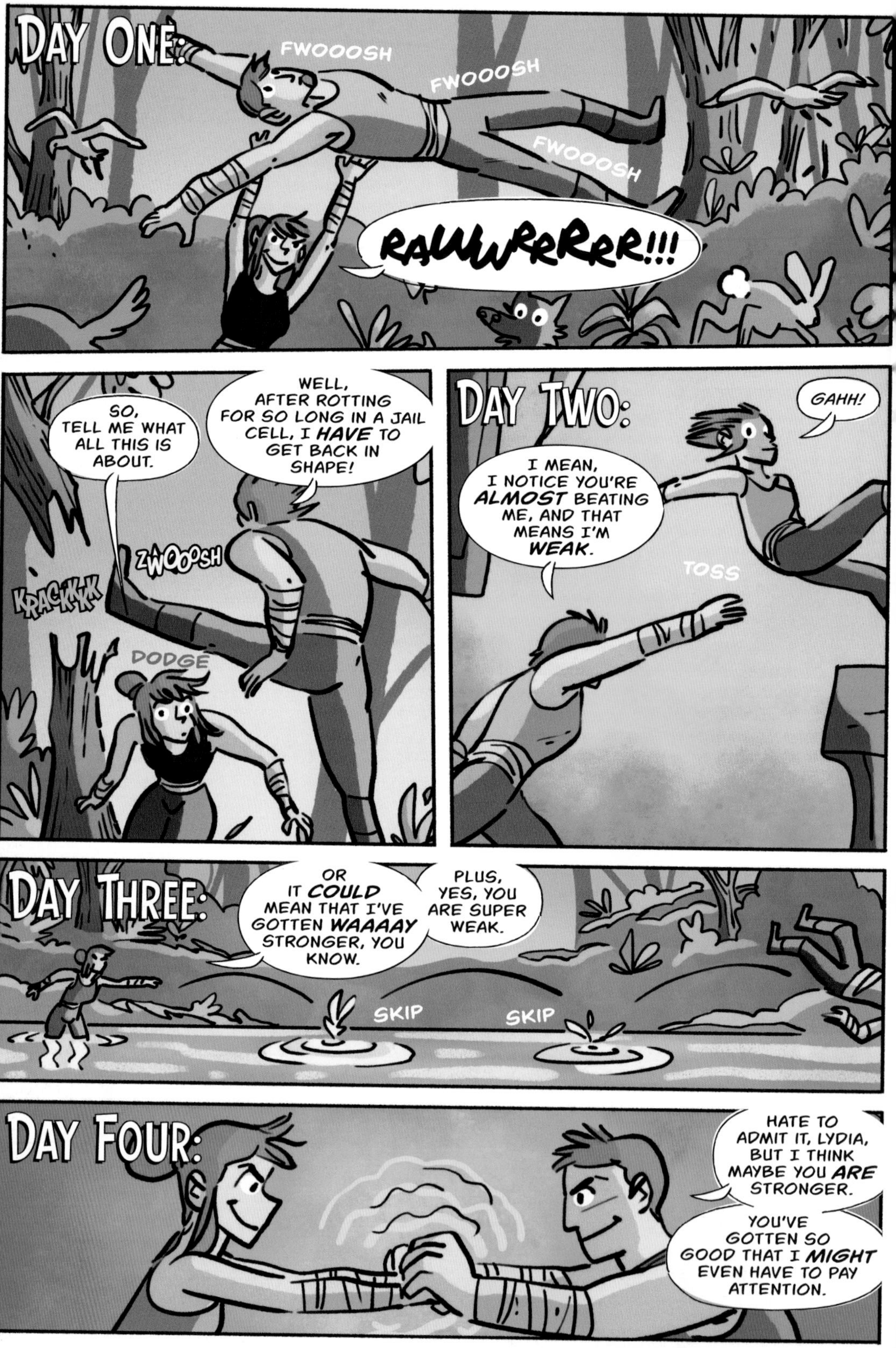
DAY ONE:
FWOOOSH
FWOOOSH
FWOOOSH
RAUUWRRRRR!!!
SO, TELL ME WHAT ALL THIS IS ABOUT.
WELL, AFTER ROTTING FOR SO LONG IN A JAIL CELL, I HAVE TO GET BACK IN SHAPE!
ZWOOOSH
KRACKKKK
DODGE
DAY TWO:
GAHH!
I MEAN, I NOTICE YOU'RE ALMOST BEATING ME, AND THAT MEANS I'M WEAK.
TOSS
DAY THREE:
OR IT COULD MEAN THAT I'VE GOTTEN WAAAAY STRONGER, YOU KNOW.
PLUS, YES, YOU ARE SUPER WEAK.
SKIP
SKIP
DAY FOUR:
HATE TO ADMIT IT, LYDIA, BUT I THINK MAYBE YOU ARE STRONGER.
YOU'VE GOTTEN SO GOOD THAT I MIGHT EVEN HAVE TO PAY ATTENTION.

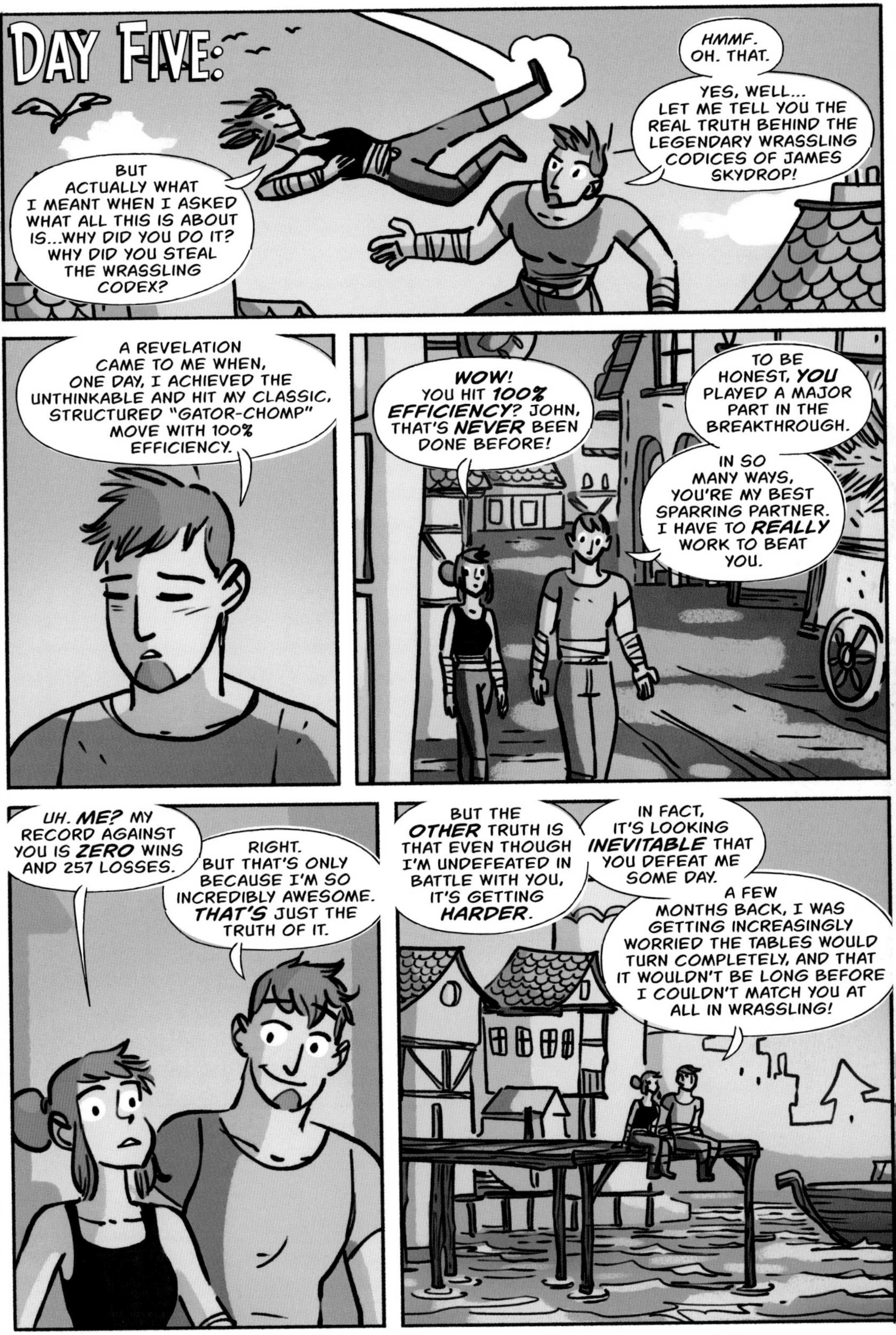
DAY FIVE:
HMMF. OH. THAT.
YES, WELL... LET ME TELL YOU THE REAL TRUTH BEHIND THE LEGENDARY WRASSLING CODICES OF JAMES SKYDROP!
BUT ACTUALLY WHAT I MEANT WHEN I ASKED WHAT ALL THIS IS ABOUT IS...WHY DID YOU DO IT? WHY DID YOU STEAL THE WRASSLING CODEX?
A REVELATION CAME TO ME WHEN, ONE DAY, I ACHIEVED THE UNTHINKABLE AND HIT MY CLASSIC, STRUCTURED "GATOR-CHOMP" MOVE WITH 100% EFFICIENCY.
WOW! YOU HIT 100% EFFICIENCY? JOHN, THAT'S NEVER BEEN DONE BEFORE!
TO BE HONEST, YOU PLAYED A MAJOR PART IN THE BREAKTHROUGH.
IN SO MANY WAYS, YOU'RE MY BEST SPARRING PARTNER. I HAVE TO REALLY WORK TO BEAT YOU.
UH. ME? MY RECORD AGAINST YOU IS ZERO WINS AND 257 LOSSES.
RIGHT. BUT THAT'S ONLY BECAUSE I'M SO INCREDIBLY AWESOME. THAT'S JUST THE TRUTH OF IT.
BUT THE OTHER TRUTH IS THAT EVEN THOUGH I'M UNDEFEATED IN BATTLE WITH YOU, IT'S GETTING HARDER.
IN FACT, IT'S LOOKING INEVITABLE THAT YOU DEFEAT ME SOME DAY.
A FEW MONTHS BACK, I WAS GETTING INCREASINGLY WORRIED THE TABLES WOULD TURN COMPLETELY, AND THAT IT WOULDN'T BE LONG BEFORE I COULDN'T MATCH YOU AT ALL IN WRASSLING!

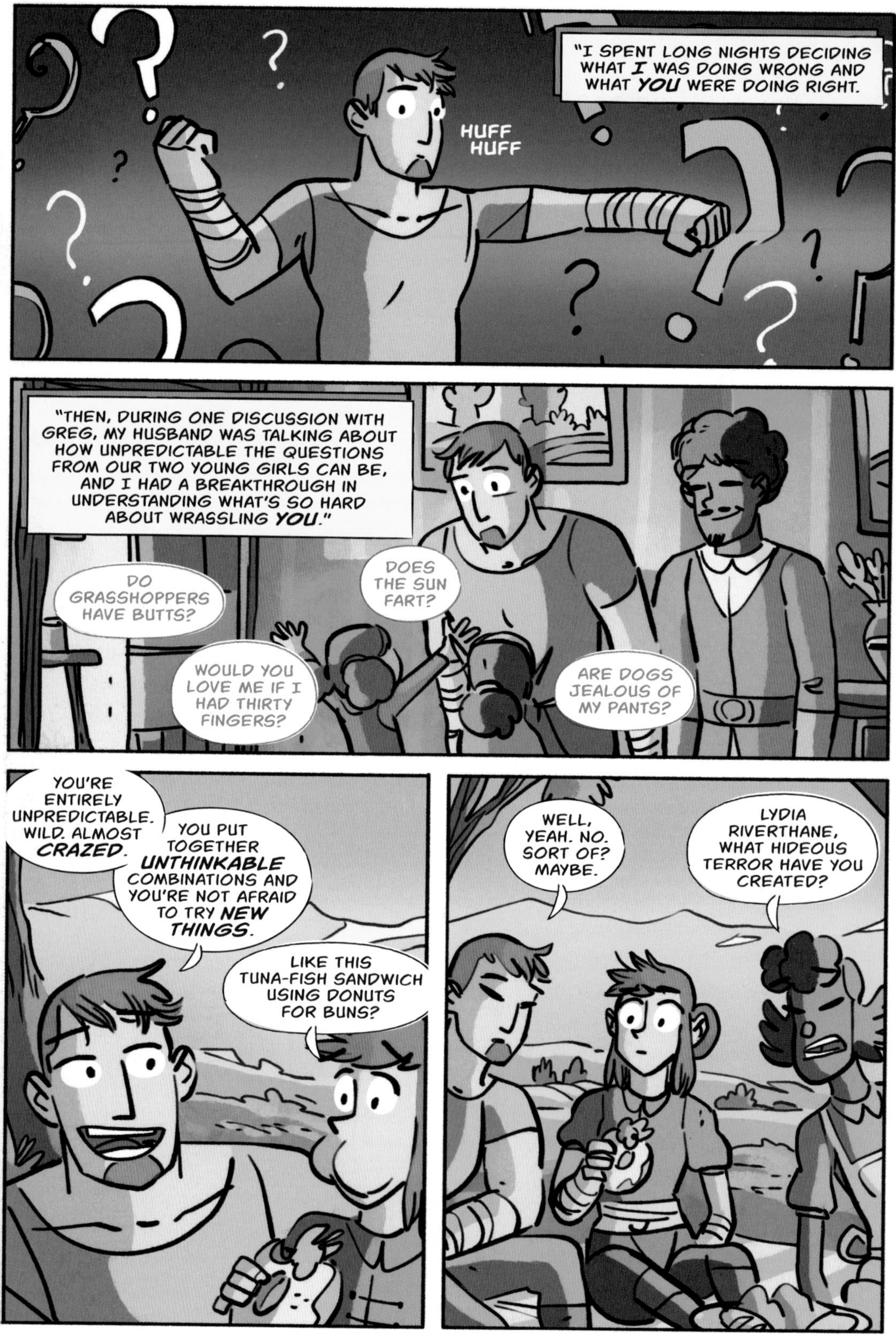
"I SPENT LONG NIGHTS DECIDING WHAT I WAS DOING WRONG AND WHAT YOU WERE DOING RIGHT.
HUFF HUFF
"THEN, DURING ONE DISCUSSION WITH GREG, MY HUSBAND WAS TALKING ABOUT HOW UNPREDICTABLE THE QUESTIONS FROM OUR TWO YOUNG GIRLS CAN BE, AND I HAD A BREAKTHROUGH IN UNDERSTANDING WHAT'S SO HARD ABOUT WRASSLING YOU."
DO GRASSHOPPERS HAVE BUTTS?
DOES THE SUN FART?
WOULD YOU LOVE ME IF I HAD THIRTY FINGERS?
ARE DOGS JEALOUS OF MY PANTS?
YOU'RE ENTIRELY UNPREDICTABLE. WILD. ALMOST CRAZED.
YOU PUT TOGETHER UNTHINKABLE COMBINATIONS AND YOU'RE NOT AFRAID TO TRY NEW THINGS.
LIKE THIS TUNA-FISH SANDWICH USING DONUTS FOR BUNS?
WELL, YEAH. NO. SORT OF? MAYBE.
LYDIA RIVERTHANE, WHAT HIDEOUS TERROR HAVE YOU CREATED?

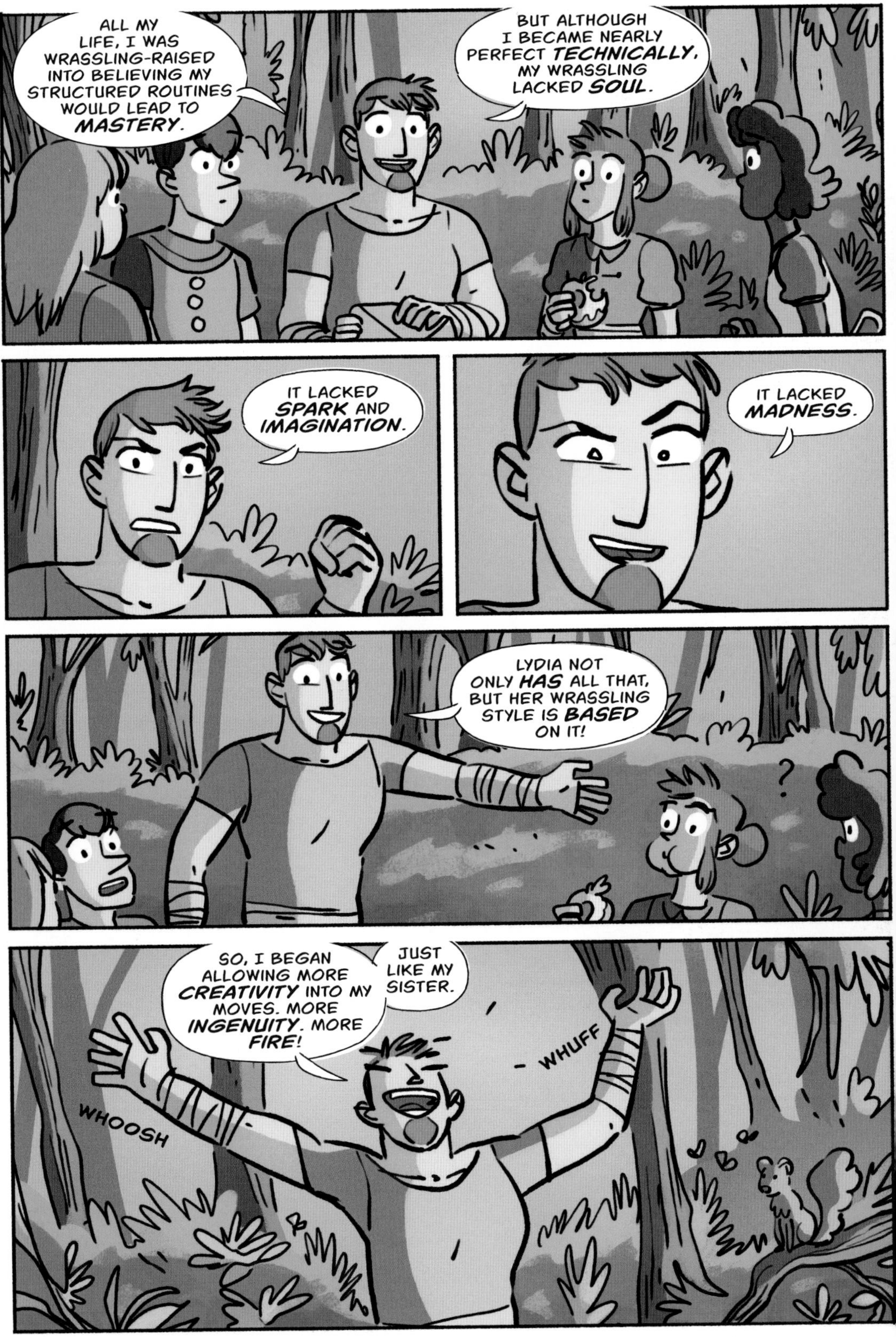
ALL MY LIFE, I WAS WRASSLING-RAISED INTO BELIEVING MY STRUCTURED ROUTINES WOULD LEAD TO MASTERY.
BUT ALTHOUGH I BECAME NEARLY PERFECT TECHNICALLY, MY WRASSLING LACKED SOUL.
IT LACKED SPARK AND IMAGINATION.
IT LACKED MADNESS.
LYDIA NOT ONLY HAS ALL THAT, BUT HER WRASSLING STYLE IS BASED ON IT!
?
SO, I BEGAN ALLOWING MORE CREATIVITY INTO MY MOVES. MORE INGENUITY. MORE FIRE!
JUST LIKE MY SISTER.
WHUFF
WHOOSH

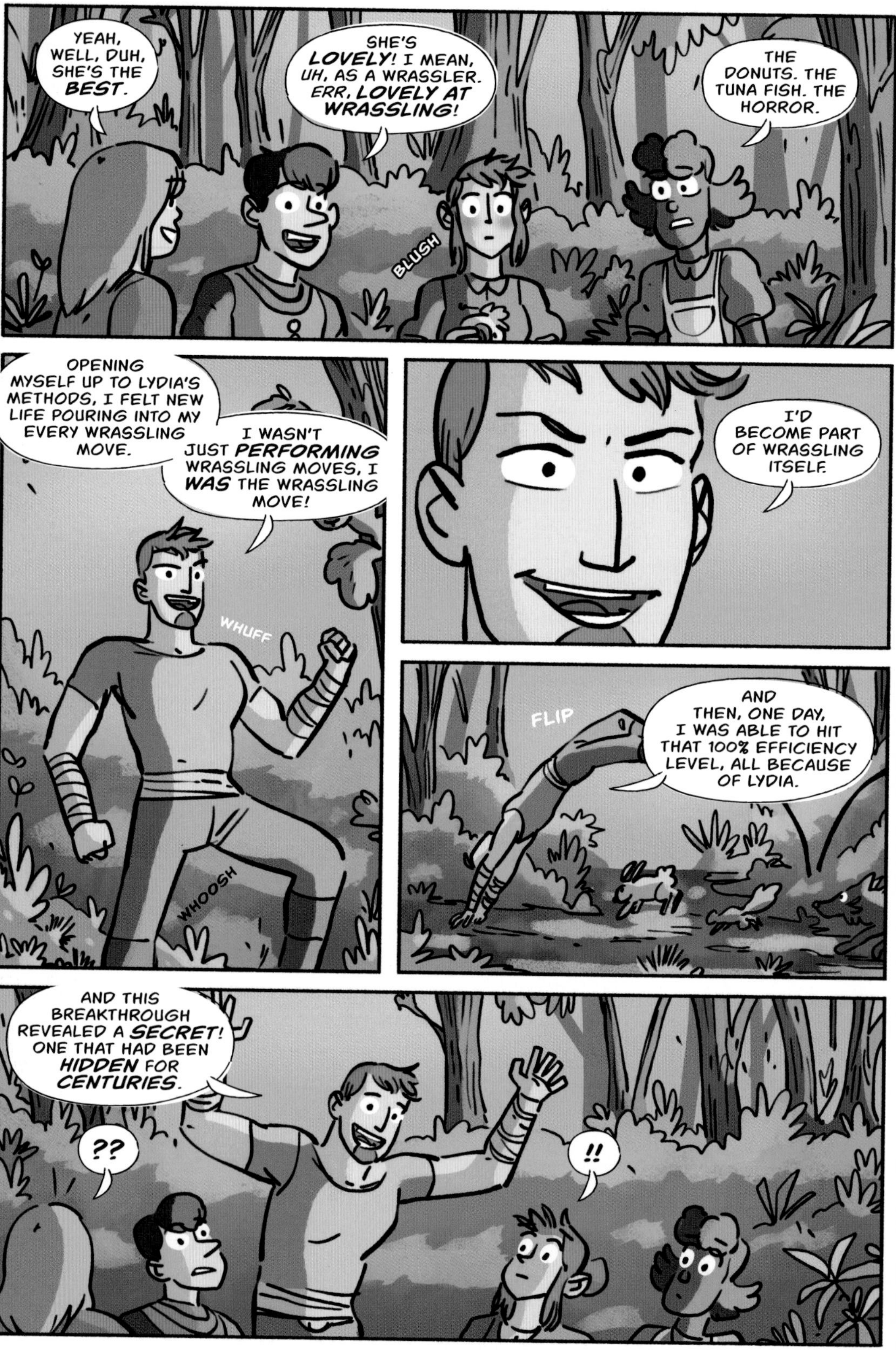
YEAH, WELL, DUH, SHE'S THE BEST.
SHE'S LOVELY! I MEAN, UH, AS A WRASSLER. ERR, LOVELY AT WRASSLING!
BLUSH
THE DONUTS. THE TUNA FISH. THE HORROR.
OPENING MYSELF UP TO LYDIA'S METHODS, I FELT NEW LIFE POURING INTO MY EVERY WRASSLING MOVE.
I WASN'T JUST PERFORMING WRASSLING MOVES, I WAS THE WRASSLING MOVE!
WHUFF
WHOOSH
I'D BECOME PART OF WRASSLING ITSELF.
FLIP
AND THEN, ONE DAY, I WAS ABLE TO HIT THAT 100% EFFICIENCY LEVEL, ALL BECAUSE OF LYDIA.
AND THIS BREAKTHROUGH REVEALED A SECRET! ONE THAT HAD BEEN HIDDEN FOR CENTURIES.
??
!!

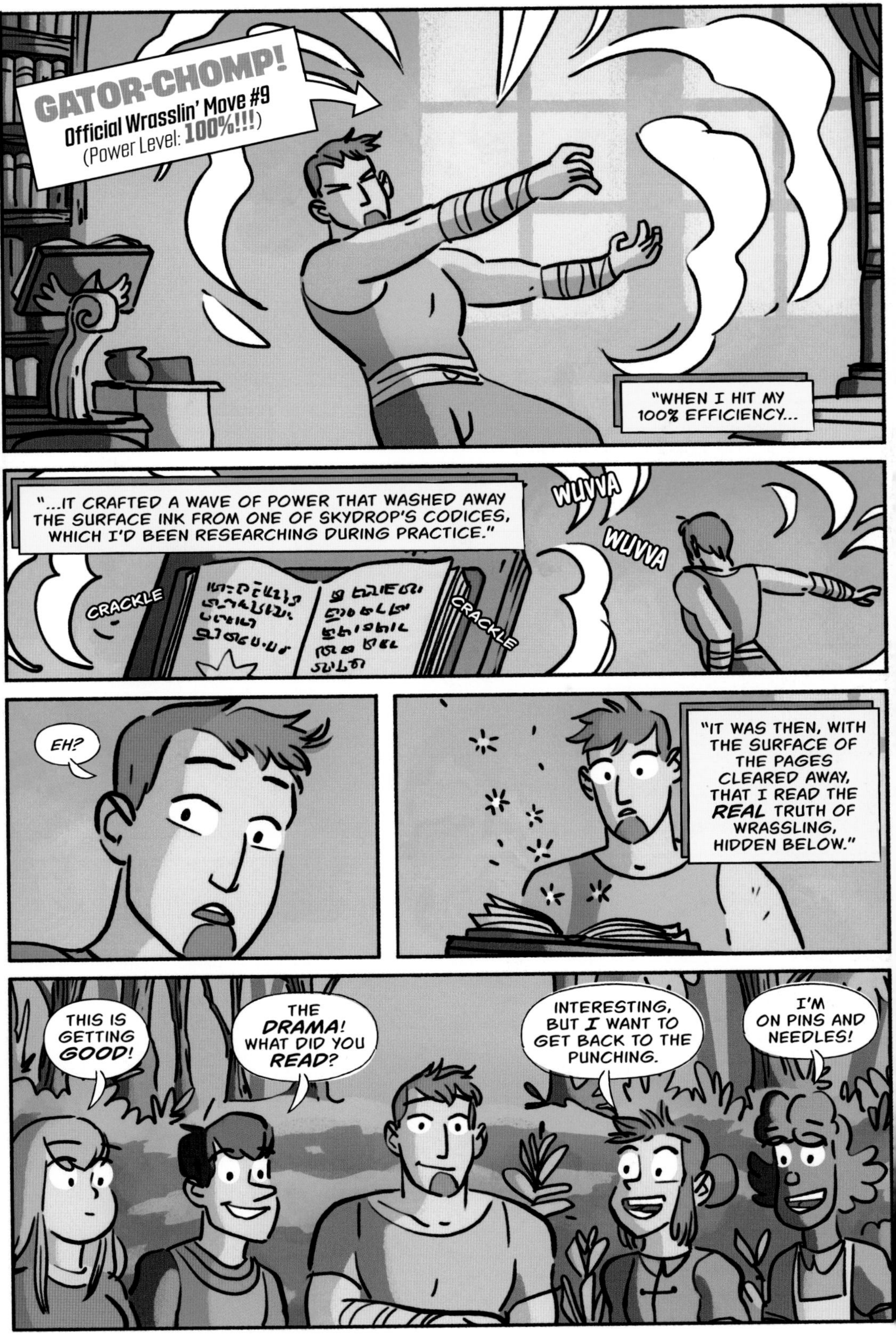

GATOR-CHOMP!
Official Wrasslin' Move #9
(Power Level: 100%!!!)
"WHEN I HIT MY 100% EFFICIENCY...
"...IT CRAFTED A WAVE OF POWER THAT WASHED AWAY THE SURFACE INK FROM ONE OF SKYDROP'S CODICES, WHICH I'D BEEN RESEARCHING DURING PRACTICE."
WUVVA
WUVVA
CRACKLE
CRACKLE
EH?
"IT WAS THEN, WITH THE SURFACE OF THE PAGES CLEARED AWAY, THAT I READ THE REAL TRUTH OF WRASSLING, HIDDEN BELOW."
THIS IS GETTING GOOD!
THE DRAMA! WHAT DID YOU READ?
INTERESTING, BUT I WANT TO GET BACK TO THE PUNCHING.
I'M ON PINS AND NEEDLES!

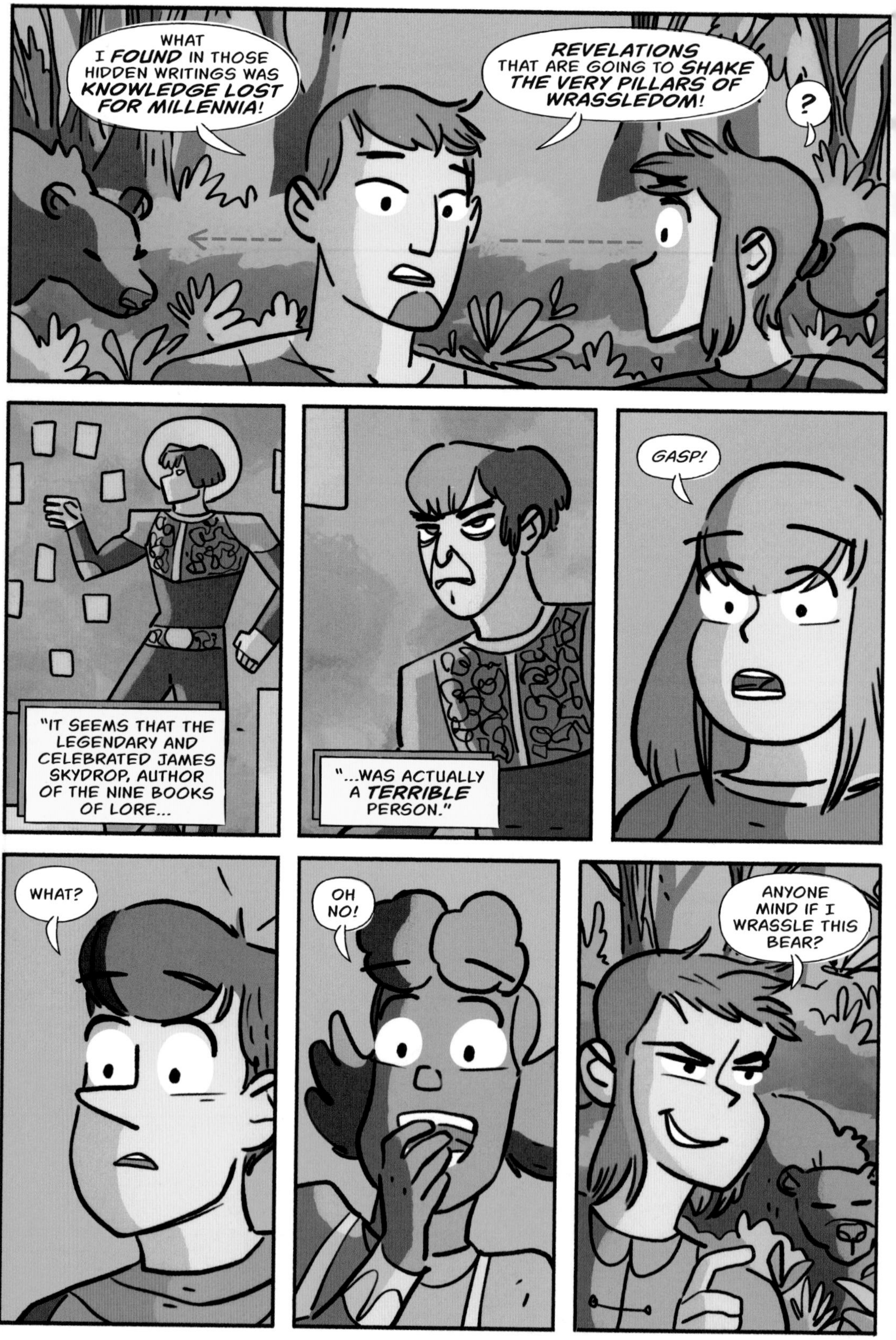
WHAT I FOUND IN THOSE HIDDEN WRITINGS WAS KNOWLEDGE LOST FOR MILLENNIA!
REVELATIONS THAT ARE GOING TO SHAKE THE VERY PILLARS OF WRASSLEDOM!
?
"IT SEEMS THAT THE LEGENDARY AND CELEBRATED JAMES SKYDROP, AUTHOR OF THE NINE BOOKS OF LORE...
"...WAS ACTUALLY A TERRIBLE PERSON."
GASP!
WHAT?
OH NO!
ANYONE MIND IF I WRASSLE THIS BEAR?

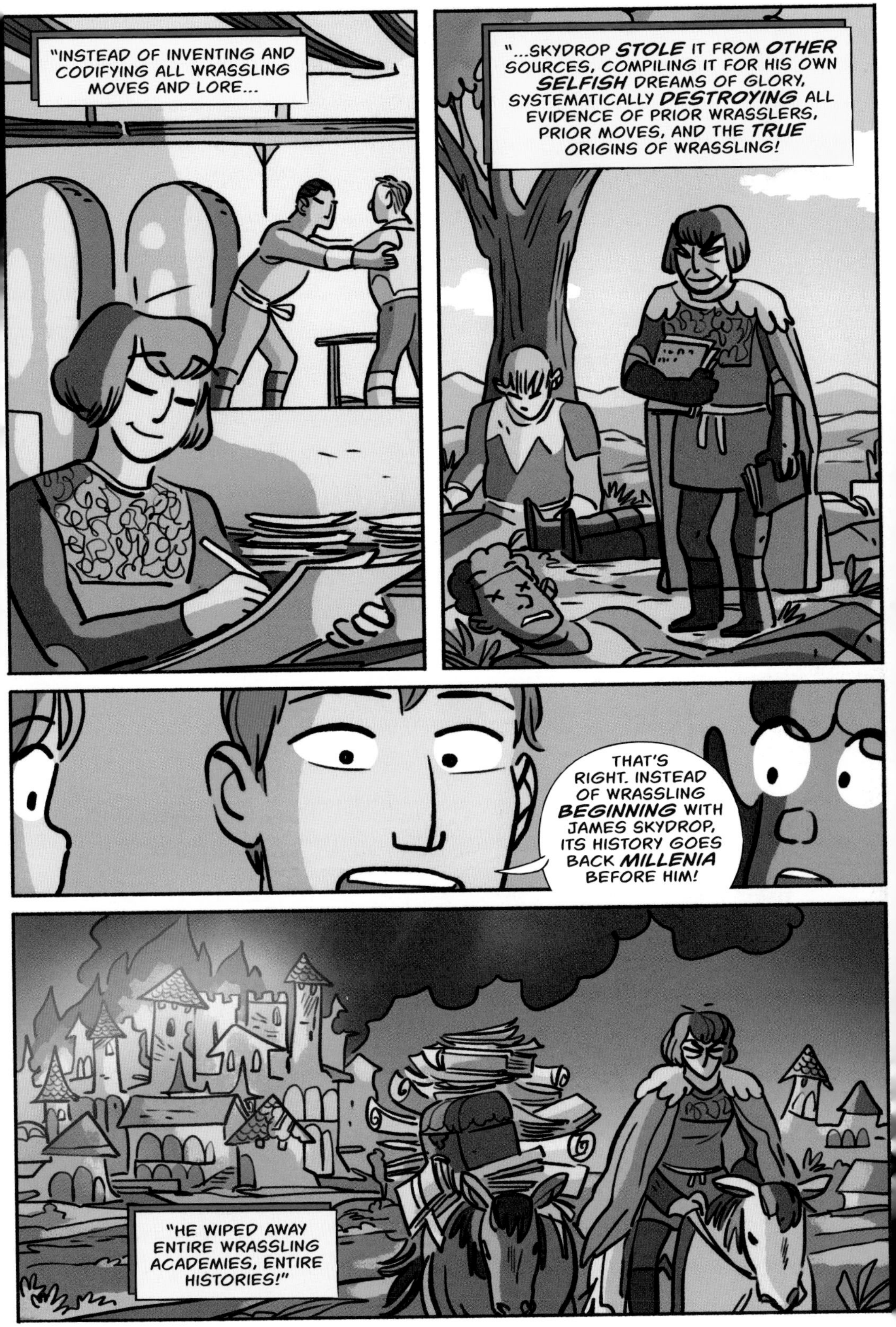
"INSTEAD OF INVENTING AND CODIFYING ALL WRASSLING MOVES AND LORE...
"...SKYDROP STOLE IT FROM OTHER SOURCES, COMPILING IT FOR HIS OWN SELFISH DREAMS OF GLORY, SYSTEMATICALLY DESTROYING ALL EVIDENCE OF PRIOR WRASSLERS, PRIOR MOVES, AND THE TRUE ORIGINS OF WRASSLING!
THAT'S RIGHT. INSTEAD OF WRASSLING BEGINNING WITH JAMES SKYDROP, ITS HISTORY GOES BACK MILLENIA BEFORE HIM!
"HE WIPED AWAY ENTIRE WRASSLING ACADEMIES, ENTIRE HISTORIES!"

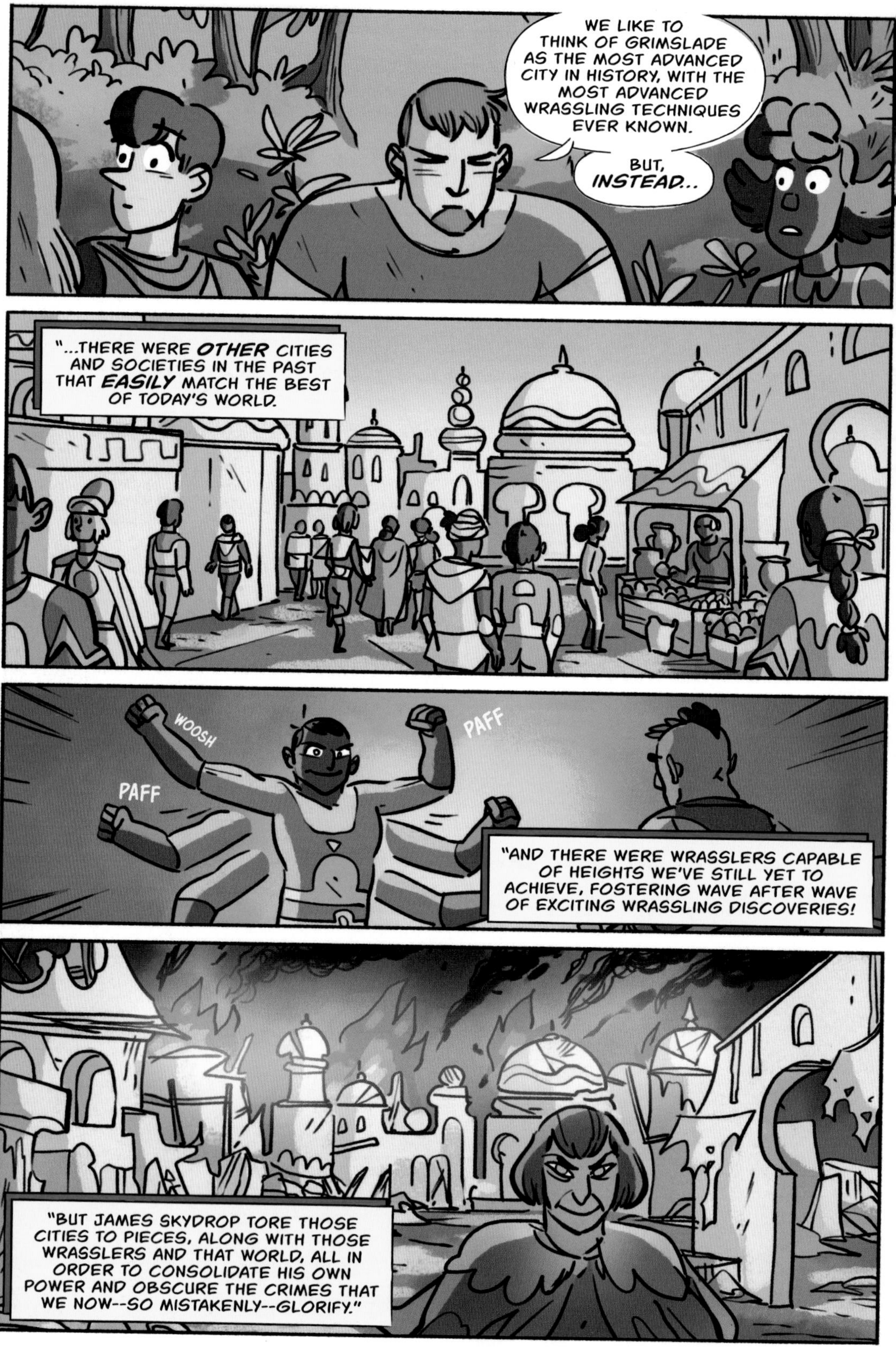
WE LIKE TO THINK OF GRIMSLADE AS THE MOST ADVANCED CITY IN HISTORY, WITH THE MOST ADVANCED WRASSLING TECHNIQUES EVER KNOWN.
BUT, *INSTEAD...*
"...THERE WERE *OTHER* CITIES AND SOCIETIES IN THE PAST THAT *EASILY* MATCH THE BEST OF TODAY'S WORLD.
WOOSH
PAFF
PAFF
"AND THERE WERE WRASSLERS CAPABLE OF HEIGHTS WE'VE STILL YET TO ACHIEVE, FOSTERING WAVE AFTER WAVE OF EXCITING WRASSLING DISCOVERIES!
"BUT JAMES SKYDROP TORE THOSE CITIES TO PIECES, ALONG WITH THOSE WRASSLERS AND THAT WORLD, ALL IN ORDER TO CONSOLIDATE HIS OWN POWER AND OBSCURE THE CRIMES THAT WE NOW--SO MISTAKENLY--GLORIFY."

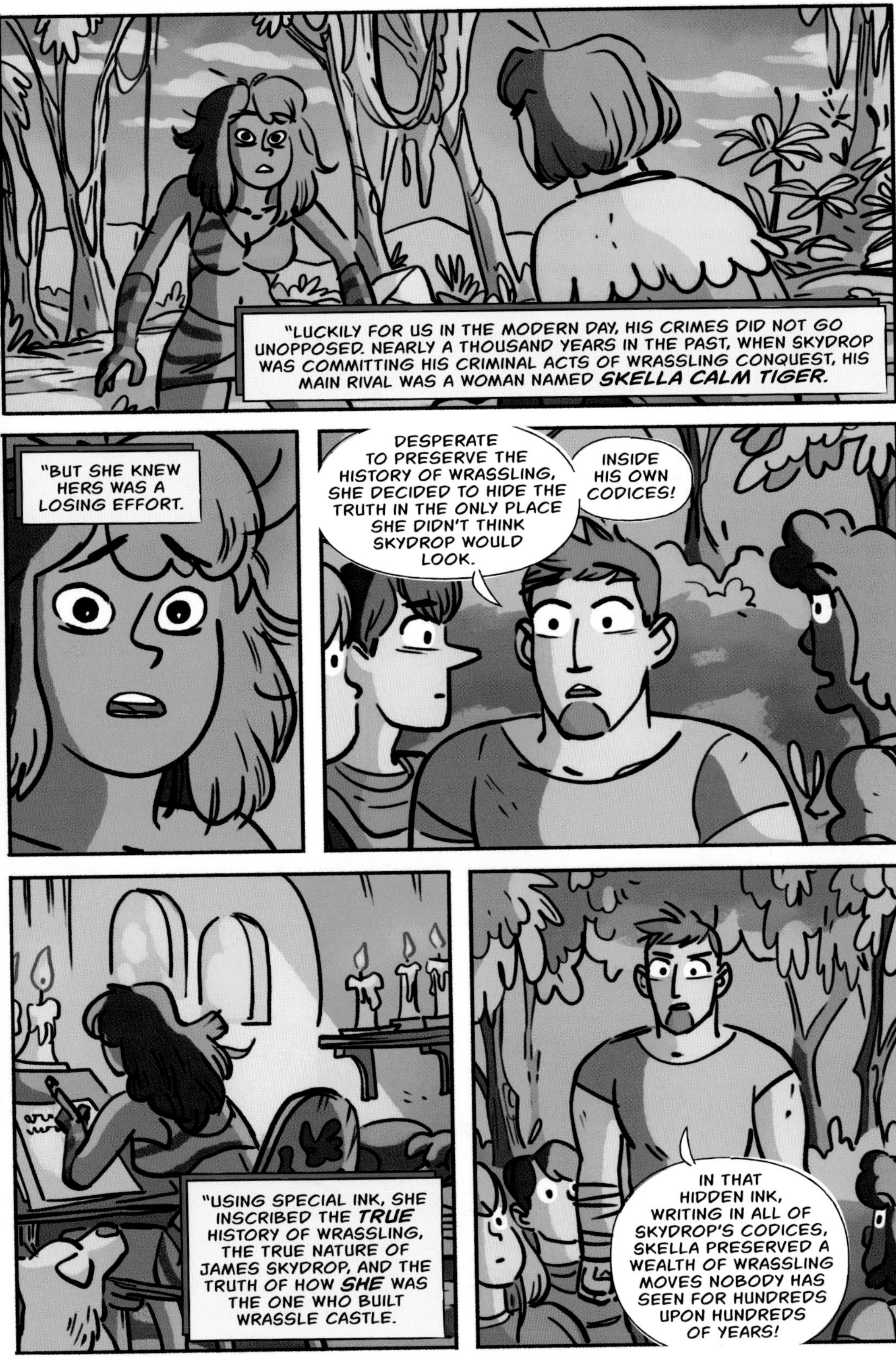
"LUCKILY FOR US IN THE MODERN DAY, HIS CRIMES DID NOT GO UNOPPOSED. NEARLY A THOUSAND YEARS IN THE PAST, WHEN SKYDROP WAS COMMITTING HIS CRIMINAL ACTS OF WRASSLING CONQUEST, HIS MAIN RIVAL WAS A WOMAN NAMED SKELLA CALM TIGER.
"BUT SHE KNEW HERS WAS A LOSING EFFORT.
DESPERATE TO PRESERVE THE HISTORY OF WRASSLING, SHE DECIDED TO HIDE THE TRUTH IN THE ONLY PLACE SHE DIDN'T THINK SKYDROP WOULD LOOK.
INSIDE HIS OWN CODICES!
"USING SPECIAL INK, SHE INSCRIBED THE TRUE HISTORY OF WRASSLING, THE TRUE NATURE OF JAMES SKYDROP, AND THE TRUTH OF HOW SHE WAS THE ONE WHO BUILT WRASSLE CASTLE.
IN THAT HIDDEN INK, WRITING IN ALL OF SKYDROP'S CODICES, SKELLA PRESERVED A WEALTH OF WRASSLING MOVES NOBODY HAS SEEN FOR HUNDREDS UPON HUNDREDS OF YEARS!

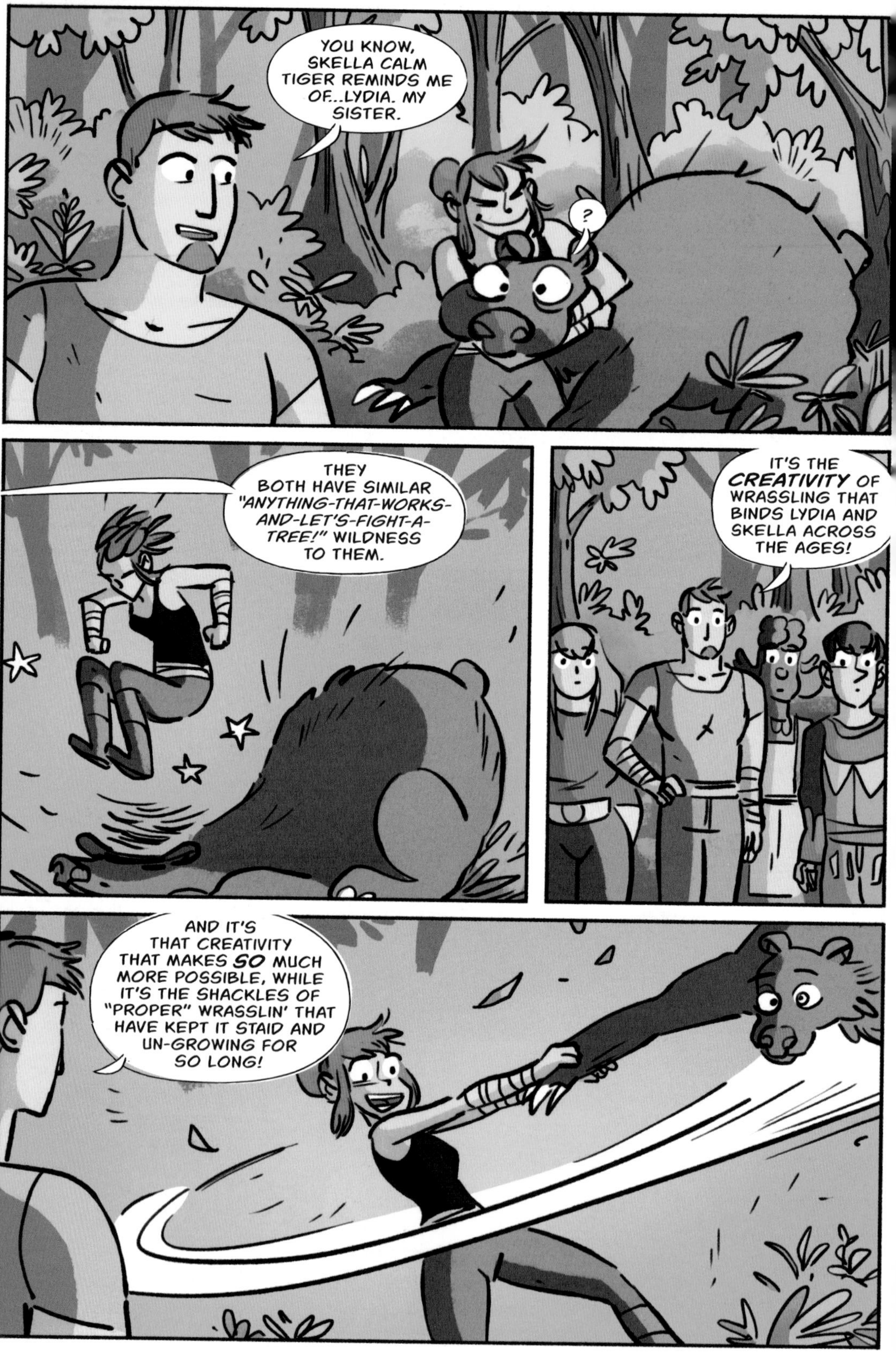
YOU KNOW, SKELLA CALM TIGER REMINDS ME OF...LYDIA. MY SISTER.
?
THEY BOTH HAVE SIMILAR "ANYTHING-THAT-WORKS-AND-LET'S-FIGHT-A-TREE!" WILDNESS TO THEM.
IT'S THE CREATIVITY OF WRASSLING THAT BINDS LYDIA AND SKELLA ACROSS THE AGES!
AND IT'S THAT CREATIVITY THAT MAKES SO MUCH MORE POSSIBLE, WHILE IT'S THE SHACKLES OF "PROPER" WRASSLIN' THAT HAVE KEPT IT STAID AND UN-GROWING FOR SO LONG!

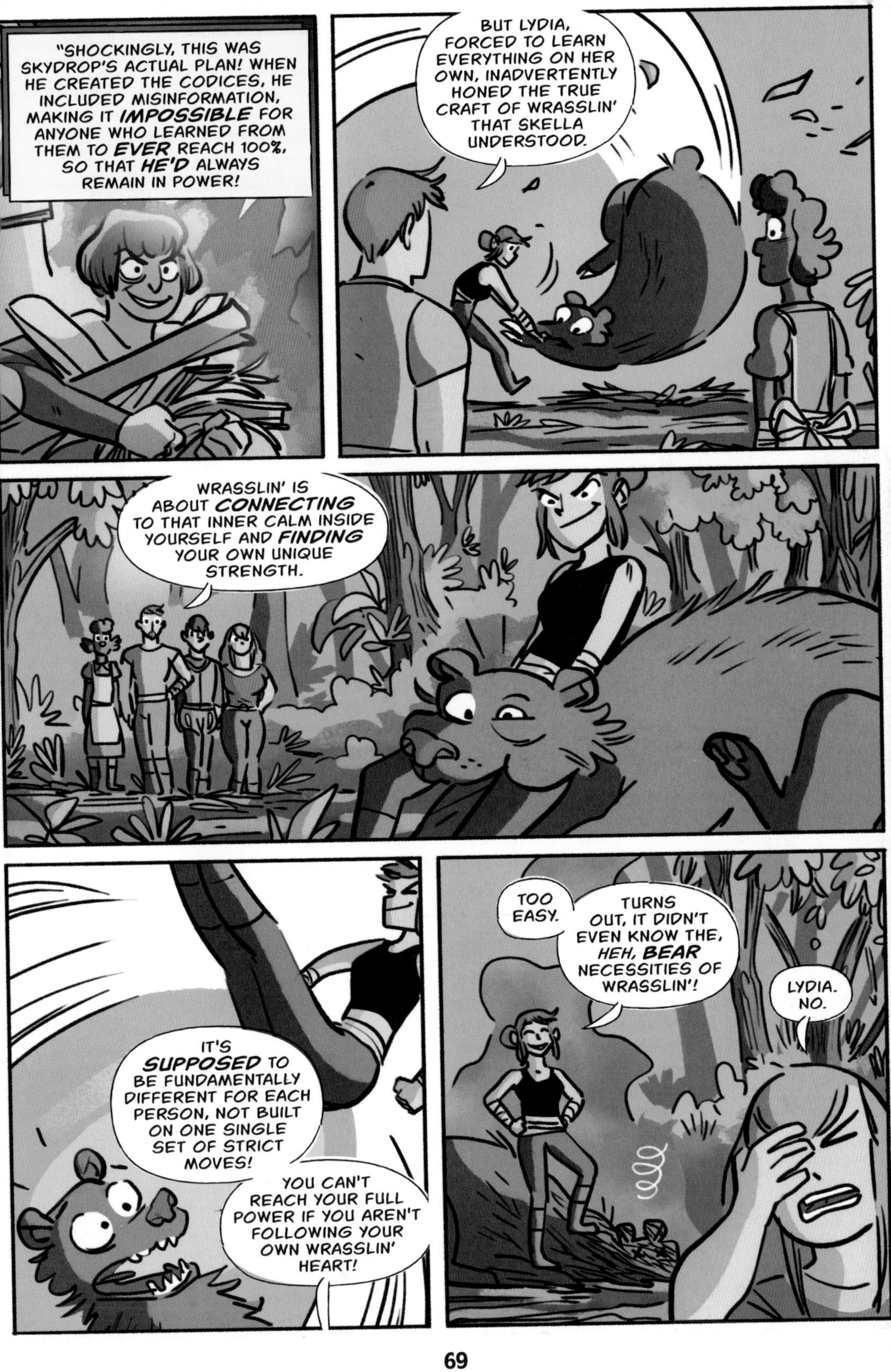
"SHOCKINGLY, THIS WAS SKYDROP'S ACTUAL PLAN! WHEN HE CREATED THE CODICES, HE INCLUDED MISINFORMATION, MAKING IT IMPOSSIBLE FOR ANYONE WHO LEARNED FROM THEM TO EVER REACH 100%, SO THAT HE'D ALWAYS REMAIN IN POWER!
BUT LYDIA, FORCED TO LEARN EVERYTHING ON HER OWN, INADVERTENTLY HONED THE TRUE CRAFT OF WRASSLIN' THAT SKELLA UNDERSTOOD.
WRASSLIN' IS ABOUT CONNECTING TO THAT INNER CALM INSIDE YOURSELF AND FINDING YOUR OWN UNIQUE STRENGTH.
IT'S SUPPOSED TO BE FUNDAMENTALLY DIFFERENT FOR EACH PERSON, NOT BUILT ON ONE SINGLE SET OF STRICT MOVES!
YOU CAN'T REACH YOUR FULL POWER IF YOU AREN'T FOLLOWING YOUR OWN WRASSLIN' HEART!
TOO EASY.
TURNS OUT, IT DIDN'T EVEN KNOW THE, HEH, BEAR NECESSITIES OF WRASSLIN'!
LYDIA. NO.

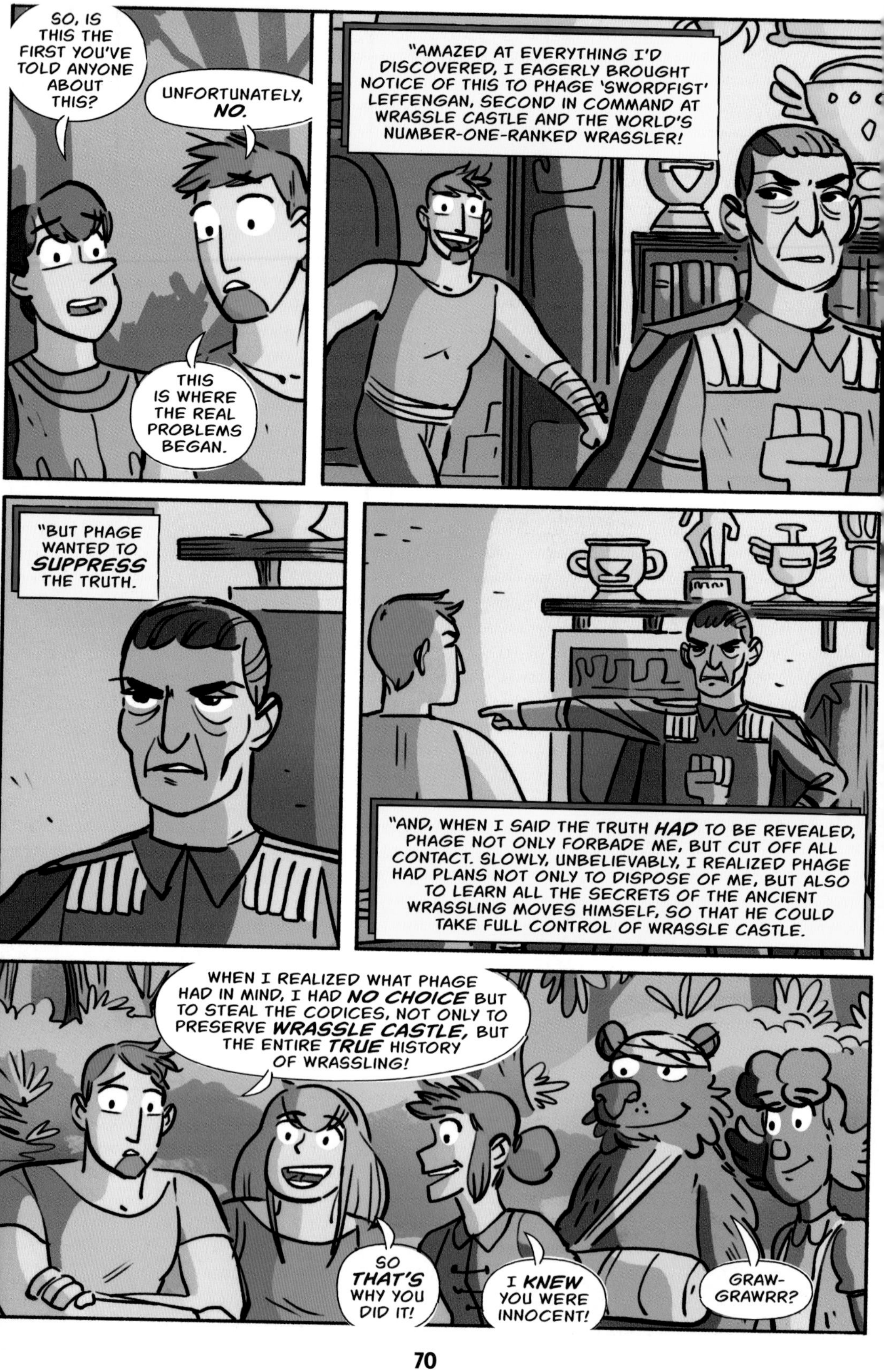
SO, IS THIS THE FIRST YOU'VE TOLD ANYONE ABOUT THIS?
UNFORTUNATELY, NO.
THIS IS WHERE THE REAL PROBLEMS BEGAN.
"AMAZED AT EVERYTHING I'D DISCOVERED, I EAGERLY BROUGHT NOTICE OF THIS TO PHAGE 'SWORDFIST' LEFFENGAN, SECOND IN COMMAND AT WRASSLE CASTLE AND THE WORLD'S NUMBER-ONE-RANKED WRASSLER!
"BUT PHAGE WANTED TO SUPPRESS THE TRUTH.
"AND, WHEN I SAID THE TRUTH HAD TO BE REVEALED, PHAGE NOT ONLY FORBADE ME, BUT CUT OFF ALL CONTACT. SLOWLY, UNBELIEVABLY, I REALIZED PHAGE HAD PLANS NOT ONLY TO DISPOSE OF ME, BUT ALSO TO LEARN ALL THE SECRETS OF THE ANCIENT WRASSLING MOVES HIMSELF, SO THAT HE COULD TAKE FULL CONTROL OF WRASSLE CASTLE.
WHEN I REALIZED WHAT PHAGE HAD IN MIND, I HAD NO CHOICE BUT TO STEAL THE CODICES, NOT ONLY TO PRESERVE WRASSLE CASTLE, BUT THE ENTIRE TRUE HISTORY OF WRASSLING!
SO THAT'S WHY YOU DID IT!
I KNEW YOU WERE INNOCENT!
GRAW-GRAWRR?

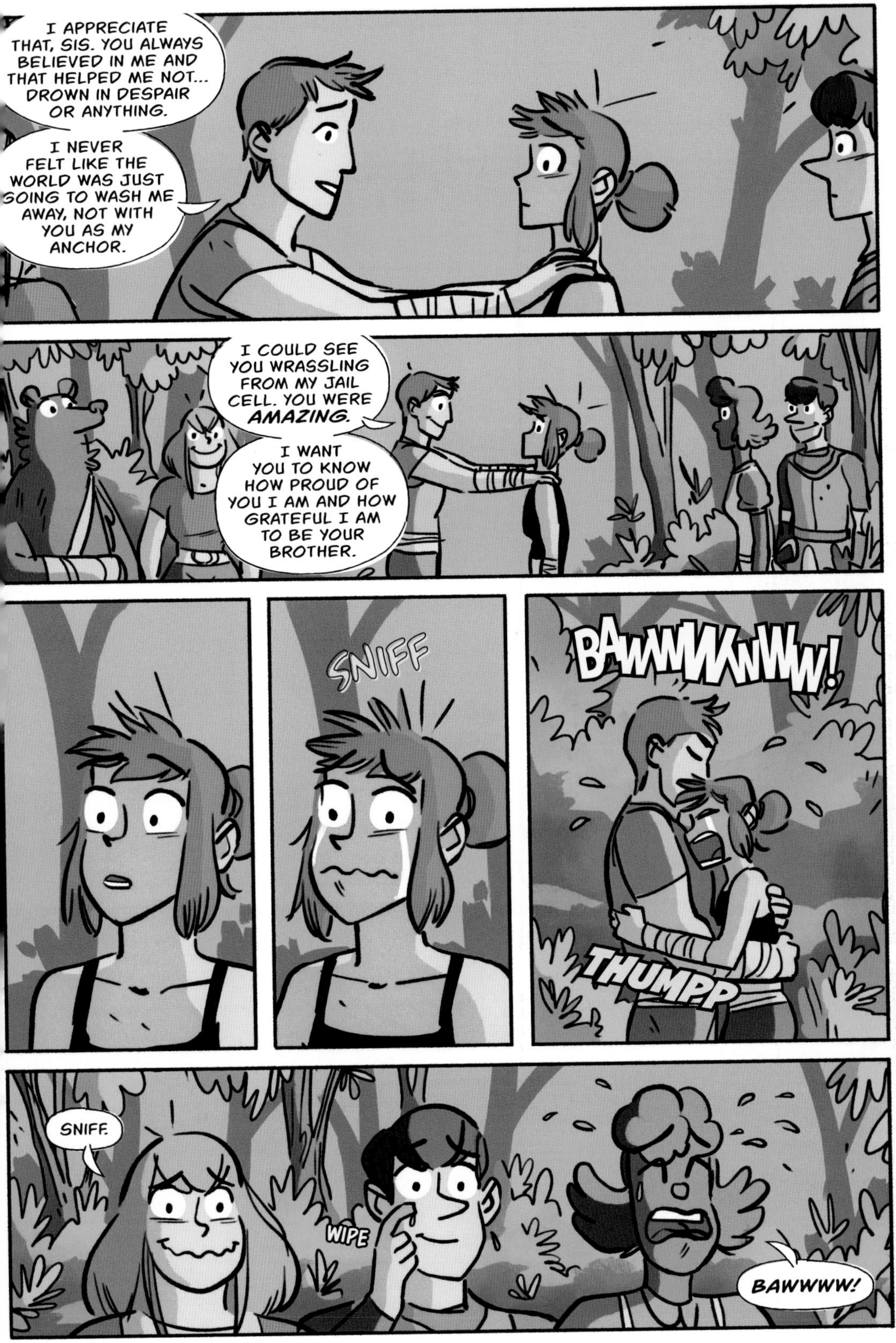
I APPRECIATE THAT, SIS. YOU ALWAYS BELIEVED IN ME AND THAT HELPED ME NOT... DROWN IN DESPAIR OR ANYTHING.
I NEVER FELT LIKE THE WORLD WAS JUST GOING TO WASH ME AWAY, NOT WITH YOU AS MY ANCHOR.
I COULD SEE YOU WRASSLING FROM MY JAIL CELL. YOU WERE *AMAZING.*
I WANT YOU TO KNOW HOW PROUD OF YOU I AM AND HOW GRATEFUL I AM TO BE YOUR BROTHER.
SNIFF
BAWWWWWWW!
THUMPP
SNIFF.
WIPE
BAWWWW!

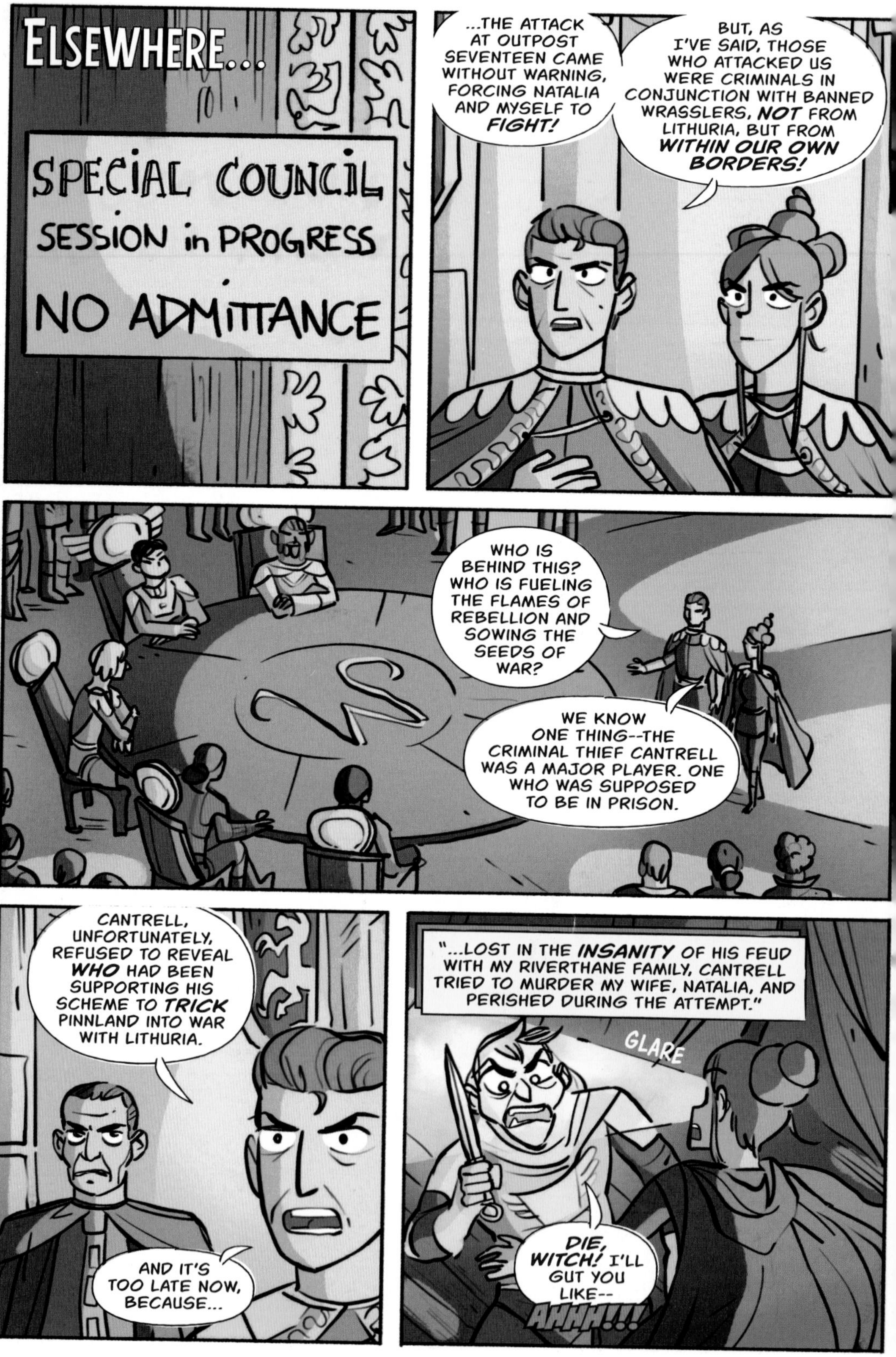
ELSEWHERE...
SPECIAL COUNCIL SESSION in PROGRESS NO ADMITTANCE
...THE ATTACK AT OUTPOST SEVENTEEN CAME WITHOUT WARNING, FORCING NATALIA AND MYSELF TO FIGHT!
BUT, AS I'VE SAID, THOSE WHO ATTACKED US WERE CRIMINALS IN CONJUNCTION WITH BANNED WRASSLERS, NOT FROM LITHURIA, BUT FROM WITHIN OUR OWN BORDERS!
WHO IS BEHIND THIS? WHO IS FUELING THE FLAMES OF REBELLION AND SOWING THE SEEDS OF WAR?
WE KNOW ONE THING--THE CRIMINAL THIEF CANTRELL WAS A MAJOR PLAYER. ONE WHO WAS SUPPOSED TO BE IN PRISON.
CANTRELL, UNFORTUNATELY, REFUSED TO REVEAL WHO HAD BEEN SUPPORTING HIS SCHEME TO TRICK PINNLAND INTO WAR WITH LITHURIA.
AND IT'S TOO LATE NOW, BECAUSE...
"...LOST IN THE INSANITY OF HIS FEUD WITH MY RIVERTHANE FAMILY, CANTRELL TRIED TO MURDER MY WIFE, NATALIA, AND PERISHED DURING THE ATTEMPT."
GLARE
DIE, WITCH! I'LL GUT YOU LIKE--
AHHH!!!

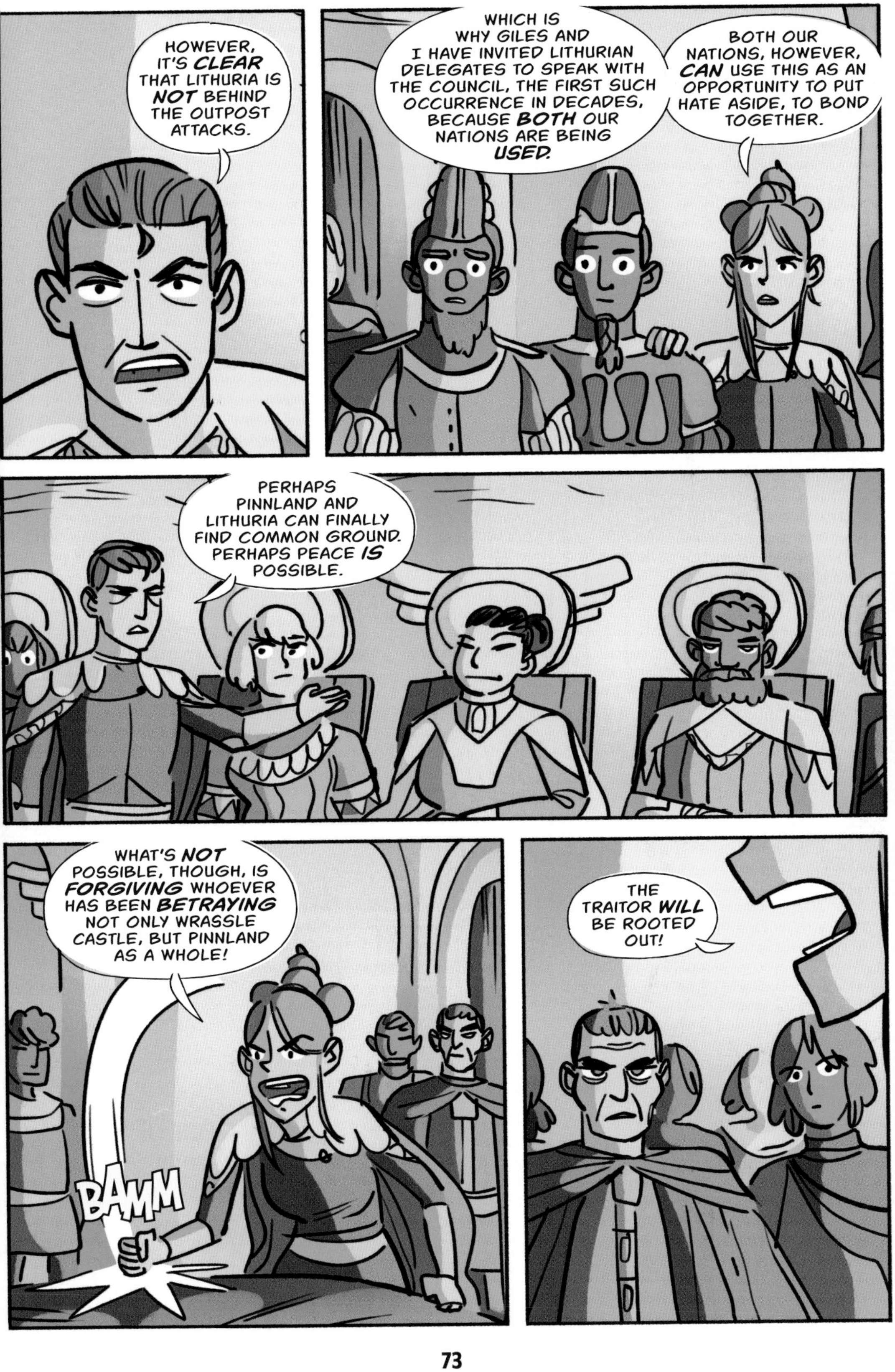
HOWEVER, IT'S CLEAR THAT LITHURIA IS NOT BEHIND THE OUTPOST ATTACKS.
WHICH IS WHY GILES AND I HAVE INVITED LITHURIAN DELEGATES TO SPEAK WITH THE COUNCIL, THE FIRST SUCH OCCURRENCE IN DECADES, BECAUSE BOTH OUR NATIONS ARE BEING USED.
BOTH OUR NATIONS, HOWEVER, CAN USE THIS AS AN OPPORTUNITY TO PUT HATE ASIDE, TO BOND TOGETHER.
PERHAPS PINNLAND AND LITHURIA CAN FINALLY FIND COMMON GROUND. PERHAPS PEACE IS POSSIBLE.
WHAT'S NOT POSSIBLE, THOUGH, IS FORGIVING WHOEVER HAS BEEN BETRAYING NOT ONLY WRASSLE CASTLE, BUT PINNLAND AS A WHOLE!
BAMM
THE TRAITOR WILL BE ROOTED OUT!

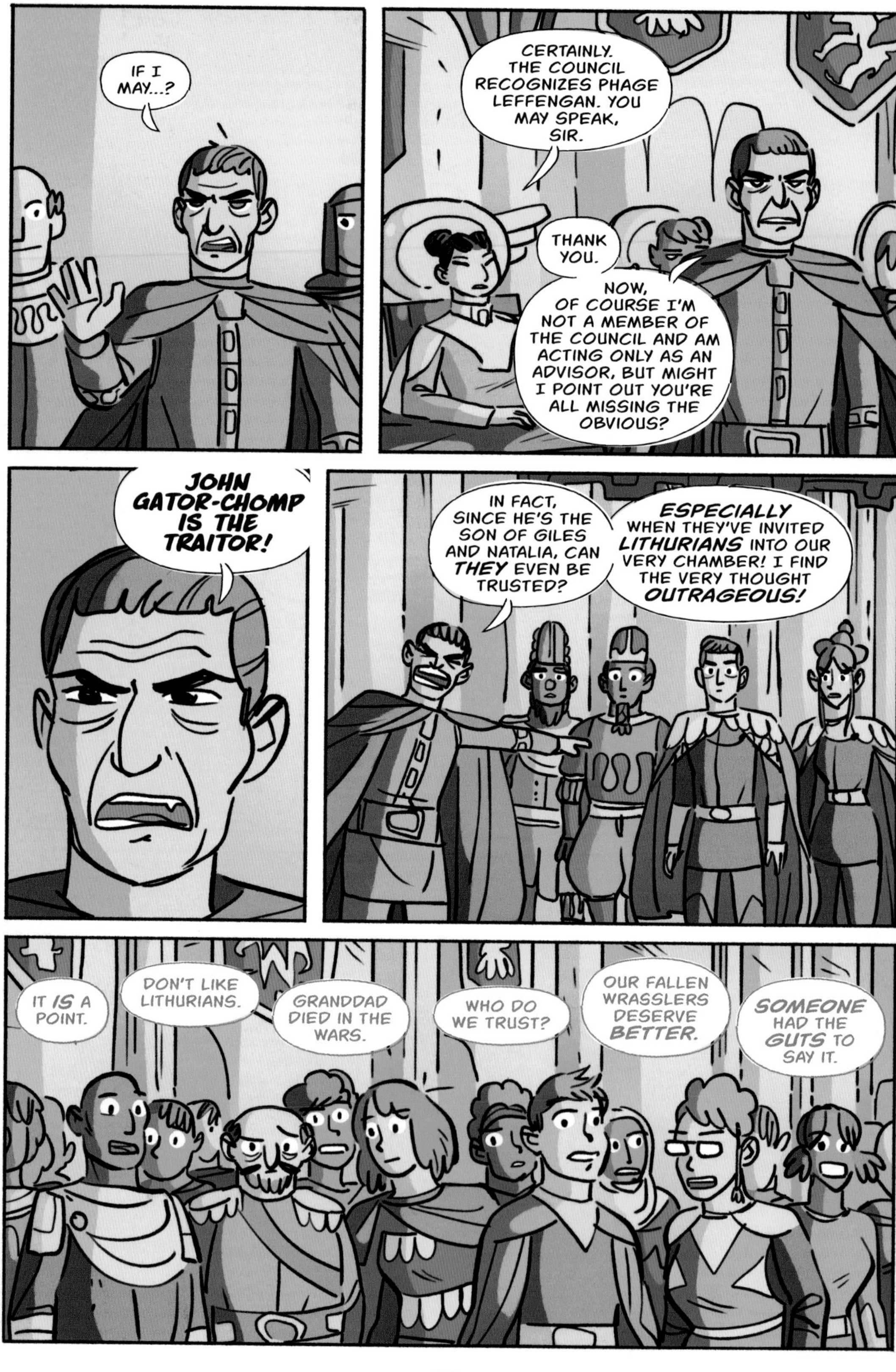
IF I MAY...?
CERTAINLY. THE COUNCIL RECOGNIZES PHAGE LEFFENGAN. YOU MAY SPEAK, SIR.
THANK YOU.
NOW, OF COURSE I'M NOT A MEMBER OF THE COUNCIL AND AM ACTING ONLY AS AN ADVISOR, BUT MIGHT I POINT OUT YOU'RE ALL MISSING THE OBVIOUS?
JOHN GATOR-CHOMP IS THE TRAITOR!
IN FACT, SINCE HE'S THE SON OF GILES AND NATALIA, CAN THEY EVEN BE TRUSTED?
ESPECIALLY WHEN THEY'VE INVITED LITHURIANS INTO OUR VERY CHAMBER! I FIND THE VERY THOUGHT OUTRAGEOUS!
IT IS A POINT.
DON'T LIKE LITHURIANS.
GRANDDAD DIED IN THE WARS.
WHO DO WE TRUST?
OUR FALLEN WRASSLERS DESERVE BETTER.
SOMEONE HAD THE GUTS TO SAY IT.

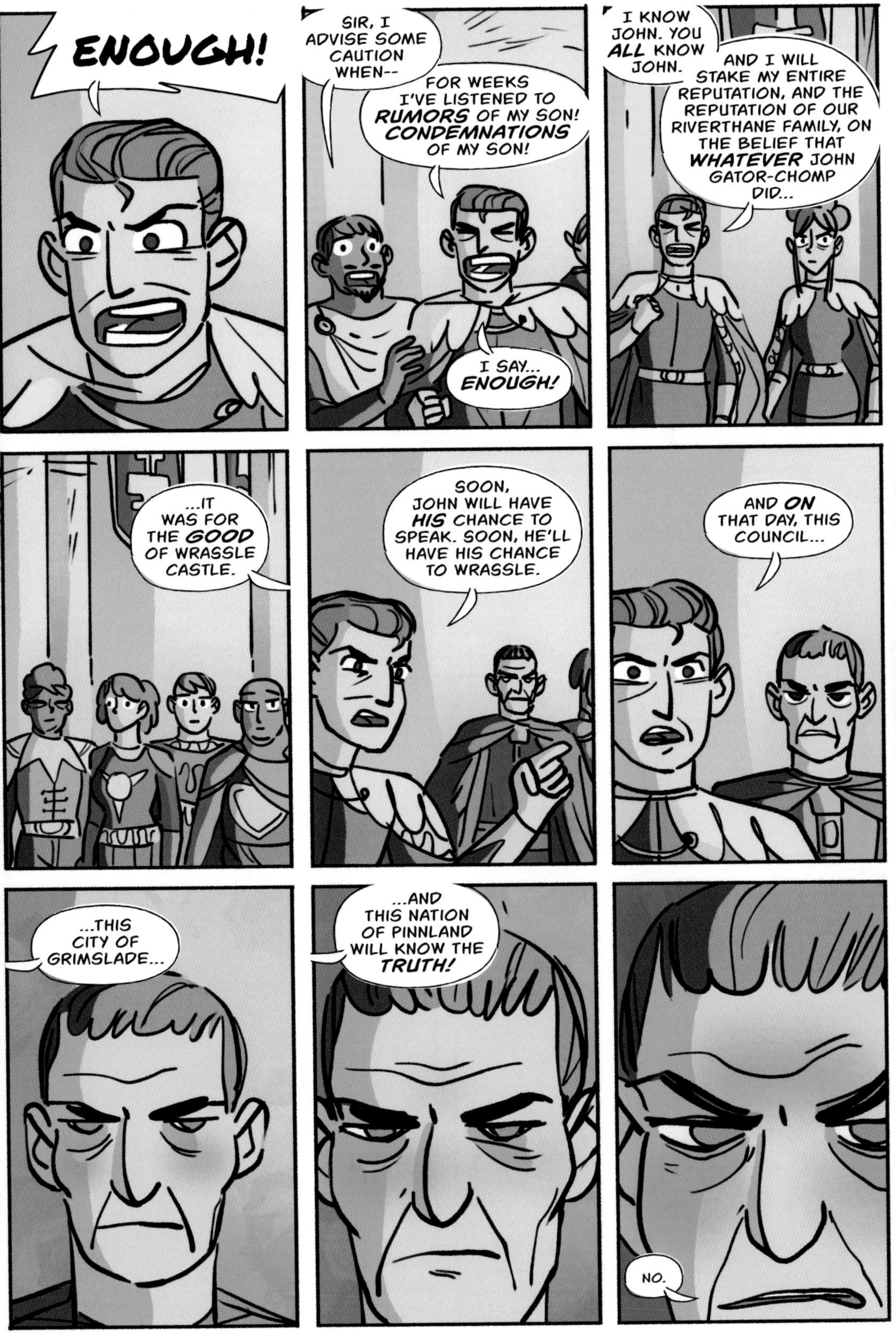
ENOUGH!
SIR, I ADVISE SOME CAUTION WHEN--
FOR WEEKS I'VE LISTENED TO RUMORS OF MY SON! CONDEMNATIONS OF MY SON!
I SAY... ENOUGH!
I KNOW JOHN. YOU ALL KNOW JOHN.
AND I WILL STAKE MY ENTIRE REPUTATION, AND THE REPUTATION OF OUR RIVERTHANE FAMILY, ON THE BELIEF THAT WHATEVER JOHN GATOR-CHOMP DID...
...IT WAS FOR THE GOOD OF WRASSLE CASTLE.
SOON, JOHN WILL HAVE HIS CHANCE TO SPEAK. SOON, HE'LL HAVE HIS CHANCE TO WRASSLE.
AND ON THAT DAY, THIS COUNCIL...
...THIS CITY OF GRIMSLADE...
...AND THIS NATION OF PINNLAND WILL KNOW THE TRUTH!
NO.

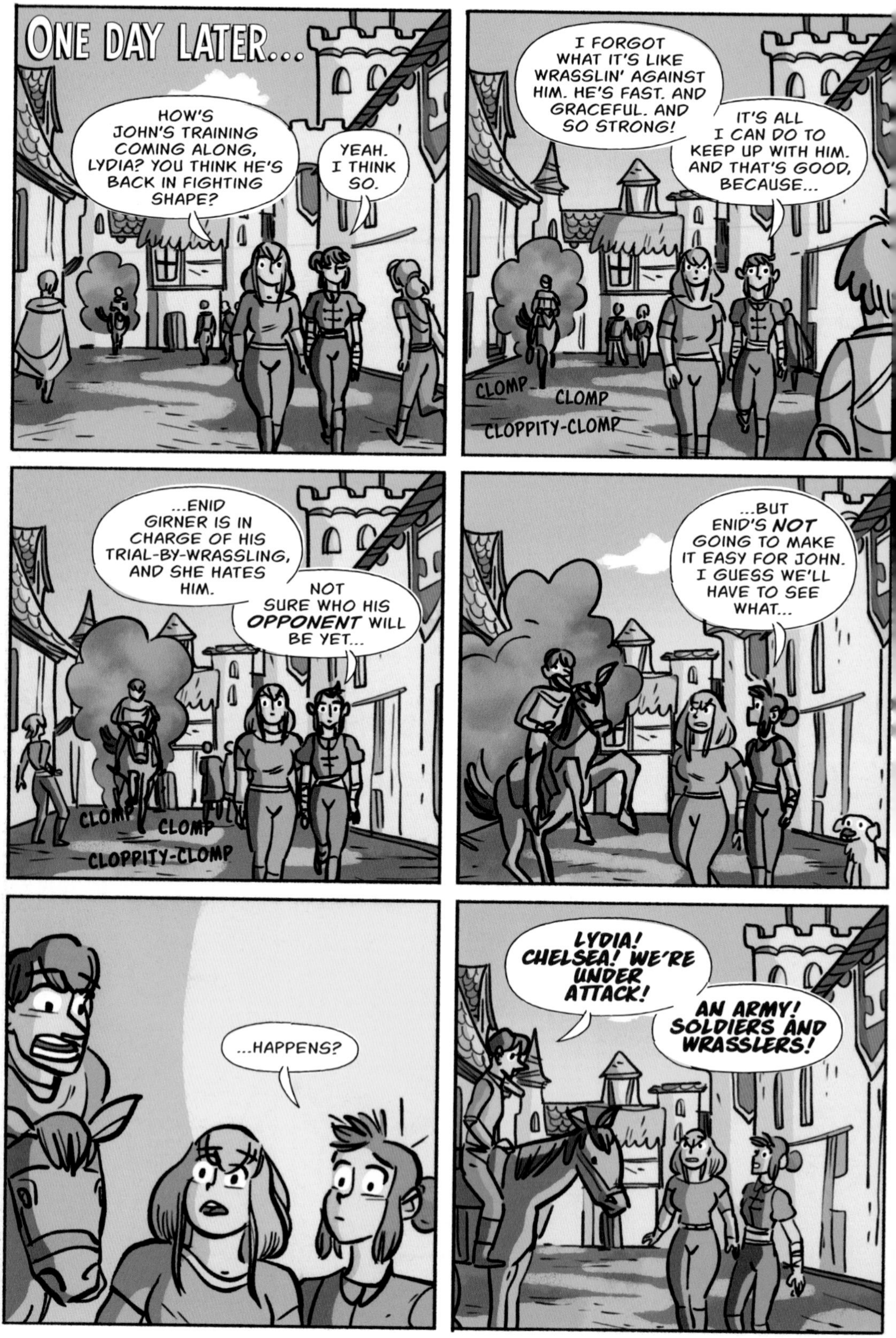
ONE DAY LATER...
HOW'S JOHN'S TRAINING COMING ALONG, LYDIA? YOU THINK HE'S BACK IN FIGHTING SHAPE?
YEAH. I THINK SO.
I FORGOT WHAT IT'S LIKE WRASSLIN' AGAINST HIM. HE'S FAST. AND GRACEFUL. AND SO STRONG!
IT'S ALL I CAN DO TO KEEP UP WITH HIM. AND THAT'S GOOD, BECAUSE...
CLOMP
CLOMP
CLOPPITY-CLOMP
...ENID GIRNER IS IN CHARGE OF HIS TRIAL-BY-WRASSLING, AND SHE HATES HIM.
NOT SURE WHO HIS OPPONENT WILL BE YET...
CLOMP
CLOMP
CLOPPITY-CLOMP
...BUT ENID'S NOT GOING TO MAKE IT EASY FOR JOHN. I GUESS WE'LL HAVE TO SEE WHAT...
...HAPPENS?
LYDIA! CHELSEA! WE'RE UNDER ATTACK!
AN ARMY! SOLDIERS AND WRASSLERS!

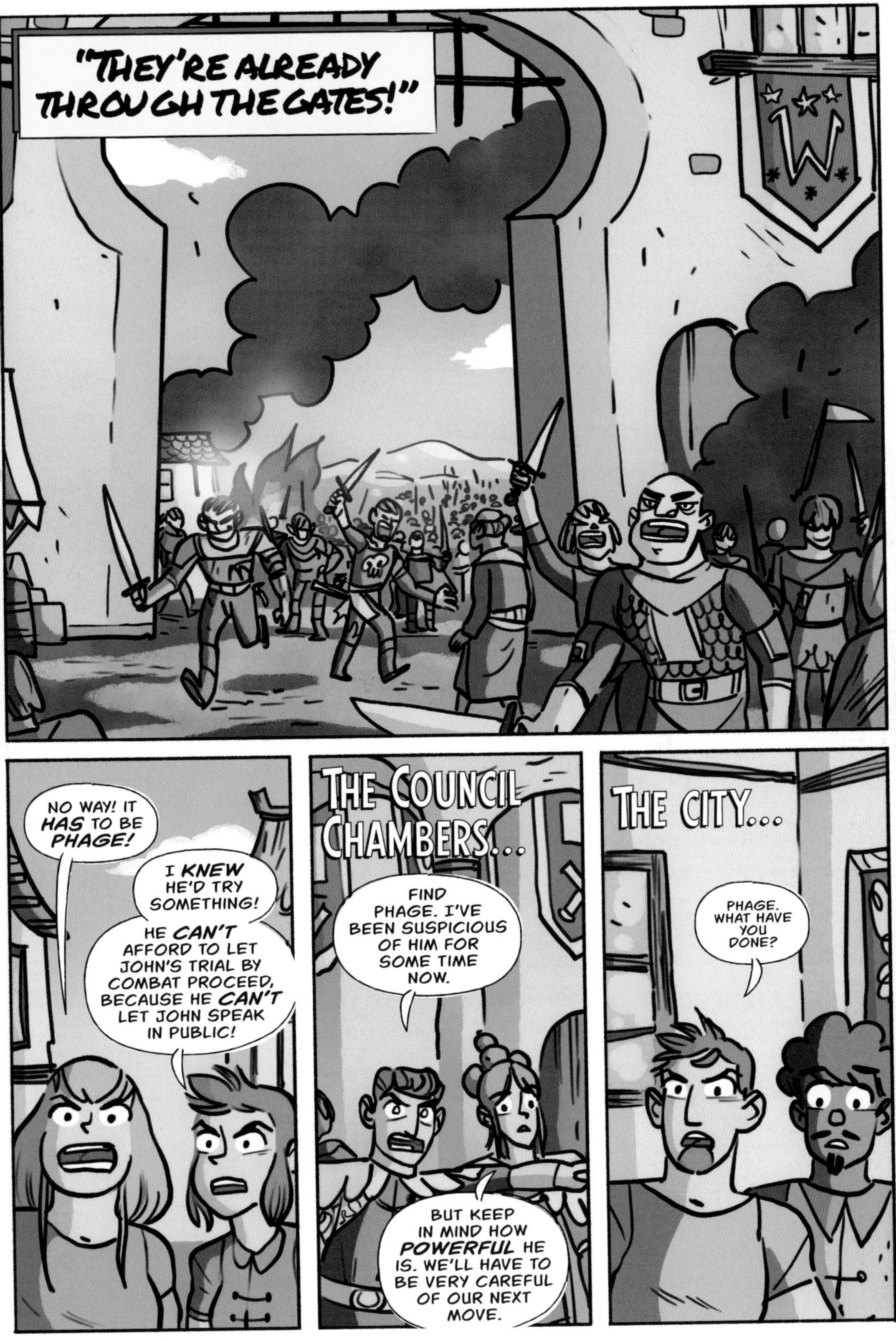
"THEY'RE ALREADY THROUGH THE GATES!"
NO WAY! IT HAS TO BE PHAGE!
I KNEW HE'D TRY SOMETHING!
HE CAN'T AFFORD TO LET JOHN'S TRIAL BY COMBAT PROCEED, BECAUSE HE CAN'T LET JOHN SPEAK IN PUBLIC!
THE COUNCIL CHAMBERS...
FIND PHAGE. I'VE BEEN SUSPICIOUS OF HIM FOR SOME TIME NOW.
BUT KEEP IN MIND HOW POWERFUL HE IS. WE'LL HAVE TO BE VERY CAREFUL OF OUR NEXT MOVE.
THE CITY...
PHAGE. WHAT HAVE YOU DONE?

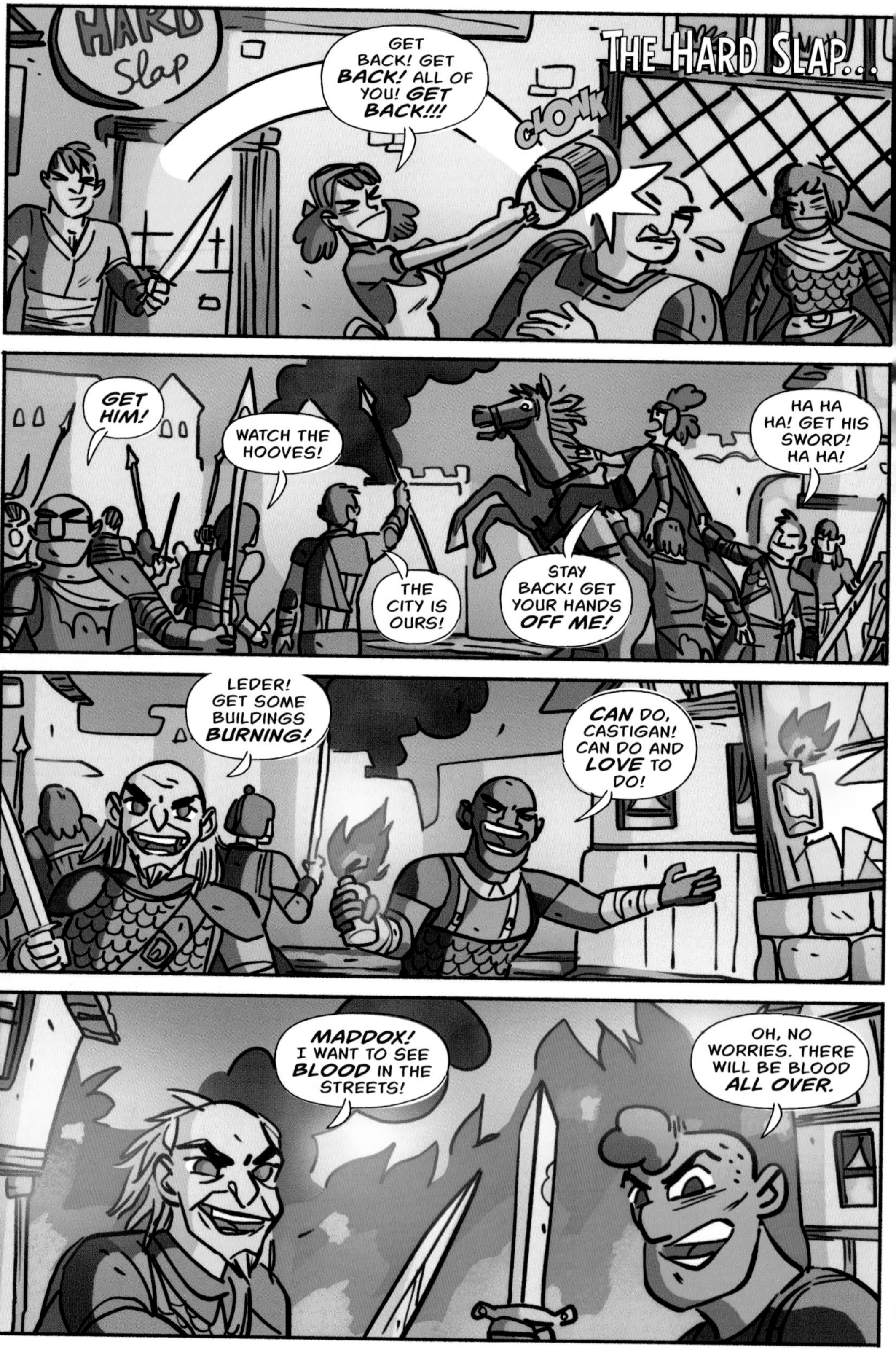
HARD Slap
GET BACK! GET BACK! ALL OF YOU! GET BACK!!!
THE HARD SLAP...
CLONK
GET HIM!
WATCH THE HOOVES!
THE CITY IS OURS!
STAY BACK! GET YOUR HANDS OFF ME!
HA HA HA! GET HIS SWORD! HA HA!
LEDER! GET SOME BUILDINGS BURNING!
CAN DO, CASTIGAN! CAN DO AND LOVE TO DO!
MADDOX! I WANT TO SEE BLOOD IN THE STREETS!
OH, NO WORRIES. THERE WILL BE BLOOD ALL OVER.

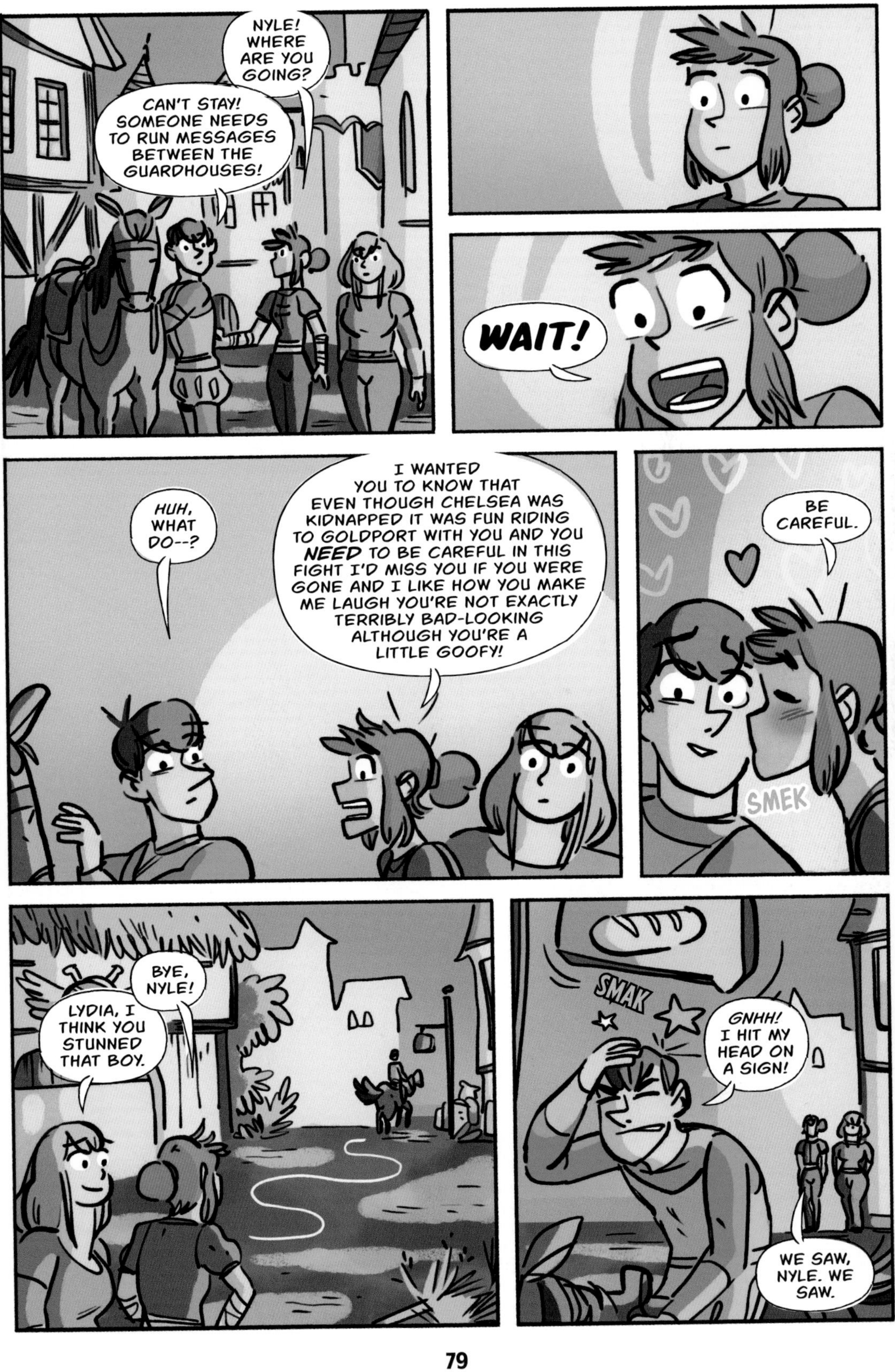
NYLE! WHERE ARE YOU GOING?
CAN'T STAY! SOMEONE NEEDS TO RUN MESSAGES BETWEEN THE GUARDHOUSES!
WAIT!
HUH, WHAT DO--?
I WANTED YOU TO KNOW THAT EVEN THOUGH CHELSEA WAS KIDNAPPED IT WAS FUN RIDING TO GOLDPORT WITH YOU AND YOU NEED TO BE CAREFUL IN THIS FIGHT I'D MISS YOU IF YOU WERE GONE AND I LIKE HOW YOU MAKE ME LAUGH YOU'RE NOT EXACTLY TERRIBLY BAD-LOOKING ALTHOUGH YOU'RE A LITTLE GOOFY!
BE CAREFUL.
SMEK
BYE, NYLE!
LYDIA, I THINK YOU STUNNED THAT BOY.
SMAK
GNHH! I HIT MY HEAD ON A SIGN!
WE SAW, NYLE. WE SAW.

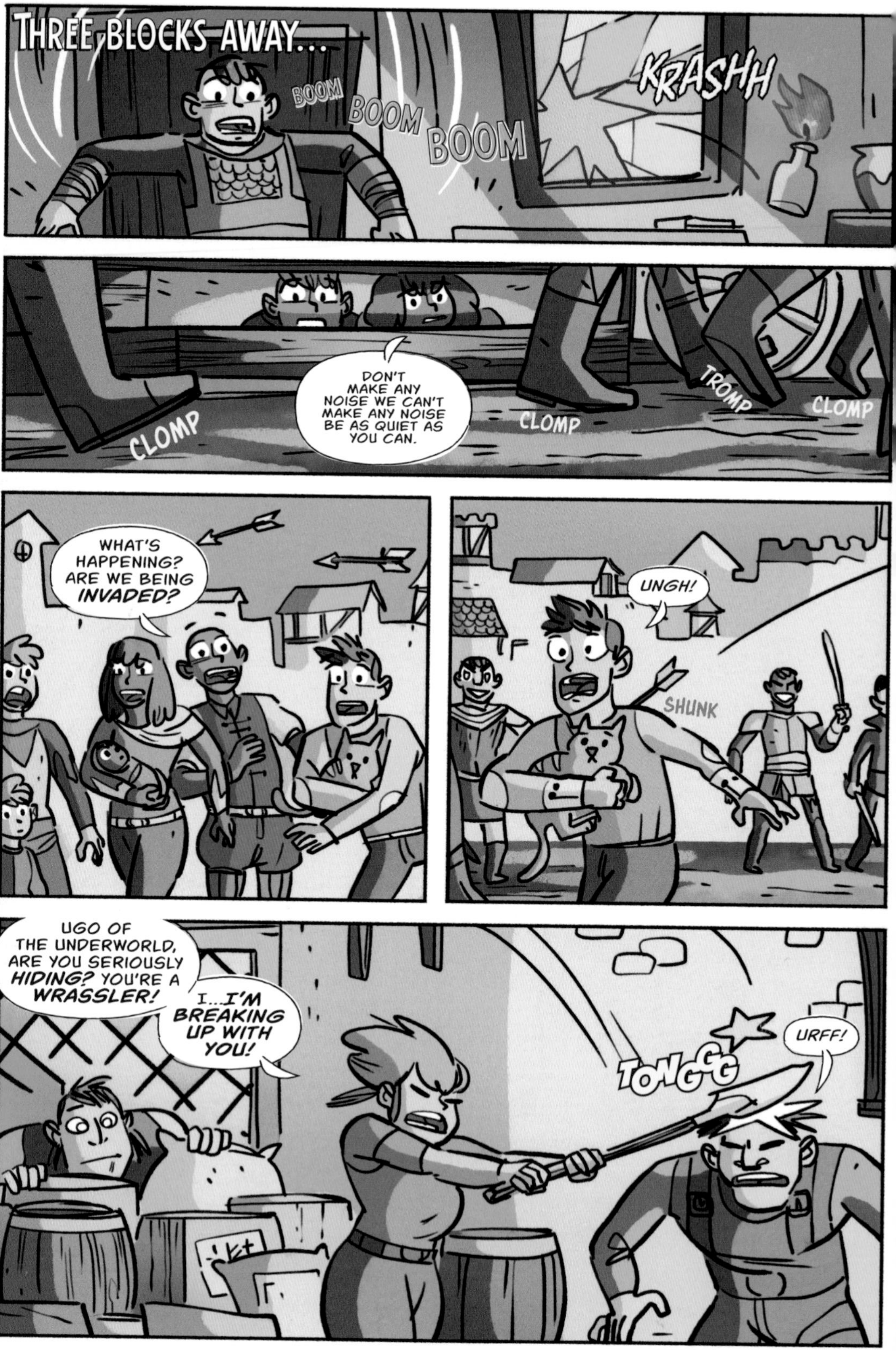
THREE BLOCKS AWAY...
BOOM BOOM BOOM
KRASHH
DON'T MAKE ANY NOISE WE CAN'T MAKE ANY NOISE BE AS QUIET AS YOU CAN.
CLOMP
CLOMP
TROMP
CLOMP
WHAT'S HAPPENING? ARE WE BEING INVADED?
UNGH!
SHUNK
UGO OF THE UNDERWORLD, ARE YOU SERIOUSLY HIDING? YOU'RE A WRASSLER!
I...I'M BREAKING UP WITH YOU!
TONGGG
URFF!

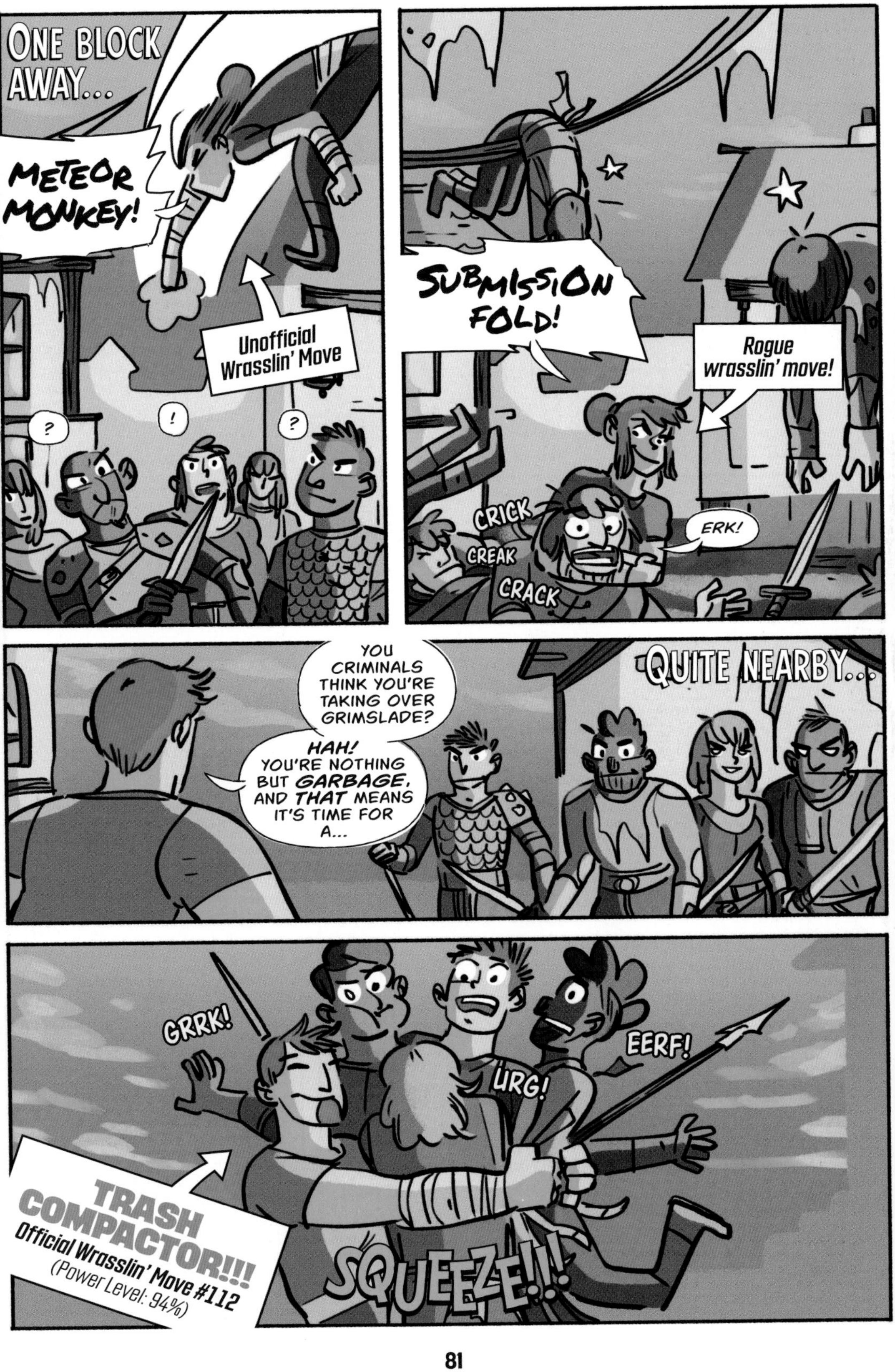

ONE BLOCK AWAY...
METEOR MONKEY!
Unofficial Wrasslin' Move
?
!
?
SUBMISSION FOLD!
Rogue wrasslin' move!
CRICK
CREAK
CRACK
ERK!
QUITE NEARBY...
YOU CRIMINALS THINK YOU'RE TAKING OVER GRIMSLADE?
HAH! YOU'RE NOTHING BUT GARBAGE, AND THAT MEANS IT'S TIME FOR A...
GRRK!
URG!
EERF!
TRASH COMPACTOR!!!
Official Wrasslin' Move #112
(Power Level: 94%)
SQUEEZE!!!

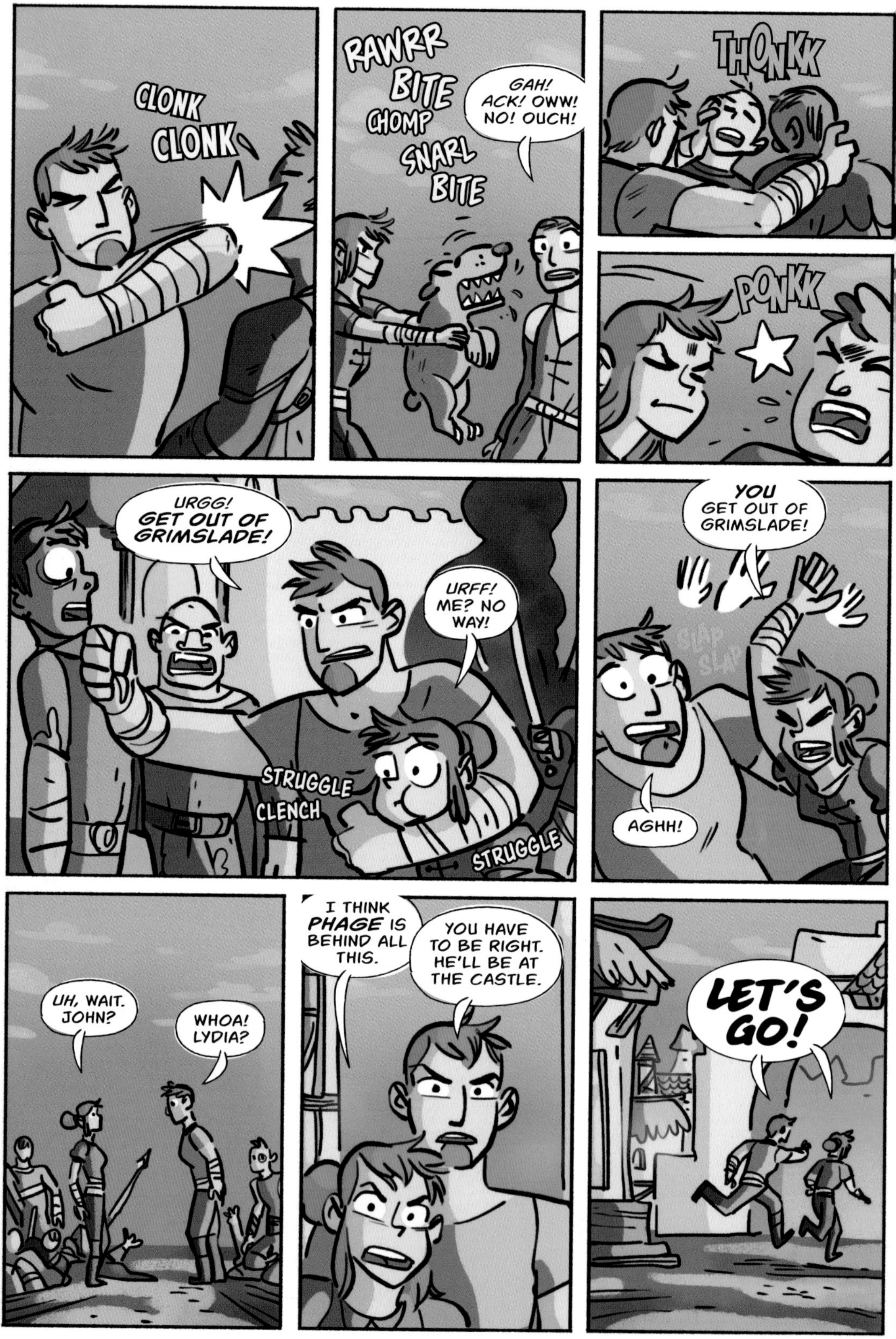
CLONK
CLONK
RAWRR
BITE
CHOMP
SNARL
BITE
GAH! ACK! OWW! NO! OUCH!
THONKK
PONKK
URGG! GET OUT OF GRIMSLADE!
URFF! ME? NO WAY!
STRUGGLE
CLENCH
STRUGGLE
YOU GET OUT OF GRIMSLADE!
SLAP
SLAP
AGHH!
UH, WAIT. JOHN?
WHOA! LYDIA?
I THINK PHAGE IS BEHIND ALL THIS.
YOU HAVE TO BE RIGHT. HE'LL BE AT THE CASTLE.
LET'S GO!

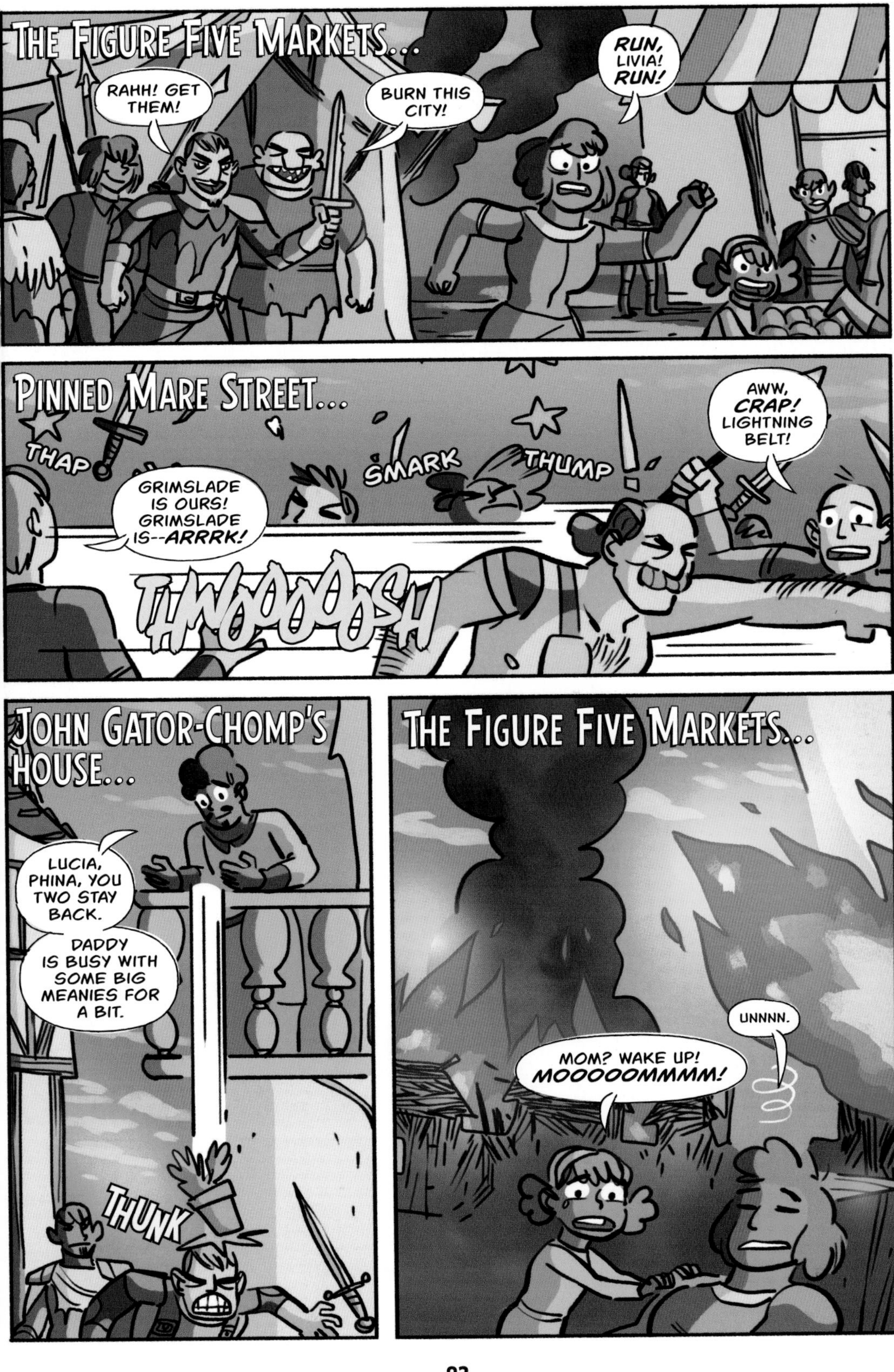
THE FIGURE FIVE MARKETS...
RAHH! GET THEM!
BURN THIS CITY!
RUN, LIVIA! RUN!
PINNED MARE STREET...
THAP
SMARK
THUMP
GRIMSLADE IS OURS! GRIMSLADE IS--ARRRK!
AWW, CRAP! LIGHTNING BELT!
THWOOOOOSH
JOHN GATOR-CHOMP'S HOUSE...
LUCIA, PHINA, YOU TWO STAY BACK.
DADDY IS BUSY WITH SOME BIG MEANIES FOR A BIT.
THUNK
THE FIGURE FIVE MARKETS...
UNNNN.
MOM? WAKE UP! MOOOOOMMMM!

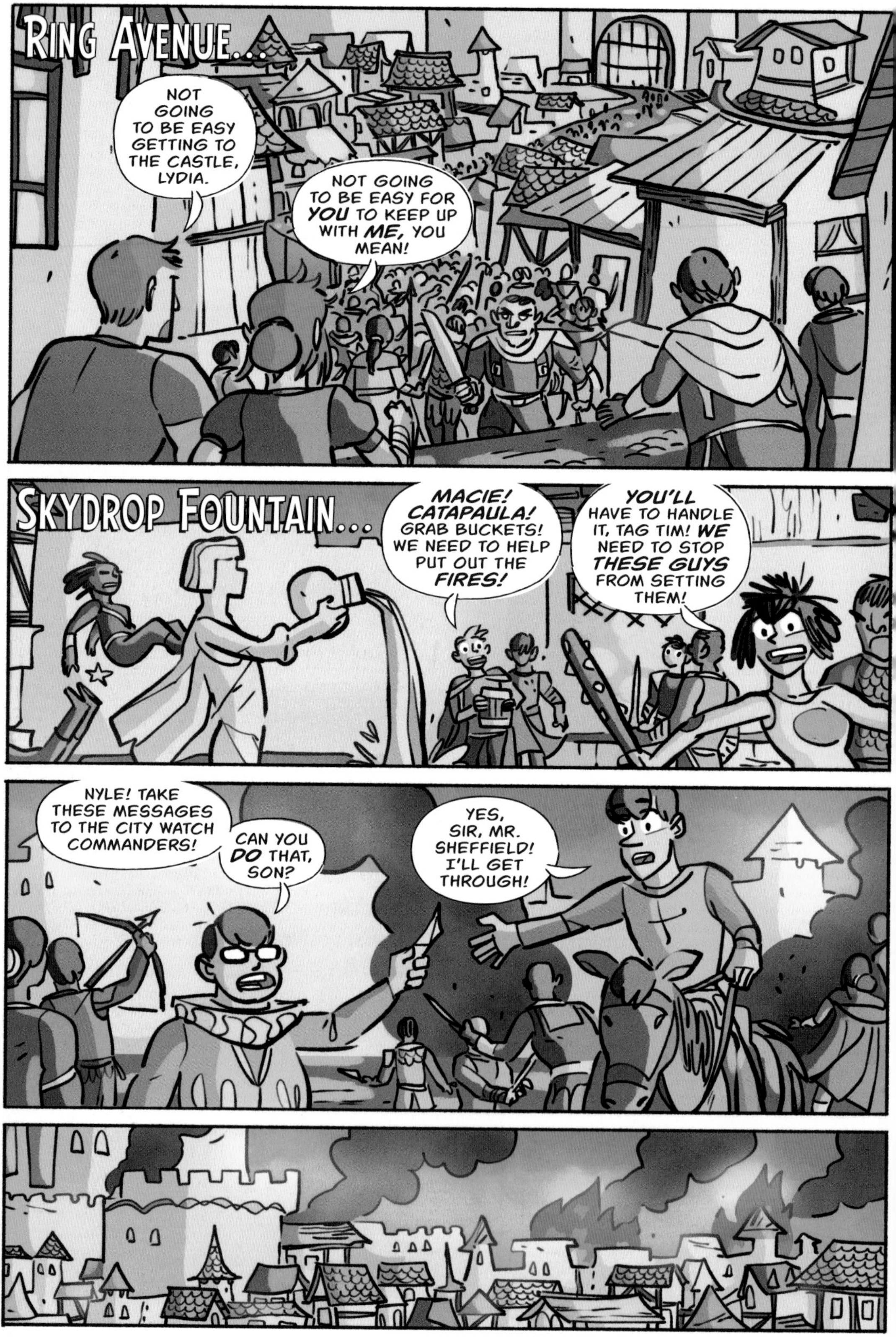

RING AVENUE...
NOT GOING TO BE EASY GETTING TO THE CASTLE, LYDIA.
NOT GOING TO BE EASY FOR *YOU* TO KEEP UP WITH *ME,* YOU MEAN!
SKYDROP FOUNTAIN...
MACIE! CATAPAULA! GRAB BUCKETS! WE NEED TO HELP PUT OUT THE *FIRES!*
YOU'LL HAVE TO HANDLE IT, TAG TIM! *WE* NEED TO STOP *THESE GUYS* FROM SETTING THEM!
NYLE! TAKE THESE MESSAGES TO THE CITY WATCH COMMANDERS!
CAN YOU *DO* THAT, SON?
YES, SIR, MR. SHEFFIELD! I'LL GET THROUGH!

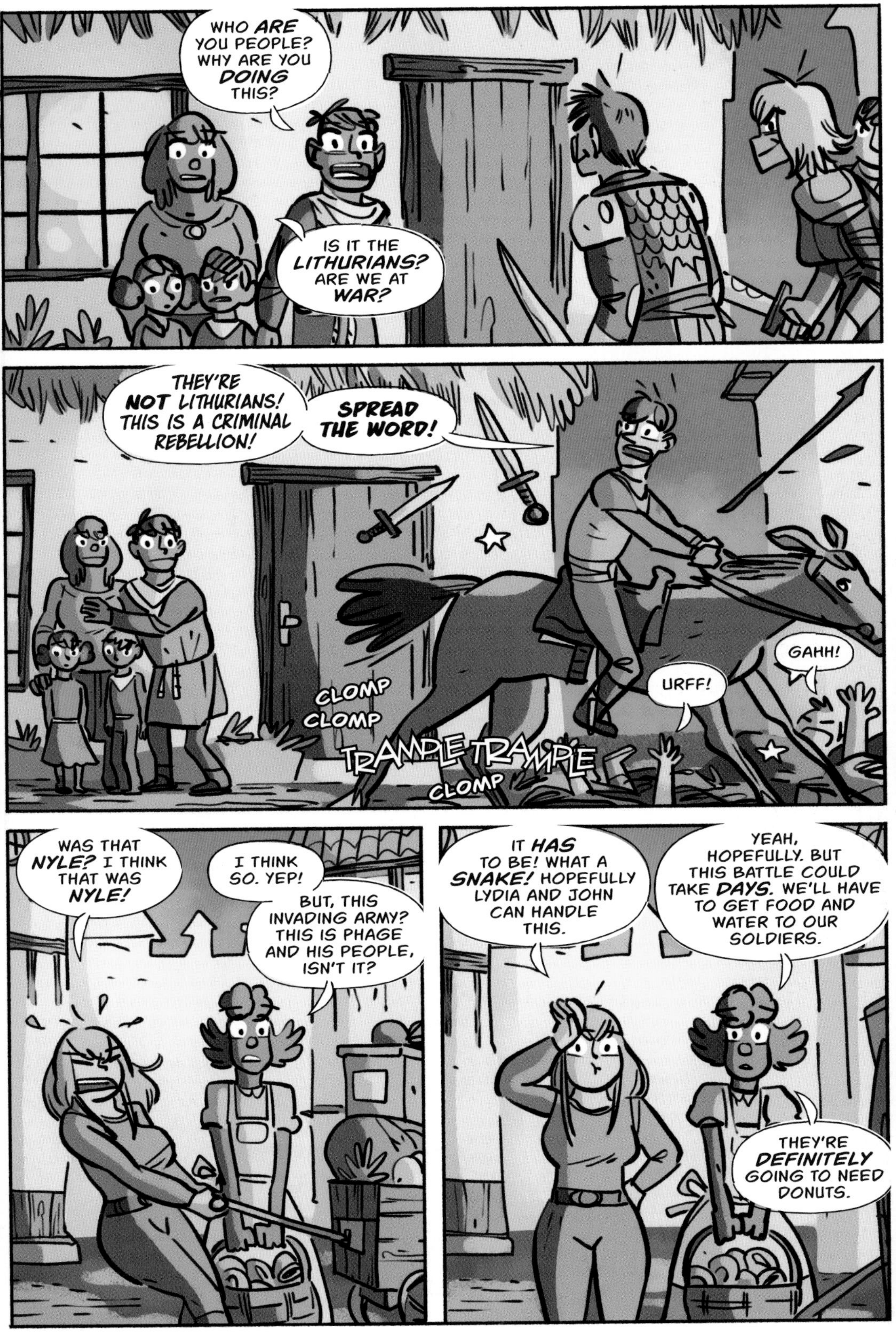
WHO ARE YOU PEOPLE? WHY ARE YOU DOING THIS?
IS IT THE LITHURIANS? ARE WE AT WAR?
THEY'RE NOT LITHURIANS! THIS IS A CRIMINAL REBELLION!
SPREAD THE WORD!
CLOMP
CLOMP
TRAMPLE TRAMPLE
CLOMP
URFF!
GAHH!
WAS THAT NYLE? I THINK THAT WAS NYLE!
I THINK SO. YEP!
BUT, THIS INVADING ARMY? THIS IS PHAGE AND HIS PEOPLE, ISN'T IT?
IT HAS TO BE! WHAT A SNAKE! HOPEFULLY LYDIA AND JOHN CAN HANDLE THIS.
YEAH, HOPEFULLY. BUT THIS BATTLE COULD TAKE DAYS. WE'LL HAVE TO GET FOOD AND WATER TO OUR SOLDIERS.
THEY'RE DEFINITELY GOING TO NEED DONUTS.

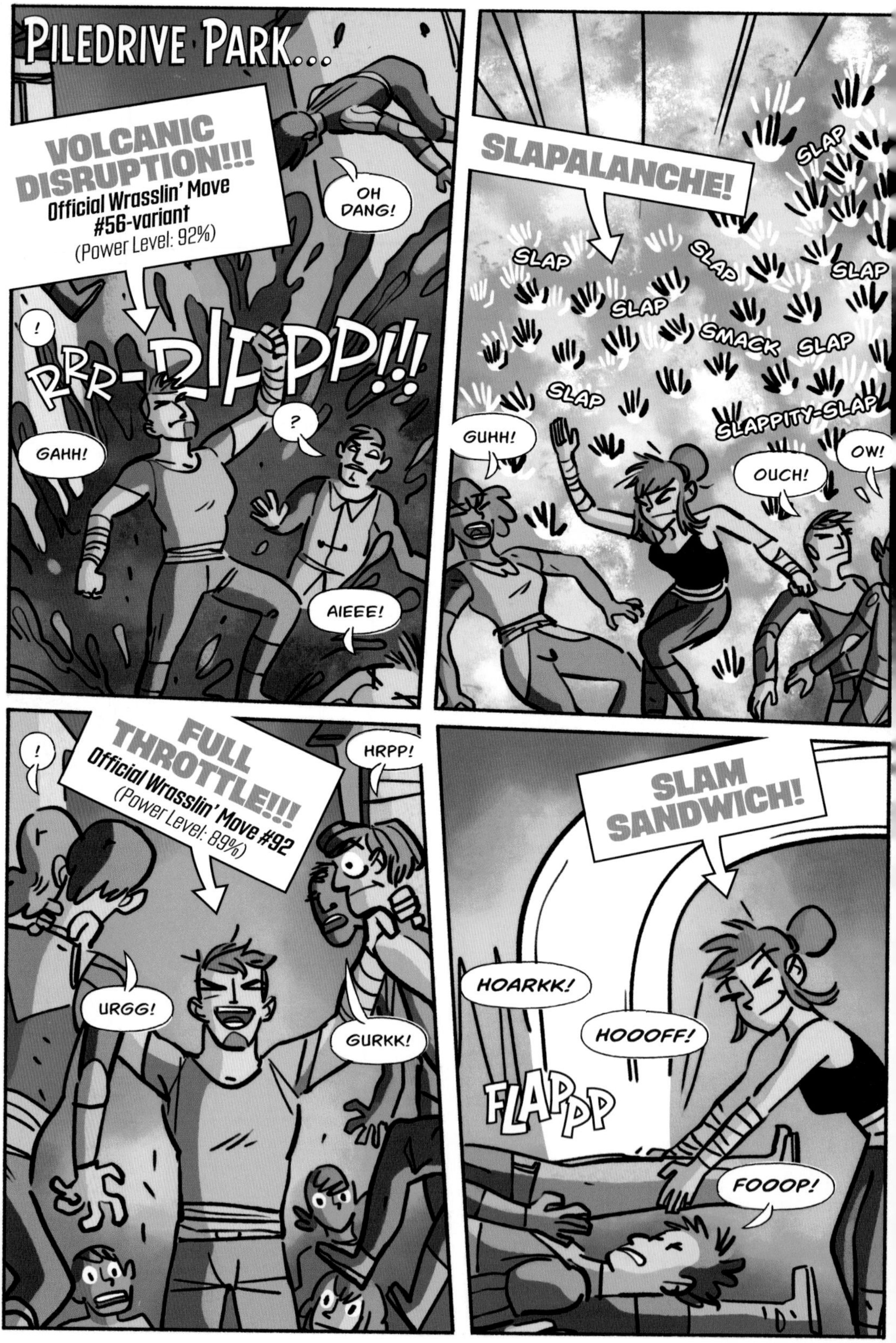
PILEDRIVE PARK...
VOLCANIC DISRUPTION!!!
Official Wrasslin' Move #56-variant
(Power Level: 92%)
OH DANG!
!
RRR-RIPPP!!!
GAHH!
?
AIEEE!
SLAPALANCHE!
SLAP
SLAP
SLAP
SLAP
SLAP
SLAP
SMACK
SLAP
SLAP
SLAPPITY-SLAP
GUHH!
OUCH!
OW!
!
FULL THROTTLE!!!
Official Wrasslin' Move #92
(Power Level: 89%)
HRPP!
URGG!
GURKK!
SLAM SANDWICH!
HOARKK!
HOOOFF!
FLAPPP
FOOOP!

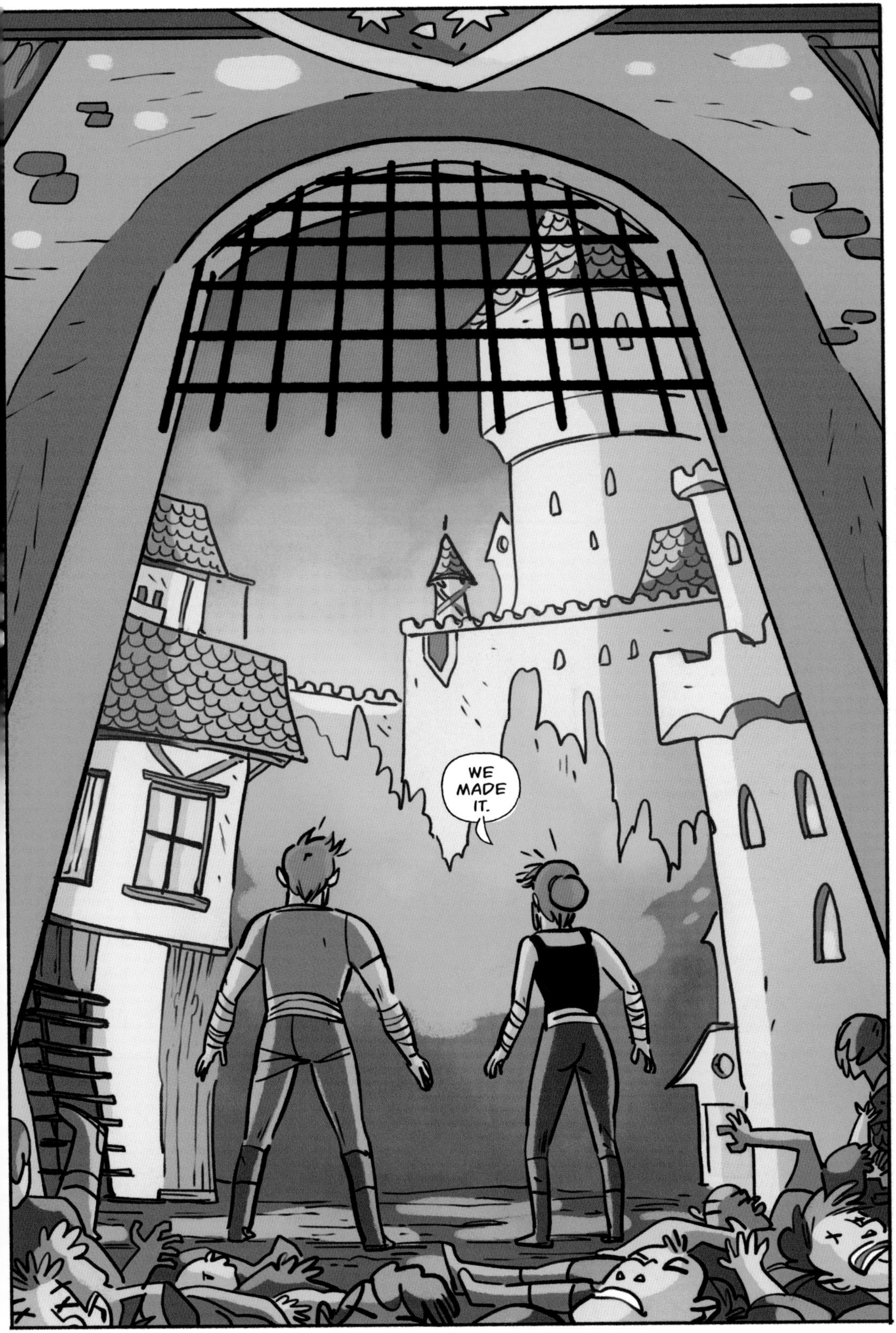
WE MADE IT.

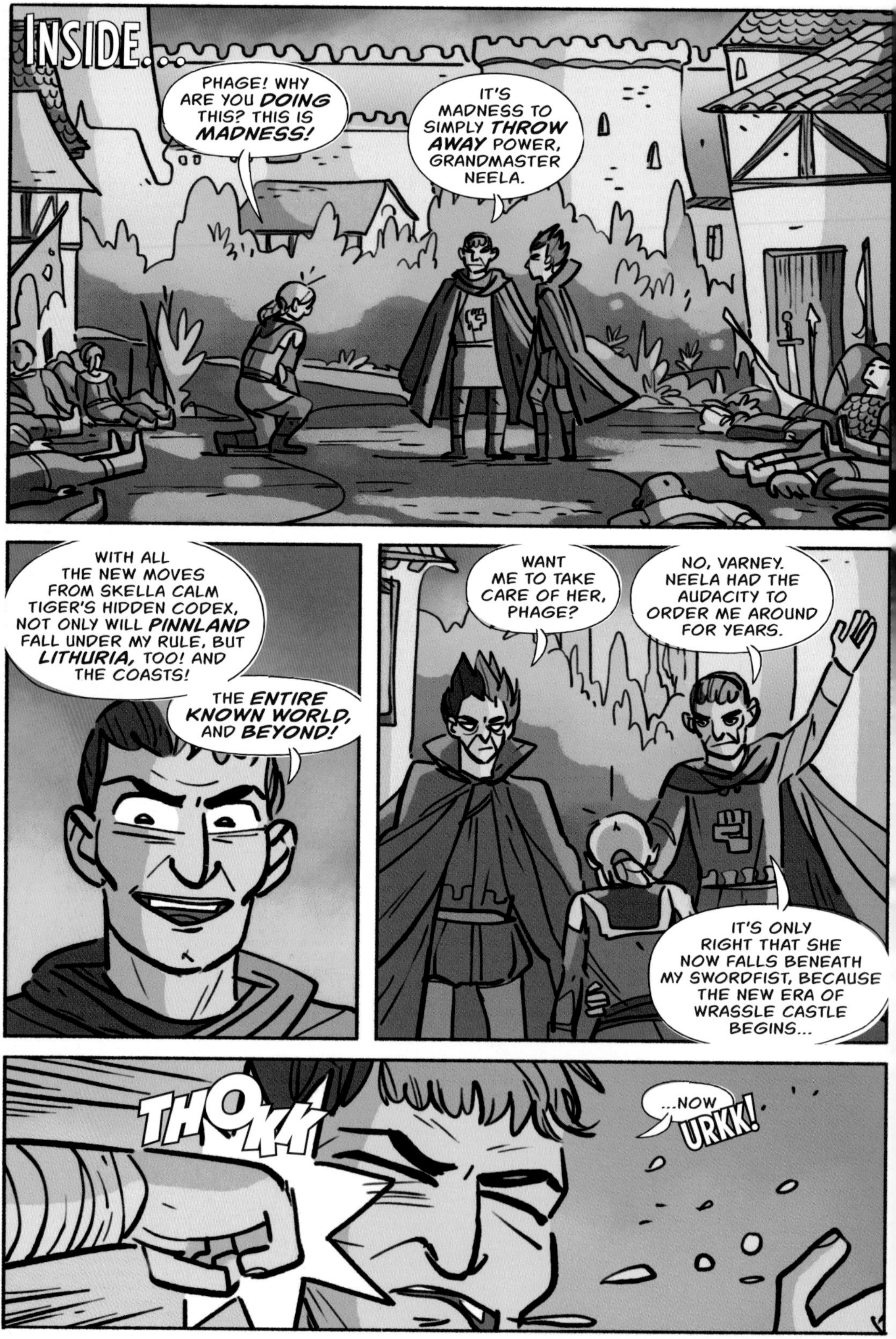
INSIDE...
PHAGE! WHY ARE YOU DOING THIS? THIS IS MADNESS!
IT'S MADNESS TO SIMPLY THROW AWAY POWER, GRANDMASTER NEELA.
WITH ALL THE NEW MOVES FROM SKELLA CALM TIGER'S HIDDEN CODEX, NOT ONLY WILL PINNLAND FALL UNDER MY RULE, BUT LITHURIA, TOO! AND THE COASTS!
THE ENTIRE KNOWN WORLD, AND BEYOND!
WANT ME TO TAKE CARE OF HER, PHAGE?
NO, VARNEY. NEELA HAD THE AUDACITY TO ORDER ME AROUND FOR YEARS.
IT'S ONLY RIGHT THAT SHE NOW FALLS BENEATH MY SWORDFIST, BECAUSE THE NEW ERA OF WRASSLE CASTLE BEGINS...
THOKK
...NOW
URKK!

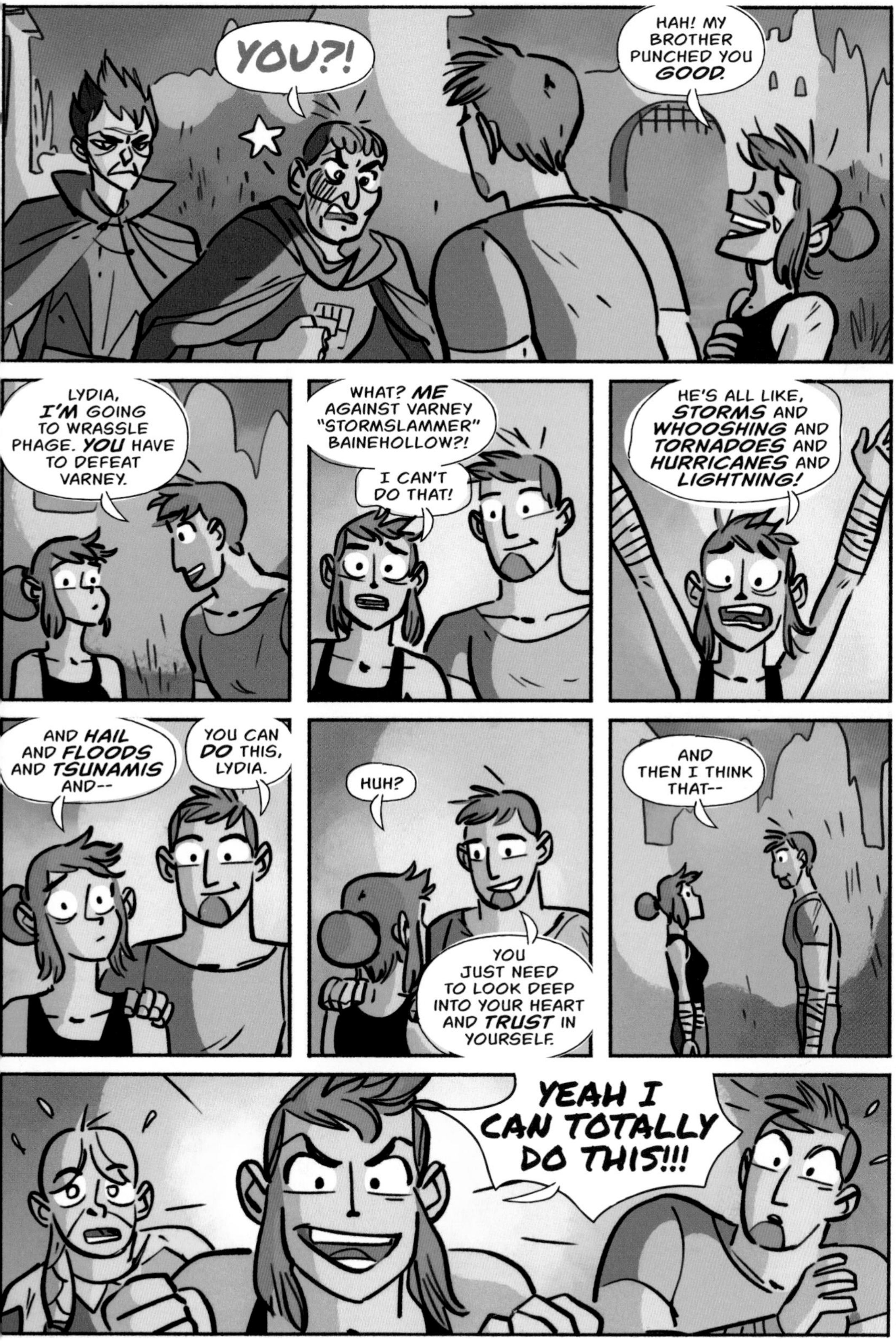
YOU?!
HAH! MY BROTHER PUNCHED YOU GOOD.
LYDIA, I'M GOING TO WRASSLE PHAGE. YOU HAVE TO DEFEAT VARNEY.
WHAT? ME AGAINST VARNEY "STORMSLAMMER" BAINEHOLLOW?!
I CAN'T DO THAT!
HE'S ALL LIKE, STORMS AND WHOOSHING AND TORNADOES AND HURRICANES AND LIGHTNING!
AND HAIL AND FLOODS AND TSUNAMIS AND--
YOU CAN DO THIS, LYDIA.
HUH?
YOU JUST NEED TO LOOK DEEP INTO YOUR HEART AND TRUST IN YOURSELF.
AND THEN I THINK THAT--
YEAH I CAN TOTALLY DO THIS!!!

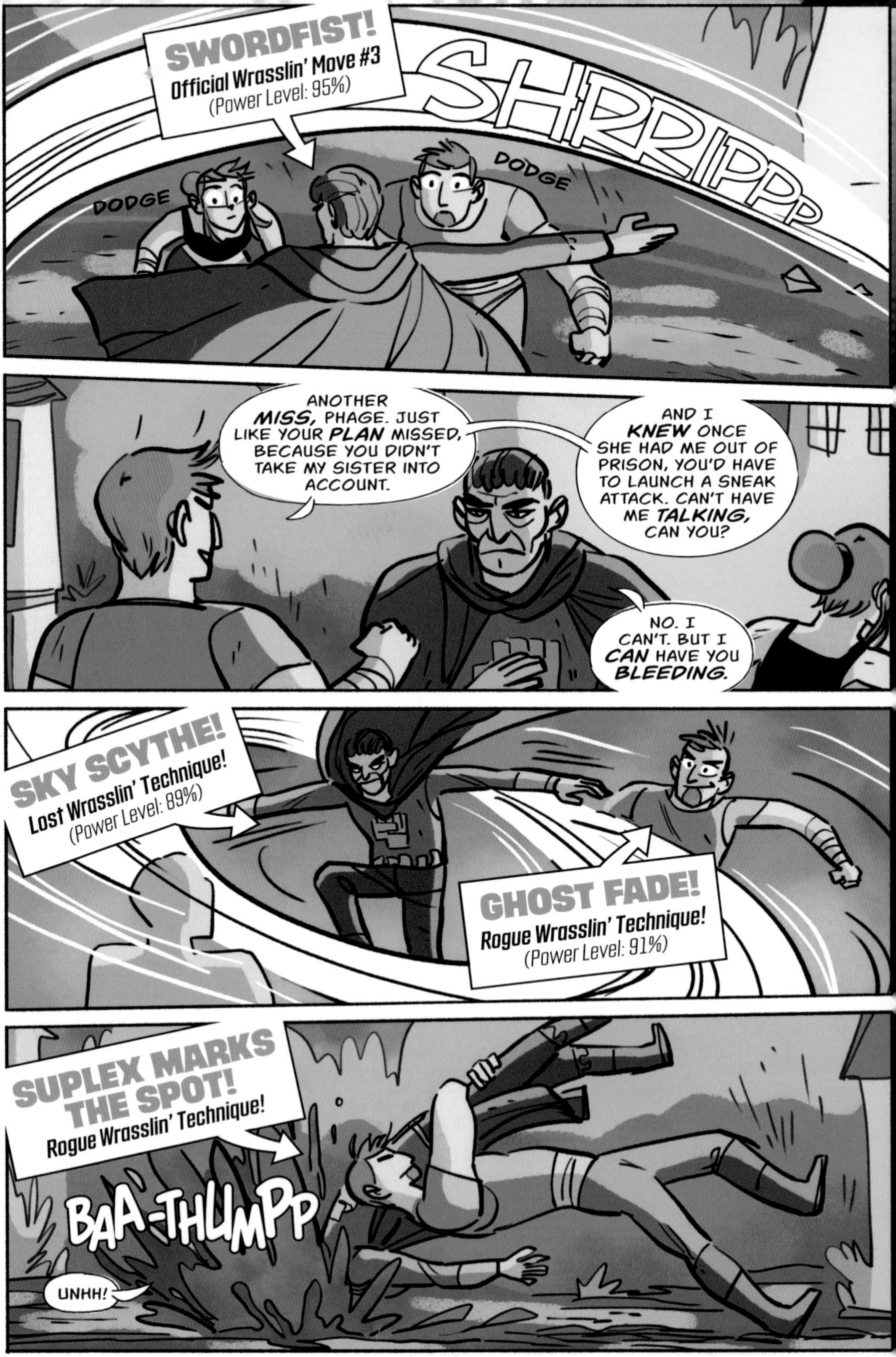

SWORDFIST!
Official Wrasslin' Move #3
(Power Level: 95%)
SHRRIPPP
DODGE
DODGE
ANOTHER MISS, PHAGE. JUST LIKE YOUR PLAN MISSED, BECAUSE YOU DIDN'T TAKE MY SISTER INTO ACCOUNT.
AND I KNEW ONCE SHE HAD ME OUT OF PRISON, YOU'D HAVE TO LAUNCH A SNEAK ATTACK. CAN'T HAVE ME TALKING, CAN YOU?
NO. I CAN'T. BUT I CAN HAVE YOU BLEEDING.
SKY SCYTHE!
Lost Wrasslin' Technique!
(Power Level: 89%)
GHOST FADE!
Rogue Wrasslin' Technique!
(Power Level: 91%)
SUPLEX MARKS THE SPOT!
Rogue Wrasslin' Technique!
BAA-THUMPP
UNHH!

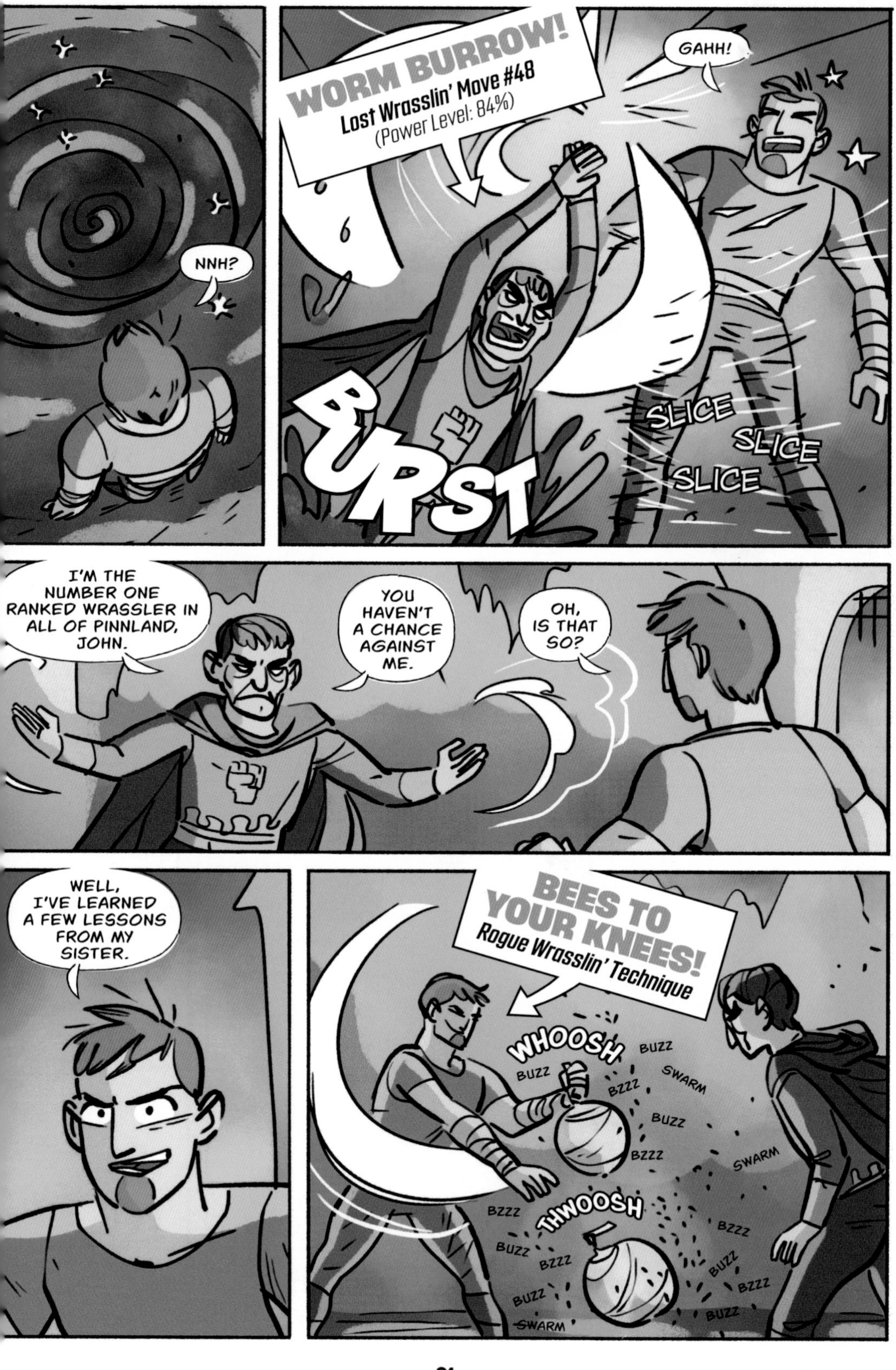
NNH?
WORM BURROW!
Lost Wrasslin' Move #48
(Power Level: 84%)
GAHH!
BURST
SLICE
SLICE
SLICE
I'M THE NUMBER ONE RANKED WRASSLER IN ALL OF PINNLAND, JOHN.
YOU HAVEN'T A CHANCE AGAINST ME.
OH, IS THAT SO?
WELL, I'VE LEARNED A FEW LESSONS FROM MY SISTER.
BEES TO YOUR KNEES!
Rogue Wrasslin' Technique
WHOOSH
BUZZ
BUZZ
SWARM
BZZZ
BUZZ
BZZZ
SWARM
THWOOSH
BZZZ
BUZZ
BZZZ
BUZZ
BZZZ
BUZZ
BZZZ
BUZZ
SWARM

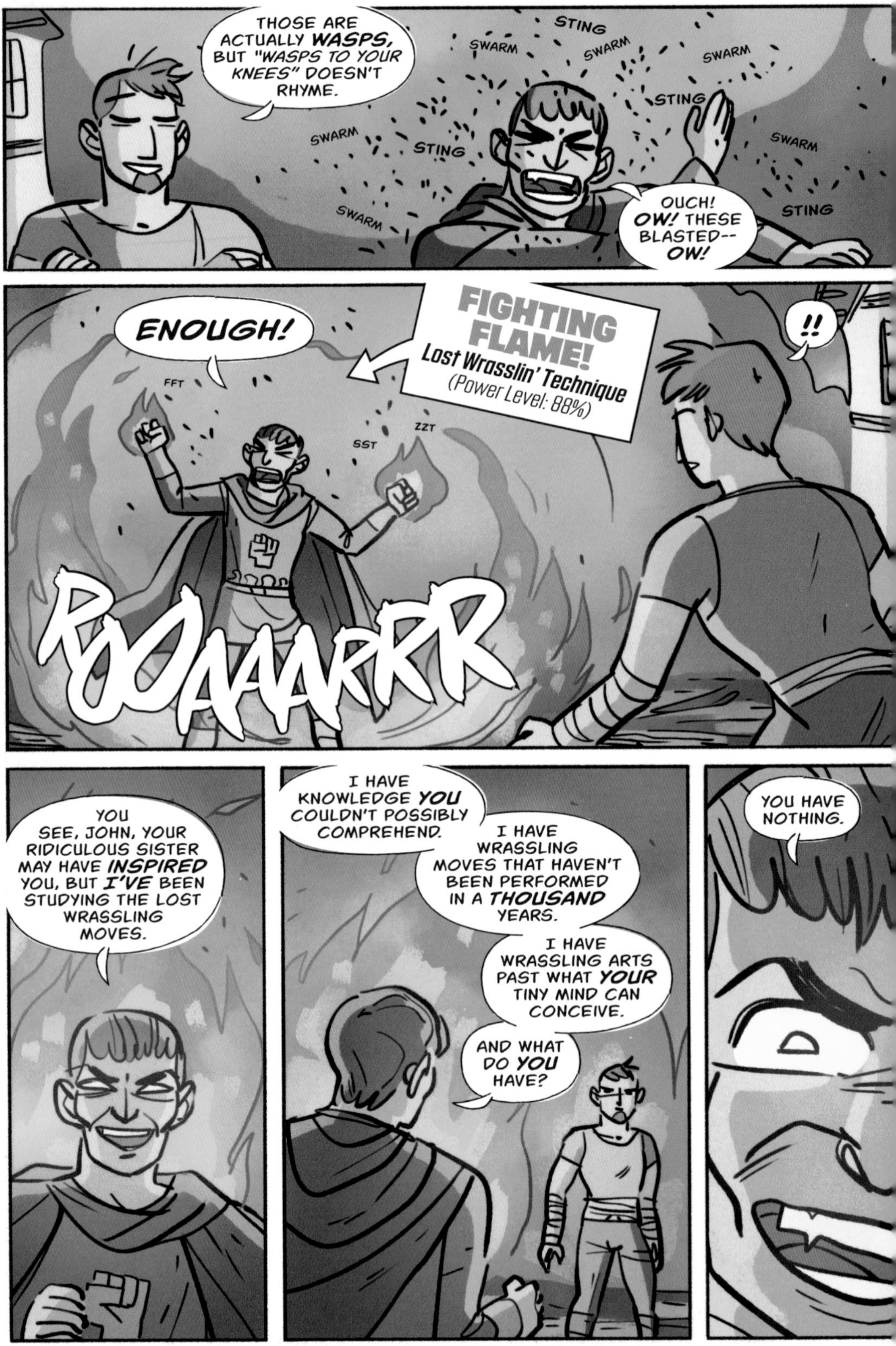
THOSE ARE ACTUALLY WASPS, BUT "WASPS TO YOUR KNEES" DOESN'T RHYME.
STING
SWARM
SWARM
SWARM
STING
SWARM
STING
SWARM
SWARM
STING
OUCH! OW! THESE BLASTED-- OW!
ENOUGH!
FIGHTING FLAME!
Lost Wrasslin' Technique
(Power Level: 88%)
!!
FFT
SST
ZZT
ROOAAARRR
YOU SEE, JOHN, YOUR RIDICULOUS SISTER MAY HAVE INSPIRED YOU, BUT I'VE BEEN STUDYING THE LOST WRASSLING MOVES.
I HAVE KNOWLEDGE YOU COULDN'T POSSIBLY COMPREHEND.
I HAVE WRASSLING MOVES THAT HAVEN'T BEEN PERFORMED IN A THOUSAND YEARS.
I HAVE WRASSLING ARTS PAST WHAT YOUR TINY MIND CAN CONCEIVE.
AND WHAT DO YOU HAVE?
YOU HAVE NOTHING.

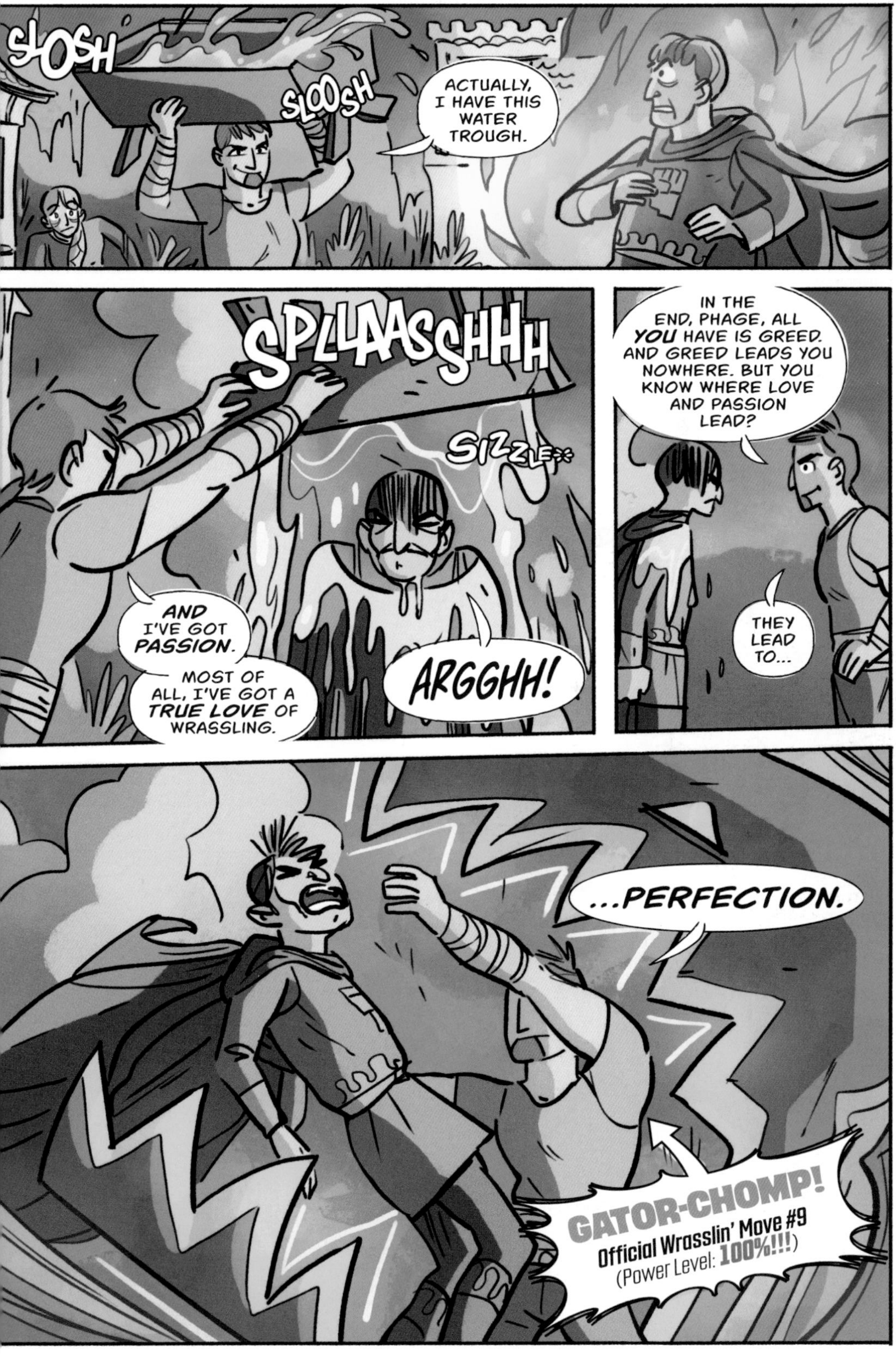
SLOSH
SLOOSH
ACTUALLY, I HAVE THIS WATER TROUGH.
SPLLAASSHHH
SIZZLE
AND I'VE GOT PASSION.
MOST OF ALL, I'VE GOT A TRUE LOVE OF WRASSLING.
ARGGHH!
IN THE END, PHAGE, ALL YOU HAVE IS GREED. AND GREED LEADS YOU NOWHERE. BUT YOU KNOW WHERE LOVE AND PASSION LEAD?
THEY LEAD TO...
...PERFECTION.
GATOR-CHOMP!
Official Wrasslin' Move #9
(Power Level: 100%!!!)

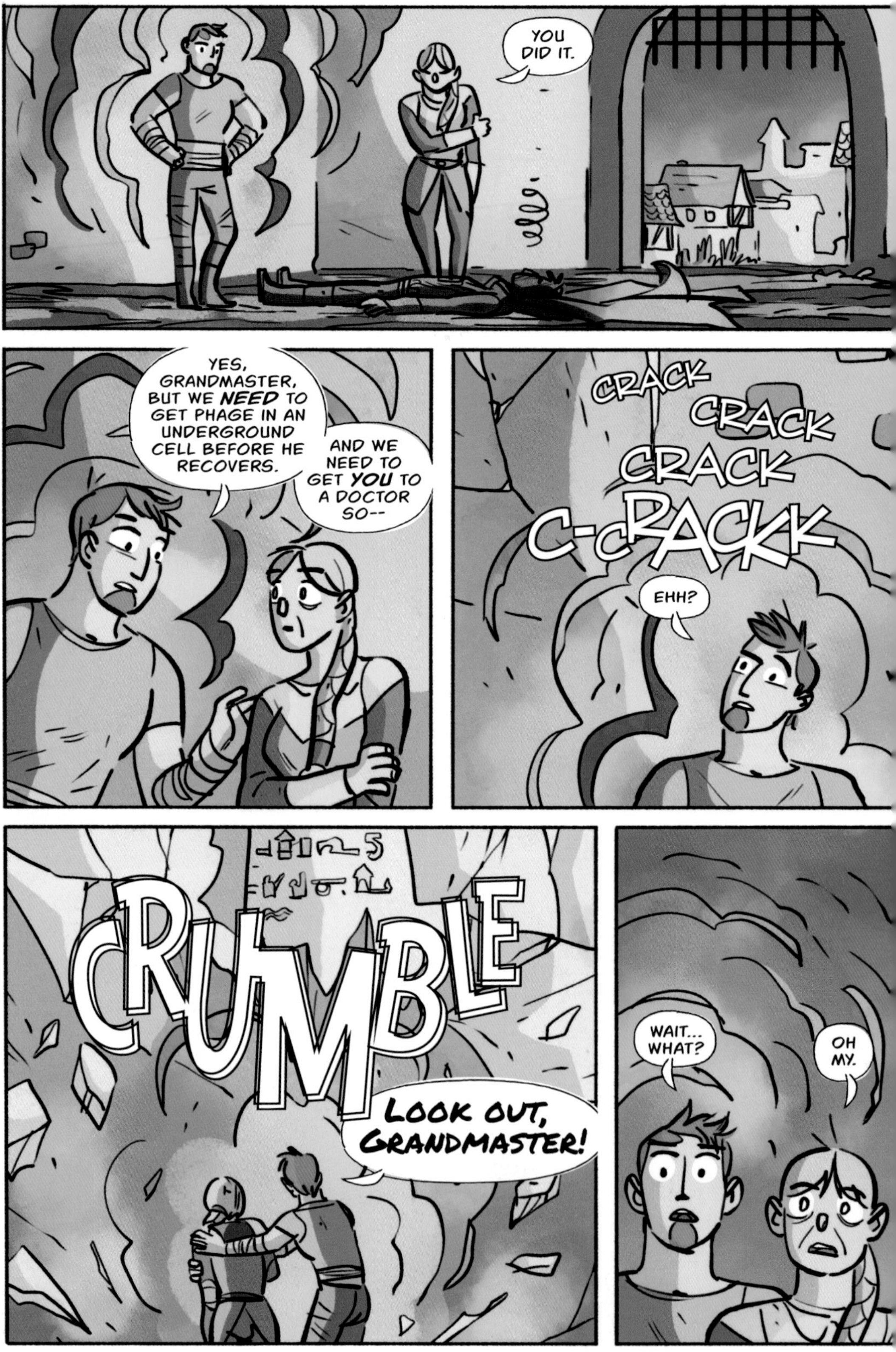
YOU DID IT.
YES, GRANDMASTER, BUT WE **NEED** TO GET PHAGE IN AN UNDERGROUND CELL BEFORE HE RECOVERS.
AND WE NEED TO GET **YOU** TO A DOCTOR SO--
CRACK
CRACK
CRACK
C-CRACKK
EHH?
CRUMBLE
LOOK OUT, GRANDMASTER!
WAIT... WHAT?
OH MY.

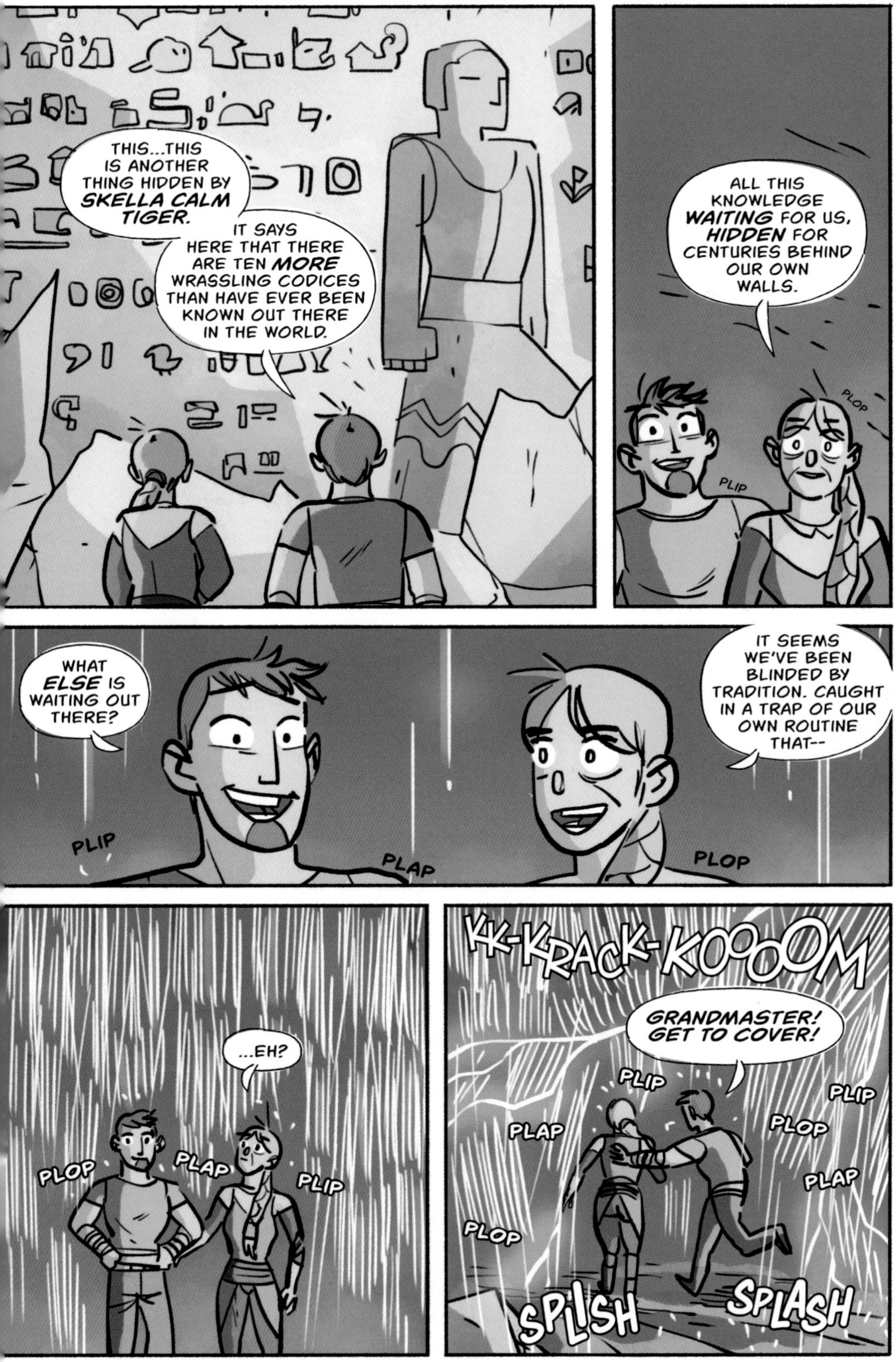
THIS...THIS IS ANOTHER THING HIDDEN BY SKELLA CALM TIGER.
IT SAYS HERE THAT THERE ARE TEN MORE WRASSLING CODICES THAN HAVE EVER BEEN KNOWN OUT THERE IN THE WORLD.
ALL THIS KNOWLEDGE WAITING FOR US, HIDDEN FOR CENTURIES BEHIND OUR OWN WALLS.
PLOP
PLIP
WHAT ELSE IS WAITING OUT THERE?
IT SEEMS WE'VE BEEN BLINDED BY TRADITION. CAUGHT IN A TRAP OF OUR OWN ROUTINE THAT--
PLIP
PLAP
PLOP
...EH?
PLOP
PLAP
PLIP
KK-KRACK-KOOOOOM
GRANDMASTER! GET TO COVER!
PLIP
PLIP
PLAP
PLOP
PLAP
PLOP
SPLISH
SPLASH

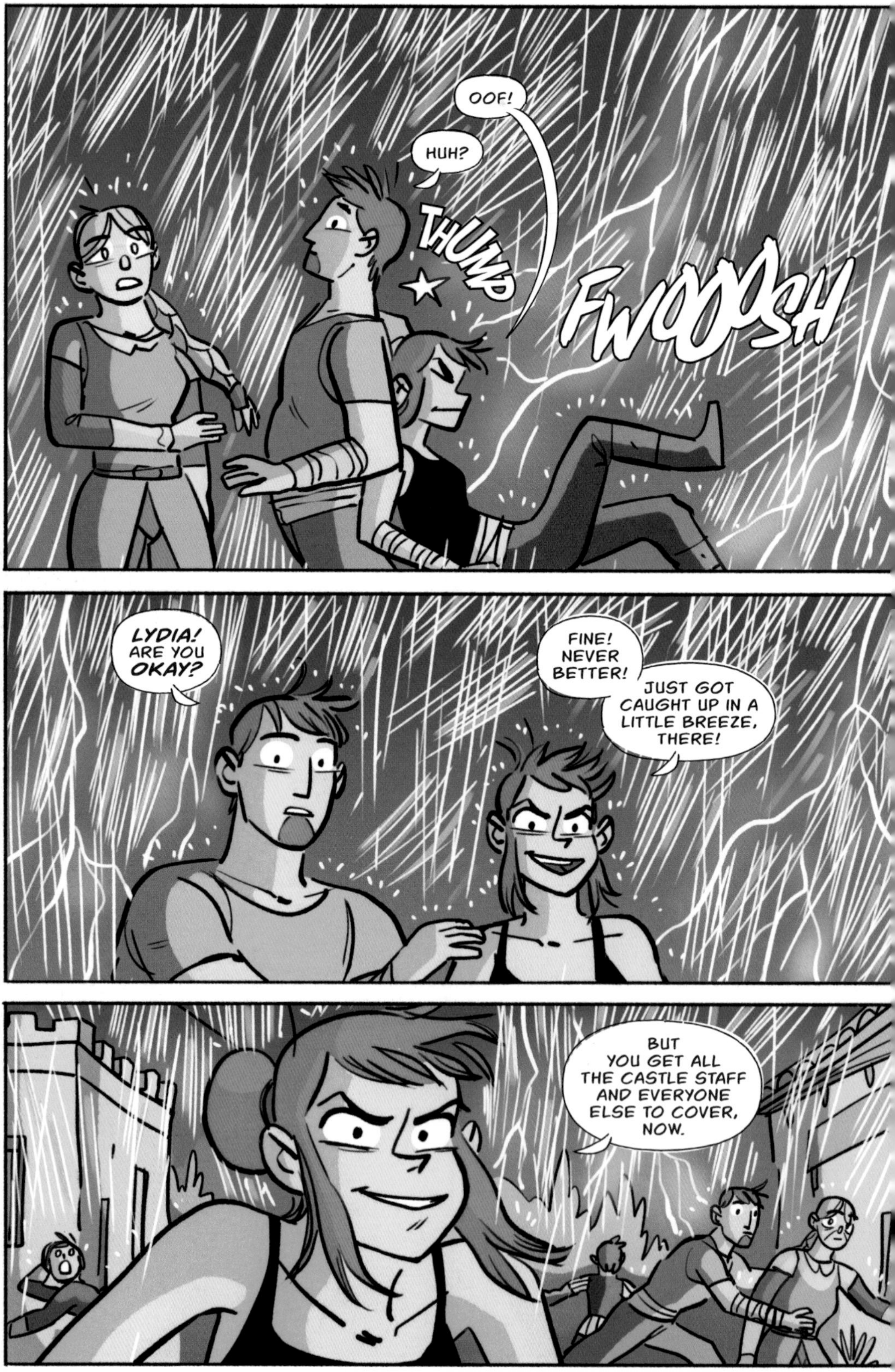
OOF!
HUH?
THUMP
FWOOOSH
LYDIA! ARE YOU OKAY?
FINE! NEVER BETTER!
JUST GOT CAUGHT UP IN A LITTLE BREEZE, THERE!
BUT YOU GET ALL THE CASTLE STAFF AND EVERYONE ELSE TO COVER, NOW.

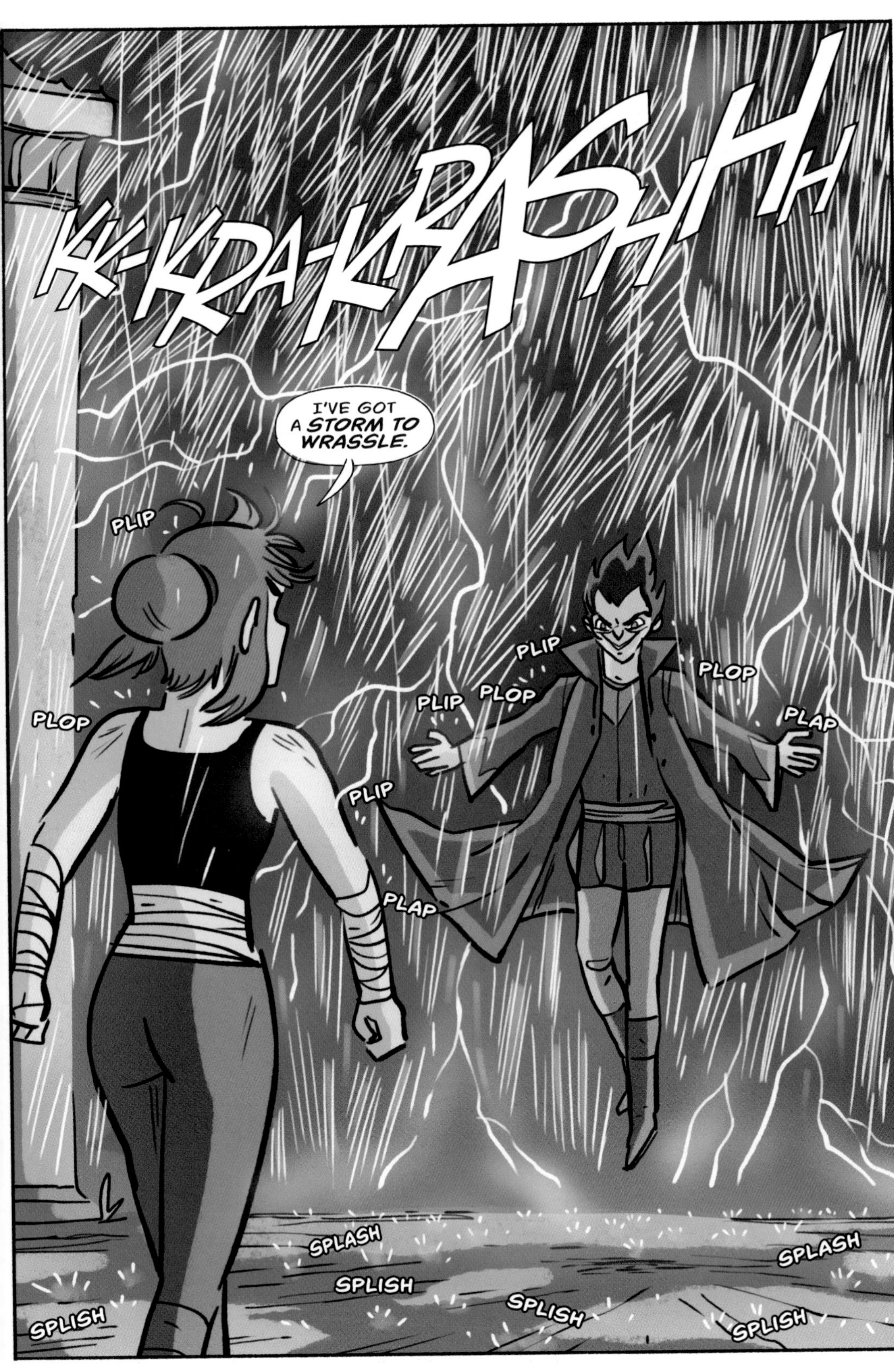
KK-KRA-KRASHHH
I'VE GOT A STORM TO WRASSLE.
PLIP
PLOP
PLIP
PLIP
PLOP
PLOP
PLAP
PLIP
PLAP
SPLASH
SPLASH
SPLISH
SPLISH
SPLISH
SPLISH

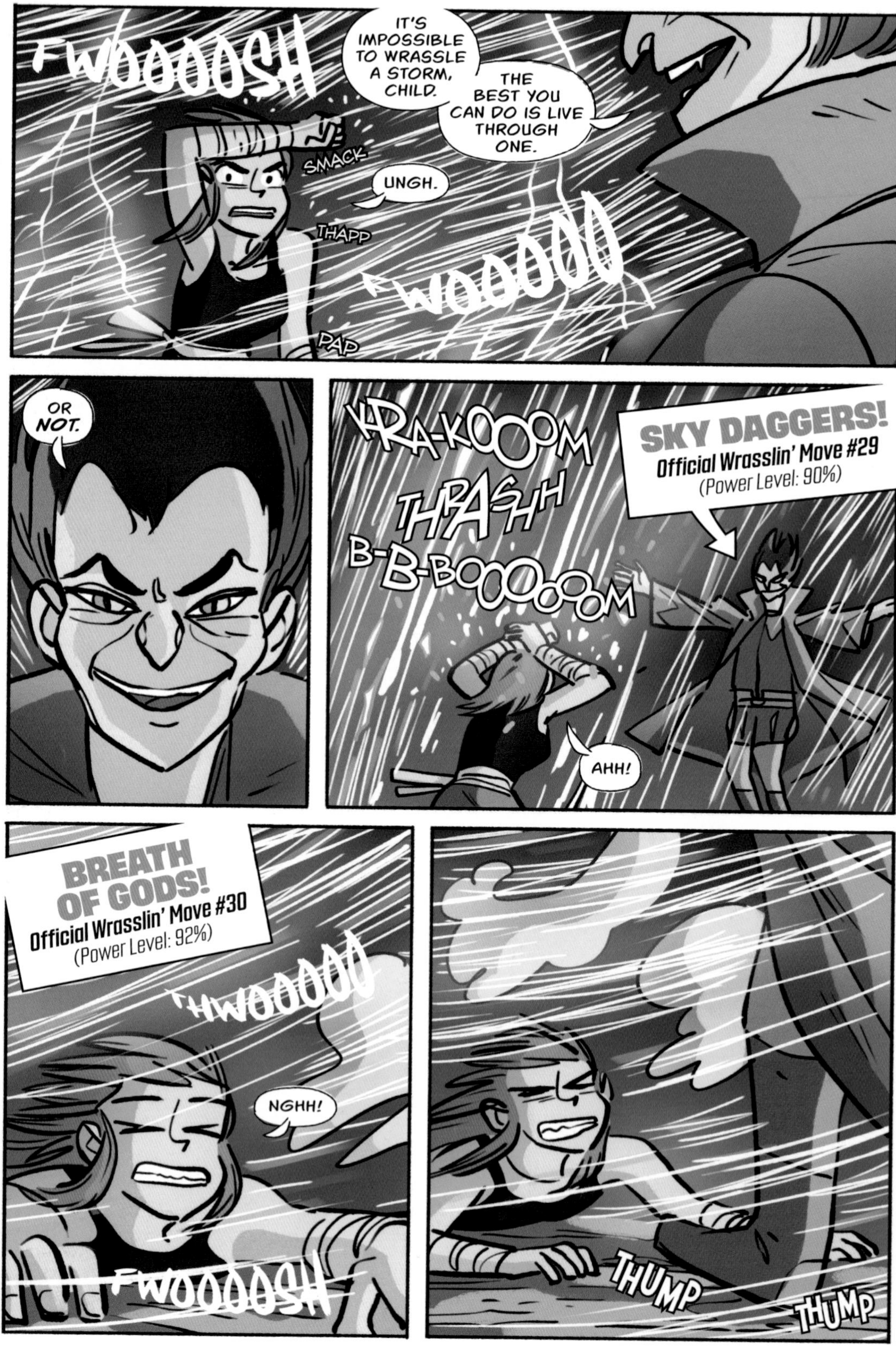
FWOOOOOSH
IT'S IMPOSSIBLE TO WRASSLE A STORM, CHILD.
THE BEST YOU CAN DO IS LIVE THROUGH ONE.
SMACK
UNGH.
THAPP
FWOOOOO
PAP
OR NOT.
KRA-KOOOOM
THRASHH
B-B-BOOOOOOOM
SKY DAGGERS!
Official Wrasslin' Move #29
(Power Level: 90%)
AHH!
BREATH OF GODS!
Official Wrasslin' Move #30
(Power Level: 92%)
THWOOOOO
NGHH!
FWOOOOSH
THUMP
THUMP

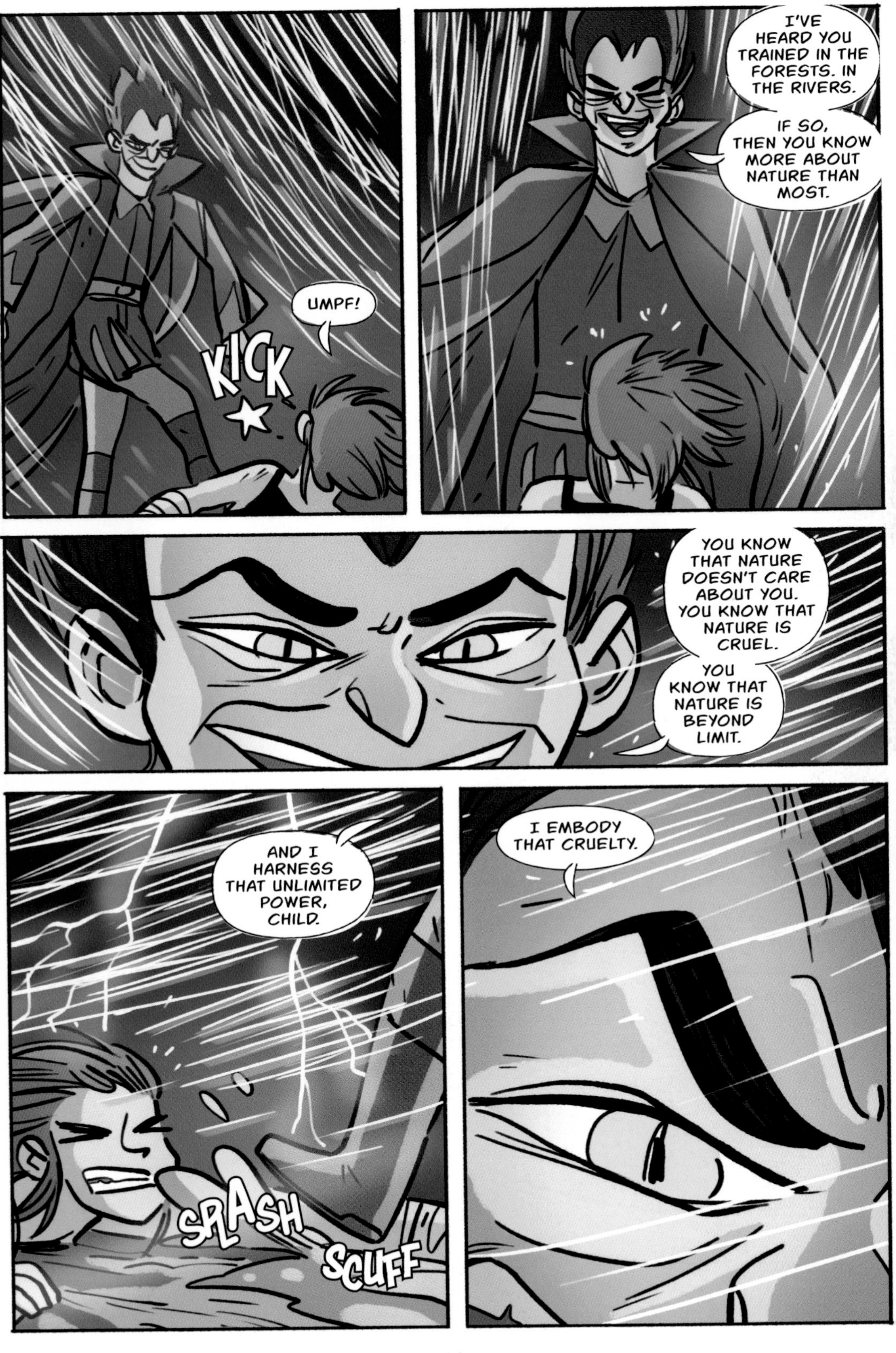
UMPF!
KICK
I'VE HEARD YOU TRAINED IN THE FORESTS. IN THE RIVERS.
IF SO, THEN YOU KNOW MORE ABOUT NATURE THAN MOST.
YOU KNOW THAT NATURE DOESN'T CARE ABOUT YOU. YOU KNOW THAT NATURE IS CRUEL.
YOU KNOW THAT NATURE IS BEYOND LIMIT.
AND I HARNESS THAT UNLIMITED POWER, CHILD.
SPLASH
SCUFF
I EMBODY THAT CRUELTY.

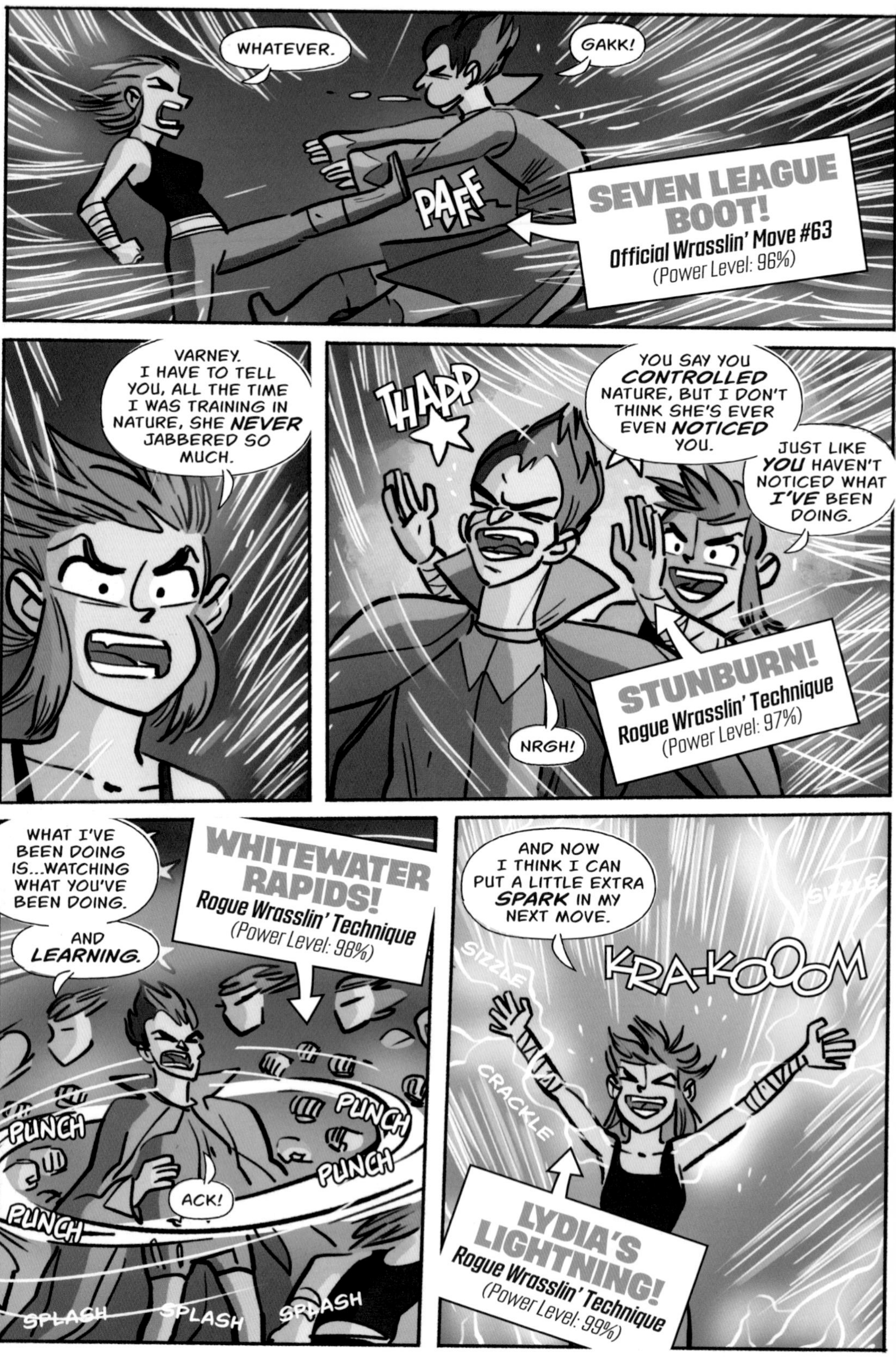
WHATEVER.
GAKK!
PAFF
SEVEN LEAGUE BOOT!
Official Wrasslin' Move #63
(Power Level: 96%)
VARNEY. I HAVE TO TELL YOU, ALL THE TIME I WAS TRAINING IN NATURE, SHE NEVER JABBERED SO MUCH.
THAPP
YOU SAY YOU CONTROLLED NATURE, BUT I DON'T THINK SHE'S EVER EVEN NOTICED YOU.
JUST LIKE YOU HAVEN'T NOTICED WHAT I'VE BEEN DOING.
NRGH!
STUNBURN!
Rogue Wrasslin' Technique
(Power Level: 97%)
WHAT I'VE BEEN DOING IS...WATCHING WHAT YOU'VE BEEN DOING.
AND LEARNING.
WHITEWATER RAPIDS!
Rogue Wrasslin' Technique
(Power Level: 98%)
PUNCH
PUNCH
PUNCH
PUNCH
ACK!
SPLASH
SPLASH
SPLASH
AND NOW I THINK I CAN PUT A LITTLE EXTRA SPARK IN MY NEXT MOVE.
SIZZLE
SIZZLE
KRA-KOOOM
CRACKLE
LYDIA'S LIGHTNING!
Rogue Wrasslin' Technique
(Power Level: 99%)

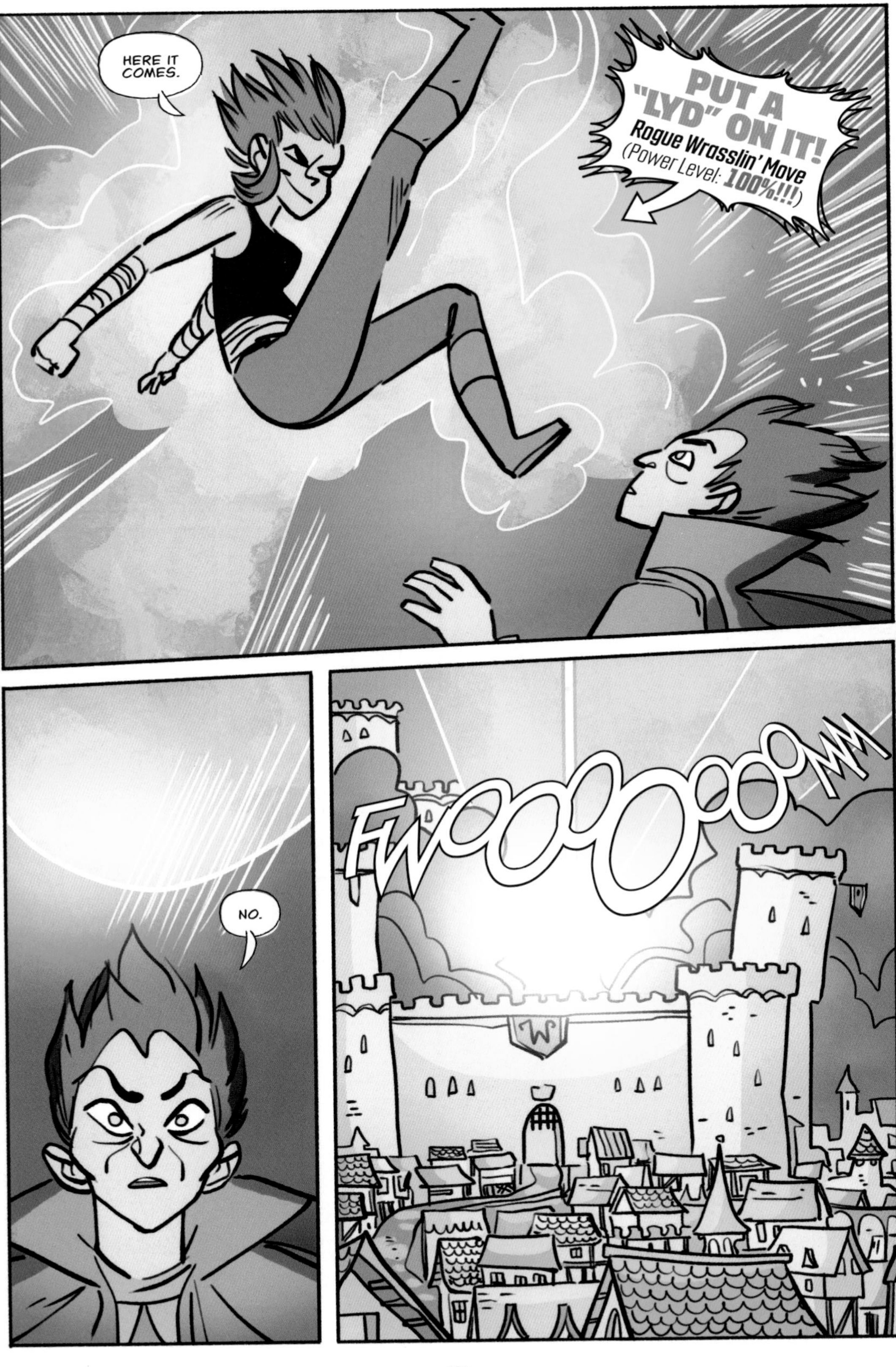
HERE IT COMES.
PUT A "LYD" ON IT!
Rogue Wrasslin' Move
(Power Level: 100%!!!)
NO.
FWOOOOOOOMM

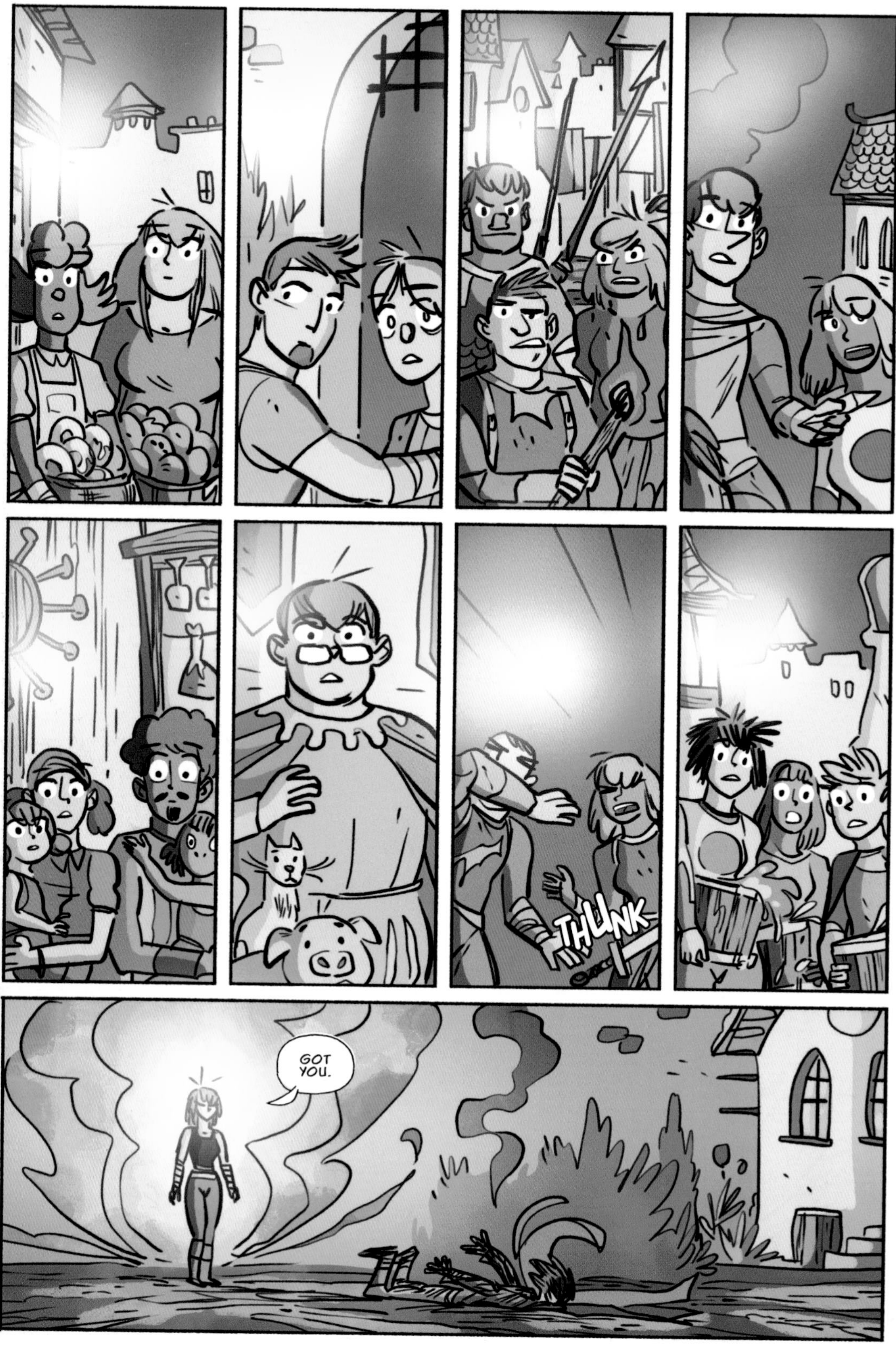
THUNK
GOT YOU.

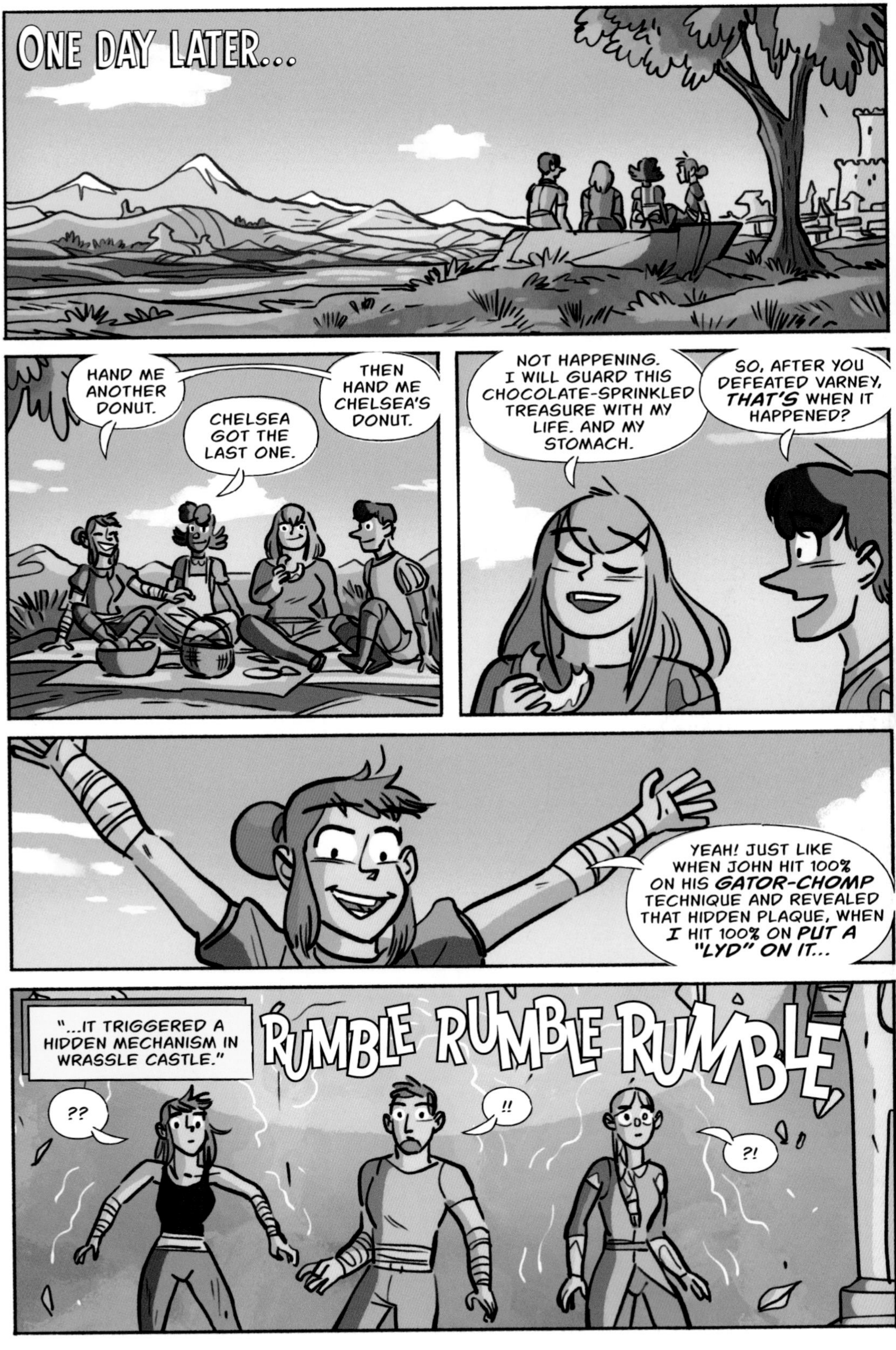

ONE DAY LATER...
HAND ME ANOTHER DONUT.
CHELSEA GOT THE LAST ONE.
THEN HAND ME CHELSEA'S DONUT.
NOT HAPPENING. I WILL GUARD THIS CHOCOLATE-SPRINKLED TREASURE WITH MY LIFE. AND MY STOMACH.
SO, AFTER YOU DEFEATED VARNEY, *THAT'S* WHEN IT HAPPENED?
YEAH! JUST LIKE WHEN JOHN HIT 100% ON HIS *GATOR-CHOMP* TECHNIQUE AND REVEALED THAT HIDDEN PLAQUE, WHEN *I* HIT 100% ON *PUT A "LYD" ON IT...*
"...IT TRIGGERED A HIDDEN MECHANISM IN WRASSLE CASTLE."
RUMBLE RUMBLE RUMBLE
??
!!
?!

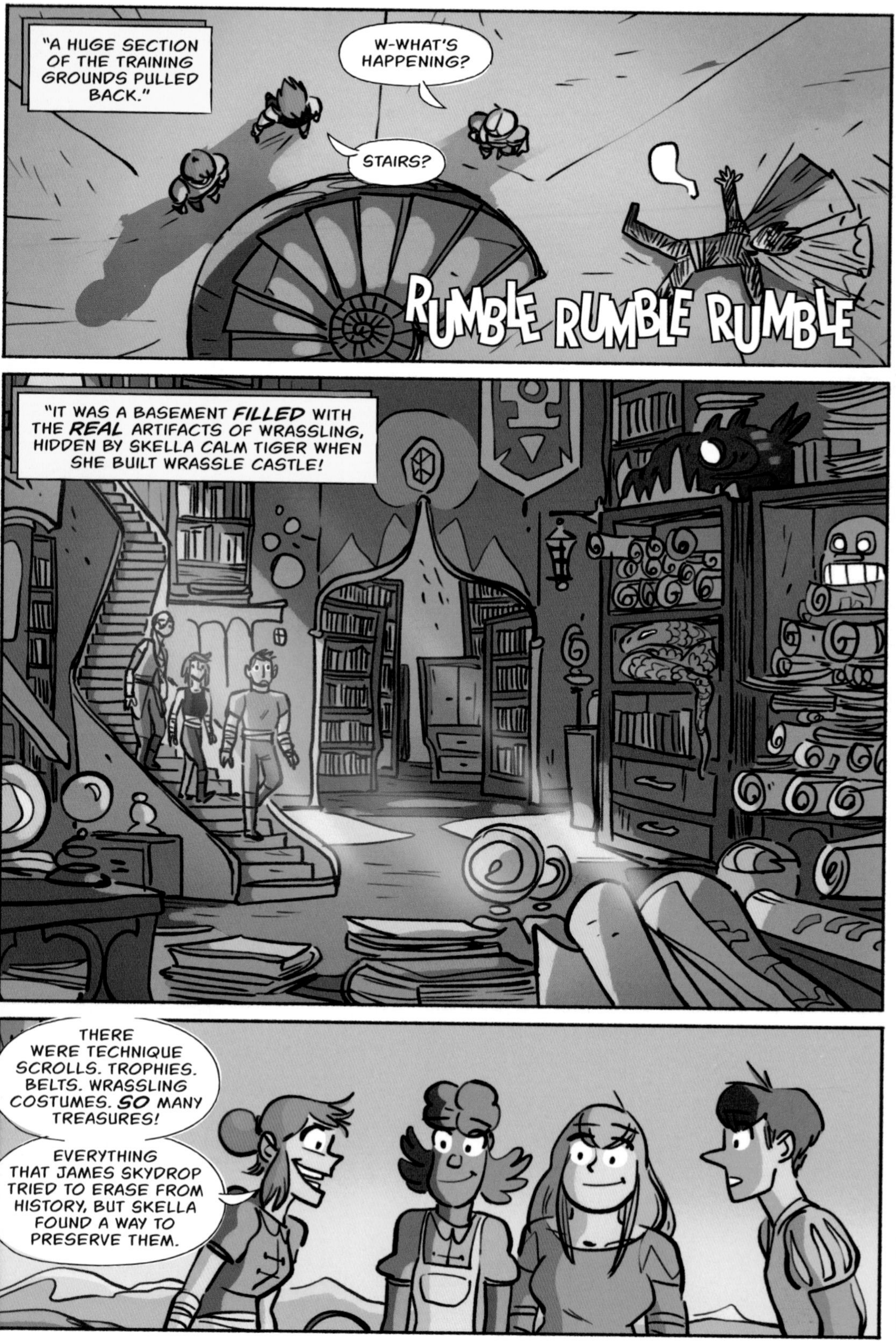
"A HUGE SECTION OF THE TRAINING GROUNDS PULLED BACK."
W-WHAT'S HAPPENING?
STAIRS?
RUMBLE RUMBLE RUMBLE
"IT WAS A BASEMENT FILLED WITH THE REAL ARTIFACTS OF WRASSLING, HIDDEN BY SKELLA CALM TIGER WHEN SHE BUILT WRASSLE CASTLE!
THERE WERE TECHNIQUE SCROLLS. TROPHIES. BELTS. WRASSLING COSTUMES. SO MANY TREASURES!
EVERYTHING THAT JAMES SKYDROP TRIED TO ERASE FROM HISTORY, BUT SKELLA FOUND A WAY TO PRESERVE THEM.

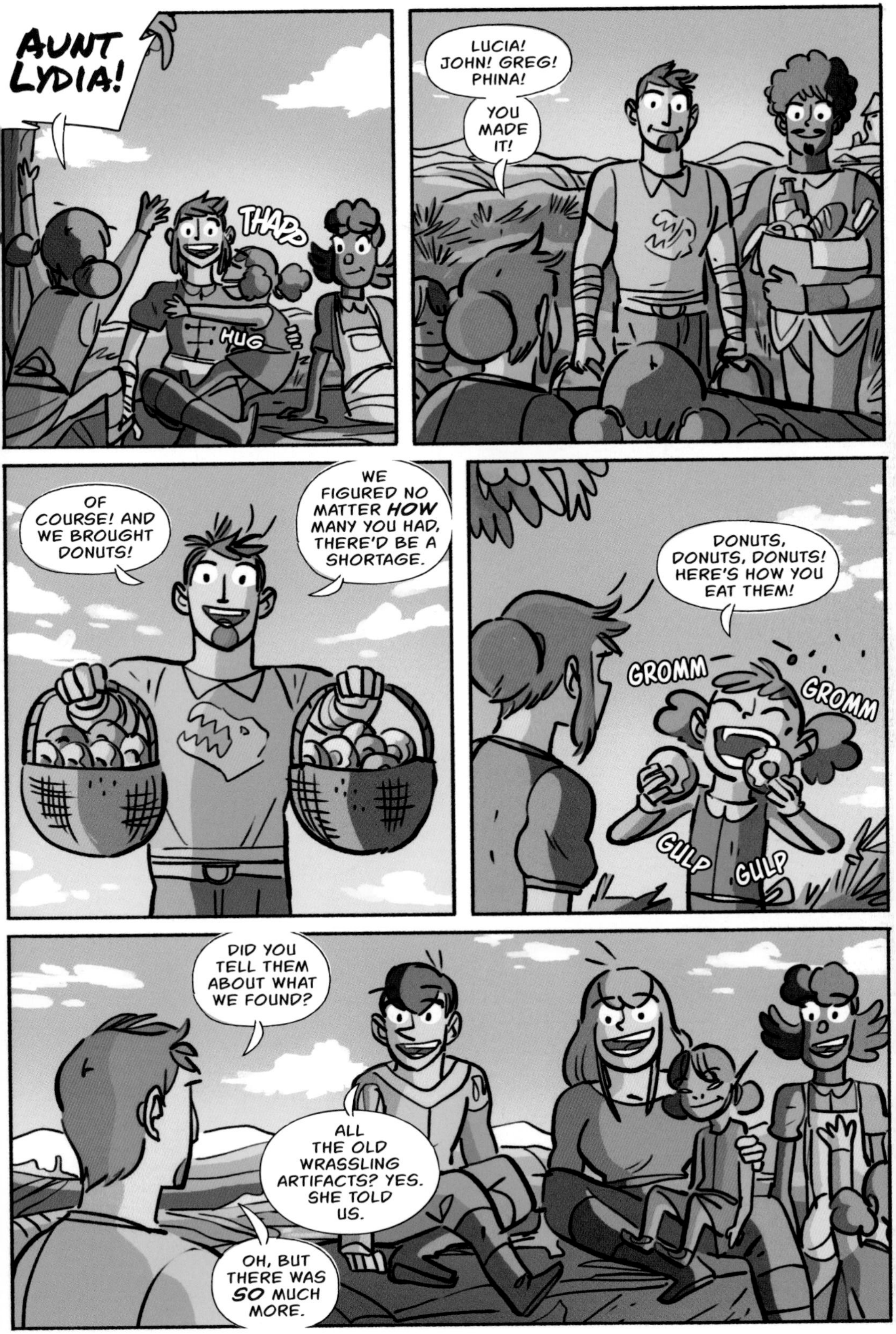
AUNT LYDIA!
THAPP
HUG
LUCIA! JOHN! GREG! PHINA!
YOU MADE IT!
OF COURSE! AND WE BROUGHT DONUTS!
WE FIGURED NO MATTER HOW MANY YOU HAD, THERE'D BE A SHORTAGE.
DONUTS, DONUTS, DONUTS! HERE'S HOW YOU EAT THEM!
GROMM
GROMM
GULP
GULP
DID YOU TELL THEM ABOUT WHAT WE FOUND?
ALL THE OLD WRASSLING ARTIFACTS? YES. SHE TOLD US.
OH, BUT THERE WAS SO MUCH MORE.

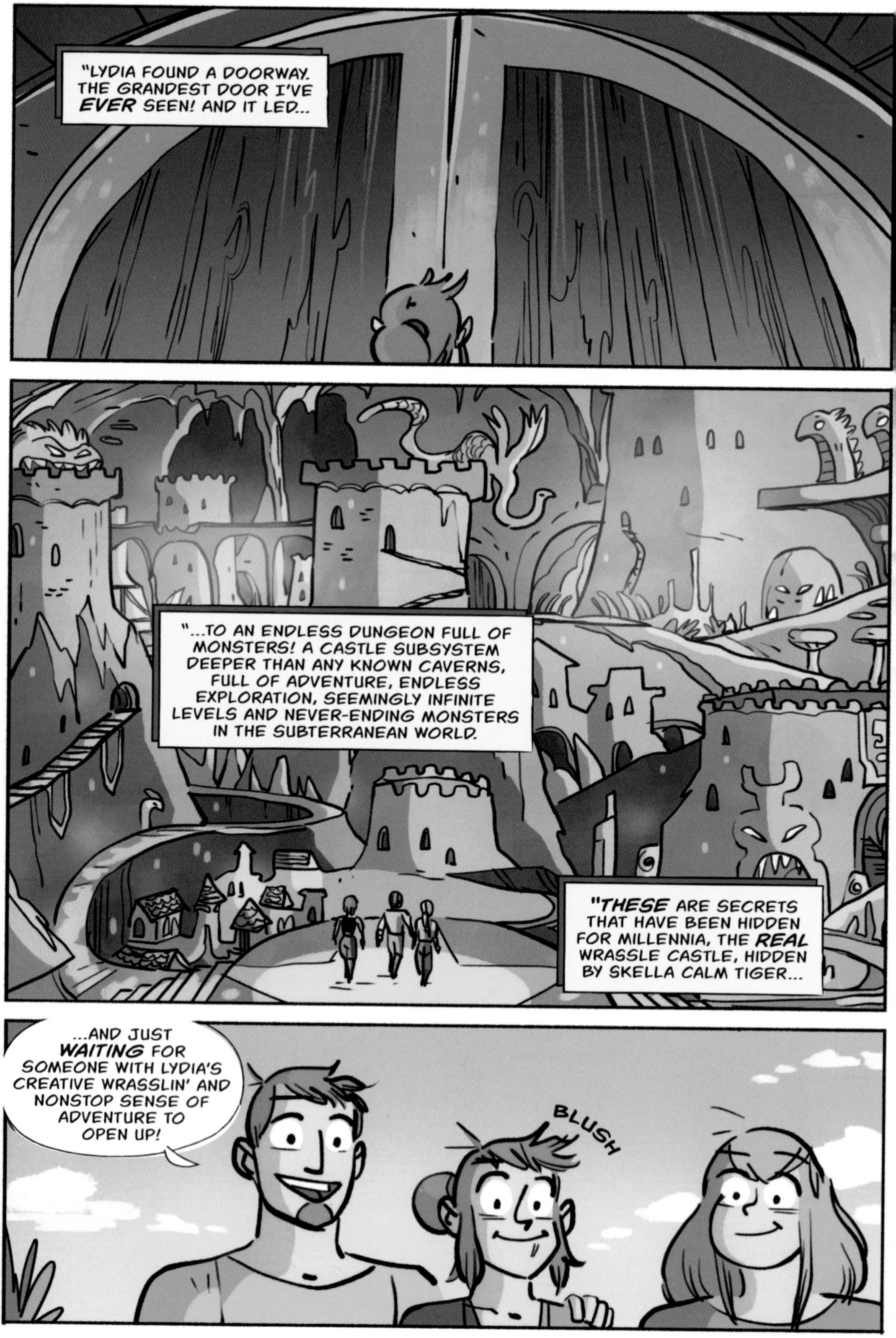
"LYDIA FOUND A DOORWAY. THE GRANDEST DOOR I'VE EVER SEEN! AND IT LED...
"...TO AN ENDLESS DUNGEON FULL OF MONSTERS! A CASTLE SUBSYSTEM DEEPER THAN ANY KNOWN CAVERNS, FULL OF ADVENTURE, ENDLESS EXPLORATION, SEEMINGLY INFINITE LEVELS AND NEVER-ENDING MONSTERS IN THE SUBTERRANEAN WORLD.
"THESE ARE SECRETS THAT HAVE BEEN HIDDEN FOR MILLENNIA, THE REAL WRASSLE CASTLE, HIDDEN BY SKELLA CALM TIGER...
...AND JUST WAITING FOR SOMEONE WITH LYDIA'S CREATIVE WRASSLIN' AND NONSTOP SENSE OF ADVENTURE TO OPEN UP!
BLUSH

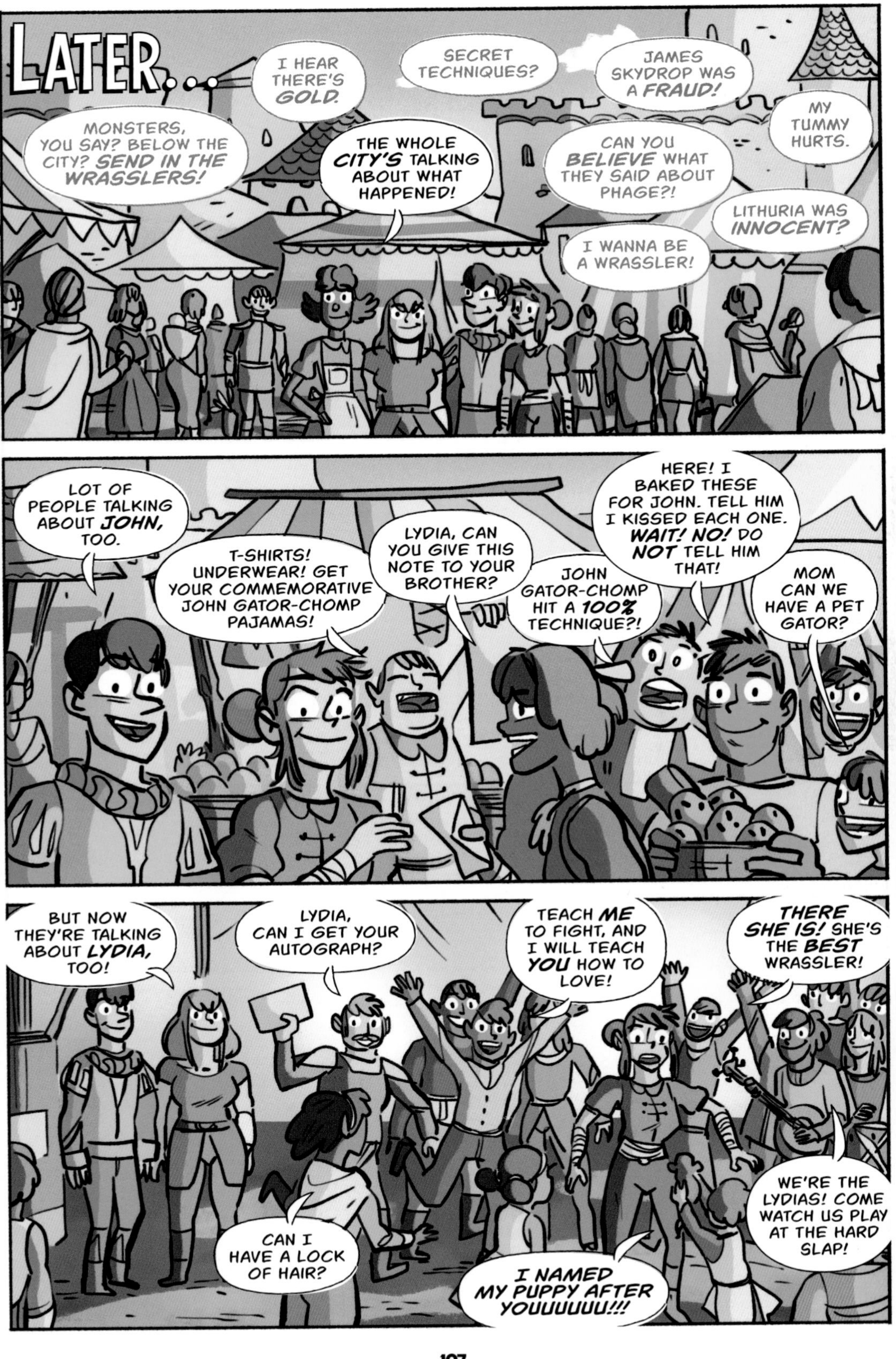
LATER...
MONSTERS, YOU SAY? BELOW THE CITY? SEND IN THE WRASSLERS!
I HEAR THERE'S GOLD.
THE WHOLE CITY'S TALKING ABOUT WHAT HAPPENED!
SECRET TECHNIQUES?
JAMES SKYDROP WAS A FRAUD!
CAN YOU BELIEVE WHAT THEY SAID ABOUT PHAGE?!
MY TUMMY HURTS.
I WANNA BE A WRASSLER!
LITHURIA WAS INNOCENT?
LOT OF PEOPLE TALKING ABOUT JOHN, TOO.
T-SHIRTS! UNDERWEAR! GET YOUR COMMEMORATIVE JOHN GATOR-CHOMP PAJAMAS!
LYDIA, CAN YOU GIVE THIS NOTE TO YOUR BROTHER?
JOHN GATOR-CHOMP HIT A 100% TECHNIQUE?!
HERE! I BAKED THESE FOR JOHN. TELL HIM I KISSED EACH ONE. WAIT! NO! DO NOT TELL HIM THAT!
MOM CAN WE HAVE A PET GATOR?
BUT NOW THEY'RE TALKING ABOUT LYDIA, TOO!
LYDIA, CAN I GET YOUR AUTOGRAPH?
TEACH ME TO FIGHT, AND I WILL TEACH YOU HOW TO LOVE!
THERE SHE IS! SHE'S THE BEST WRASSLER!
CAN I HAVE A LOCK OF HAIR?
I NAMED MY PUPPY AFTER YOUUUUUU!!!
WE'RE THE LYDIAS! COME WATCH US PLAY AT THE HARD SLAP!

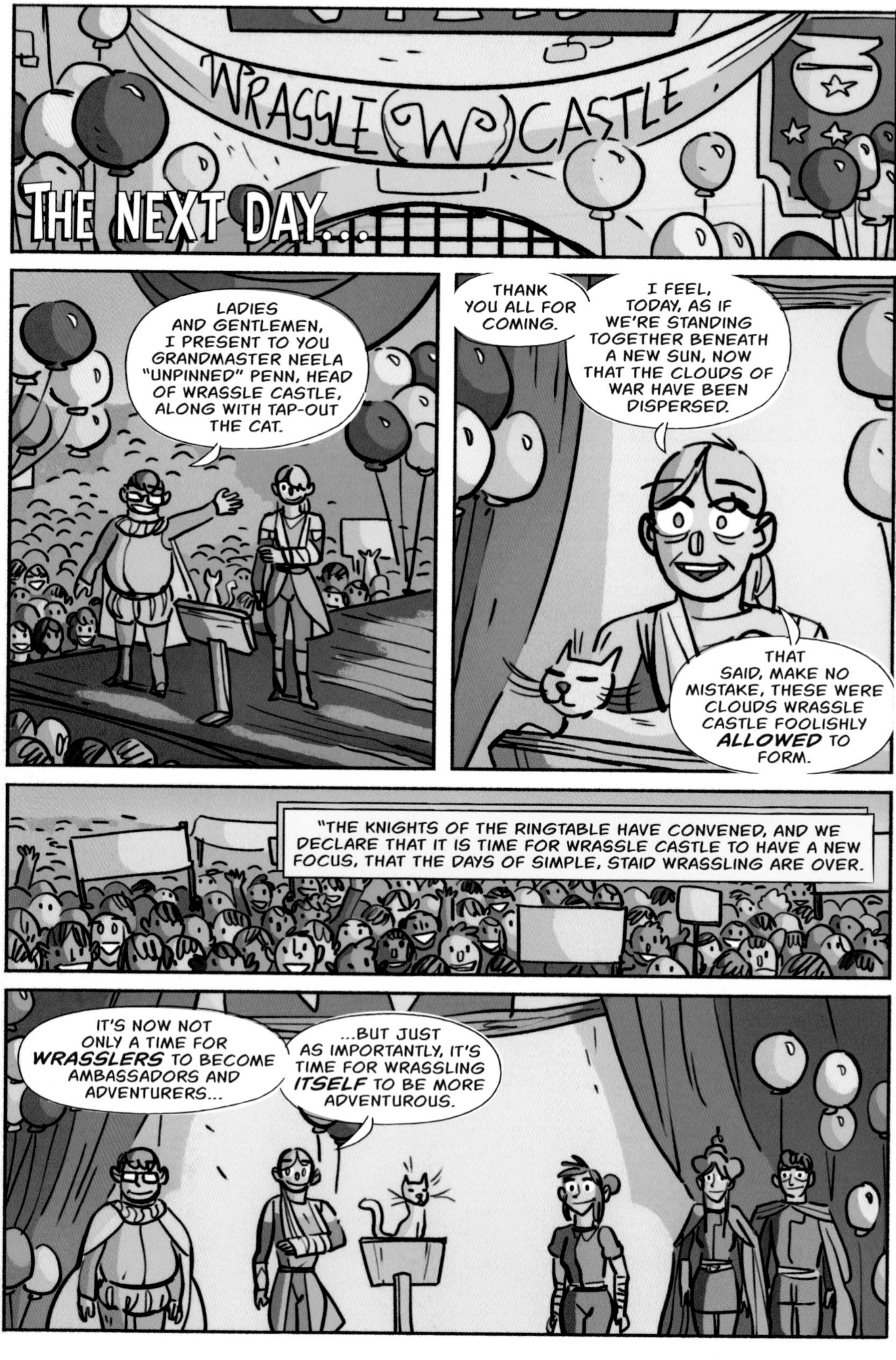
WRASSLE (W) CASTLE
THE NEXT DAY...
LADIES AND GENTLEMEN, I PRESENT TO YOU GRANDMASTER NEELA "UNPINNED" PENN, HEAD OF WRASSLE CASTLE, ALONG WITH TAP-OUT THE CAT.
THANK YOU ALL FOR COMING.
I FEEL, TODAY, AS IF WE'RE STANDING TOGETHER BENEATH A NEW SUN, NOW THAT THE CLOUDS OF WAR HAVE BEEN DISPERSED.
THAT SAID, MAKE NO MISTAKE, THESE WERE CLOUDS WRASSLE CASTLE FOOLISHLY ***ALLOWED*** TO FORM.
"THE KNIGHTS OF THE RINGTABLE HAVE CONVENED, AND WE DECLARE THAT IT IS TIME FOR WRASSLE CASTLE TO HAVE A NEW FOCUS, THAT THE DAYS OF SIMPLE, STAID WRASSLING ARE OVER.
IT'S NOW NOT ONLY A TIME FOR ***WRASSLERS*** TO BECOME AMBASSADORS AND ADVENTURERS...
...BUT JUST AS IMPORTANTLY, IT'S TIME FOR WRASSLING ***ITSELF*** TO BE MORE ADVENTUROUS.

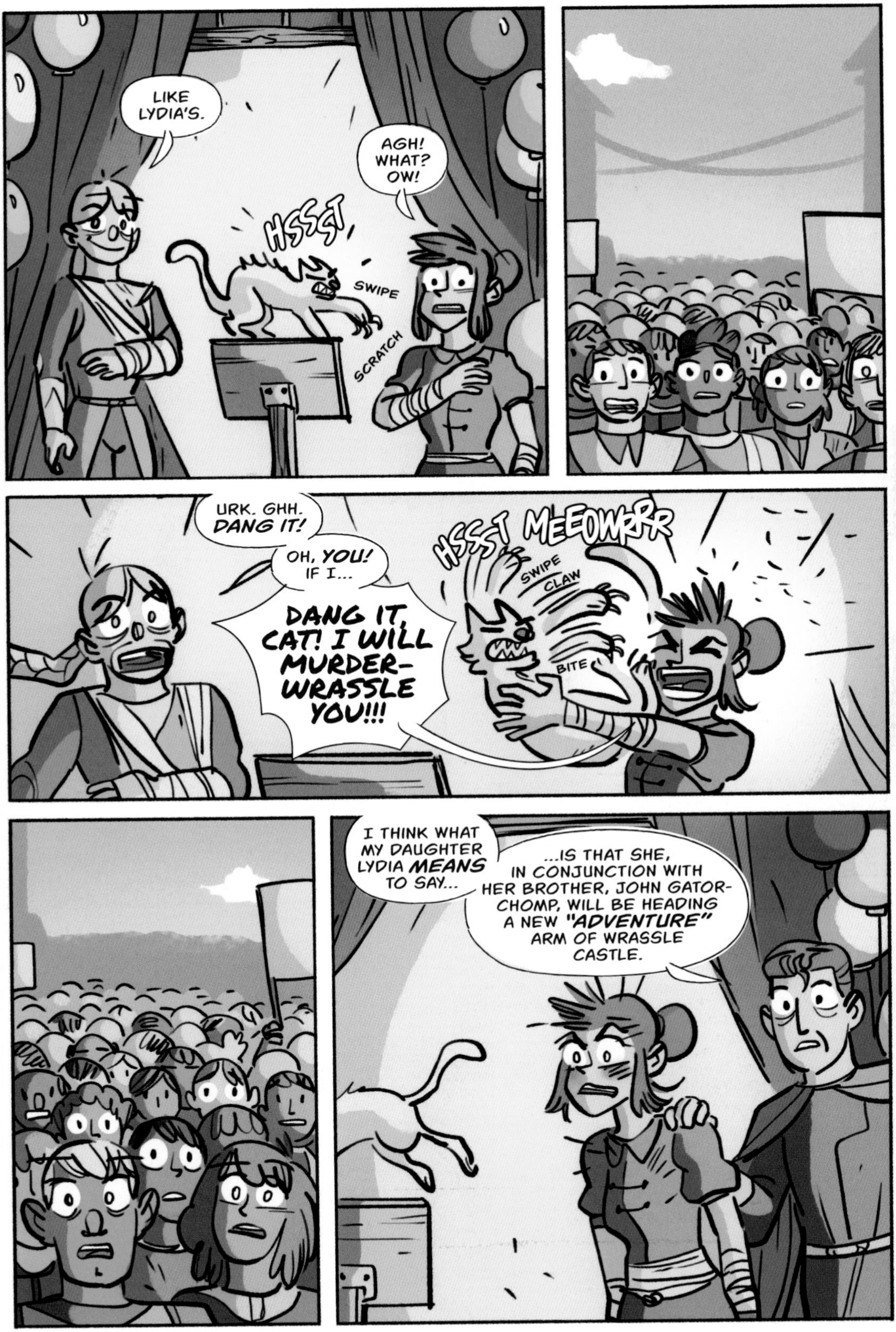
LIKE LYDIA'S.
AGH! WHAT? OW!
HSSST
SWIPE
SCRATCH
URK. GHH. DANG IT!
OH, YOU! IF I...
DANG IT, CAT! I WILL MURDER-WRASSLE YOU!!!
HSSST MEEOWRRR
SWIPE
CLAW
BITE
I THINK WHAT MY DAUGHTER LYDIA MEANS TO SAY...
...IS THAT SHE, IN CONJUNCTION WITH HER BROTHER, JOHN GATOR-CHOMP, WILL BE HEADING A NEW "ADVENTURE" ARM OF WRASSLE CASTLE.

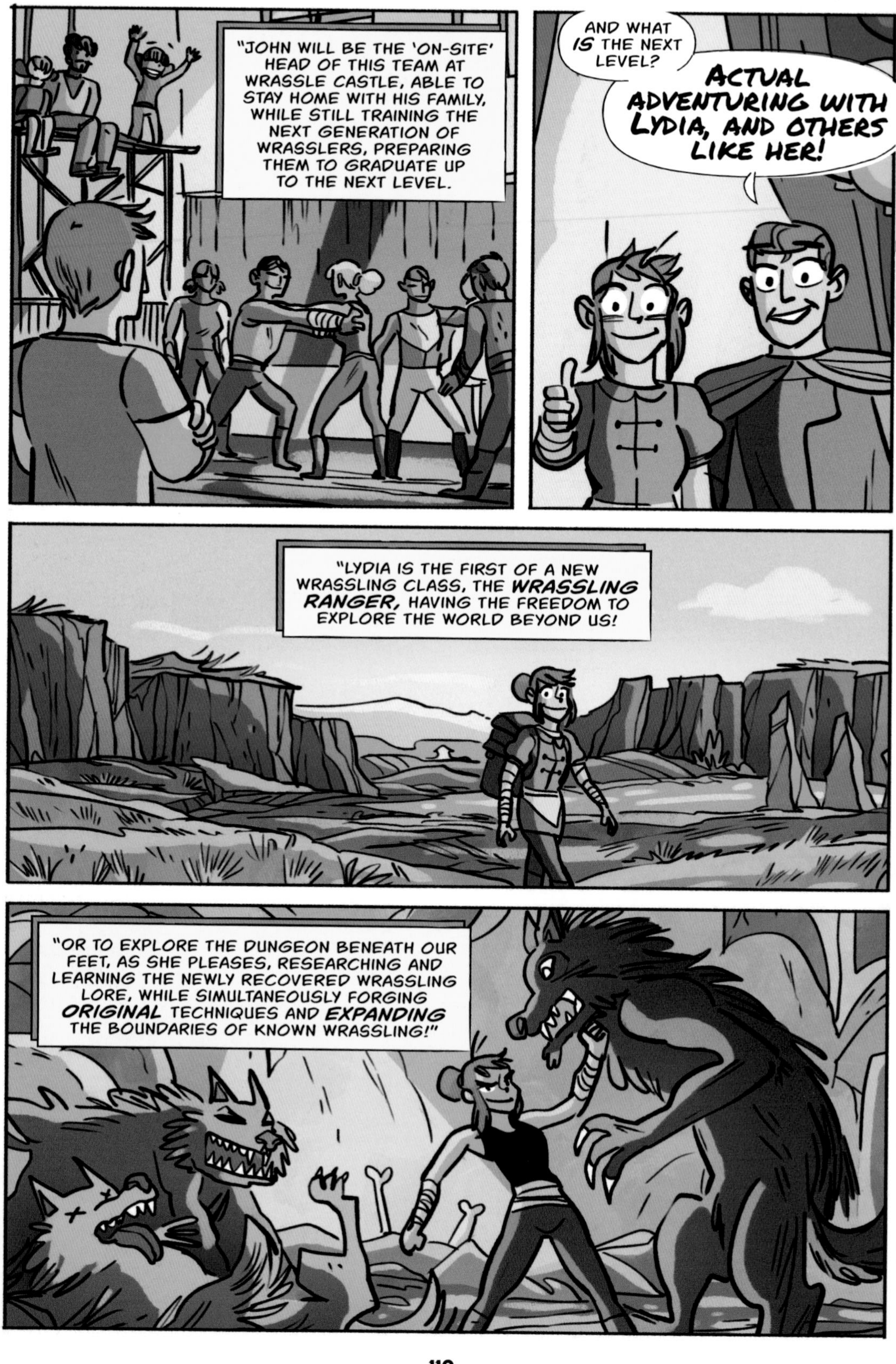
"JOHN WILL BE THE 'ON-SITE' HEAD OF THIS TEAM AT WRASSLE CASTLE, ABLE TO STAY HOME WITH HIS FAMILY, WHILE STILL TRAINING THE NEXT GENERATION OF WRASSLERS, PREPARING THEM TO GRADUATE UP TO THE NEXT LEVEL.
AND WHAT *IS* THE NEXT LEVEL?
ACTUAL ADVENTURING WITH LYDIA, AND OTHERS LIKE HER!
"LYDIA IS THE FIRST OF A NEW WRASSLING CLASS, THE ***WRASSLING RANGER,*** HAVING THE FREEDOM TO EXPLORE THE WORLD BEYOND US!
"OR TO EXPLORE THE DUNGEON BENEATH OUR FEET, AS SHE PLEASES, RESEARCHING AND LEARNING THE NEWLY RECOVERED WRASSLING LORE, WHILE SIMULTANEOUSLY FORGING ***ORIGINAL*** TECHNIQUES AND ***EXPANDING*** THE BOUNDARIES OF KNOWN WRASSLING!"

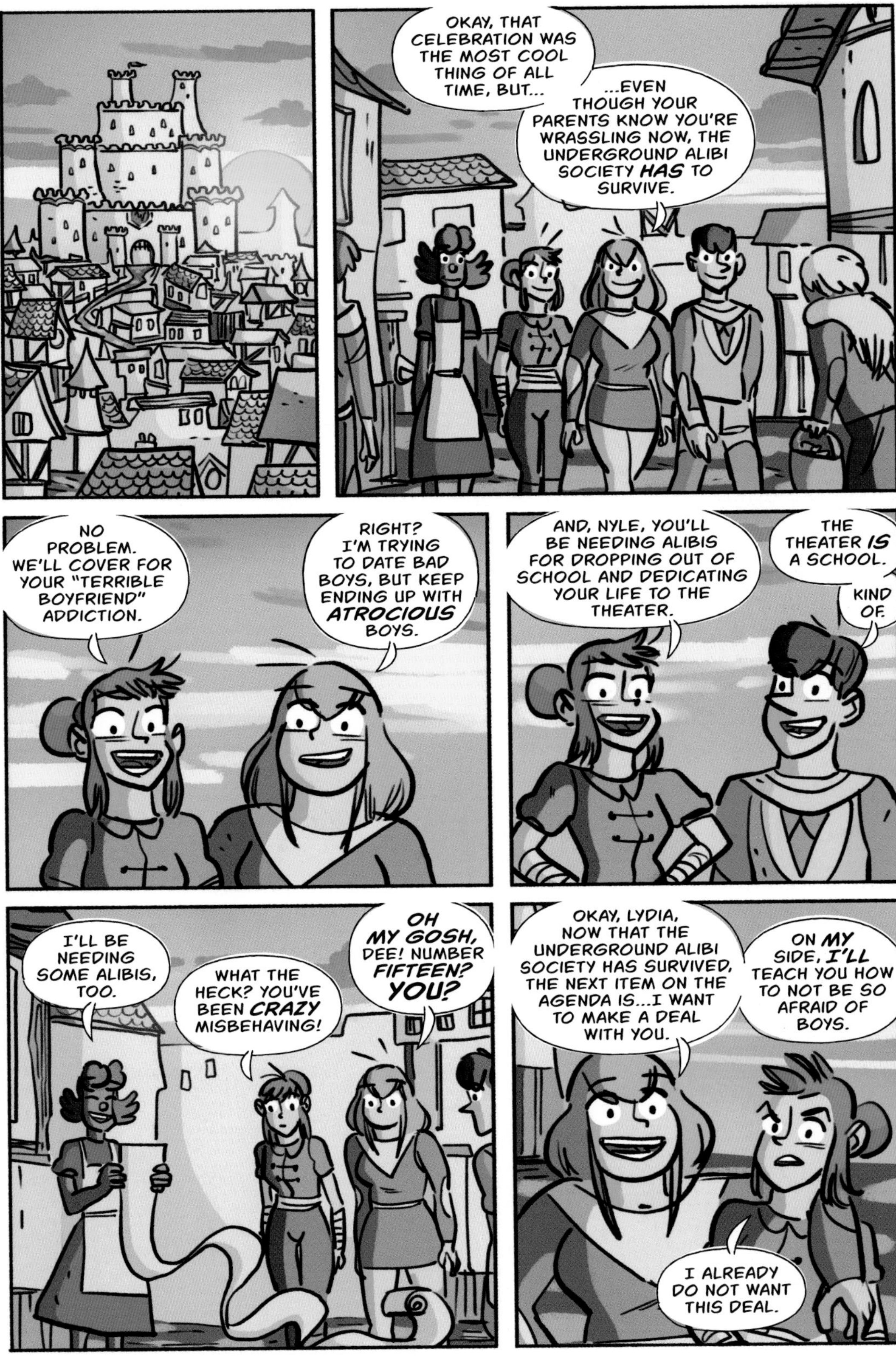
OKAY, THAT CELEBRATION WAS THE MOST COOL THING OF ALL TIME, BUT...
...EVEN THOUGH YOUR PARENTS KNOW YOU'RE WRASSLING NOW, THE UNDERGROUND ALIBI SOCIETY HAS TO SURVIVE.
NO PROBLEM. WE'LL COVER FOR YOUR "TERRIBLE BOYFRIEND" ADDICTION.
RIGHT? I'M TRYING TO DATE BAD BOYS, BUT KEEP ENDING UP WITH ATROCIOUS BOYS.
AND, NYLE, YOU'LL BE NEEDING ALIBIS FOR DROPPING OUT OF SCHOOL AND DEDICATING YOUR LIFE TO THE THEATER.
THE THEATER IS A SCHOOL.
KIND OF.
I'LL BE NEEDING SOME ALIBIS, TOO.
WHAT THE HECK? YOU'VE BEEN CRAZY MISBEHAVING!
OH MY GOSH, DEE! NUMBER FIFTEEN? YOU?
OKAY, LYDIA, NOW THAT THE UNDERGROUND ALIBI SOCIETY HAS SURVIVED, THE NEXT ITEM ON THE AGENDA IS...I WANT TO MAKE A DEAL WITH YOU.
ON MY SIDE, I'LL TEACH YOU HOW TO NOT BE SO AFRAID OF BOYS.
I ALREADY DO NOT WANT THIS DEAL.

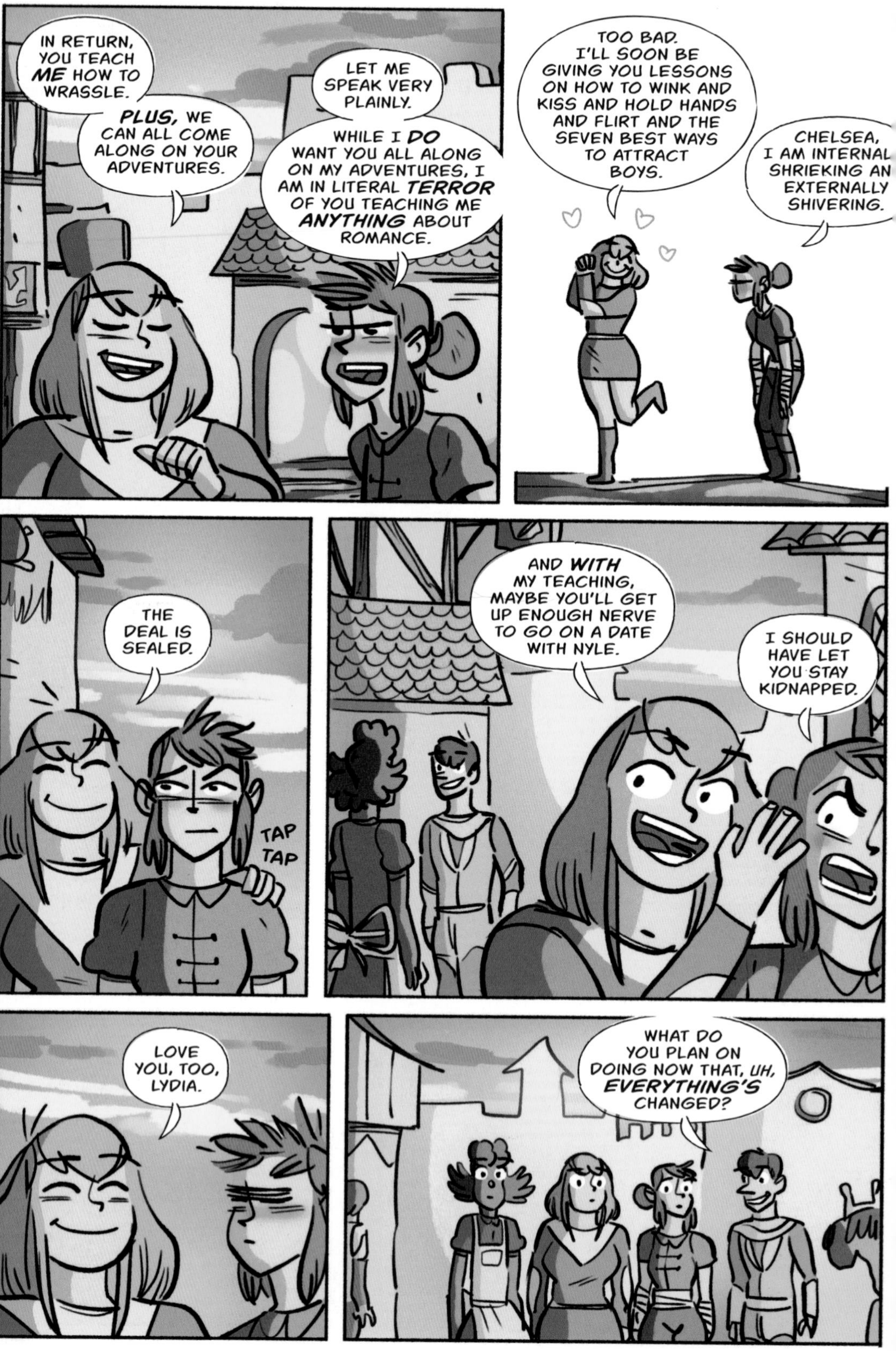
IN RETURN, YOU TEACH ME HOW TO WRASSLE.
PLUS, WE CAN ALL COME ALONG ON YOUR ADVENTURES.
LET ME SPEAK VERY PLAINLY.
WHILE I DO WANT YOU ALL ALONG ON MY ADVENTURES, I AM IN LITERAL TERROR OF YOU TEACHING ME ANYTHING ABOUT ROMANCE.
TOO BAD. I'LL SOON BE GIVING YOU LESSONS ON HOW TO WINK AND KISS AND HOLD HANDS AND FLIRT AND THE SEVEN BEST WAYS TO ATTRACT BOYS.
CHELSEA, I AM INTERNAL SHRIEKING AN EXTERNALLY SHIVERING.
THE DEAL IS SEALED.
TAP TAP
AND WITH MY TEACHING, MAYBE YOU'LL GET UP ENOUGH NERVE TO GO ON A DATE WITH NYLE.
I SHOULD HAVE LET YOU STAY KIDNAPPED.
LOVE YOU, TOO, LYDIA.
WHAT DO YOU PLAN ON DOING NOW THAT, UH, EVERYTHING'S CHANGED?

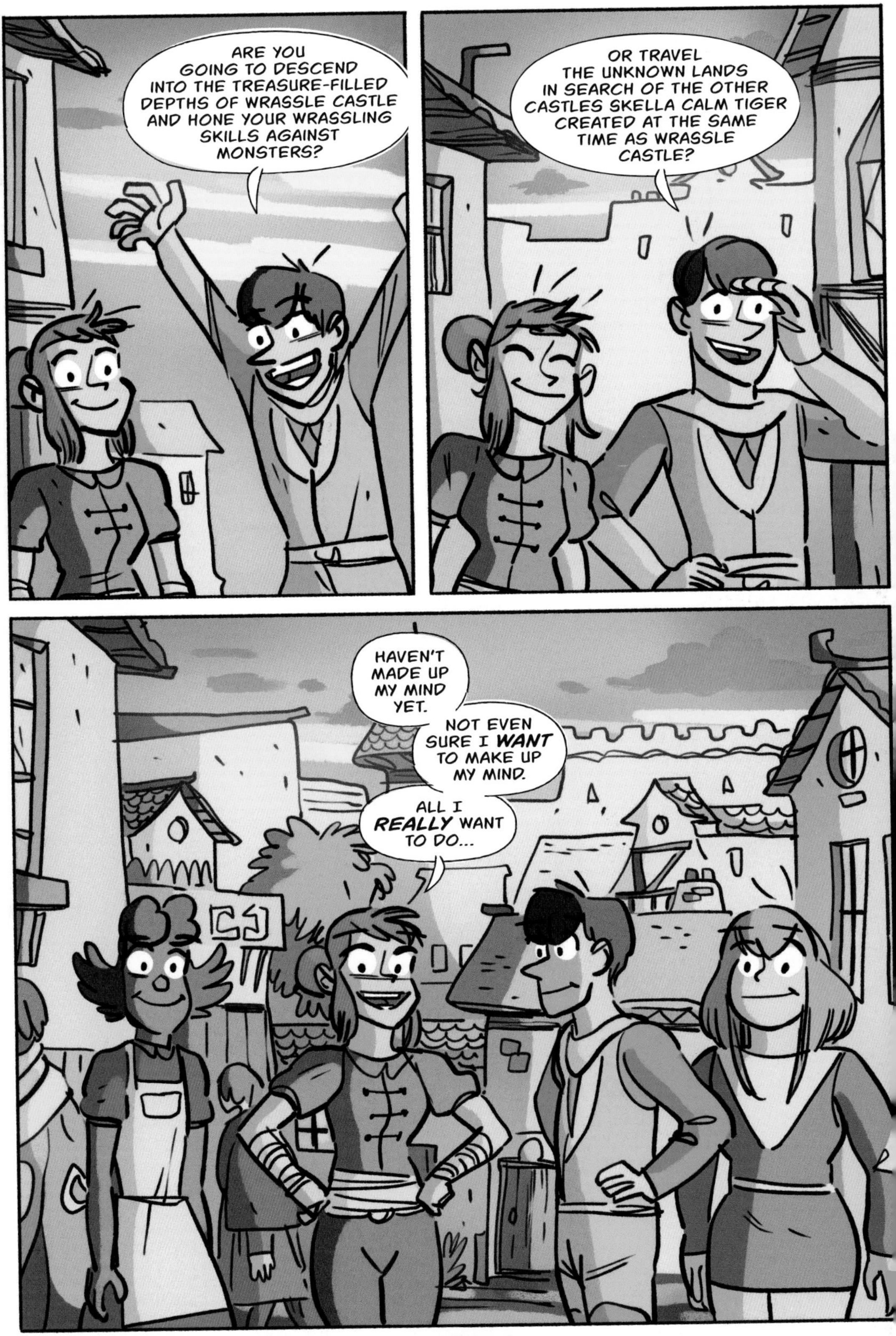
ARE YOU GOING TO DESCEND INTO THE TREASURE-FILLED DEPTHS OF WRASSLE CASTLE AND HONE YOUR WRASSLING SKILLS AGAINST MONSTERS?
OR TRAVEL THE UNKNOWN LANDS IN SEARCH OF THE OTHER CASTLES SKELLA CALM TIGER CREATED AT THE SAME TIME AS WRASSLE CASTLE?
HAVEN'T MADE UP MY MIND YET.
NOT EVEN SURE I *WANT* TO MAKE UP MY MIND.
ALL I *REALLY* WANT TO DO...

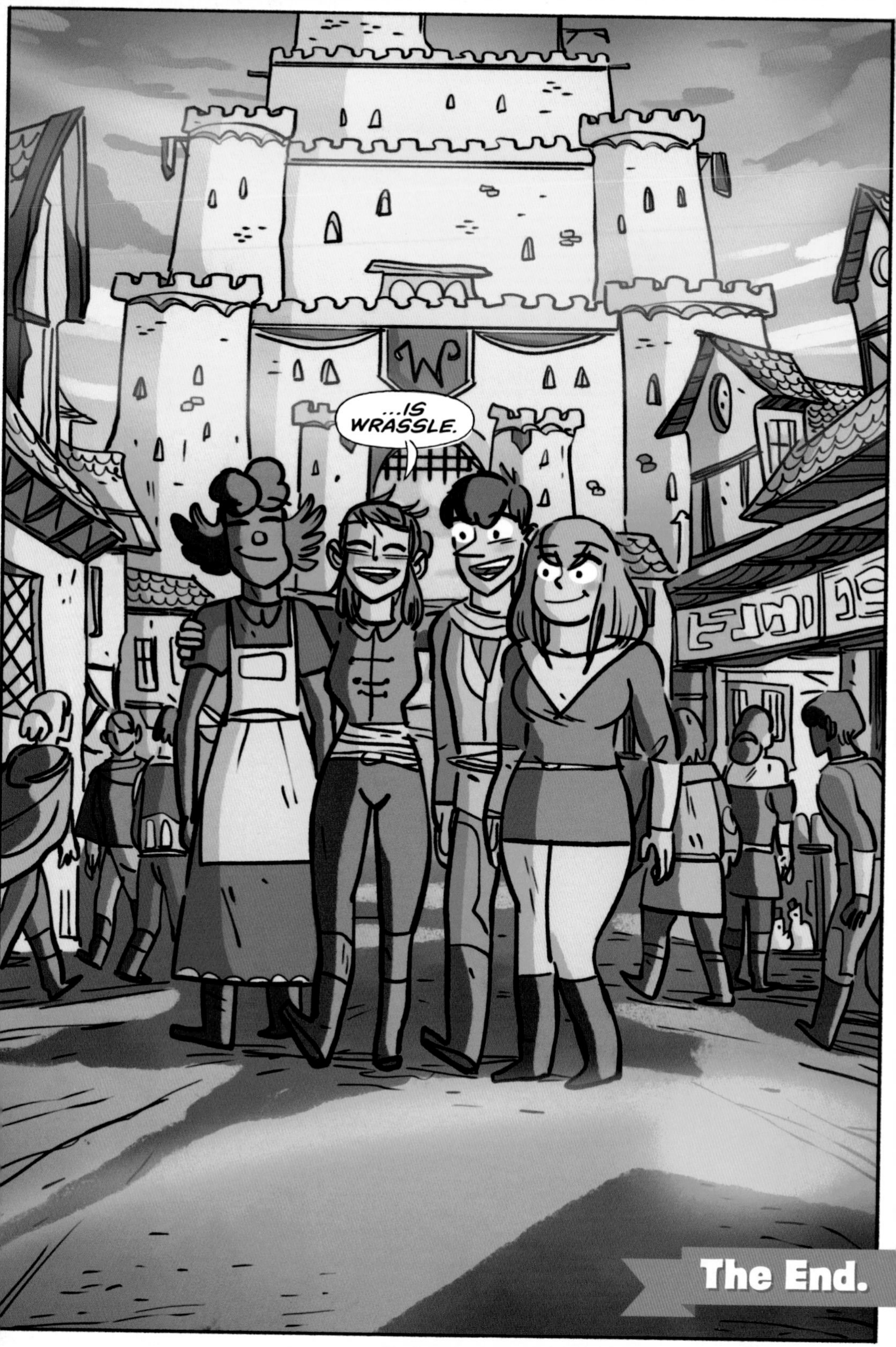
...IS WRASSLE.
The End.

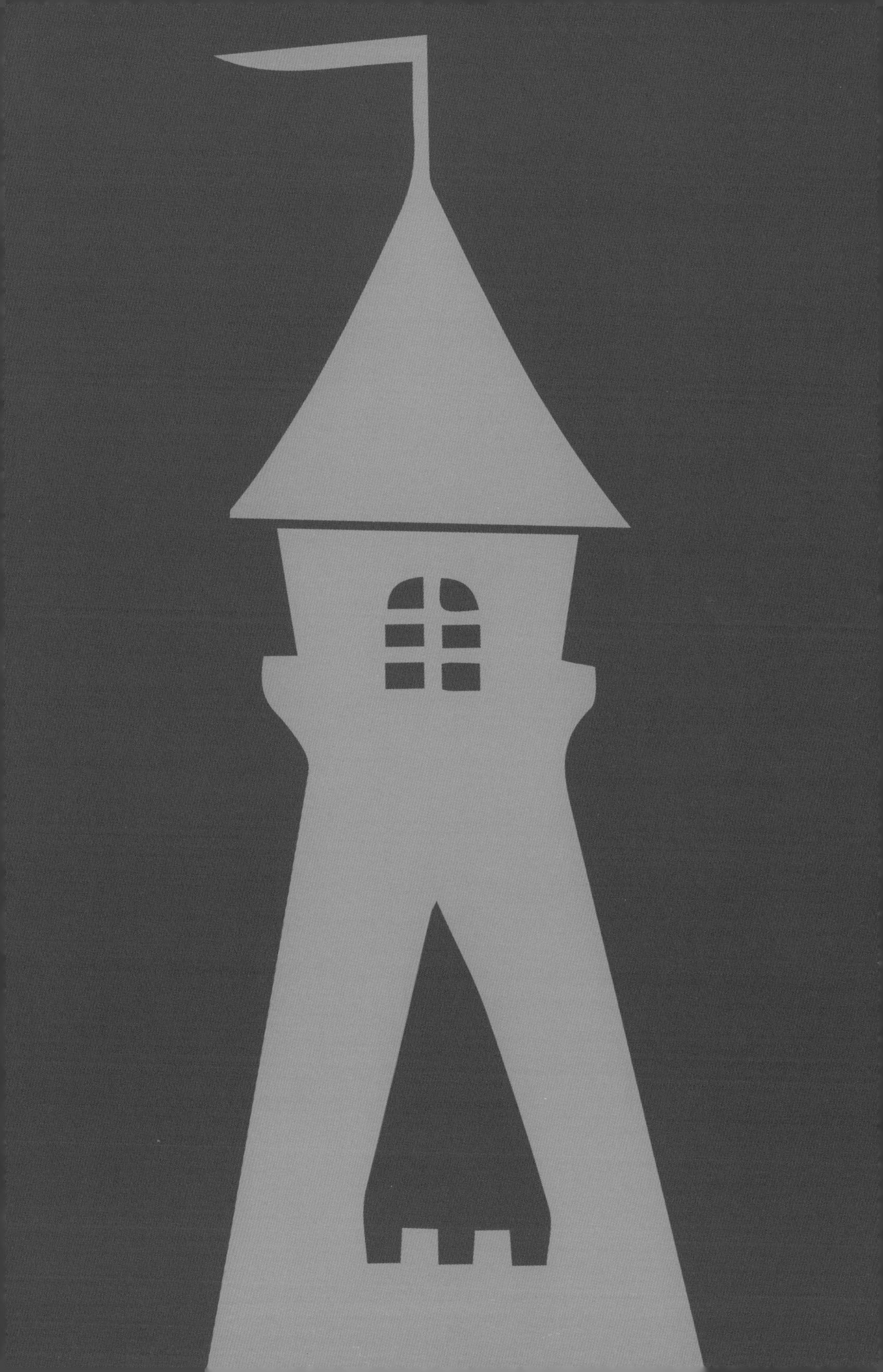

AUTHOR'S CORNER

WHEN WE FIRST CAME UP WITH THE TITLE "WRASSLE CASTLE," I WAS OVERJOYED. "IT PRACTICALLY WRITES ITSELF!" I DECLARED. WHILE THAT TURNED OUT TO NOT BE ENTIRELY TRUE, CREATING THIS WORLD HAS BEEN A PURE JOY THAT I AM SO GLAD TO SHARE WITH YOU!

- COLLEEN COOVER

"WRITE WHAT YOU KNOW," THEY SAY, BUT I WROTE A STORY ABOUT WRASSLING WITH BEARS WHEN ALL I'VE EVER PERSONALLY WRASSLED ARE MY BROTHER MIKE, A FEW DOGS, AND THEN ONE SHEEP, THE LATTER OF WHICH DID NOT GO WELL, BUT I SUPPOSE WHAT THIS BOOK IS REALLY ABOUT IS FRIENDSHIP AND ADVENTURE, AND THOSE ARE TWO THINGS I'VE ALWAYS HELD AS PARAMOUNT IN LIFE AND THAT I HOPE YOU'LL ALL FIND WHEN READING WRASSLE CASTLE.

- PAUL TOBIN

WHEN I STARTED WORKING ON WRASSLE CASTLE, I THOUGHT IT WOULD BE
JUST SILLY FUN AND LOTS OF PUNS (WHICH IT IS!), BUT AS I DELVED DEEPER
INTO THE SCRIPT, I REALIZED THAT THIS SERIES WAS MUCH MORE THAN
THAT: A CAST OF INCREDIBLE CHARACTERS, A WORLD FULL OF WONDERS
AND MAGIC, A STORY ABOUT NEVER GIVING UP, WORKING HARD TOWARD
YOUR GOALS, AND MAKING MEANINGFUL FRIENDSHIPS. OUR BOOK IS NOT
JUST FUN AND FIGHTS, IT'S GOT HEART!

- GALAAD

COLLEEN COOVER

AGE: STILL COUNTING.
NATIONAL RANKING: ALSO STILL COUNTING.
OCCUPATION: WRITER
SIGNATURE MOVE: TRUTH BOMB
(HIGHEST POWER LEVEL: NUCLEAR)
STRENGTH: 15
DEXTERITY: -99
SOMETIMES UNCOMFORTABLE HONESTY: 20

FAVORITE FOOD: UNDISCLOSED FOR PASSWORD
SECURITY REASONS.

HOBBIES: KNITTING.

NOTES: COAXED FROM THE COMFORT OF HER
COMIC-DRAWING CAVE BY THE PROSPECT OF
CO-WRITING A FANTASY WRASSLIN' ADVENTURE,
COLLEEN HAS BEEN TRAINING HER AUTHORING
MUSCLES BY BENCH PRESSING COMPUTER
KEYBOARDS AND EATING RAW WORD DOCS
FOR BREAKFAST.

"MEAN" COLLEEN

PAUL TOBIN

AGE: SEVERAL YEARS OLD
NATIONAL RANKING: 7,898,653 (ON A GOOD DAY)
OCCUPATION: WRITER
SIGNATURE MOVE: NAPALANCHE
(HIGHEST POWER LEVEL: 98%)
STRENGTH: 20+
DEXTERITY: 20+
SELF AWARENESS: 3

FAVORITE FOOD / NEWSPAPER STRIP COMBO: PEANUTS

HOBBIES: INDOOR ROCK CLIMBING, OUTDOOR BIKE
RIDING, ALLDOOR COOKIE EATING.

NOTES: AS A FERAL CHILD IN THE IOWA WILDERNESS,
PAUL WAS RAISED BY A KINDLY PAIR OF PULP
MAGAZINES AND EVENTUALLY JOINED HUMAN SOCIETY
AFTER PASSING THE LEGALLY-REQUIRED POTTY
TRAINING TEST ON ONLY THE FOURTH TRY. HE ENJOYS
FRENZIED STORMS AND AN ASTONISHING RANGE OF
THINGS MOST PEOPLE CONSIDER STRANGE.

"TEN TOES" TOBIN

GALAADOR

AGE: UNDISCLOSED.
NATIONAL RANKING: OFF THE CHART.
OCCUPATION: DRAWS COMICS
SIGNATURE MOVE: EXPLOSIVE PENCIL OF DEATH
(HIGHEST POWER LEVEL: DEADLY)
STRENGTH: AVERAGE
DEXTERITY: NATURAL 20
ABILITY TO BEFRIEND CATS: EXCEPTIONAL

FAVORITE FOOD: ANYTHING THAT CONTAINS
SUGAR, EGGS, BUTTER, FLOUR OR ANY
ASSORTMENT OF THOSE.

HOBBIES: CRUSHING PENCILS, LIFTING
DRAWING TABLETS.

NOTES: ONCE DEFEATED VEGETA IN SINGLE COMBAT.
OR WAS IT IN HIS IMAGINATION?

"ÚLTIMO DISEÑADOR EXTRAORDINARIO"

REBECCA HORNER

AGE: ETERNAL
NATIONAL RANKING: LOW!
OCCUPATION: COLOURIST, CAT WRANGLER
SIGNATURE MOVE: BEFUDDLE!
(HIGHEST POWER LEVEL: ?!?)
STRENGTH: AS MUCH AS THESE NOODLE ARMS
CAN MUSTER
DEXTERITY: SOMETIMES!
EXCLAMATION POINT USAGE: INCREDIBLE!!

FAVORITE FOOD: ANY KIND OF TOASTED SANDWICH

HOBBIES: JIGSAW PUZZLES, JUGGLING CAT
TOYS, RETRIEVING JIGSAW PIECES FROM
LIGHT-FINGERED FELINES

NOTES: CAN BENCH PRESS UP TO 2 CATS AT ANY
GIVEN TIME!

"RABBLE ROUSIN" REBECCA